A PLANET OF WRATH AND TEARS

ALSO BY COLIN ALEXANDER

LEIF THE LUCKY NOVELS

Starman's Saga: The Long Strange Journey of Leif the Lucky
Murder Under Another Sun
The Lucky Starman

OTHER SCIENCE FICTION AND FANTASY NOVELS

Princess of Shadows: The Girl Who Would Be King
Complicated: The Interstellar Life and Times of Saoirse Kenneally
Accidental Warrior: The Unlikely Tale of Bloody Hal
My Life: An Ex-Quarterback's Adventures in the Galactic Empire

MYSTERY NOVELS

Lady of Ice and Fire
God's Adamantine Fate

A PLANET OF WRATH AND TEARS

COLIN ALEXANDER

A LEIF THE LUCKY NOVEL

A PLANET OF WRATH AND TEARS:
A LEIF THE LUCKY NOVEL

Copyright © 2023 by Colin Alexander

All rights reserved, including the right of reproduction in whole or in part
in any form. No part of this book may be used or reproduced in any manner
whatsoever without written permission except in the case of brief quotations
embodied in critical articles and reviews.

ISBN 978-1-7361984-7-6 (ebook)
ISBN 978-1-7361984-8-3 (trade paperback)

This novel is a work of fiction. Names, characters, places, and incidents are
either the product of the author's imagination or are used fictitiously and
are not to be construed as real. Any resemblance to actual events, locales,
organizations, or persons, living or dead, is entirely coincidental and beyond
the intent of the author.
Cover art by Alejandro Colucci
Interior formatting by Mariska Maas (Rubre Art)

Aficionado® and BRICKS AND STONES are each trademarks of the
publisher.
www.aficionado.com

For Cello, who always believed even when I didn't

PROLOGUE

FIRST CONTACT WAS NEVER SUPPOSED TO BE LIKE THIS. TRUST ME.

First contact, that moment when humans meet intelligent beings from elsewhere in the universe, has long been a dream of astronomers and space scientists as much as it has been a staple of Hollywood vids and science fiction writers. Some have cast it as a moment of magic, others as an awful nightmare. From one extreme to the other, however, all of them have pictured it as a time that would change the trajectory of human history. None imagined it the way it really turned out. I wouldn't have imagined it, either, but I lived it. I really should learn to look before I leap.

No matter how you view the event, some stories need to be told and this is one of them. I'll do the telling. It's not because I'm any good at it. I'm a reluctant storyteller at best. I don't have any natural talent for entertaining, and people have made comments to that effect when I've tried in the past. They've said much the same about my knack for empathy and even my sense of humor. However, I'm the one who needs to talk about this because I was there for all of it—and I'm still alive. I suppose that last bit is a little remarkable since I was born in 2038, joined the US Army in 2055 for seven years of fighting in the

Troubles, then survived two starshots and the return to a war-torn planet—and that was before any of this happened. That's more than I can say for anybody else.

This story is more than the plain facts of the first contact. It is a tale of the decisions we made and the consequences that followed. We all make choices—from the trivial to the profound—and whatever choice we make precludes us from knowing how it would have turned out if we had chosen differently. Sometimes we choose based on desire, sometimes from a sense of duty. Often it is a mixture, with a bit of impulsiveness thrown in. Regardless of how we do it, each choice comes with its own cost. I've made my decisions, and I'll live with them and the results.

I hope you can too.

Leif Grettison

EARTH
AD 2252, EFOR

PART I

I must go down to the seas again, to the lonely sea and the sky,
And all I ask is a tall ship and a star to steer her by

John Masefield, "Sea-Fever"

CHAPTER ONE

"**B**RICKS AND STONES WILL HIDE THE BONES," CHANTED THE CHILDREN IN THE back of the McClintocks' wagons. "Bricks and stones will hide the bones!"

I had ridden fusion-powered ramjets at light speed to the stars, landed on strange worlds and explored their mysteries. Now? I jounced in the saddle, moving at the speed of horse across what used to be the eastern United States, and when I dismounted, watched out for horse droppings in the road.

How the mighty had fallen!

The children of the families that made up the small wagon train had been singing those words ever since the three of us joined the motley collection of wooden vehicles and people. That was on the road into the last farming community that had been dug out of the ruins that remained of old, dead East Saint Louis. When we first slowed our pace to ride with the train, the children had not only sung but scampered out of the wagons to pick buildings near our route. They'd rush into them to play bone hunter. Each kid would search their chosen building, and the one who found the most human bones won the game. I could still hear their shouts in my ears.

"I've got a whole skeleton! That's a bonus! Counts double!"

"It's missing a hand. Doesn't count. It's not whole."

"The hand's there! It's just a couple of fingers gone! Does too count!"

"You can't count past ten anyway!"

Kids. Bare Bones McClintock, the train leader with a mien as skeletal as his name, put a stop to the bone hunting as soon as the town's buildings were out of sight. "Back in the wagons!" he yelled, riding his horse forward and back along the line of wagons. "If you get lost in those buildings and something happens, we'll never find you. You'll just be another set of bones. You hear me now!" Then he galloped ahead of the train to where a man waited for him in front of a small farm that had been carved out of the concrete-and-brick wilderness. We held back and waited, per his earlier instructions.

The younger ones did climb back into the wagons among their families' stores and furniture, pulled the canvas across wooden frame-works to make them like tents, and chanted "bricks and stones" with the fervor of a church choir. Maybe it was the increasing chill in the air that drove them under cover, or maybe they were paying heed to McClintock's warning. Our surroundings had turned spooky as the dead urban zone surrounded us. East Saint Louis wasn't even a real city—not to me. I had grown up around twenty-first-century New York. Nevertheless, on all sides of us stretched out an unending pile of concrete and brick, except for this farm. Silent except for birds overhead, winging south ahead of the winter. Blank windows stared at us.

"There are ghosts behind those windows!" one of the older children shouted while we were waiting for Bare Bones to come back. "Ghosts of the people from before—and they're staring at you!"

It was enough to make me shiver. I had plenty of my own ghosts without having a dead city watch me. The younger ones shut up and hid among the furniture, casks, and burlap sacks in the wagon beds.

I looked over at Caleb Peterson where he sat on his horse, a few feet from me at the tail end of the wagon train. He was a man who had started off thin, based on the size of his clothing, and had recently become even thinner, given how loosely those clothes now hung on him. His face, shadowed by a broad-brimmed hat, bore its usual worried look, one of the few expressions he seemed to have.

"Explain something to me, Caleb," I said.

"What?" Lids drooped over his eyes. The corners of his mouth drooped as well, not hidden by his scraggly brown beard.

"You rode into Eastview right after our harvest as though all the hounds of hell were after you. Earthbase had received some mysterious signal from a star humanity never went to. They needed you to find a crew of starfolk, who they knew had just come back—well, it had been over a year, but never mind that—in hopes that the starfolk would help Earthbase figure out what to do. Except there was no crew of starfolk. Just me. I was the sole survivor from the *Dauntless*. Do you remember what I said when you found me in Eastview?" I went on before he could answer. "I said that if someone out there"—I thrust a hand at the sky—"is trying to get in contact with us, that's about the most important thing that's happened since Noah's ark. I rushed like crazy to leave and we rode like hell from what used to be Pennsylvania. But we meet these wagons and now we're going to bump along no faster than them. What happened to the idea of *urgent*?"

Caleb couldn't, or wouldn't, tell me what Earthbase expected me to do about this signal—and for all I had puzzled about it, I couldn't figure that part out—but being given a personal invitation to the most momentous event in history was not something I was going to turn down. Or miss because we dawdled.

Caleb's chronic frown deepened. "I know. I know. But you heard what was said back in that town. There are robbers on this road now. These are families. They have little children." His eyes went to the wagon in front of us. "I'm a scout. I can't let them ride into trouble."

"So we're doing it along with them." I looked at the pistol holstered on his belt and the rifle sheathed by his saddle. "Caleb, have you ever had people shooting at you, trying to kill you?"

His head snapped around to face me so fast that he inadvertently turned his horse. "No."

"Let me tell you something. Knowing what you're doing and doing the right thing doesn't mean you live through it. Survival is often a matter of luck. You ever kill anyone? Intentionally, I mean."

"No." His stare seemed to go through me.

Shit, I thought. I wouldn't let families with kids ride into an ambush either. If there was dirty work to be done, though, I had a feeling I was going to be the one doing it. I've always had a knack for putting myself in those situations.

I wondered what McClintock and the man were saying. The man he was talking to supposedly knew about the road ahead. I'd have preferred to go with him, but Bare Bones hadn't wanted company for the conversation. He was the leader, as he said, and the people in the wagon train were his responsibility.

So we sat on our horses while the teams in harness took a rest from pulling the heavily laden wagons, stamping their hooves on the cracked concrete of old Interstate 70. Meanwhile, the children summoned up courage against ghosts and again peeked out from under their canvas covers. Once more they defiantly sang, "Bricks and stones will hide the bones!" at the ruins. Those words were a slang expression that meant "never." Yes, I thought as I looked at the empty buildings, when 650 million people or so across North America all died within the span of two to three years, a lot of bones were left lying around. It might not be forever, but it would be a long, long time before they were all hidden or turned to dust.

Finally, Bare Bones galloped back from his conference with the farmer. His leather coat flapped loosely over a homespun shirt and pants.

"This is not good," Bare Bones said. "It's not just a couple of high-waymen hiding in the ruins. That man"—he pointed to where the farmer had stood—"said a group of them robbed his farm. Told him and his wife they would be coming back for food, and if they didn't get it, they'd burn the place. He said his wife heard some of them talking when they didn't know she was listening. They're all officers from the old president's guard, who ran away when the starman led the army into New Terra." His black eyes burned holes in me. "Now they've put a roadblock on the bridge to collect what they call tolls." He spat into the dirt.

"Maybe it would be wiser for you to turn back," I said.

He glared at me. "Not possible. We sold everything to make this move—including our land." He spat again. "There is no place to go back to."

I was familiar with burning bridges behind me. "We're here," I said, nodding at Caleb. "Maybe we can help."

"Yeah," McClintock said. "You're sure that's the only bridge open to the west side?" He addressed the question to Caleb.

"Yes," Caleb said. "One side of the Stan Span is intact and open across the Mississippi. The other is choked with wrecked cars. We've used that bridge as a trade route, and that's how I came East. There are other bridges still standing over the river, but they're all blocked, same as the other side of the Stan Span—filled with cars that drove into each other during the Tribulation. You can pick your way through those on foot or maybe lead a couple of horses through, but you'd never get the wagons across. Don't know why this one stayed clear, but it did."

Bare Bones fingered his beard where it hung down over his chest. "And now the clear bridge has a barricade and robbers. You said you came east this way. You didn't see them?"

"No, but things have obviously changed since I came through." Caleb was quiet a moment, then he said, "The men and women in your train are armed, and maybe a couple of the older children can shoot. There are three of us and our rifles. Maybe we can make them stand aside."

Unfortunately, Caleb's idea made no sense, which wasn't surprising given his lack of experience. "If these are former New Terran soldiers, which is what it sounds like, they will have military equipment," I said. "They could have a machine gun."

"I don't see your point," Caleb said. Bare Bones looked from one of us to the other.

"You need to listen to Leif." Those words, from behind Bare Bones, came from the third man riding with me and Caleb. No Nonsense Johnson had been at the front of the wagons but came back to us while we talked with Bare Bones, as if he was afraid of missing some secret. He wore a homespun shirt and twill pants, much like mine, also with a pistol at his belt and a rifle in a sheath by his saddle. That armament was pretty much standard outdoor wear on the eastern border of New Terra—what used to be Western Pennsylvania—where we had been living. When I left Eastview with Caleb, No Nonsense had joined us to have an adventure. I stood out among them not only by my size—a well-muscled six-three—but by my red hair, blue eyes, and on most days, clean-shaven face.

"Leif's talking about a gun that fires very fast," No Nonsense said. "Never stops as long as you hold the trigger down. I saw them in the fighting in the East. It could kill all of us in less time than it takes me to say this."

"But then there's nothing we can do, even with you here," Bare Bones said. "We'll have to give them whatever they want and hope it's not more than we can spare."

"Maybe the farmer is exaggerating," Caleb said. "But even if bandits have put a barrier across the bridge and have a weapon like that, there's something we can do. Before the road gets to the bridge, there's a place where the ruins stop. It's trees and brush from there to the river. I'm a trained scout. I can see if there's a way I can get behind them before you come up. A man with a rifle at their rear will change the situation."

Spoken like a man who has never done anything close to that.

"If there's any sneaking around and getting behind some enemy position to be done, I'm the one who'll be doing it," I said.

Spoken like a man who has never known when to keep his mouth shut. Well, that was true. But what was also true was that I was the one best suited for that type of job. Back in the fighting during the Troubles two centuries ago, I had been an Army Ranger. If there was anyone who could pull off a crazy stunt, it was me.

Bare Bones frowned and his heavy eyebrows knitted together. "I never believed in a lucky starman, not really," he said. "I guess I better hope the stories are true."

"This has nothing to do with luck," I said.

He spat to the side again and rode back to the lead wagon of his little train. I grimaced. Since the wars that ended our civilization, a myth had sprung up that people who went to the stars were lucky, and when they returned, they brought some of that luck back with them. The belief that I was a lucky starman had played a big role in the revolution in New Terra. I had become tired, however, of being everyone's lucky rabbit's foot.

"I'd say the man is nervous," No Nonsense said. "He was jittery when we first met him because he heard there was some kind of trouble on the road. Now he's sweating but good."

"Give the man a break, No Nonsense," I said. "We may be facing a fight."

"So what?" No Nonsense shot back. "We've faced worse than this. You know what you're doing, and I've learned."

No Nonsense spoke with all the assurance a cocky seventeen-year-old can manage, which is considerable. He was a tall young man, almost reaching my height, and since the previous winter, his frame had filled out with muscle. He had a broad face that smiled often. Freckles dotted skin that had lost its summer tan. Even though he was months from his eighteenth birthday, his beard had already come in full and bushy, and he was inordinately proud of it.

He was the eldest of Charity Montgomery's children, the family I had found when I returned to Earth a year ago and then left almost three weeks ago because of Caleb's impossible message about a signal from the stars. What didn't show on the surface was No Nonsense's itch for adventure. It had led him into New Terra's army with me and through battle to victory and revolution. And now here. I looked at him, sighed, and wished he had stayed home—but there was no talking sense into a seventeen-year-old boy. I should know.

"Why is this thing called the Stan Span?" I asked Caleb as a way of not talking about gunfights or luck.

"You'll see the name on signs," Caleb said. "There was someone named Stan who must have been important before. That's all I can tell you."

Shouts came from ahead of us, and the wagons creaked into motion.

The road to the stars ran across a bandit-infested bridge. Oh, joy. "Okay," I said. "Let's go see what we've bought into."

CHAPTER TWO

OUR WAGONS PLODDED WESTWARD ON THE ROAD. THE BRIDGE CAME INTO view as the sun was in the west and half-hidden by a broken bank of gray clouds. Suspension cables stretched from two giant towers to the roadway. Its width was even greater than the four lanes still distinguished by barely visible paint. For now, anyway, it still looked ready to carry traffic. I wondered how long it would stand that way.

We brought the wagons to a halt where the old buildings helped to provide a screen from the river. The remaining ground out to the riverbank had been open before the wars. Now trees and bushes occupied most of it. I was more interested in the roadway that led to the bridge. The road ascended on concrete pillars as it ran up to the bridge to arc across its span. This was an elevated roadway. Caleb hadn't mentioned that salient point. I prefer to know about my problems in advance.

The old road signs were still there, white lettering on green. STAN MUSIAL VETERANS MEMORIAL BRIDGE. Well, that was where "Stan Span" came from, although I had no idea who he had been. The left-hand side that went eastbound back in my day was filled with a mass of wreckage, as Caleb had said. Smoke was rising from behind a barricade on the old westbound side. I left the wagons and, along with Caleb and No Nonsense, worked my way on foot from tree to tree until we had a better view.

"So, the farmer had it right," Caleb said. "They can't be living there, though. That doesn't make sense."

"I'll agree with that," I said. "They've got to have a camp somewhere else, and people who'll mingle in the frontier communities and pick up word of travelers. Then they head out here when they know someone is coming."

"We have to get past them," Caleb said.

"Probably not as simple as tossing a solid dollar or two into a bucket," I replied. "You didn't tell me this damn road was elevated."

He shrugged. "I didn't think it mattered."

"All details matter." I sighed.

No Nonsense picked that moment to ask, "Do they have machine guns?"

"Can't tell from here." I wished for my old combat visor with its magnification and thermal detector. My implanted chip could give me a little magnification on its projection field, which I could see like a heads-up display, but not enough to be useful in this situation. While I was wishing, I wished for my old squad, who knew what they were doing. But wishing for what I couldn't have wasn't going to help.

"There's only one way to find out," I said, "and there's only one way to do this. They set their position on the open side at the point where the wrecks block the eastbound lanes. It's still over land. See where those trees are, close to that pillar?" I pointed. "I can get up the tree and onto the roadway, among the old cars. I'll be on the other side from them, but I will be behind them. If you have Bare Bones bring the wagons down the road while I'm doing it, they'll be watching you. Just go slow so I have enough time to get into position."

I slung my rifle and took off, using the foliage to conceal myself from those at the barricade. Their eyes would be on the road, looking for the wagons they were expecting. When those wagons rolled into view, the bandits would be fixated on them.

Within a few minutes, I reached my target tree by the pillar. I had to count on Bare Bones not arriving at the barricade before I was ready. Knowing how fast those wagons could move, I used my chip to set a timer on my field. Coordination was so much simpler in the days when everybody had a phone. Now, once you were physically away from somebody else, you had to hope that they would do what they were supposed to do and that they would do it on time. As much as our chips and phones had annoyed me, there were times I missed them. However, phones no longer existed, and I was the only one with a chip. I pushed the concerns away. My first task was to get up that tree.

I was ten years old before I ever climbed a tree, because I spent most of my childhood in and around New York City and my vacations had been in Iceland. No trees I could try climbing in either place, although for vastly different reasons. It was only after my mom died when I was nine, and my father started moving around the country, that I encountered trees. I fell out of the first one I climbed and needed stitches, which interrupted my father's schedule and his drinking—the latter being more important to him. Not that I'm bitter about any of that. Falling out of that first tree made me keep trying, with varying degrees of success and injury. In the end, Ranger school fixed whatever climbing problems I had. This tree wasn't challenging.

The trunk was sturdy enough for me to climb to the open metal framework that formed part of the roadway's superstructure. I got a grip on the flange of a massive I-beam and put my weight on it. The old metal held. I did a pull-up and managed to get my feet onto it. From there, I extended myself up and found my next grip point at the base of a stanchion supporting the guardrails. One more pull-up and a heave let me swing a leg over the railing. Large flakes of rust came off as I rolled over the top of the guardrail and dropped flat on the concrete on the other side. I waited for a shout or a shot, which would indicate I had been spotted. Crickets.

Where were the wagons? I could hear hoofbeats and wagon wheels on concrete. Of all times to move the wagons quickly, Bare Bones had picked now. They were early; I wasn't in position. I needed to move fast.

I squeezed through gaps between the dead cars to keep myself below the cover they provided. If there were no gaps, I rolled over hoods and trunks, trying not to show against the sky any more than necessary. Some of the vehicles held skeletons. I had spent long enough in postapocalyptic America that they were nothing more than part of the background.

Bricks and stones, as they say.

Shouts came from the blockaded westbound side. I heard demands to halt. I covered the last few feet to the guardrails beyond what had been the breakdown lane and tucked myself behind the hood of a wrecked car. It was a good covered firing position. The skull of a skeleton in the front seat was looking directly at me, but no one else was.

My rifle was a replica of the old 1873 Winchester that people of the twenty-third century produced as one of their standard weapons. This is a lever-action rifle with an eleven-bullet magazine. It requires a round to be chambered after each shot, but the lever action allows it to be fired rapidly. My pistol was a semiautomatic with a ten-bullet clip, but given the range, the rifle was a better bet.

A quick scan of the westbound side showed me that I was behind the position of the barricade. I had a decent view. The barrier had been constructed from logs chopped out of the woods and debris taken from wrecks. One section of the barrier looked like it could be pulled to the side to allow passage. I counted ten men behind the barricade, all wearing the dark gray serge overcoats of officers in the New Terran army. Their clothing had seen a lot of wear. Yes, they probably had been officers who fled the capital at New Terra when the president was overthrown—men whose prior actions gave them reason to fear vengeance after a revolution.

Small tents had been set up behind the barricade as well, and smoke still curled up from a now-extinguished campfire. It looked like they camped here for a few days when they knew wagons were coming down the road.

The barricade faced east. Travelers coming from the west would encounter these men only by chance. It would have been nice if a group from the west had come through and torn the site apart, but wishing for impossibilities wouldn't make them happen. What did matter was a tripod-mounted machine gun in the middle of the makeshift wall. It covered the road in front of the wall through a firing slot. The machine gunner was well protected against anyone on the other side of the barricade, but his position was open to the back.

"What is it you want?" I could hear Bare Bones even if I couldn't see him.

"The toll!" a hoarse voice shouted. "Twenty percent of everything of value."

"That's outrageous!" Bare Bones shouted back.

Don't get crazy, I thought.

"It's a lot cheaper than dying," the hoarse voice answered. "And don't think about raising a gun. We've got a machine gun and we'll kill every one of you, down to the children. Drop all your weapons on the road. Now!"

"We'll take a woman too!" another voice yelled out. "A young one. Not used." A laugh followed from several of them.

I hate robbers. I hate rapists supremely more.

Hollywood—back when there was a Hollywood—produced countless vids in which the hero, as a way of showing he's a good guy, refuses to shoot first, or shoot the bad guy from behind, or shoot the bad guy from hiding, despite these scruples putting themselves and their friends into peril. That's bullshit; it's not reality. If our hero acts that way, nine times out of ten they will be a dead hero with dead friends. When you have the shot, you take it.

Maybe I'm not a good guy.

I shot the machine gunner through the back of his head without warning. Blood and brains splashed around the firing slot. While the man closest to the gunner was dealing with the shock of seeing a head blow open, a quick pump of the lever chambered another round, and I shot him too. I didn't want anyone helming that weapon. One man spun around at my first shot. He fired wildly and a car window near me shattered. I shot him in the chest.

Taking advantage of the confusion among the enemy, No Nonsense jumped on top of the logs that formed part of the barricade. He had recovered his rifle and fired down at the bandits. One of them screamed and fell. Weapons dropped and hands went up in the air.

.   .   .

IT DIDN'T TAKE US LONG TO PULL BACK THE SLIDING PORTION OF THE BARRICADE, smash it to pieces, and roll the wagons past it. The four men we shot were dead. We heaved the bodies over the side of the elevated road. That left us with six prisoners.

"What do we do with them?" Caleb asked.

"We'll take their horses," Bare Bones said. "Maybe they can reach wherever their real camp is on foot, or get to one of the towns to the east. Not our concern."

"Yes, it is," Justice Served McClintock said. She was standing next to Bare Bones, a bolt-action rifle cradled in her arms. "Our wagons can't move fast. A man on foot can move faster. They could track us. What happens when it gets dark, especially if we haven't reached the Settlement Association camp? We need to finish this."

"No," I said. "I won't shoot a disarmed prisoner, and I won't let you do it either."

"Then what?" Bare Bones asked. "Justice is right. We have to protect our families, and you can't take their words they'll go back east."

He had a point, but there are some things I can't accept. I stared at the prisoners. I doubted they would have shown us any mercy, but still …

"All right," I said. "All six of you. Coats off. Drop them on the ground now."

They stared at me, fear and questioning in their faces.

"Do it now!" I shouted. "Whatever I say, do it immediately, if you want to live."

Six serge coats hit the pavement.

"Now your boots and socks." When those had been pulled off, I said, "Drop your pants."

A few minutes later, six skinny bare asses shivered in the chilly wind. Giggles came from the wagons.

"Okay," I said to the six. "We're taking your clothes. If you're thinking about tracking us as you are, I'd think again. If you're smart, you'll get to some camp or town to the east as fast as you can. Better get going."

We watched until they had made their way, barefoot and shivering, down the causeway and out of sight into the trees. From the bridge, we dumped their clothes into the Mississippi. Their weapons, including the machine gun, went into the wagons.

With the erstwhile highwaymen gone, the bridge was open in front of us. Only one car was visible on our side of the span, rammed into a side guardrail.

Out of curiosity, I dismounted next to the car and peeked through the windows. A coffee mug still sat in a holder, but I saw no human remains.

"I wonder where they went," I said to Caleb and No Nonsense.

"Probably jumped and made a quick end of it," Caleb said.

"Aren't you the cheerful one," I replied.

When he said nothing else, I remounted and spurred the horse away from the car. From the bridge, we had a good view of Saint Louis on the west side. The city was depressing. The scale of it, silent and ruined, pressed down like a great weight that would squeeze the life out of any creature with the temerity to intrude. Beyond our horses and wagons, the only sounds came from the river lapping against the piers below. I looked across the Mississippi to the arch. From this distance, it stood there seemingly untouched by time. A thick wood had grown up around its base, where there had once been open land for a park. More buildings marked the skyline to the west.

Bare Bones dropped back to come even with me. "The Settlement Association camp is supposed to be by the arch," he said. "We'll stop there for the night. You're welcome to share the camp with us."

I checked the distance between the sun and the horizon, then assessed the crawling pace of the wagons. As much as I wanted to pick up our pace, even if we left the wagons that moment and went on our own, we were not going to be free of the city by nightfall.

"We'll join you," I said.

CHAPTER THREE

THE SETTING SUN FOUND A CRACK OF CLEAR SKY BETWEEN THE GRAY CLOUD BANK and the horizon. It lit up the sky and the undersides of the clouds in streaks and sheets of purples and reds. Red light poured across the words painted around the base of Gateway Arch as we rode in. On each side, I saw the lines of the Prayer of the Hungry and the Cold that I had seen painted on so many buildings in the East.

> *To hell with the future*
> *We're doomed by our past*
> *May God in His mercy*
> *Be kind at the last.*

Unlike many places I had seen those words, this paint could not have been more than a few years old. It had scarcely weathered. Smoke billowed up from a campfire in front of two small but sturdy log buildings. The sign above the door of one read SETTLEMENT ASSOCIATION. The one on the other building read GENERAL STORE.

McClintock brought the wagons to a stop in the cleared area beneath the arch. While adults unhitched the horses and cared for them, children tumbled out of the wagons and ran, shrieked, and played, as kids will do when no adult is giving them chores. My kids would have been the same way. Yes, I thought of them as *my* kids, and that felt right. The saying was—and I had discovered that the church also preached it—that family was where you found it. I had found Charity and her children the day I landed on Earth. Despite my initial intent to travel on to Earthbase—and later having to go to war—I had gone back to Charity's farm. I had found a family to join. I would be there now, except for a message from a distant star and the urgent need of Caleb and Earthbase for starfolk.

I sighed—only to myself, I think—as I thought of Charity, the farm, and that squad of kids. I would head back there once I had done whatever I could do about this signal from the stars. What I could do was still unclear to me, but I would figure out something. I had to do that much. I had told Caleb about how important and unique the opportunity presented by the signal was for humanity—but it was more than that. I had been to the stars twice. And although I'd paid a price in doing so, it was a rare privilege, one purchased by the efforts of thousands and the fortune of the world. There is a duty that comes with privilege like that. As cynical as I had become about duty after years of deployments and combat, the concept was still embedded in my mind—even if it sometimes felt like a burden. I didn't think I could explain that to Caleb, or even to No Nonsense.

I had duties to Charity and the kids also. I had told Charity I was coming back. She had given me a long kiss and said she would pray for safe travel and a quick return. Elvy, my little thirteen-year-old imp with the odd jade-green eyes the townspeople called feral eyes, had been a different matter. She had found me, or I had found her, in a raider ambush right after I had parachuted to Earth. I killed those raiders and she had come with me to Charity's family and stayed as one of Charity's daughters. I winced at the memory of her reaction to my departure.

"You're lyin'!" she had shouted at me. "You're not comin' back! I know it. You're not." The polished jade green of her eyes had been as hard as real jade. She had turned her back and avoided me until I rode off. I hadn't seen eyes like hers since we were west of Old Pennsylvania. I missed them and her.

I guess family can be complicated at times.

I allowed myself to imagine her reaction when I reappeared at the farmhouse. *See*, I would say, *I've come back. Just like I said.*

Maybe that would be childish. Maybe I should bring something back for her. I tried to think of what that should be, and my gaze swung to the general store.

"Leif!"

Caleb's shout cut through my reverie, and my daydream dissolved into thin air like the smoke from the campfire. He was standing between the fire and the log houses in a group composed of No Nonsense, Bare Bones, Justice Served, and a man I did not recognize. Judging by how they looked at me, I was expected to join them.

"Leif," Caleb said when I reached the group, "this is Praise Worthy Jefferson, who is running the station here this season. I was just telling him about you."

Inwardly, I groaned.

"So, you're Starman Leif," Praise said. I could hear wonder in his voice, and my insides groaned again. He was a thin man, as were almost all I had met since my return, with dark brown skin and a clean-shaven face. He wore a sturdy pair of wool twill pants and a stained homespun shirt. "The stories about you have even crossed the Mississippi. They're all calling you Leif the Lucky. Did the old president and his senators really flee when you walked into Government Plaza in New Terra and told them to be gone?"

"They had run off before I arrived," I said, "and I think it was the army of forty thousand that was filling that plaza and the city streets that did it. That state was ripe for a revolution. With all the stories and fables people tell about lucky starmen, I made a good excuse to revolt. That's all."

It was an odd thing. It felt like a lifetime ago—or even a life in an alternate universe—when I fought Miles Richmond, a crazy man who was threatening to destroy humanity's antimatter production facility. I killed him and inadvertently turned him into a martyr who was credited with launching humanity's interplanetary and interstellar settlements. The notoriety from that had left me longing for the day when I could be introduced without someone remarking that I had killed Saint Miles, as he had come to be called. Well, that day had come, only to be replaced by people hailing me as the lucky starman who had won a war and led a revolution. Was a day ever going to come again when the response to *Hi, I'm Leif Grettison* would be only, *Glad to meet you?*

"Modest man," Praise said. "Still, you can be sure I'll talk about the day you camped at my station. Even though I should be angry at you."

He didn't look angry. He looked ready to laugh.

"Why?"

He did laugh. "With the Formation Wars over and an actual honest government in New Terra, folks are pouring out to settle new land. Most of them, though, are going into the old open borderlands in the East. Not so risky as crossing the Mississippi, so traffic's down here—and that was even before we had bandit trouble. If you've rid us of them, and maybe you have, that'll count as a good deed. But it's lonely here, I'd say, and my goods don't sell." He pointed back at the store then slapped his hands together. "Well, the association promised to give me a station in the East next year, so this will become someone else's problem." He laughed again.

One of the children whooped "Bones!" Justice Served started in the direction of the voice, trying to see into the gloom that had gathered under the trees.

"They can't have gone as far as the buildings," Justice Served said.

"No, they didn't," Praise replied. "They don't have to. This area around the arch, people from the city came here. Nobody knows why, of course. Maybe they were hoping for boats to take them down the river, not that it would have helped them. Whatever the reason, they died here. Dig anywhere and you'll find graves, so they must have buried the dead at first. Later on, though, they were just left where they died. You can still find bones up top if you look."

"Any idea what killed them?" I asked. "Or who?"

Praise shrugged. "Probably starved. Or froze. Or both. It was the Tribulation. Dead is dead."

Dead is dead. The catchall phrase everyone used in a world where so many had died in such a short time that any death was unremarkable. I remembered finding piles of skeletal remains in what had been an airport parking garage. How long before they all turned to dust and people forgot?

"If you'll excuse me," Justice Served said, "I'm going to see to it that the children are all back in the wagons for the night."

"Yes. We'll want to start with the first light," Bare Bones said. "Newtown's letter said they had homes waiting for families that hadn't come, that's why we're on the road so late in the year. But a home and stores for the taking don't do us any good if we're caught in a snowstorm on the way. The days are short, and the sooner we get there, the happier I'll be."

"We'll part ways, then," Caleb said. "I want to be off at first light as well, and we have a long road west. We will need additional supplies." Caleb took Praise Worthy by the arm and walked with him to the general store. At least Praise would sell some of his goods.

Bare Bones and Justice Served went off at the same time, yelling to the other families to round up their children, an action on par with herding a flock of cats. They were good people, I thought, but we would go our separate ways, as Caleb said, and never see each other again. I had done exactly that in the past with everyone I had known on Earth. It's the nature of a starman. Well, it was before I became a grounded starman. If nothing else, that allowed me some sense of permanence.

I took the opportunity to disengage from the others and sit alone by the fire. By the calendar it was still October, but it was cold in the evenings and snow was a risk. The nuclear strikes and resulting firestorms in the wars that ended civilization in 2137 had thrown so much ash and dirt into the atmosphere that the sunlight had been blocked, and temperatures had fallen around the world. The Three Years' Winter, people called it. That was why most of the population had starved and frozen: no power, no heat, no transportation, and no food. The climate remained much colder than I remembered, back when we worried about global warming.

I had beef jerky in the pack I was carrying—no need to go back to the saddle packs for something to eat—but thinking about the wars and the mess we had made of Earth took my appetite away. It often did that. Instead, I felt for the secret pocket that Charity had sewn into the waistband of my pants, using a piece of the parachute that had brought me down to Earth. In there, safe in the smoothest fabric available on this current Earth, was where I kept the printed pic of me and Yang Yong.

By firelight, I gazed at the picture of the two of us together in the meadow on High Noon, the planet we had explored on the first starshot. Yong died on our return from our second star mission, killed while preventing a malware-infected ship's computer from crashing a starship fully loaded with antimatter fuel into one of the remaining population centers on Earth. I sometimes thought she had seen that death as a release, an atonement for her part fighting in the Troubles and paving the way for those who had wrecked the world. I forced the thought away. She was a hero; she was my love.

"You still look at that picture."

With a start, I realized No Nonsense had walked up behind me. His voice held only respect, however. There was none of his usual smart-ass teenaged tone. "I remember when you told stories about her at the farm."

"I loved her, No Nonsense. It's not something I can describe very well. I don't think it's something you would understand. Not yet, anyway."

"Leif—"

"Don't." I cut him off without taking my eyes from the picture. "Please don't give me that 'dead is dead' line that everybody uses. It doesn't feel like that, and it never will."

"I wasn't going to say that." No Nonsense folded his frame and sat down easily on the ground—the way I used to be able to do—next to me. "We all understand. Ma does. She likes you. She wants you to come back, and she wants you to stay when you do. She wants it to be your family also, but she understands how you feel and it's okay. The other children understand too. Well, maybe not the little ones, but I know Elvy does. We know the woman in the picture was special."

I slid the picture carefully back into its pocket. Then I rested my arms on my knees and stared back into the fire. I didn't say anything. I was getting empathy and support from a teenage boy.

What had happened to my world?

CHAPTER FOUR

I T WAS ASTONISHING HOW LONG IT TOOK TO PASS THROUGH THE RUINS OF SAINT Louis, which wasn't even one of the largest cities of my time. It took, in fact, almost an entire day's travel to go from the Gateway Arch to the I-70 crossing over the Missouri River. Of course, we were traveling on horseback. Even after a year, I found I needed to periodically reset my expectations.

The deserted city stretched out on either side of the highway as far as I could see. From a distance, it all looked intact; it was the silence, broken only by the occasional cry of an animal, that seemed out of place. Up close, however, it was different. Wherever the ground had not been paved over or built on, tall weeds, bushes, and some trees had grown up. Even in the highway itself, a formidable barrier against nature clad in concrete and asphalt, grass had found its way into cracks, and the road had begun to break up in places. As elsewhere, wrecked, charred, or simply deserted cars dotted the road.

No Nonsense reined in by a pair of cars, one a burned-out hulk, the other whole and untouched, with skeletons visible inside. "This is strange," he said. "How does one of these catch fire, without any fire anywhere else, and then this other one, it's fine, but the people just sat inside and died. Why didn't they get out?"

Caleb came back to where we had stopped and rode around the two vehicles. He shrugged. "It's anybody's guess what happened. These cars, they all had computers in them. I've heard stories that the computers, when they went mad before they died, could make a car catch fire to kill the people inside, or they could seal the doors and windows so the people were trapped and then the car could do something to the air inside. But no one knows the truth of what happened during the Tribulation."

Caleb paused and I thought about what he had said. If cars with malware-infected computers could deliberately crash, they could probably also ignite their batteries and incinerate their occupants. Maybe even seal their occupants in airtight prisons. People's ordinary tools, appliances, and possessions had been connected by the chips and phones of our civilization, and many of them had been weaponized. The ingenuity of that time in pursuit of random murder was as amazing as it was revolting. During the final cyberwar, people died in terror of the mundane.

"I think computers were evil incarnate," Caleb said.

"No," I said. "Computers were machines. People were evil."

"Then I doubt anything has changed." Caleb pulled on the reins and turned his horse back to the west. "Come on. I would like to cross the Missouri before dark. The bridge that carries this road is standing and open."

·　　·　　·

As Caleb said, that river crossing presented no problems and we continued west on the old interstate. Each day blended into the one before and the one following. The old road was easy enough to follow. Even where dirt had blown across the concrete and grass and weeds had taken root, the roadway was obvious. Two broad open paths ran east and west with a shallow depression that had been the median between them.

Even a century and more of time had not been enough to break up the thick concrete and substructure to the point that trees could take root and grow. If that were not enough of a trail to follow, plenty of road signs still stood. As important as the open road, the weather held. It was cold even in the sun, but the scattered clouds above were thin as tissue.

Kansas City, when we reached it, was almost identical to Saint Louis. Dead, hollow, and silent. Only the signs were different. We crossed the Missouri yet again and left Kansas City behind for the plains of Kansas, where the world became flat as well as empty. The wind blew past us, burning our cheeks and rattling the few remaining road signs. Grass waved in the wind, and sometimes birds that had not gone south flew overhead, but that was about it for signs of life. Even the ruinscapes were gone. We saw only the sad and derelict relics of a few buildings here and there. While there had been a boom in the area adjacent to Earthbase, most of western Kansas was pretty depopulated back in the twenty-first century. Where we were riding had been nearly vacant by the time of the wars in the twenty-second.

When darkness fell, we would light our campfire, eat a meager meal, and curl into our bedrolls to stave off the increasing bite of the cold night wind. At my insistence, we set a watch through each night.

Caleb grumbled about that for the first few days. "There's not much point to it," he said. "Not enough game on the plains for any large predators. Anyway, it's people who are really dangerous, and there are none in the Empty Lands."

"Times change," I said.

"Not out here," Caleb responded. "At least, not yet. I'm a senior scout. We scouts know this land. The Three Years' Winter was very harsh here. Almost everything died. It became a desert not too far north of here. It's still empty. That's why it's important to carry adequate food. You can't rely on catching enough to feed yourself."

"How many senior scouts like you does Earthbase have?"

"Certified? Like me? Not many. A dozen to two dozen at any time. I'm certified to go anywhere, even into the eastern states, and to guide traders out to Earthbase. It takes training and a willingness to be alone."

"I'm not disputing what it takes to be one of you," I said. "My point is that this land is vast. Two dozen of you can't know what is happening out here or how it may be changing. Open land is attractive. Just look at the folks we came across the Mississippi with."

"Where they settle is barely out of sight of the river," Caleb protested.

"That's for now," I said. "Next, some will settle just past sight of where the towns are now, where they can still have plenty of open land. And then the next group will settle just beyond them. And it will go on like that."

"It won't matter." Caleb tossed a branch into the fire. "We have plenty of local scouts who go out on the plains, even if they're not certified for long distance, and there are more juniors who will grow up and be seniors, and then there are Blues who support what we do even if they're not scouts."

"Blues?" I asked.

"I'll explain about colors when we get there. Blues are on our side." He busied himself with something inside his pack that appeared to need attention.

"You should listen to Leif," No Nonsense said. "He knows a lot from before."

"Before is gone," Caleb replied. "It has nothing to do with now."

I suppose Caleb was right. We were never bothered at night. I did want to know what he meant about Blues and what it meant that they were on his side. But Caleb proved as resistant to talking about colors as he had been about providing any further details on the message from the stars.

·   ·   ·

Most of the nights were clear, and it was impossible not to look at the stars when it was my watch. The sky was dark in a way it had never been when I was young, when the glow of city lights washed out all but the brightest stars. The sky now let millions of stars twinkle along-side the brilliant band of the Milky Way, a huge bracelet of fairy dust thrown against blackness.

On those clear nights, I would look up and wonder *who* sent us this signal and what message it contained. What were they like? Did they look mostly like us, or were they like what a dinosaur would have evolved to if not for an asteroid that hit Earth, or even something amoeboid that manipulated its world with muscular pseudopods? Did they play sports or vid games? I could never form a clear picture, but then again, no one has ever said I could write fiction.

I wondered, too, about what we would do when I reached Earth-base. They must have somehow preserved much of their computer capacity. I saw us arguing over possible meanings of an uncertain translation and debating what to include in the message we would send back. In my imagination, I always managed to find a way to sign my name, Leif Grettison, to the return message—a graffiti artist approach to interstellar communication. Our message would take decades, maybe longer, to reach the aliens, and I assumed I would be long dead by the time their next signal came back. The people here who received it would need to puzzle out why the aliens were asking, *Who is Leif Grettison?* Okay, it was a pleasant and harmless conceit.

One of those nights, I looked over at No Nonsense lying on his back, rolled up in his blanket, head pillowed on a pack. I thought he was asleep until I saw his eyes blink. He was staring at the star-spangled sky.

"Are you okay?" I asked. "Are you thinking of home? Do you miss the farm?"

"No, no," he said. "I mean, sure I miss Ma some, but I was always going to leave and she knew that. No, I was thinking about the stars. I still have trouble believing you are a starman—and I've known you more than a year—and that you had adventures out there, up there. God, what I'd give to do that. Now, don't laugh at me," he said quickly. "I know I'll never do it. But I will see the mountains beyond the Empty Lands, and that'll be grand enough for me. Maybe I'll find a girl, like you did, and have that adventure with her. That would be spectacular, don't you think?"

"It's a good way to die in a strange place," I said. He and I had had this conversation before.

"And that's worse than dying in the same place you've always been 'cause you never went anywhere or did anything?" He laughed. "You're getting to be an old man, Leif."

"Go to sleep, No Nonsense."

When I was sure he was sleeping, I looked back at the sky. I didn't want to look at the stars, but I couldn't help myself. I found it hard to believe myself, lying by the embers of a campfire in what had been Kansas, that I had gone out to them. I wanted to see the stars of Heaven or High Noon but I couldn't. I didn't know where to look or if they were even overhead, and I wasn't sure they were bright enough if they were. I had walked on the worlds that circled those stars, though. There were people on those worlds now—some of them, maybe on Heaven, descended from ones I had known. Did they wonder about Earth?

I had never planned to be a starman. In truth, any plans I made had been short term at best. I joined the army because after my mom died, my father was usually broke and drunk. And if I survived combat, the army would pay for college. I'd never had a plan for what I would do with my life beyond getting a job and not being broke. I put in an application for the BerthRight Lottery because people I knew were doing it, and how I ended up winning that berth on the first starshot had been no plan of mine.

To the extent that I had come up with a plan after that, it was to fly through the universe forever with Yang Yong. But civilization imploded, she died a hero, and I was riding a horse across Kansas. Even this crazy ride hadn't been a real plan. Not one of my making, at any rate.

Caleb had shown up in Eastview, the town nearest Charity's farm, with this wild tale of a message from a star that Earthbase couldn't interpret. He said they needed a starman's help to deal with it. I couldn't—wouldn't—say no to that, not to something that important and not to the concept of duty it brought with it. But it wasn't as though I had planned what I was doing. Maybe the best plan I could make for the future was to go back and live on the farm with Charity and raise kids.

Like I know anything about raising kids.

I wanted to talk to Yong about all of that. I wanted to hear her voice, but she kept her counsel to herself. My ghosts were silent those nights on the plains. I could feel only the weight of the stars above me.

.   .   .

WE TURNED SOUTH TO EARTHBASE IN THE SAME PLACE I HAD IN **2069, 183** YEARS before, when I had self-driven my car out to join the first starshot. The exit sign on the highway was still there.

The secondary road that led to Earthbase and the city of Tribune was mostly covered over with dirt and grass. My implanted chip had a road map from 2097 and a compass app. Both showed the direction; however, I had no intention of disclosing the existence of the apps or my chip. They did confirm to me that Caleb had no trouble keeping us on the right course.

It was Caleb's behavior after we made the turn that I found interesting. He pulled a small metal shield out of his pack, maybe three inches long by two wide. It was coated with blue enamel. He pinned that to his jacket as we rode.

"What's that?" I asked.

"My color" was the answer.

"That's not very helpful," I said.

"It shows I'm blue," Caleb said.

"That isn't much more helpful." I tapped my chest and then waved at No Nonsense. "What are our colors?"

"You don't have colors. You're not from Earthbase." Caleb kept his eyes on the road ahead.

"Oh, so is this some secret society you're part of? Does it have a secret handshake to go with it?" There might have been an edge in my voice.

"Can this wait till we get there?" I could tell from the rigidity in the way Caleb now sat in his saddle that he was acutely uncomfortable. "I shouldn't be the one to talk about this."

"Just like the signal from the stars," I said.

"Yes." The word was bitten off short.

"Okay," I said. "You're the boss."

"No, I'm not," Caleb said. "That's the point."

CHAPTER FIVE

THE FOLLOWING MORNING, CALEB TOOK TIME TO GATHER ARMFULS OF BRUSH and start a smoky fire. It sent a column of gray-white cloud into the otherwise flawless blue canopy above us. Using a blanket he pulled from his horse, he cut the pillar of smoke into a series of puffs.

"Who are you signaling?" I asked.

"Earthbase. I also want to let any scouts who are outside, particularly with animals, know that we are here."

"I gather you're not worried about anyone else seeing your signals," I said.

"Of course not." Caleb stood up straight and folded the blanket. "I told you, there's no one else anywhere on these plains."

"Then why bother with the signal?" I asked. "We could just ride in and when we show up, we can't be anybody else."

His shoulders tensed; he stared at me with that worried look of his. After a long moment, he said, "Maybe the training was from before, when it did matter, and now it's no more than habit." He kicked dirt into the fire. "I never thought of it that way."

"We all have our habits," I said. "Now that we've announced our arrival, though, we might as well get there. Have you decided what you're going to say about not finding more starfolk?"

Its purpose accomplished, Caleb smothered the fire with more dirt. "I doubt I'll say more than they can see." He pushed hair away from his eyes and adjusted his hat. "I hope you can help. Even if I only have one of you."

The three of us let our horses pick their own pace south along the old road with the packhorses trailing behind. It wasn't too long before I could see the buildings of Earthbase poking up from the flat plain of Kansas and outlined against the sky. My memory told me Earthbase had been much smaller when I drove down this road in 2069, but I hadn't arrived by road in 2097, and for all I knew, the view was no different than it had been in that year. What was different now was a low gray line across the buildings that became visible as we approached in the afternoon. A wall. Had Earthbase been enclosed by a wall? I couldn't remember.

While I was trying to puzzle this out, I spied a single rider headed toward us from the southwest. Recognition must have been mutual, because whoever it was spurred their horse into a gallop at the same time I spotted them. The distance between us closed rapidly. Caleb reined in at the other's approach, so No Nonsense and I stopped as well. Since Caleb made no move for a weapon, I assumed he was confident in his assessment that people from Earthbase would be the only ones to see his signal.

The other rode hard right up to Caleb before reining in abruptly, a maneuver that had the horse rearing up with dirt and rocks flying. It was a woman in the saddle. She pushed a broad-brimmed leather hat back from her head and let it dangle from a strap around her neck. Her face was smooth and unlined, a young face. No older than No Nonsense, I would bet. Fair skin was still tanned, except for where the hat would sit across the top of her forehead. Bouncy auburn curls festooned her head from the top, where the hat had been unable to squash them, and hung down to her shoulders. She had light brown eyes and a slight upturn at the end of her nose. Her attire was all leather, down to gloved hands that held the reins and dusty, well-worn boots in the stirrups. There was a pistol at her belt, but no rifle by the saddle. Pinned to her jacket was a blue enamel shield, the same as Caleb wore.

"Shoshanna," Caleb called out to her, "they stuck you with cattle and sheep duty?"

"Someone has to do it!" she yelled back with more force than the distance between them warranted. "And while I'm doing it, which has been more days this fall than I want to count, I can watch for you coming back. You took your damned time about it. Mario and Yaeger are hissing around Landrieu like cats in heat, wanting him to do something, but no one will say what he should do. The Reds just sit there like there's no thought at all in their heads, which is probably true. So, it's all your damned fault, and aren't you even going to introduce your sister to whoever the hell they are?" She flung out an arm at me and No Nonsense.

This Shoshanna had a flair for the dramatic.

Caleb laughed, possibly the first real laugh I'd heard from him since we'd met. "I would if you would ever give me a chance to get a word in." He turned his horse to face us and got it to back up so he was side by side with her. "This is my sister, Shoshanna Peterson, a scout—but a junior scout, as she is still at the delicate age of seventeen."

Now that they were next to each other, I could see the similarity in their faces.

"Far from delicate," Shoshanna said, and aimed a backhand slap at Caleb from her saddle. "And I usually go by Sho."

"As in Sho-off," Caleb said.

"You'll pay for that," she replied. Then she walked her horse over by mine. "This is all you brought back?" she said over her shoulder to Caleb. "All that time and only this?"

Well, I thought, *I'm pleased to meet you too.*

"That's all there is, Sho," Caleb said.

She turned to face me. "You're a starman." It was a statement, not a question.

"Yes. Leif Grettison."

"Good. Maybe." She moved her horse next to No Nonsense. "You're not," she said. "No way."

"And that's the truth. I'm No Nonsense Johnson and I'm riding with Leif for now. I'm off to see the plains and the mountains beyond."

"What for?" she asked. "Nothing there but dead towns and dead cities and deader bones. I won't say Earthbase is a lively town, but parts of it can be. Depending on what people you're with." She gave No Nonsense a careful visual inspection, and I didn't think it was the same way she would check over one of the cows. "I like that beard." A little smile formed on her lips, enough to cause dimples.

No Nonsense turned a delicate shade of pink, but he was also looking hard at her. The leather outfit she wore was fitted closely enough to showcase broad shoulders and a trim form, even on horseback.

Caleb noticed the looks. Hell, anybody within half a mile would have noticed. "What happened with Devin Whelan?" he asked. "I would swear I heard you declare he was the love of your life. More than once!"

"I was young then." Sho laughed easily. "After you rode out, he started acting like he owned me. Turned out to be a real turd."

Caleb's face turned grim. "What did he do? I'm back now. He'll see you've got an older brother who can do what needs to be done."

"As if!" She threw her head back, and this laugh was loud enough to startle the horse into rearing.

Caleb peered at her as she brought the horse back under control. "What did you do?" he asked.

"Beat the shit out of him," Sho said. "Pretty public too."

"Ah." Caleb smiled. "And perhaps that's why they've got you out counting cow chips. Not that you're desperate to catch the first glimpse of your brother on his return."

"There could be some of that involved." Sho had the grace to look a bit guilty.

I moved my horse over next to No Nonsense's. He was still admiring her figure on horseback. "You know," I murmured, "I'm pretty good with emergency first aid, but there are some pieces I can't put back together. You might want to think about that."

"I know how to take care of myself, Leif," No Nonsense said.

I'd heard that line before. Hell, I'd used that line before.

"Yeah," I said. "Sure."

"Brandon can watch the dumb animals by himself for a while." Her comment to Caleb brought my eyes back to her. "I'll ride in with you. There are people, and not only Greens, who are very unhappy you rode out. There's strength in numbers. You only brought back one, though, so maybe they'll only laugh at you."

"Wait a minute." I broke into the brother-sister exchange before Caleb could reply. "You told me you were sent to find the starfolk, and I'm sure you said you weren't the only one sent out. Now your sister is saying people are unhappy you went, and it sounds like you're the only one who did. What's the truth?"

Caleb shifted back and forth in his saddle. "Scout leadership did say I should go."

"Some of them. Mario only, I bet. Privately," Sho said. "The board never agreed. You left before they could meet on it."

"Which means they never said no," Caleb said.

"Why would that even be a question?" I asked.

"It's complicated," brother and sister said together.

"I don't know what could be so complicated," I said, "but sitting out here on our horses won't make it uncomplicated."

"True." Caleb pulled on the reins to turn the horse toward Earth-base.

That was when something else from his exchange with Sho tickled my mind. "One more question before we go," I called to them. "What did you mean when you mentioned Greens and Reds. What are they?"

"Other colors," Caleb said, and gave his horse a kick.

CHAPTER SIX

As we neared Earthbase, I saw that the wall was poured gray concrete, stained by time, sun, and weather so that a pattern of irregular blobs of white to dark gray ran along its length as far as I could see. Flowing waves of brown and orange ran down from its top, where rusted remnants of razor wire showed. The only barrier those would likely pose today was the risk that anyone trying to scale the wall would contract tetanus for their trouble. More disturbing, as I scanned the top of the wall, were the platforms that had been placed every few hundred feet.

"Those are gun emplacements," I said. "I don't see soldiers, though. Are they all automated? Do you have that tech here?"

"No, no," Caleb said. "That's all old. Goes back to the Tribulation, to the Three Years' Winter. Even before it, I think. The guns are still there, but even if they still have ammunition, I doubt they would work. I don't think there's anybody old enough to even remember when they were last fired."

"But they were fired," I said, picking up on the way he phrased his last sentence. "What happened here? That wall won't stop an army, certainly not if they have any kind of artillery. What's the wall for, and why all the guns?"

"It's stories," Caleb said.

"That doesn't tell me anything."

He sighed as we rode under the muzzles of weapons that tipped over the wall at crazy angles. "During the Three Years' Winter, after the wars, there was no food and no heat. We had supplies in Earthbase, though. Not a lot. Barely enough to survive. The people who lived in this area tried to storm Earthbase and take what we had. The stories say the guns were almost out of ammunition when the mobs gave up. All around the wall, it used to be called the Bonefield."

"It still is," Sho said. "Dig a little, you'll find them. We don't need those guns anymore. There's nobody left out here except us."

"Base security will get mad at you if you say they don't need guns," Caleb said.

"Hah!" shouted Sho. "That's only so they have jobs and can look important."

We rode to an opening that had been built into the concrete wall. Two armed men stepped out to block the way as we came close. They wore dark gray pants of heavy wool over leather boots, and lighter-weight shirts dyed a pale blue were visible under their serge coats. Each of them wore a shield similar in size to Caleb's and Sho's, but the enamel was green. It was the weapons they carried that caught my eye, however. M8s! I hadn't seen one of those since we left the colonists on Heaven.

Caleb and Sho dismounted before they reached the guards and walked ahead of their horses the rest of the way. I decided to copy them and was gratified to see No Nonsense come to the same conclusion.

"Well, well, Caleb Peterson," I heard the guard closest to us say. "What are you bringing us? Not traders, obviously. Must be starmen or refugees. You had no authorization to bring anyone. Or even to go."

"You're a guard on gate duty, Ramón Ugarte," Caleb snapped. "Not an administrator. Everyone knows a ship came in and they didn't land here. It's the scouts' job to find them when that happens, and that's what I did."

"Not that it's happened since you were born. Everybody knows that the situation is different now. Ever vigilant. That's our motto at base security. Now more than ever."

"Your motto should be 'Ever vigilant, ever unready!'" Sho shouted.

Ramón glared at her, then focused back on Caleb. "You needed permission, and you didn't get it. Plenty say that you wouldn't have got it."

"My brother doesn't need your permission to do his job, or for you to tell him what a scout's job is." Sho stepped between Caleb and Ramón. "I'll bet the only ones saying he wouldn't have gotten permission are Greens too stupid to have any job except base security. You think carrying that gun when you have duty makes you a big man? It doesn't." She held her hand out, palm down, at the level of her chin, which was about the height Ramón's head came to.

Ramón didn't move. "How does it feel to hide behind your little sister?" he asked Caleb. "And what are you going to do, Sho? Punch my teeth out the way you did to Whalen? I would say the scouts need discipline and better administration."

Sho looked like she would be happy to do some punching then and there, but that's not a move I recommend against a man carrying an assault rifle. Clearly, these were not old friends, and I was getting more than a whiff of internal politics.

I stepped up to be even with Sho but well to the side, so that if Ugarte brought the rifle up, he wouldn't be able to cover both of us.

"How are you carrying an M8?" I asked. "I haven't seen one since I left."

That drew Ramón's attention to me. "It's an M8c," he said. "We've always had them. Is that your way of telling me you're a starman? Neither you nor him"—he pointed at No Nonsense—"look old enough."

That stopped me long enough for Caleb to speak. "The others have been here, what, thirty-three years for the last crew? That's why they look old, idiot."

My ears perked up at that. A starship crew had been at Earthbase for thirty-three years?

"I'm Leif Grettison from the *Dauntless*, if you know the ship's name."

Ramón shrugged. "People may have mentioned a ship's name. Can't say I recall it. What about him?" He gestured at No Nonsense again. "He looks too young for sure, and we don't take refugees. What story did you give Caleb?"

Thankfully, No Nonsense didn't rise to the provocation. He gave Ugarte the same line he had used before about riding with me and then heading west.

"You can talk to the Red administration about how long you can stay and whether you can buy provisions. We've had a couple of trade groups from the East this fall. Maybe the Reds will work out something for you too. For us in security, it's ever vigilant." He tapped the stock of his rifle. Then he pointed at me. "Any starman who comes in needs to see the chief administrator."

"You recite that as though you do it every other day," Caleb said. "I'll show Leif where he needs to go. May we now pass your eternal vigilance?"

From Ramón's face, I think he wanted to think of some reason to keep us standing outside the wall, but he lacked the imagination to come up with one. Instead, he ground his teeth, growled, and made a gesture to the other guard. That man retreated to the rear of the opening in the wall, where I could see a rusted chain-link fence in the shadows. He shoved it to the side with a loud squeak and walked through the gap, leaving it open for us. Before we reached it, I heard hoofbeats pounding away from us on the other side.

I inspected that fence as we walked up to it and then guided our horses through the opening. I think it would have been proof against rabbits, but I'm not sure it would have stood up to a deer.

On the other side of the wall, we were at the top of the Avenue of Heroes. I remembered this road from my two stays at Earthbase. Once, a grand sign had arched over the roadway, welcoming one and all to the J. Robert Mitchell Earthbase. No trace of that sign, or of J. Robert Mitchell, remained. *Sic transit gloria mundi.* To our right was the spur of pavement that led to the maglev station, where I had arrived from the Garden City Airport in 2097. The building was still there, or the tumbledown wreck of it was.

Caleb followed my gaze. "The tunnel was blown up and blocked during the Die-off, when the mob tried to break in. Base security keeps a guard there, but nobody else pays any attention now."

We saddled up again and rode slowly past the monument to Apollo 1, with its statues of Grissom, White, and Chaffee. It was odd riding a horse down the avenue beyond, past the statues of Armstrong, Aldrin, and all the other early astronauts and cosmonauts. The statues to the Russian and Chinese space explorers had had tar thrown over their faces, and half of them had been knocked off their pedestals.

"I'm not sure how much good those guards do you," I said, mostly to take my mind away from the rows of statues. "With the land around you empty, they don't have anything to do. However, if New Terra actually sent a force out here, they wouldn't be able to defend the place."

"But they are ever vigilant," Sho said, and it was impossible to miss the sarcasm in her voice.

"Do their weapons work?" I asked.

"Every one of the old guns is test-fired once a year," Caleb said. "We also manufacture our own modern rifles and pistols using the same designs as the states in the East. It has been a law since the time of those mobs that every adult must have a weapon, and every family must have a weapon for every child age twelve or older, although people don't carry them all the time as they do in the East."

"Does it matter?" Sho asked. "They'd be lucky to hit the wall from a distance of ten feet. They had to watch me, a junior and a girl, win the riflery competition this summer."

The rest of the way down the avenue, Caleb and Sho kept up a derogatory and sophomoric exchange about the skill, training, and dedication of base security. I tuned it out. No Nonsense didn't say anything, but I saw he had positioned his horse so that he could keep his eyes locked on Sho. I knew what he was thinking. More precisely, I knew he wasn't thinking. I looked at the three of them and sighed. Kids.

In my mind, I could hear Petey from my old platoon speaking to me. *Hey, Sarge, what happened? You get transferred to day care duty? Maybe you can get back with us. We're headed out on a recon and then I hear we'll get some rest at Schwarzkopf.*

Sure, Petey, I could hear myself say. *I'll be with you guys at Schwarzkopf.*

And I had been. Where that last attack had killed everyone in the platoon. Except me.

There were times I wondered why I hadn't died with the rest of them. Thought I should have died there. Wondered if it would have been better if I had.

At the end of the avenue was the monument to Starshot I, a grandiose mass of granite, marble, and bronze. It hadn't been finished when I was last at Earthbase. I dismounted in front of the life-sized statues of the pilots: Peter Bush, Vasily Kuznetsov, and Yang Yong. I had eyes only for Yong and had to fight to keep them from misting. Now I was glad I hadn't died at Schwarzkopf. If I had, I wouldn't have had the chance to love her. Loving Yong was worth everything that had happened, all the way to the agony of losing her when the *Dauntless* exploded and she died. Sometimes I thought it wouldn't matter so much if I died now, but then I would remind myself that as long as I lived, I could still love her—and as long as I lived, in a way, so did she.

A few minutes passed before I noticed that the others had dismounted and were grouped around me. It was No Nonsense who interrupted my daydreaming.

"That statue," he said. "That's the woman in the picture you keep, the one you look at all the time. She's the one in your stories."

"Yes." It was an effort to say that one word.

Caleb walked over to the bronze plaque on the other side of the marble base that held the names of the thirty-three of us who flew on the mission. He rubbed at the verdigris that coated one of the names.

"This is your name," he said. "Your name is on this plaque."

"Yes, it is," I said.

Sho walked over to stare at it past Caleb's shoulder. "It's spooky being around starfolk sometimes."

"Sometimes, it's spooky being one." That snapped me away from my memories and back to the present day. I wasn't going to stand there and be maudlin with a bunch of kids. "Okay. Who's the chief whatever I need to see so I can find out about this signal and what I can do? Where do I find him or her?"

"Chief Administrator Landrieu," Caleb said. "He's the head of the board of directors that runs Earthbase. He keeps an office in this building for important meetings. It's also where the board meets." He pointed to the large structure past the monument that I remembered as the International Space Commission administration building. "Sho and I will take your friend to the scout barracks and see that he has a place to stay and is taken care of."

"Thanks," I said. "No Nonsense, you make sure you don't get yourself into something again that I'm going to have to get you out of."

"That's never happened before," he said.

Seventeen-year-olds have short memories. Sho had a smile on her face.

CHAPTER SEVEN

THE OLD ISC BUILDING WAS STILL IMPOSING FROM A DISTANCE. WHEN I approached the entrance, though, I could see that the automatic sliding doors had been removed and replaced with a wooden frame that held a hinged wooden door. I turned the handle, pushed, and it opened. The inside, with its high ceilings, was dimly sunlit through windows that hadn't been cleaned for a century. The fans that hung from the ceiling didn't move. It was, however, warmer inside than out, which was interesting in the absence of any fire.

A young man in woolen clothing and a green badge was waiting for me in front of the long curve of the old reception desk. My footsteps echoed off the dirty and scuffed marble tiles as I walked over to meet him.

"Base security sent word of your arrival," he said. "The chief administrator is here today and would like to meet with you."

He led me around and behind the reception desk, not to the elevator but to a staircase. We walked up two flights of shadowed steps that were hard to see in places. The hallway where we came out was likewise dim, its only light coming from windows in empty offices with open doors. We walked down the corridor to where it ended at a door with a black marble plaque next to it. The light was subdued enough that I had to look closely to read the engraving: CHIEF ADMIN-ISTRATOR, INTERNATIONAL SPACE COMMISSION.

The chief administrator stood up when I entered his office. He was situated behind a large desk with a polished fake wooden top that had only a pen and a few sheets of paper on it. He held his spare frame stiffly and was a good four inches shorter than me. Close-cropped salt-and-pepper hair capped a brown face whose parentage was mostly Black. A woven wool shirt over twill pants, both light gray, fit loosely. At first, he rested his fingertips gently on the desktop. Then he extended one hand, palm up, to indicate one of the chairs in front of the desk. I took it without saying anything. The seat cushion lacked most of its cushioning. He sat down again after I was settled, steepled his fingers, and gazed at me.

I took a moment to look around while he did that. His office was a large corner one, so some stereotypes had survived even an apocalypse. Its windows had been cleaned in the not-too-remote past, so it was well illuminated. The track in the carpeting from door to desk was as beaten down and hard-packed as any horse trail I'd seen. The couch, chairs, and coffee table at the far side of the office were coated with a layer of dust thick enough to date back to that apocalypse.

"I'm Chief Administrator Christian Landrieu," he said at last. His baritone rang with authority. "Please tell me your ship and destination."

It struck me suddenly that I had carried this goal in my mind for more than a year; that I would report to Earthbase and complete our mission. I had created it after I lost Yong, mostly as a way of having a purpose for a life that hadn't ended but lacked any other reason for being until I met Charity and the kids. I'd long since abandoned and forgotten the whole idea, but now I was actually being asked to do it. Old habits and drill kicked in.

"Exoplanetary Scout Leif Grettison reporting," I said. "I'm from the *Dauntless.* Our mission was to deliver reinforcing colonists and supplies to Heaven." I added the New Gliese Catalog NGL number for the star, since Heaven was the name the colonists gave to the planet, and Earthbase wouldn't know it. "The mission was carried out successfully. It is my conclusion that at the time of our departure, the colony was functioning well and should have been able to survive. Unfortunately, we met multiple attacks on our return to the solar system, and the ship was destroyed. I am the only survivor. I will provide a full and detailed report verbally or in writing, whichever you prefer."

He actually relaxed as I said that. I could see the rigidity leave his spine with my first two sentences.

"I don't need the detail," he said. "I didn't even need as much as you already said. The name of your ship and your target are enough to establish that you're not a fake. In the current state of the world, no one except one of the crew could know those items." He pushed his chair back from the desk. "So, Caleb has actually brought us back a starman. I'll hope it turns out well, and I'll apologize for any less-than-enthusiastic welcome. It wasn't always like this."

He stood up and walked over to one of the windows, beckoning for me to join him. "Can you see out there at the horizon, just left of that tall building?"

I looked, saw nothing but lower buildings and plains beyond. "What am I supposed to see?"

If a laugh could be sad, his was. "Maybe it's only because I know it's there. It's the very top of the tail fin of the spaceplane from the *Invincible*. When they came down, thirty-three years ago, we gave them a celebration that lasted for days. I was a young man then. I remember it well."

"What about the *Daredevil*?" I asked. "They were the first ship to Heaven and would have returned several months before us."

"I know that," Landrieu said. "They sent a signal as well. Then a message that they were going to try to refuel, doubtless after they realized what happened here. Nothing more."

Well, that fit what we had deduced on the *Dauntless*. "It's possible they did refuel and left for one of the colonies," I said. "However, it's most likely that they were destroyed by one of the traps we encountered." I was thinking of the mines and the booby traps in space around the antimatter production facility. Only Yong's consummate skill as a pilot, plus a little luck, had allowed us to survive.

"Why didn't you respond to any of our calls?" I asked while his eyes were fixed on the scene beyond his window. "I don't know if it would have changed the outcome, but maybe, just maybe, we would have made different choices."

"We can't." The words were delivered flat and hard. Landrieu returned to his desk and sat. Without another option, I went back to the chair I had originally taken and waited for him. The corners of his mouth turned down and he tapped an index finger on his desk. "The receiver net is an isolated system. That was done—it was set apart somehow—at the time of the wars, to preserve it from whatever happened to all the computers. That's in the stories we tell here. I can't tell you, actually, what the receiver is or where it is, but there is a station in the building we still call the tech center that is labeled for it. That station still works. We generate enough power from the solar panels to keep it functioning. Everything else in the tech center, and that includes any transmitter, was integrated with all the rest of the computer systems. Like all of them, it was ruined in the wars. We couldn't repair the systems then; we certainly can't now."

"What's the good of a receiver with no transmitter?" That seemed like a logical question to me.

Landrieu favored me with a wry smile. "I don't pretend to know what people were thinking in the middle of the Tribulation. Maybe they believed knowing that a ship was coming was the most important thing. Maybe they did the best they could in the mess they were in, and this is what they could manage."

"I see." I didn't, not really, but that seemed the best thing to say. "What about this signal from another star, though? Of all the things that could be important, having beings around another star trying to talk to us would be at the top of my list. Caleb came to find starfolk because of that, and that's why I came here. He wouldn't tell me anything more except that I'd be told when I got to Earthbase. Well,

I'm here, and you seem to be the person who should know. What did it say and who said it?"

"We don't know the answers to those questions. None of them." There was nothing evasive in his tone or his face, but after a few seconds of looking me straight in the eyes, he turned in his chair to gaze out the window at the white clouds in the sky. "I can tell you the star it came from. At least, I can give you the NGL number, and as I'm sure Caleb told you, I can assure you that we never sent a ship there. Beyond that …" He blew out a hard breath and slammed a palm down on the arm of his chair. Then he turned back to me.

"Listen. We first noticed this signal had been received when your ship transmitted. That's how I knew your ship was the *Dauntless*. This other signal wasn't on a frequency the starships used, nor any of the old solar system stations or interstellar colonies. Because of that, it didn't generate an alert in the receiver's system. Now, please understand, I don't know precisely what a frequency is, not the way you do, I'm sure. To me, it's only some sort of specific channel you communicate through. There are many different ones, I guess. Anyway, we only found the signal because they were training a base security junior on how the system works. Found it by accident, if you will. When they told me about it, I had them check again because the system knows—I don't understand how—to store anything that's a signal, not some natural phenomenon—and I don't know how it knows that either. We found out that this message had been repeating every two months or so for fifteen years. We had never noticed." He shook his head.

I went bolt upright in my chair. The message had been coming from the stars for fifteen years! "Nobody noticed it for fifteen years? Seriously? How is that possible?"

"Base security is responsible for checking the system every day," Landrieu said. "I suppose 'ever vigilant' becomes less so with time." I heard more resignation than anger in his voice. "That system was designed to alert us to signals from starships, stations in the solar system, or colonies—not totally unexpected ones out of wherever. They also told me something about it being an odd frequency—again, whatever that means. I suppose checking this system is a bit of useless habit from the past, and there is so much else that must be done every day to keep this community going and viable." He paused and stared at his hands as if reminding himself not to go off on a tangent. "Never mind that. What matters is that we can't decipher it. Maybe the old computer systems could have, but they are all dead. Then the signal stopped about six months ago. That's the longest gap in fifteen years."

"What did you decide to do?" I asked. "You're saying you don't even have a transmitter to do anything with." His story sounded bizarre.

"Nothing really. That's the answer to your question." He moved his hand across his face as though shoving the questions away. "There's nothing to do. That's what I told our board. There's no decision to make. It's a fact, something that happened. We'll put it in the records we keep. Nothing more than that."

"But you did send Caleb. You have something in mind. You must."

"We don't even understand the message, much less have anything to work with."

"Wait a minute. Someone around a distant star is calling us and we're not going to do anything? That's crazy, impossible."

He paused, then all trace of authority vanished from his voice. "It was Mario who started the trouble. Mario—you'll meet him, I'm sure—is the senior administrator for the scouts, which makes him one of the Blue directors." Landrieu stopped abruptly. He inspected me carefully, as though he was trying to ascertain my character from across the desk.

He pressed his lips together and narrowed his eyes; a man who has reached a decision. "I am going to tell you the situation. The *whole* situation. You need to have a full, unvarnished picture before all the Colors get at you—and they will, each with their own self-serving version." He cleared his throat. "Mario said that we need to respond to the signal, that whoever lives around that star must have picked up evidence of our civilization from before and that they expect a response. That if we don't respond, they might come here. We're in no shape to deal with them the way we are now. I know Mario's game. We agree to a project like that, and he'll push for a Blue to take my seat, say that's necessary to oversee it. The chief administrator has no Color, or gives it up if they have one, in order to serve all of Earthbase. That is what I have done and all before me did. Mario figured a project to reach back to the stars would be sufficient reason to change that."

Landrieu shook his head again. He was looking everywhere except at me. "I'm not the only one who could see through him, and that set everything off. The Reds—Paula Bischoff is their senior—say that if we do respond, it is likely to bring aliens down on us. She doesn't want to do anything. Sydney, she's the senior Green, and Barttleby, who's the junior and will follow Sydney, they claim not to care if we respond or not. As long as we do what she wants on trade and security. What that really means is that the Green votes will go whichever way is best for Sydney and her desires for power here, and those desires do not include a Blue as chief. Or me, frankly."

He massaged his temples with his fingers. "To get Sydney and the Green votes, Red would have to give up increasing the traders coming here. That's dear to them but anathema to Sydney. They haven't taken that step, because they don't think Mario will give up enough to Sydney to get her votes. Meanwhile, we can't even send a signal to a returning starship. We can hardly manage a transmission to another star. They're all using the signal as a means to different ends. The argument was really about politics here and who is in charge."

"But we're talking about the stars, about contact with aliens," I said. "It's a once-in-a-lifetime opportunity. All this infighting doesn't make sense."

"Yes, it does. We may have been Earthbase in the before, and we still call our town by that name, but we're really nothing more than a community in the middle of nowhere that just needs to survive and is often closer to the line on that than I like to think. Oh, the signal is interesting, don't get me wrong. Before the wars, it would probably have been our most important issue. Not now, though. It can't be. We need to protect our people. We need to keep the Colors out of the chief administrator position. I had the argument stopped, had us back to the business we need to manage with the rivalries at an impasse. Caleb sabotaged that when he rode out, and I'm sure Mario told him to do it, knowing it would break the political impasse—not that any Blue will admit it. We had picked up through our traders stories about—well, we thought it was a whole crew, but I guess it was you—in the battles in the East." He managed a tight grin. "Lots of stories, in fact. It's hard to believe people believe in that stuff about a lucky starman."

"Yeah. Amazing," I said. "But I'm here to do *something* about the stars. I can't see that I have anything to do with your political mess."

"You have a lot to do with it. Or you will. Knowing Mario, I'll bet he figured that if we're confronted with a new starship crew, they would side with him, say we have to respond to the stars. That's how you're already leaning, isn't it? Sydney would be forced to agree. She won't tell a new crew of starfolk they don't know what to do about the stars. She'd look foolish and she can't abide that. That would give Mario the vote he wants at not too high a political price." Landrieu's eyes darted around his office as though looking for an exit he could sneak through. Finally, he looked back at me and cleared his throat. "The truth is, this won't end well. We can't afford this turmoil now. I thought I had it controlled and then Caleb upset everything."

Listening to this logorrhea, my head was starting to spin. I could remember many e-books and vids about the imagined first contact between humans and an alien species. This didn't fit any of them. How could a signal from the stars be turned into nothing more than a political gambit? And what were those politics? I needed to understand them if I wanted to do anything about the signal from the stars.

"What do you mean by all these colors? I've been hearing about blue, green, and red, and none of it makes sense. What are they?"

"Oh." He looked up at the ceiling. "Yes, you came here thinking it was about a message from the stars and I need to explain colors. Lord in Heaven. They are teams, ball teams."

It took me a moment to process what he said. "Excuse me? Ball teams? Are you serious?"

"Well, they started as teams. I know, it sounds crazy. But we are very isolated, have been since the Tribulation. People need something to take their minds off work and off how close to the edge we have always lived. So we play crossball. Blue, Green, and Red. Those are the teams. Players, and those who support the teams, which is nearly everybody, identify with one of the colors. Over the past thirty years, give or take, they have also become political factions. Today, most of base security is Green. Scouts are Blue. Reds are almost all farmers and artisans. The board is evenly divided among them, with a chief, as I said, who has no Color."

He shook his head. "We used to work together, but over the years, the board has become as partisan as the teams on the field. Each one is aiming to be the controlling faction. This is our problem here. Not the stars. Does that make sense now?"

This all sounded so wrong, so insane. Somebody out there in the galaxy was trying to make contact with us. Who were they? What were they saying? That's what was important. That's why I'd ridden a damned horse halfway across what used to be the United States. I couldn't have come all this way to find out no one cared.

I searched Landrieu's face for some sign that he was joking, but there was none. "No. It doesn't make sense. What is crossball, anyway? I've never heard of it."

"It will be easier to describe if you see it, and you probably will. It gets very intense, for the players and the supporters. But the game is no longer the issue with the Colors. More properly, it's not the only issue."

"And what about the stars?" I asked. My voice was starting to rise, and I think my irritation was justified. "I can tell you what I think about putting your politics before the stars, but I can see it won't matter. What matters is that someone sent for me, I'm here, and I want to talk about the signal from the stars. Fifteen years late or not."

"You are here," Landrieu agreed. "If it were up to me, I wouldn't have dragged you out here. All that's done is stir up the pot again. But Caleb's done it and it can't be undone. I've told you all of this because you will be sucked into it. The factions will try to use you." Landrieu paused and I could almost see gears turning behind his eyes as he thought. "Maybe there is some way you can help fix this," he said at last.

"What am I going to fix? Your politics, or the call from a star?" I was close to barking at him.

"Maybe both." His eyes narrowed again. "If there were a way we could respond to the signal, one that I could put forward, one that does not need the Colors, maybe that would change the situation. Talk with the other starfolk who are here. They understand the tech, and maybe they can figure out what might still be usable. See if you can come up with an idea that will give me a chance to let the air out of Mario's balloon and divorce the star signal from Sydney's scheming. That will leave Mario without a cause and Sydney with no leverage. I'll get a positive vote from the board that will leave me in position to make the directives."

He mulled it over, then nodded. "Yes. It's worth a try. If communicating with the stars is important to you, this is your opportunity. I will give you a few days, then I will have the full board meet with you. They really won't have a choice in that." He gave me a pained smile. "We are a small and insular community, and I am responsible for all of it. I promise you, I take that responsibility seriously. My ancestors go back here long before the Tribulation. One of them, Jonathan Robinson, came here in 2095. I need to do the right thing for everyone, not leave it to the Colors and their scheming."

The name Robinson pricked a memory. I sat up even straighter and forced some dust out of the seat cushion. "This ancestor of yours," I asked, "did he go by the name of Jack?"

Landrieu stared at me. "Yes, he did. I only know that because he was the first of my family at Earthbase, and my grandfather told me about him when I was a boy. Grandpa said there was a story in the family about that nickname, that it had some old meaning. I don't think even he knew what it was. How did you know?"

It was my turn to sigh. "I met him here when I came back from Starshot One in 2097. He was a young man then. Jack was the name he used."

Our eyes locked together and stayed that way. Neither one of us spoke for a couple of minutes. I had just told him that I met his great-great-great-grandfather when that worthy was a young man. It is the little details like this that drive home what venturing into the universe and playing with relativity really mean. Temporal alienation is nothing more than a fancy name for when your mind says the situation is insane.

Finally, Landrieu said, "I'll have someone show you where the starfolk from *Invincible* live so you can talk with them. They've always kept to themselves, and I think I understand that now."

CHAPTER EIGHT

T WAS A FIFTEEN-MINUTE WALK FROM THE OLD ADMINISTRATION BUILDING, ACCOM-panied by the man with the green badge who had taken me up to Landrieu's office. I hadn't spent enough time in Earthbase in 2097 for the structures to look familiar, but the difference I noted was the lack of people on the streets going about their business. Earthbase wasn't a ghost town, but it was quiet compared with my memories. The buildings had a vacant, dilapidated appearance. Cracks and fissures had appeared in many of the concrete structures, some crudely patched, others not at all.

I did see young children running around and playing in those otherwise empty streets. That, too, was different. Earthbase had been a place where people came to do their jobs, but their families lived in nearby places like Tribune. Not anymore. One street had been taken over by a group not yet into their teens who were running around, screaming, in a game that reminded me of lacrosse. I wondered if this was the crossball game Landrieu had referred to in his dissertation on the Colors. Their shouts at least dispelled the silence and gave the place some life.

One thought kept pounding in my head over and over as I walked, rising above the penny-ante politics. *They don't have a transmitter! They don't have any kind of a transmitter, let alone one that can send a message to the stars.* We had a message from a particular star, but Earthbase didn't know what it said and had nothing they could use to respond. It wasn't important to them.

Having Caleb send up a smoke signal to the stars wasn't going to work. But how could we not do anything? I couldn't throw my hands in the air and give up. I hoped the starfolk who were here could tell me something different.

My destination was a five-story building that might have been the same one I had stayed in years before. My guide left me there. As with the administration building, the automatic sliding door had been replaced with a hinged wooden one. Above the lintel, someone had painted STARFOLK's HOME on the concrete in sloppy white letters.

Past the door, a short corridor led to a choice between an elevator and a staircase on the left and the entrance to a caf on the right. The interior was warm. The door to the caf was open and I could see that it was occupied. I strolled in.

Six people, four men and two women, were seated around one of the tables. Six sets of eyes focused on me the instant I walked in. One of the men stood almost immediately. He was a burly white man half a foot shorter than me with a crease under his jaw suggesting the beginning of a double chin. A handful of tattooed golden stars made a constellation on his right cheek. He walked around the table and met me halfway.

"Shane Crystal, pilot-in-command of the *Invincible*, Starshot Twenty-two," he said.

The hand Shane extended was large with a wide wrist, but the muscles that once thickened the hand had shrunk and left hollows. I shook his hand.

"Landrieu sent a runner to tell us you had come in," Shane said. "If you want to move in, you're welcome. We have plenty of room."

"Thanks," I said. "I haven't thought that far. I'm Leif Grettison, Exo-planetary Scout from the *Dauntless*, Starshot Fifteen."

"Welcome, Leif." Shane pointed out the others at the table. "Magdalena Cruz, our copilot."

"Magda, please." A short, very thin woman struggled out of her chair to stand and wave to me. Even from halfway across the room, I could see the swollen knuckles and deviated fingers of her hands. A tattooed lightning bolt arced over her right eyebrow.

The others stayed seated as Shane went through brief introductions. Max Berringer, a man with loosely hanging jowls, was the ship's senior physician. Kwame Stevenson, a trim man of my height, was the junior ship systems engineer, and Hope Blanco and Ian Gross were the nuclear engineers. Like Shane and Magda, all wore the small facial tattoos that had been the style in the New Golden Age. From their voices, I thought Max was German and Ian English, while Kwame and Hope were American. That probably didn't matter anymore.

Silence descended after Ian's hello. They looked at me while I looked at them. I understood why. I saw gray hair on all of them, almost white on Magda, a few dark streaks in the gray on Shane. Faces were wrinkled, skin loose. Magda's hands betrayed rheumatoid arthritis. They were ... old.

"You've been here thirty-three years?" I asked.

"Yes," Shane said. "We left the solar system in 2117 for NGL 38152. That's a K-type star, fifty-one light-years out. Set up the colony on the sixth planet. Returned in 2219 and found, well, the same as you did, obviously."

I did some quick mental calculations. They had left on their starshot nineteen years after I went out on the *Dauntless*; they had been teens or younger when I left. But they had flown only 102 light-years compared with my 152, and that brought them back thirty-two years earlier than me. They had *aged* those years. I knew they were having the same thoughts.

"Would you like to have some coffee with us?" Shane asked, breaking the awkward silence.

"Coffee? You actually have coffee?" My voice must have slid up an octave. "I didn't think there was any coffee left in what used to be the US."

They all smiled. "Earthbase has all the stores for missions that never went out," Kwame said. "The people here now don't seem to drink coffee, so while the supply isn't unlimited, it will probably last our lifetimes."

With that, Max went to a pot sitting on a hot plate and poured me a cup.

"Coffee." It was my first cup of coffee in over a year. It had been packaged over a century ago, lacked enough strength to be bitter, and tasted like dilute turpentine. It was marvelous. "And you have electricity and heat."

"Solar panels supply some power here," Kwame said. "Not a lot; this isn't like the times we remember. No phones, for example."

"Phones?" I had become so accustomed to a world without them, I had to stop and think for an instant. "You have power, you said."

"Yes," Kwame said, "but the batteries in the phones are good for twenty-five years, max. Ours are dead, and the ones that were here are even deader. Anyway, there's no network they could connect to, same as our chips. And yours." I nodded at that. "So they do what they can here—a little manufacturing, mostly clothing and some weapons, a few systems that support the community, deep artesian wells for water, other agricultural systems like irrigation, and some simple medical supplies. But it's not a lot. They take care of us, though. Very well, actually. We're almost privileged." He tapped the fingers of his hands together. "The problem is that there's nothing for us to do. That can be wearing, or it was when we were younger."

"Age catches up with you quick without medical supplies," Magda said. She was looking at her hands on top of the table. "Unlike the coffee, those have been used up or have expired and lost potency. What they can manufacture here now is pretty limited."

"How many came back with your ship?" I asked. I did not want to get into a pity party about age and relativity.

"We're all of them," Shane said. From the way his eyes sharpened when I asked the question, I guessed he was as glad to have the conversation diverted as I was. "All the construction and exploration people stayed with the colonists. So did one of our docs."

"I'm surprised," I said. "We brought reinforcements for a colony, and the colonists told us that the first crew, including the construction people, couldn't wait to go back. In fact, they had so much trouble finding volunteers for the ships that the colonists weren't, shall we say, the best suited for what they needed to do."

Shane gave a derisive laugh. "That's the difference nineteen years made. By the time we went, anybody and everybody could see that the Treaties were breaking down, and every sane person was afraid of what was going to come. Our volunteer call was so oversubscribed that we needed a lottery at the end. The construction team jumped at the chance to stay. We even talked about all of us staying and, maybe"—he gestured at the otherwise empty caf—"we should have. Although we found out when we landed back here that the reinforcing ship never went out. Earthbase does have some records. Oral history at first, now written down. Anything that was electronic is gone or useless. Anyway, Starshot Twenty-three was delayed for two years by the politics and the funding situation with the treaty breakdown. When they did launch, it was only a research team to Alpha Centauri. And that was the last."

"I know that," I said. "We got into GSY Station when we returned, and I saw some ISC records."

Shane shuddered. "We didn't try that. Just went for the landing here, risky as that was with almost empty fuel tanks. The runways here hadn't been maintained, of course. A section had heaved up and we didn't know. It was a damned miracle I was able to bring the space-plane in without casualties."

I listened to Shane recount his heroism and thought that the most Yong would have said was that the landing presented a few issues. I didn't say that, however.

Magda jumped into the temporary break in the conversation. "I hope our colony survived without the second ship. There's no record here of any signal."

"I know there were messages from High Noon and a couple of other stars in the ISC system on the station, but I don't recall if the star you mentioned was one of them. What I can tell you is that there were no messages at all in the last fifty years. So, given the distance to your star, maybe it's that the system here broke down and your colony is fine."

"The Earthbase receiver could have picked up a message," Magda said softly.

The atmosphere in the caf turned gloomy again.

"Right," I said, perhaps a bit too loudly. "Earthbase did pick up a transmission. From somewhere else. And nobody seems to have a plan to do anything about it. Which is why someone went to find me and bring me here. So let's not talk about the past. We know that's a bad deal. What do we do now? About this transmission? Landrieu told me if we can come up with an idea, he'll take it forward."

Again, they appeared grateful to have the conversation refocused, and the signal was what I wanted to talk about in the first place. The five of them at the table looked to Shane.

"Well, we don't know," he said after a moment. "We've all listened to it, and none of us can make anything out of it. It can't be natural, though. The frequency it's on, the timing and its duration, none of that fits anything I know about cosmic radio pulses. We've discussed it half to death and we're convinced it was sent by some intelligence out there. There's no functioning AI here, so forget trying to interpret it."

"What star did it come from?" I asked. "Are there planets? What do we know?"

"We know damned little," Shane said. "The star is NGL 23845, which I'm sure tells you as little as it tells us. The receiver is actually a separate radio telescope array, and it's not within Earthbase. The people here don't seem to realize any of that. None of us remembers where the array is located—that wasn't important before. It doesn't have its own database, and of course, its link only brings in the information it collects. It's not connected to the computer systems, which is why it still functions. Any information about that star was in the databases, and they're all kaput."

"How far away is this star?" I asked. "Do we at least know that?"

"No, the NGL information was all electronic, as were almost all other records," Shane said. "However, we scoured the nearby stars for any hints of activity during the SETI program, and again back when ISC was looking for starshot targets. This star has to be out a hundred light-years or more."

Shit. That was a long way away. Well, not really on a galactic scale, but it was farther than our starshot to Heaven, and that was the farthest humanity had gone. Wait a minute. "If they are a hundred light-years away, they would have sent that signal not long after the wars. They could have been responding to stuff we generated in the solar system before the wars." I thought of all the old jokes about another species picking up early Hollywood shows. "But if they're farther away, say twice as far or more, signals from here would have had to start out in the eighteenth century or before. That can't be. We didn't have the tech to transmit *anything* that far back."

"That's part of the point," Shane said. "Suppose they're sending signals to stars with likely planets, and if they don't get a response, they assume it means *they* can colonize that planet? How would we like being on the receiving end of that? We do need to reply."

"Hang on," I said. "If they're waiting for a response to make a decision and then they're going to come, they won't get here for centuries. We should be able to handle it then."

"Do you really think so?" Max asked. "Look at the mess now. Who can say it will get better?"

"And that's assuming they're no more advanced than we got to be," Shane said. "Suppose they have faster-than-light capability. They could be here a lot sooner than centuries."

"If they have FTL capability, they could be here now," Magda said.

I looked at their worried faces. "You know, if they—whoever they are—have FTL, they would be far enough ahead of us that we're probably fucked no matter what we do. If they want to fuck us, that is. That's not the point, though. If there's somebody out there around some other star who's trying to talk to us, we ought to reply, if we can.

But what I got from Landrieu is that the only possibility is if you and I can come up with something. So, can we?"

"Really?" Shane cocked an eyebrow. "Our *fearless leader*," and he put a heavy dose of sarcasm in those words, "wasn't interested in having us come up with anything before. He let us listen to it, obviously, and asked if we could figure it out and did we know anything about the star. When we said no, he said thank you—and that was it, as far as he and the board were concerned. He simply doesn't give a shit."

"That's not fair to Christian," Magda put in. "It's not like he rules Earthbase. The board of directors makes the policy and the laws. Christian can only issue directives to execute those decisions. The board is two Greens, two Blues, and two Reds. On this, they're hopeless. It's all about political infighting. It's not just him."

"Sorry, Magda; it's a leader's job to lead despite problems and despite pressure. Believe me," Shane said, "I know." I rolled my eyes, internally. "And that's what he's not doing. He's wrapped up in this eternal argument about who will dominate their board. The only importance of the signal to him is if it leads to a board majority—specifically, one opposed to him." Shane turned to face me. "Now you've shown up, though, and I guess that's messed up the political calculations enough that he thinks doing something would be a good idea. I won't argue with the reason if it leads to action. I think that means we need to talk to Mickey." He scanned the others, who remained quiet. "Okay. Come with us, Leif, and talk to Mickey. He's the one with hands on what passes for electronics these days."

"Who is Mickey?"

"Of course." Shane pounded a fist into his other palm. "Mickey was our senior ship systems engineer. He married an Earthbase woman and moved into the community, the only one of us who did. He's got a family and a grandchild now."

I'd almost had a family before I got sucked into this.

"By all means, let's go pay him a visit," I said.

CHAPTER NINE

S HANE TOOK ME ON THE WALK BY HIMSELF. MAGDA BEGGED OFF BECAUSE IT was a long way and her joints wouldn't take it. Max didn't want to walk that far without a good reason. The others merely smiled and shook their heads.

Shane set a brisk pace, more like a forced march. Then he apologized for it. "I want to get back before the sun starts to go down," he said. "There're virtually no electric lights in Earthbase anymore, a combination of not enough power generation and, frankly, no lights that are any good. So these streets get pretty dark. I don't see that well in dim light now. Max thinks I'm growing cataracts. Should be routine to take care of that, but not now. Nothing to do about it, and I have to adjust."

I wasn't complaining about our speed, but I decided to keep my thoughts to myself. This wasn't the sort of conversation I expected to have with starfolk.

As we moved to the side of Earthbase away from the main entrance, I saw more people. The place was busy. The buildings changed, too, but in an odd way. Many of them were unfinished, with bare girders from ground to sky or sticking up from a finished lower story. Here and there, I saw foundations without any other work done. Many of these structures were incorporated into buildings made of salvaged brick, concrete chunks, and wood. They were similar to the construction I had seen in the town of Eastview and other places in the East. I asked Shane about it.

"ISC approved a five-year plan in 2115 that was going to double the size of Earthbase by 2120. I don't know what they were thinking. Streets were laid out and buildings started, but most of the construction here stopped even before we left," Shane replied. "Congress passed the Military Renewal Bill in 2116. One day there was money for new construction at Earthbase, and the next day there wasn't."

"But why are the people here putting up these slapped-together buildings with salvaged junk? It can't be like the East, where people would tell me they were afraid of the wires and electronics in the old buildings. And it's not as though the old buildings here are full of bones."

Shane shrugged. "The old buildings were built to be really airtight for the air-conditioning and heating systems we used. The windows don't even open in most of them. The air-conditioning and heating systems need electricity, and there's not enough electricity. Makes the old buildings tough to cool in the summer and smoky if you build a fire in winter, even if you chop holes in places. Some of the concrete is badly cracked, bad enough to worry that some of them will fall down. The wonders of going with the lowest bidder." He forced a laugh. "People will move into them for shelter in really bad weather, but that's about it. They work with what they've got. Come on, this is the Earthbase market. Mickey's shop is in the next block."

Mickey's shop turned out to be a small brick building set on a foundation of concrete blocks that were mortared together. A hand-painted sign over the door read I FIX ELECTRONICS. Inside, a small man with long, thinning gray hair sat at a rough wooden workbench. He was bent over a modern-looking circuit board and was using tweezers to insert a component when I walked up. Behind him, two boys in their teens sat at a separate bench, their eyes and hands everywhere except on the circuitry and papers in front of them.

The old man looked up at me. Bright blue eyes were set close to a straight, thin nose. His pale skin had only a few wrinkles, but did hold a few burst capillaries on his cheeks. He brushed loose strands of gray hair off his forehead and pressed his lips together. It was not the friendliest face I had ever seen. A red shield was pinned to his work apron.

"Leif Grettison off the *Dauntless*," I said, because he obviously wasn't going to speak first. "I literally just reached Earthbase today, and I'm told you're the person to speak to about a signal and about sending a signal."

"Yes, I've heard about your arrival. Word of certain things travels fast—you might say at light speed, even without phones." The accent I heard was Russian.

Mickey turned and caught the eyes of the two boys in the shop. He made a quick jerk of his hand toward the door. In an instant, they were off their bench and gone.

"Apprentices." He shook his head slowly. "Don't know anything when I get them. Don't want to learn. Don't want to work. Expect it all to come to them by osmosis, and they don't know what that is either."

"Yeah," I said. "Kids today."

That loosened up the set of his features a bit. He poked at the board he had been working on. "We had another failure in a cluster of panels," he said. "Kansas weather is not kind to components." He looked over at Shane. "Is this something you need to hear, or are you just bringing him over?" His tone went flat.

"I'm going to head back," Shane said. "When you're done, if you can have one of the kids here guide Leif back, that would be good. Assuming he's going to spend the night in our building, of course."

"Of course," Mickey said.

No further words were spoken until Shane had nodded and vanished out the door.

"Want to tell me what that was about?" I asked.

"What?"

"Oh, come on!" I was annoyed and I didn't care if it showed in my voice. "I've seen guns come out over exchanges that weren't as cold as that. What did he do? Sleep with your wife and brag about it afterward?"

That brought something I could call a smile to his lips. "That would have been a simpler matter to deal with," he said. "To start over, I'm Mikhail, not Mickey. Mikhail Sitnikov." He turned to extend a hand to me and I saw a small tattoo at the angle of his right jaw. White bar over blue bar over a red one. The colors had faded and the formerly straight lines of the bars had sagged with his skin, but it was still the Russian flag.

I shook his hand. "Good to meet you, Mikhail. That name is a better match for the accent."

"Yes, you can still hear the accent even after all this time." He pushed the circuit board to the side. "I was the only Russian on a Euro-American ship. In 2117, that was … uncomfortable. When we returned to the solar system and saw—well, you know what we saw— it was worse. And what about you, Leif Grettison? You are from the same era, and I would take you for an American."

Did the old hatreds never go away? I chose my words with care. "I'm even older. I flew on Starshot One in 2069 and I fought in the Troubles before that." I could see him stiffen and I shook my head. "I used to kill people because of the emblems on their uniforms or shirts. I gave that up." I thought of Yong. "I fell in love with a woman who flew attack planes for China. I'll fight if I need to—trust me on that— but it won't be because of where somebody comes from."

I could see him relax. Then his eyes widened. "Now I recall that name," he said. "It was you and Miles Richmond. You could say you're responsible for all of this."

"I would *not* say that."

"I agree." He gave a short laugh. "That wouldn't be fair."

"No." I believed he had a good idea of what unfairness could be. "What is it like for you here? This used to be the USA."

"As far as the people here are concerned, I'm a starman and that's all they care about. I moved into the community as soon as I could, and I have as little to do with the *Invincible* crew as I can manage. This business of the signal is the first time I've had anything to do with them in years."

"They seem to think you're the one to figure out how to send a reply signal. Can you?"

"Maybe. Maybe not." He picked at a splinter sticking out from the top of the workbench. Then he stood up and shoved his hands into the pockets of his work apron. I towered over him, so he had to tilt his head up to meet my eyes. "The spaceplane we took down from the *Invincible* is still out on the field. If you give Shane the opportunity, he'll tell you in great detail how he managed to land it despite running out of fuel and its power going out and how we had only one broken leg as a consequence."

He gave me a wry grin. "I'm not going to go on about that. Point is, the systems on that spaceplane are quite dead. However, there are other spaceplanes here in the hangars. You know, they use those hangars as barns for the animals, especially through the winters. The cows and such share space with the spaceplanes, but there should be fuel stores, not just hay. The starships that returned, like the *Invincible*, were left in orbit and powered down. If I can bring the system up on one of the spaceplanes, it may be possible to signal one of the orbiting starships. The reactors on them may be adequate after a century. If I can get one to wake up, maybe we can have it boost a signal. There's also another idea I have, but I'm not ready to discuss it yet. So, maybe, if you're asking. Maybe not, if it's Shane."

"Do Landrieu and his board know you could do this? It didn't seem that way when I talked to him."

"He doesn't know, and neither do they. None of them have ever come to talk to me. Shane can't go to the board on this without me, and I won't go *with* him."

"Are you sure of this? If I'm asking, that is."

"No, not at all. I'd have to get into one of the spaceplanes and see what I can do for a transmission, and I'd need to try raising a starship.

If I can do that, I'll need to play around and see if I can get one to transmit and how much power I can put into a transmission. It's not like there are any computers down here I can use for a simulation. I haven't worked with a ship system in thirty-three years."

"Okay," I said. "At least that's something. Thank you for your time."

"Don't mention it." He put a hand on my arm as I turned to go. "One thing you should understand, though. I'll see what I can do about sending a signal. Just don't expect me to do anything for Shane."

I nodded. "I get it," I said.

"Good. Now, are you going back with *them* or are you staying with whoever you came in with?"

I had to laugh at that. "You know, I hadn't even thought that far. I rode in with Caleb Peterson and his sister, Sho. And with a friend of mine from the East." I couldn't think of a better way to describe No Nonsense at that moment. "I'm actually not sure where my horse and things went."

For the first time, I saw a genuine smile on Mikhail's face, followed by a real laugh. "So, you know those two! Well, that changes everything. As it happens, the Green juniors have a crossball challenge match against the Blue juniors tomorrow early. You'll want to stay out here. My wife will make arrangements for you tonight."

"I heard about crossball from Landrieu," I said. "I've got no idea what it's about."

"Of course not. But you'll see." He pulled his hands out and rubbed them together. "I'm Red myself, but I always like a good game. Sho is still a junior, so she'll play. And trust me, Sho will put on a show."

Mikhail pulled closed the wooden door to his shop, the bottom of the door scraping against the ground. The CLOSED sign he hung on the door was probably a greater deterrent to any entry while he was away than the puny latch that held the door closed. Judging from the waves and greetings as we walked out of the market area, Mikhail was both well-known and well-liked among the community.

Mikhail lived in a small cottage set among numerous others of similar size, about five minutes' walk from his shop. A cloud produced by all the chimneys hung over the neighborhood. The lower third of the walls of Mikhail's home was built of the same concrete blocks I had seen in other construction, with brick filling in gaps in the concrete. Yellow light flickered from two glass windows in the front, the bottoms of whose frames sat on the concrete. Strips of siding, not all the same color, covered the walls from the concrete to the eaves under a steeply pitched roof. A brick chimney spewed a column of smoke to join the cloud from the others.

"I built most of this myself," Mikhail said as we reached his front door. "This was even before I married Rosann. It was my way of showing I was worth marrying, even though being able to handle electronics is a valuable skill here. That chimney"—he pointed up—"was a bitch to do. Thank God some people from Earthbase helped, which is more than I can say for any of the *Invincible* crew."

Inside, it was warm, almost hot, but not smoky, proof that the chimney had a good draft. A drywall with a door cut into it divided the cottage in half. A woman stood by a woodstove near the hearth, tending three bubbling pots. From her cheery face when she saw Mikhail walk in, this had to be Rosann Sitnikov. She was of Mikhail's height, with a round face and gray hair pulled back into a bun. A bright red apron covered her shirt and pants. A younger woman, around thirty I guessed, was focused on the stove. A girl of maybe four years sat on the floor nearby, playing with a doll.

The room suddenly shifted. So did my balance. Instead of Rosann, I saw Charity by the stove. Instead of one child on the floor, I saw a half dozen scattered around the living area. Instead of a blank wall across from the fire, I saw a gun rack that also held a banjo.

"My wife, Rosann and my daughter, Svetlana," Mikhail was saying, "and also granddaughter, Deirdre."

I stared, seeing other people.

The women said their hellos, and that was enough to pull my mind back to Mikhail's cottage in Earthbase. I hoped none of them could see the shake I felt in my body. It had been a flashback, like the ones I still got when a bird low on the horizon would morph, without warning, into a Chinese J-45 superstealth attack plane and I would be back on the defense line at Camp Schwarzkopf, about to be bombed. I'd never had one about Charity and the kids—never had one about anything other than combat. I wondered what that meant, while I struggled to introduce myself without giving away that my mind had gone elsewhere.

"Mischa, I had no idea you would bring a guest—and the new starman, for that matter." Rosann stirred a pot automatically. "I have a stew, and that will be enough food—but, really, we should have better. You could have brought something from the market, since I could not have known," she added in a gentle rebuke.

"Stew will be fine," I hastened to assure her. "More than fine."

"It is not the food that is most important anyway," Mikhail said. "It is the drink." He clapped me on the back and went through the door in the drywall. He returned with a large jug. "The *Invincible* crew could never forget that I am Russian, and I choose to remember that also. The proper drink is vodka." He brandished the jug. "I distill this myself. It is quite good."

"I can't drink, Mikhail. It's a medical thing." I don't usually lie about why I don't drink, but I didn't want to go into my alcoholic excuse for a father. I didn't think Mikhail would find that an acceptable reason.

His face showed surprise. He pushed the thinning hair on top of his head from one side to the other. Then he shrugged.

"I'll drink for us both, then, and we'll pretend you drank yours." He poured two cups full and shot both of them down.

"Don't mind Mischa," Rosann said. "I have water that you can drink. It's good water, too, and safe, and that's because of the system Mischa set up and keeps running. Everyone in Earthbase is grateful to him for that."

I had a cup of the water Rosann offered while Mikhail matched me with another one of his vodka.

"The people of Earthbase, yes," Mikhail said. "But that does not include Shane and his crew."

"Mischa, Shane is not here."

I matched another cup of vodka with one of water.

"He was at the shop," Mikhail said. "Enough to give me indigestion. The vodka will cure it."

Rosann ushered me to a seat at the table that was next to the fire. Mikhail seated himself. The table and chairs were well-made of solid wood, sanded smooth and polished. Rosann was telling me that Mikhail had made them for her after they were married, while Svetlana gathered up Deirdre and said goodbye. Rosann ladled stew for the three of us, and a glance at the pot told me that the amount of stew was the reason Svetlana had decided to leave.

"Mischa, I know about Shane, but you should eat some along with the drink."

Mikhail grumbled at her but took a spoonful of the stew.

"Mischa will go on about Shane and that crew," Rosann said to me. "I once thought that as the years went by it would hurt less, but it does not. They are not very nice people."

"My wife is generous to a fault," Mikhail said. Another vodka went down his throat. "However, she didn't have to live with them on a ship. Magda was a decent in-system pilot, but never would have been at the top of an ISC list. Max flew with Shane on a Mars flight. Kwame was nothing more than a systems supervisor at one of the moon bases. One way or another, they all owed Shane for their positions, and he made sure they knew it."

"And you?"

"That was a Roscosmos thing. I was told, not asked. They don't exist anymore, anyway. And you're not Russian to understand this," he said to Rosann. He shifted his seat to face me and downed another cup of vodka. Droplets of sweat stood out on his forehead and might not have been solely due to the heat from the fire.

"Shane would be an asshole even if he wasn't an American. Shane the Magnificent. He was pilot-in-command and you did what he said. He'd snap his fingers and Magda and the rest of them would jump. I think the construction people stayed with the colony so as not to have another flight with him." Another cup was drunk.

"That landing at Earthbase. He should have changed his approach. It's not as though the problem with that runway was subtle. But we were coming down, because that's all he could think of after we saw what had happened. And then, after he wrecked us, and somehow we crawled out of that spaceplane and it never caught fire, and we looked at the mountain in the runway that he missed seeing, then it was all about Magda should have warned him, or one of us should have seen it on the screens, and it was the damned Russian who blocked the critical view before he committed to his approach and we should have known we were out of fuel but the damned Russian wasn't monitoring the tanks and he couldn't make any changes once he'd committed us and he shouldn't have trusted a fucking Russian to check anything and it was a mark against his record—like anybody still has a record— because he had a fucking Russian on *his* ship who made sure to sabotage him when it mattered the most—and I will be damned in hell before I do anything again for that jumped-up, posturing, flimsy excuse for a real pilot and that so-American and so-European crew and—"

Even nuclear submarines come up for air at some point, but Mikhail didn't. He finally ran down, battery drained. His arms slid forward across the table, and he put his head down. A snore told me he was asleep. Rosann leaned over and kissed the top of his head.

"Shane must have said something," Rosann said. "He usually doesn't get this bad."

"Well, Shane did," I said. "It wasn't good, but it wasn't that much. I guess there's a lot of history."

"Yes," she said. "I wish it was like the rest of history that nobody knows anymore." She sighed. "You can have our bed in the back room tonight. I'll stay out here with Mischa."

"No, that's not right," I said. "Let me help you get him to bed. Then, if you can give me a blanket, I'll do perfectly well in front of the fire."

CHAPTER TEN

WE WERE UP EARLY THE NEXT MORNING TO SEE THE BIG GAME. FROM THE expression on Mikhail's face, I didn't think he would do well if there was any cheering. Rosann fed him some soup before we left, although I wasn't sure it was going to stay down. Past the Earthbase market, the unfinished buildings of Earthbase gave way to open fields about a ten-minute walk from where Mikhail lived. Rosann was rubbing Mikhail's back every third step of the way. Svetlana and her husband joined us as we walked, each holding one of Deirdre's hands.

Our destination was a playing field approximately the dimensions of a soccer pitch, which had been marked off at each corner with concrete blocks painted red. At each of the long ends, a goal had been set up. This consisted of an eight-foot-wide opening between two tall vertical pipes that held a crossbar about five feet off the ground. Another crossbar ran between the pipes about ten feet off the ground. Netting covered the back of both openings. Judging from the number of people—adults and children—who were there when we arrived and who streamed in afterward, this game was a big deal. Nearly all the spectators wore a shield with blue, green, or red enamel.

The players were all teenagers, which fit what Mikhail had said about them being juniors. They stood around loosely grouped into the two teams, roughly half boys and half girls. No one wore a uniform; clothing was a mixture of wool, loosely woven or homespun, and leather for all. But the teams were obvious, as one group wore brassards of green cloth on their right arms, the other side blue. None of the players wore padding or a helmet. Within each team, they talked and laughed together, but I didn't see anyone from one side approach the other.

Each player's equipment was a wooden shaft about five feet long. At one end was a hoop with a netted back that made it look like a lacrosse stick. The other end had a small paddle shape carved into a shallow cup. My mom was Irish, and I had watched vids of hurling with her when I was young. That end of the staff did look like a hurley. There was no uniformity among the staffs. Each one had clearly been handmade. I recalled the children playing in the street when I had walked in from the administration building. They had been carrying sticks that looked like this.

A gray-haired man in a black shirt ran onto the field and blew a whistle. At that, the players positioned themselves, ten to a side. Green took one half of the field, Blue the other. The man in black tossed a small hard ball into the middle of the field, and the action started. Nobody explained the rules to me, so I had to figure them out as I watched. A player could run with the ball in the lacrosse-style net, held in their hand or balanced on the concave part of the paddle. Scoring was accomplished by flinging the ball from the basket into the lower net or striking it with the hurley end and knocking it into the upper net. That was simple. What I found confusing was all the flipping from basket end to the hurley end.

"If you're running with it in the basket, you have to flip it into the air and strike it over the bar to score," Mikhail said when I finally asked. "If you have it in your hand or on the paddle, you have to toss it, catch it with the basket and fling it into the lower net."

Then what they were doing made sense. I was impressed by the players' coordination and vision of the field. They ran fast and they played rough. Body checks, slams, and hacks with the staff went up and down the field. The crowd screamed itself hysterical with each score, and there were as many body checks, along with fisticuffs, among the spectators as on the field.

It was obvious how Sho came by the epithet Sho-off. She was fast. No defender could stay with her. I watched her plant a foot, give a juke and a spin, and leave an opponent sprawled in the dirt while her shot went into the net. She shot both arms into the air and screamed at the sky. That was too much for the Green boy who had been left on the ground. He picked himself up, ran at her, and took a swing at her head with his stick. Fortunately, she ducked and blocked it with her own stick. Blues in the crowd roared disapproval while Greens jeered at them. More fights started among the crowd.

"Both hands on the staff and at least a foot apart to hack, you dickhead!" Svetlana shouted along with others.

Sho turned her back on the boy and started back toward where play had resumed, but suddenly she pivoted, jaw clenched, and ran at that Green. She started a high swing with the basket of her stick aimed at his head. He raised his stick to block her, but she pulled back as the sticks made contact, spun hers, and snapped the paddle end up between his legs. The boy folded in the middle, retched, and collapsed on the ground.

The game stopped. The entire group of players crowded together, Blues in a phalanx protecting Sho while the Greens tried to push through to reach her, all of them screaming in each other's faces. Open warfare seemed likely.

"That's two balls in the net!" Rosann screamed with all her lungs, but the crowd was so loud, she couldn't be heard more than a few feet away. Mikhail was holding his head in his hands. Svetlana, her husband, and Deirdre were yelling something, but the words were lost in the din.

The man in black who had started the game shoved his way in between the two sides. A brief tongue-lashing that I could not make out was administered to both teams. The moaning boy was carried to the side of the field, and the two teams separated. After a conference among Greens outside the playing area, another boy slipped on a green brassard and joined the Greens, so the sides were even again at ten each. Play resumed as though nothing had happened.

"Now, if these were seniors playing," Mikhail shouted over the crowd noise with his mouth an inch from my ear, "they wouldn't get them separated so easy and we'd have a proper brawl for a few minutes. And work for the doctors afterward!"

The Blues won, sixteen to twelve. I was surprised no one had been killed, either on the field or in the crowd. Mikhail's family took him back to his house, where they could nurse his hangover, and I left them to that task. I made my way over to where I saw No Nonsense standing with Sho and Caleb.

"Damn near took your damned head off," Caleb was saying when I arrived. "I'll be looking up a couple of them later."

"I paid him back myself," Sho said. "I don't need you to do it for me."

No Nonsense had a look of adoration on his face. I decided I would need to speak to him as soon as I could get him away from Sho. Preferably also without Caleb around.

Caleb kept turning to me as if he wanted to tell me something, but before he ever did, he would turn back to fuss over his sister.

"How did you get this?" he asked Sho, almost touching a finger to where her lip was split.

"During the game. Obviously." She brushed his hand away. "I'm not your ten-year-old little sister anymore who got thrown when her horse got spooked."

"We need to get you cleaned up," Caleb said. "That's going to look ugly."

"I think it looks fine," No Nonsense said.

"You're no help," Caleb said to No Nonsense.

Then he finally spoke to me, half over his shoulder. "Look, Leif, the scout senior administrator wants to speak with you. He's also one of the Blue directors. He's pissed that I only brought one—you, that is—but he does want to talk to you. I'd take you over there now, but I really have to get this sister of mine cleaned up. There is always a party the night after a game, and heaven forbid Sho should miss a party."

"I can take care of Sho," No Nonsense said.

"Bricks and stones," Caleb said.

"Sho can take care of Sho," said Sho.

It didn't seem she was going to have that option, as she ended up being escorted from the field with Caleb on one side and No Nonsense on the other. The scene would have been funny enough to laugh at; however, as they walked away I was left with the realization that I wouldn't be speaking to this very important scout right away. Nor would I be able to have a talk with No Nonsense. I was sure No Nonsense was going to be at this party, and I wanted to talk to him about Sho before that happened. I had no intention of trying to chaperone No Nonsense at whatever kind of party this was going to be.

I looked around the rapidly clearing field in frustration and tried to figure out what to do. I wasn't going to impose on Mikhail's family for a second night. I didn't want to witness another drinking marathon along with a repeat recitation of the sins of Shane and his crew.

That was when I felt a gentle touch on my right arm from behind. A woman's voice said, "May we speak for a minute, Starman Grettison?"

I turned to find a tall woman with silver-blond hair twisted into a loose braid that fell in front of her right shoulder, a sharp contrast to her dark gray serge overcoat with a green shield pinned to it. That coat was wide open, revealing a sharp taper from broad shoulders and bust to her waist—a striking figure, and one I couldn't miss seeing. Her face was an oval, pale and pink in the chill air, the corners of a rosebud mouth curving up in an easy smile as soon as she saw my eyes on her. That smile did not touch her eyes, however, which were two chips of stone-hard pale blue.

I tried to place her among the people I had seen and spoken to since I arrived at Earthbase and couldn't. "I'm sorry," I said. "Have I met you?"

"No." The smile broadened but it still didn't change the eyes. "In a small community like ours, anyone who comes in from the outside will be immediately recognized. So, I know who you are, even if you do not know me. Yet. I'm Sydney Yaeger, senior administrator for base security. I am also the senior Green member of the board. I really would like a brief conversation."

What I really would have liked was breakfast, but Yaeger didn't seem the type to be pouring coffee or flipping pancakes. "Here and now is fine."

Her eyes flicked to each side as if making sure that no one was close enough to be eavesdropping. "Good enough. You came in yesterday with a pair of our scouts. Not the most discreet pair, I might add."

I wondered if her eyes would ever blink. "They seem like nice kids."

The smile vanished and her lips pressed together. "Caleb is old enough to know better. Everyone has heard about you and your traveling companions. Did you have a productive discussion with Landrieu?"

"How does that concern you?"

"Everything to do with the safety of this place and its people concerns me."

"Ah yes," I said. "Ever vigilant. I've heard."

"No. You haven't. Not really." She spat on the dirt at her feet, then ground the spittle into the earth with the tip of her boot. "Look there." She grabbed my upper arm and tugged for me to turn around. That left me facing the wall that ran around Earthbase. It was not that distant from where we stood. I could see the old razor wire and useless gun emplacements on top of it.

"Earthbase was where men and women left from to go into space, to the moon and to the stars. Those are the stories, and they are also the truth. But that was long ago. We still call it Earthbase because, well, what else would we call it? But our people are only the remnant of what was here before. We no longer look outward. We are self-contained, self-sufficient. We have crops and animals that started from the banks the original Earthbase intended for the stars. They serve as well here. The few items we need that we do not make ourselves, we can obtain in trade from the East, but we send people there to do the trading. We do not need to bring eastern traders here. We are small in size and few in number compared to the East. We are vulnerable. My primary concern is our security. What do we do about these traders from the East? What do we do about the East itself? To be blunt, the East is closer and more dangerous than the stars."

She stopped and gave me a searching look. When I said nothing, she tapped an index finger against her lips. Her face would have been a good one for a poker table.

"Maybe that signal was sent by another intelligent race," she went on. "So what? I personally do not care one way or the other about the signal. Only a narcissist would think we are so important that some other race is waiting on tenterhooks for our answer."

She had a point. Although, listening to her speak, that wall looked less like a fortification against danger and more like a self-imposed prison. "Maybe whoever sent the signal doesn't care if we respond," I said. "Maybe it's not even possible. Why is it an issue for us to try? Someone *has* sent us a signal. We can't just let it go. We can't do that. We owe it, if not to ourselves, then to everyone who worked to give humanity a place in the wider universe. This has never happened before and it may never happen again. If we try and we can't, that's something else. At least we will have tried."

"Projects take resources. I told you that the East is important and not so far away." She paused, as if considering her next words, so I waited for her. "Our scouts want to make more journeys to the states east of the Mississippi. They encourage more traders to come across the Empty Lands to reach us. This trend, this mindset, is a danger. Today, the Empty Lands are our real defensive barrier, the wall beyond this wall." She pointed at the physical one. "We need to shelter behind it."

"I don't think you can do that," I said. "People are already crossing the Mississippi to settle. People will come here eventually, whether you encourage them or not."

"If we open ourselves to it, then it will become a certainty." Her voice was as hard as her eyes. "If we avoid it, at least there is a chance. You can see what will happen to us if we allow it." Cold blue eyes bored into mine. "Landrieu is going to schedule a meeting of the board. Ostensibly, it is to decide on our response, or nonresponse, to this signal we have detected. However, the discussion will be broader than that, much broader. I will see to that. You will be at this meeting, because it was your arrival and who you are that triggered it.

"Depending on what plan is proposed, depending on the resources it would take, depending on how it can affect what I have told you is important, depending on all of that, but especially the last, I could be persuaded when it comes to the signal. I could vote one way or the other. The other Green vote will go with mine. Please think about what you are going to say. Your words will affect votes. If you can see Green leading the way and managing what is important to this small town, you can have the signal back to the stars you want. I trust that we understand each other."

I told her that I understood her completely. I did. I assured her that I would think about it very carefully and that I would speak at the meeting if I was invited.

The smile came back to her face, again missing the eyes. "Good. Now, you might want to skip the party they will be having tonight. It can be unfortunate for people from away who don't know how things are done here."

I tried to appear as though I were still listening to what she said, but part of my mind was thinking back to the old history of the American West and the consequences of that expansion for the people who had lived there first. I doubted there would be a way to stop the current push west any more than there had been back then. However, she had made it clear that anything to do with the stars would hinge on giving her what she wanted. She wanted to be in charge and run Earthbase her way. Did I care if her approach would work, as long as we did what we needed to do about the stars? I would be back in New Terra, at the farm. It wouldn't be my problem.

As soon as she had wrapped her coat around herself to conceal her figure, I thought I might be up for going to a party. I have a long history of doing things I have been advised not to do.

Yes, the results have been mixed.

CHAPTER ELEVEN

B Y THE TIME I FINISHED WITH Sydney, Caleb, Sho, and No Nonsense had
disappeared. I walked back to the market and went from shop
to shop, examining everything from wool pants to meat pies.
Nobody I questioned knew where the trio might be.

Mikhail did not return to his shop, so I retreated to what I
mentally dubbed the Old Starfolk's Home. Unfortunately, I discovered
quickly that I had little in common with the crew of the *Invincible*
beyond having gone to the stars. They had all grown up during the
New Golden Age, that period of time people then called the best in
human history, the dawn of permanent peace and prosperity, which I
now knew to be nothing more than a head fake between the fighting
of the Troubles and the final wars known as the Tribulation. I had
spent roughly a year in the New Golden Age between starflights, and
I hadn't fit in. The crew of the *Invincible*, on the other hand, waxed
nostalgic—endlessly nostalgic—for those days. They spent much of
their time reminiscing about it. Again, I didn't fit in. None of it meant
anything to me.

Part of me said that I shouldn't blame them. They had spent
thirty-three years sitting in a building with nothing to do in a world

where *they* didn't fit. The rest of me, however, wanted to scream at them that they should have gotten off their asses and found something to do, the way Mikhail had. Unfortunately, the time for that had probably passed. Thirty-three years of staying apart, trapped in a nostalgia bubble, is a big hill to get over. I could see why Caleb and the scout leadership that sent him wanted newly arrived starfolk to put in front of the board.

In addition to the crew of the *Invincible*, there was one other surviving occupant of the building. Her name was Ruth Jones and she had flown in the *Indomitable*. That ship had left Earth in 2113 and returned in 2189. She had been a young woman of twenty-eight when she left, but her bio age was now around ninety-two, allowing for hib and awake time on her journey. Short and curly white hair made a contrasting cap over a dark brown face that was all wrinkles around sparkling eyes. She had grown up in the same New Golden Age as the *Invincible* crew, but she had already been back at Earthbase for thirty years by the time they returned. She didn't mesh with them, and no one else from her crew who had returned to Earthbase was still alive. That left her lonely, so I sat and talked with Ruth. She was a little unsteady on her feet, with swelling in both ankles above the soft slip-on shoes she wore, but she was a lively ninety-two, full of stories and questions for me. Her mind would wander at times and her memory was hazy on many things, but she was a pleasant old lady who was glad of someone to talk to. I sat and listened to her and drank coffee until my nerves jangled.

. . . .

MY OPPORTUNITY ARRIVED WITH LUNCH. AS KWAME HAD SAID WHEN I FIRST ARRIVED, Earthbase treated the starfolk as privileged guests, almost celebrities. In that sense, their practice of keeping apart probably helped. Someone brought fresh food from the market every day, and a series of kids came by the Starfolk's Home throughout the day, asking if there were errands to be run or chores to be helped with. A steaming basket of meat pies arrived for lunch. Along with the basket and the kids who brought it came an eight-year-old little urchin who hung around after they left. She waited for me to select a meat pie, then boldly stepped in front of me and asked if there was anything the new starman needed done. I asked her to find No Nonsense—the man from away I'd ridden in with—and tell me where he was. The girl came back a little before dusk and waved for me to follow her.

A light flurry of snow was coming down from leaden skies when we headed out. The accumulation was enough that we left footsteps in the snow, and the girl was able to kick up sprays of it in front of her. I was glad that someone found fun in the setting. The grayness of the evening weighed on my spirits. Our destination was a pub built of brick and plywood in the new part of town. I spotted the faded lettering stamped on one sheet of the plywood that helped frame the entryway, TRIBUNE CITY WORKS. I suspected a lot of the salvaged construction materials Earthbase depended on came from expeditions to the local ruined areas. No, Senior Administrator Sydney Yaeger, Earthbase was not nearly so self-sufficient behind its wall as you liked to pretend.

Before I went in, the girl gestured for me to bend down. Then, as if she were a conspirator in a spy show, she whispered to me where I could find the party afterward. As soon as she finished, she winked and scampered away.

Okay, I thought. That's a hint.

The interior was smoky and dim. I needed a couple of minutes for my eyes to adjust. When I could see, I took in the whole place with one glance. It had only a small number of tables, again with plywood for tops, set close to the fireplace. Seating was on benches rather than chairs. The floor was poured concrete with a spiderweb of cracks running through it. No Nonsense was seated at the table closest to the fire. A steaming tureen, which had to be soup or stew, was in front of him, and a foam-topped mug was by his right hand.

I climbed over the bench and sat down next to him. "Evening, No Nonsense. How are you?"

No Nonsense looked up and wiped a bit of foam from his whiskers. "Damned good right now, Leif. I know you don't drink, but I can get you some of this stew. Not as good as Ma's, but plenty of meat in it." He spooned a large helping of it into his mouth. "They actually take solids here, although Sho said she'd help if there were any problems with money."

Solid dollars—stamped metal coins, as opposed to money recorded only in electronic systems that had vanished when the computers died—were the coin of the realm in New Terra. Apparently, they were accepted for payment in Earthbase. Yet more evidence that Sydney's image of Earthbase did not match reality. Financial systems weren't at the top of my mind at that moment, however.

"Yeah, can I talk to you about that girl?" I asked.

The spoon paused on its way to his mouth. "Sho? Sure. What do you want to know?"

"It's not that I want to know anything. I think you should be careful about her."

That was enough to divert No Nonsense's attention from the stew. He put the spoon down and wiped his mouth with his sleeve. "What are you talking about?"

"No Nonsense, I've seen the way you look at her. I also see how she acts. What do you think you're doing?"

No Nonsense smiled. Damn near split his face. "Leif, I am in love with this girl. Plain and simple. She's perfect. She's beautiful. She's tough. She likes me too."

I could see from the level of the foam in the beer mug that it was nearly full. This was coming out cold sober. I'm not sure which would have been worse. "No Nonsense, you have known her for what—two days?"

"More than enough."

I put a hand on his arm and tried to sound earnest. "You're going to get hurt. I'll bet every guy who wears Blue is after her."

"So what? I'm the one she likes. No offense, Leif, but you should have a rocker by the fire next to Ma." He laughed at his own joke.

I decided to try another tack. "This place has wires and electronics, you know. I know how you feel about that stuff from before." No Nonsense had, in fact, been petrified by the wiring and electronics in a simple tractor engine at the farm. "I'm sure Sho works with that. If you hang around her, you're going to have to deal with it."

He shrugged. "We talked about it yesterday, right after you went to see that guy in the building by the monument. Sho's okay with it. And if it's no problem for her, I'll get used to it. It's not a problem."

Of course, a guy can't show any weakness in front of the girl he likes. I knew where the macho stuff came from. Sometimes my life would have been simpler without it. At least it would have been safer.

"What about Caleb? Her parents?"

"Caleb's okay. It's not like he doesn't know. She never mentioned parents. Look, Leif"—he set his face in a stubborn pose—"this is perfect and it's going to work perfectly, and I don't need you trying to tell me otherwise, because you don't know. I love her. That's what I know." He got up from the bench. "Now, I'm going to be at the party with her tonight. If you're there, you'll see." He left most of his beer and a bit of the stew on the table.

How had I become the one trying to give fatherly advice?

·   ·   ·

I MADE THE BEST OF THE SITUATION AND HAD A BOWL OF THE STEW MYSELF. BY THE time I finished it, the snow had stopped falling and it was getting dark. The pub's other patrons were picking up and leaving. It was a curious time for a pub to empty out, but I caught snippets of conversation and could tell the others were headed for the party. All I had to do was follow them.

I could hear the cacophony, a mix of music, song, laughter, and shouts, long before I caught sight of the place. I had the impression that the post-game parties were as much entertainment for the town as the game was.

The venue was a building for which only the girder framework of the first two stories had been erected at the time construction stopped. Much more recently, someone had roofed over the first floor with canvas that now sagged in the middle under a layer of snow. With luck—and no more snow—it would stay up for the remainder of the evening. Additional sheets of canvas had been dropped over three of the sides. The result was a huge tent, or maybe a canvas cave was closer to the mark. Three sheets of wood, each illuminated by a lantern and leaning against a post in front of the open side, carried the message in white paint: NO COLORS OR WEAPONS INSIDE.

The place was already packed by the time I arrived. My first impression was that every inhabitant of Earthbase from mid-teens to forties was in there. Trestle tables near the open side held a row of barrels that were dispensing beer into an unending succession of mugs. At the back canvas wall, two men and a woman were strumming away on banjos and singing their lungs out. The banjos were similar to the one Charity had at her house, but even though I couldn't make out the words, I doubted those were the same songs she sang. I'm sure it wasn't the Beatles—a group that had been played endlessly during the Centennial of Rock in 2069—either.

In between the beer and the musicians, a crowd of people were gyrating side to side and bouncing up and down in some version of dance. Another crowd encircled the dancers, and a steady flux moved from one group to another. It could have been a keg party at the college I attended after I left the service. The primary difference here was the lack of speakers to amplify the sound. Even without that, the music and the voices blurred into waves that beat against my skull. It was relaxing. Yes, just as in my memories of long-ago parties, men paired up with women, or with other men, and some women paired with women.

In the middle of this mob, I saw Sho. It was impossible to miss her. She was dancing, or prancing, or spinning in the center of the dancing circle, and people gave her space to do it. She held a mug of beer on high in one hand. With her gyrations, foam slopped over the side and sprayed on anyone who was too close. A swarm of boys danced around her. If the large crowd of dancers was the cytoplasm of the party's cell, Sho was in its nucleus. Then she changed course and danced her way through the crowd to the edge. She found No Nonsense there, looped an arm around him, and pulled him into the center of the dancing maelstrom, all the while sloshing some of the beer in the general direction of his mouth. Did No Nonsense have a clue what he was getting himself into? I doubted it.

"Thinking of doing some dancing yourself?" The gravelly voice from behind me cut through the din.

I turned to find a short man with shoulders seemingly as broad as he was tall. What impressed me immediately about his face was his nose. This was a mountain of a nose. It rose from below his forehead in a triumphal aquiline arch and broadened as it reached his mustache, as if buttresses were supporting that arch. The end was flattened a little, possibly squashed at some time by a door or a punch. Puffy bags made for narrowed, rheumy eyes. The mouth under the mustache was a crescent with the points aimed down. This was not a happy face. The accompanying mop of hair and full beard were grizzled.

"Mario Abbruzzese," he said.

Ah. This was the Mario I had heard of. "Are you asking?" I grinned.

"No." He didn't.

He did extend a hand, so I shook it and gave him my name. "I'm not much of a dancer anyway," I said. "Never was, and this crowd looks a bit young for me. At least the ones who're dancing."

"That wouldn't stop others," Mario said.

I shrugged. "Is that why you're here?"

"No." He regarded me for a second. "I'm the senior administrator for the scouts. Just keeping an eye on things."

I looked away from him at the crowd. In keeping with the order on the boards outside, I did not see a single enameled shield. Some were dressed in leathers, some in the wool that base security wore, most in a mélange of clothes that did not fit any type of uniform. They all mingled together. "You mean because of the game this morning? The incident with Sho?"

"No, no. That's forgotten. Except for the jokes circulating that the boy will never have children." He gave a short laugh that was mostly absorbed by his beard and mustache. "Beer and youth, however. Old folks and beer too. You never know."

"That dynamic I understand."

"It also seemed like a good opportunity to meet you. Without being obvious about it." His eyes stopped roving around the crowd and focused on mine.

"Would that be the reason I was able to find a child to take me to meet my friend at the pub and give me directions to this place?"

"Of course." He cleared his throat. "You spoke with Yaeger after the game. There is already as much conversation about what the two of you said as there are jokes about that boy's nuts. I would rather have the chance to speak with you at some length without it being the subject of everyone's speculation."

"Here?"

"Of course not. Just saying hello here. Some of the scouts will be out tomorrow to take care of the animals. That is part of their duties. Some of the old hangars make excellent barns. The scouts, naturally, require supervision from time to time. I'll send your friend from the East over with a horse and directions where to bring you. Then we can talk. Also, I want to show you something."

"Does this have to do with politics or the stars?" I asked.

"Both. See you then." He gave me a friendly pat on the shoulder and moved away.

CHAPTER TWELVE

N O NONSENSE CAME TO FIND ME THE NEXT MORNING AS THE SKY WAS JUST beginning to brighten. He showed no apparent ill effects of the night before, for which I hated him. If he were a horse, he would be champing at the bit. Speaking of horses, his was tied up outside the Starfolk's Home and he had another one for me. My talk with Mario was obviously going to take place early.

We rode out of the walled town of Earthbase and headed for the old runways where airplanes and spaceplanes had once landed. The clouds that had brought yesterday's snow were gone. A bright sun, still close to the horizon, sparkled in a clear sky, although that sunshine did little to alleviate the chill in the air. The wind had blown the light snow of the previous day completely away from some areas and piled it up in ridges and dunes elsewhere. Where the ground was bare, I could see patches of concrete from the runways. Most of them were covered, however, by dirt that had blown across the plains over the years and by grass that had grown in that dirt. Give nature a little more time and you would need to dig to find the runways.

Silhouetted by the rising sun was the lander from the *Invincible*, stark against the sky. It tilted at a crazy angle, one wing up in the air.

Part of the landing gear must have collapsed when they crash-landed. I remembered Mikhail saying the crew had come out with only one broken leg for injuries. They had been lucky.

No Nonsense was not heading for the wreck of the spaceplane. He turned his horse to leave that behind us and rode in the direction of one of the huge hangars that sprouted from the field. Incongruously, as we approached the hangar I heard the moos of cows and the baas of sheep. The hangar doors were open. Men and women were busy going in and out through them. A solitary man sat on his horse at a distance and watched the proceedings. No Nonsense took me over to him, then let out a whoop and galloped toward the hangar.

I was not surprised to find that the man waiting for me was Mario Abbruzzese. He was bundled against the cold in a heavy wool coat. A knit wool cap was pulled down to his ears and a broad-brimmed leather hat sat on top of the cap. He turned in his saddle to face me as soon as No Nonsense had ridden away. The corners of his mouth still drooped.

"Your friend is very eager to help with our work, even though we have not asked it of him."

No Nonsense had been a good worker at the farm, but it had always been at Charity's direction. "Why do you think would he do that?"

"Gives him a chance to impress Sho," Mario said. "He's rather obvious about it."

"And is she impressed?"

"Hard to say. I'm not sure hauling hay to feed cows will do it." Mario gave a faint chuckle. His lips leveled out and lifted the edges of his mustache enough to reveal a missing tooth. "She's a hard girl to impress."

"And what do her parents think?"

"They don't." His mouth turned down again. "Her ma died in childbirth when she was three, and so did the baby. We lost her pa in a blizzard eight years ago, when the wind busted open the doors on one of the hangars and we had to rescue animals." He pointed at a structure farther out on the field. "Caleb raised her, mostly. Whatever raising she didn't do herself."

"They didn't find another family?" I asked. "What about the saying 'Family is where you find it'?" Three of Charity's children were hers, but the rest had found her, one way or another. Elvy had joined the family simply by saying she would stay.

"The Church of All Saints of the Apocalypse," Mario said. "That's from them, and that's fine for away from here, if that's what people want. We don't have that church here, nor any of their crap. We name our children the way children used to be named, and we have normal families. There's no church here anymore." A judge pronouncing sentence could not have been more final.

Sometimes I have a knack for saying the wrong thing.

"You said you wanted to talk about politics and the stars. What would you like to say?" Might as well get the conversation back on track.

"Yes." Mario managed to draw that word out into several syllables. "Caleb was sent to find us a crew of starfolk. He came back with you. He does not understand, of course, what is below the surface. Young people are impetuous and often don't." Mario's saddle squeaked under him as he adjusted his position. "What do you know about the way Earthbase is governed?"

"You have a chief administrator," I said. "That's Christian Landrieu. You also have this board, and he's head of the board. Who is actually running the place and who has the real power, that I don't claim to understand."

"A fair statement." Mario was looking at the hangar while he spoke to me. "Power often depends on who the people are. The board votes to decide on what should be done; the chief administrator then has the authority to issue whatever directives they consider necessary to implement the board's decisions. You can take a narrow or a broad view of that authority, if you take my meaning.

"Christian is a good man, mostly, but not a strong one. Each Color has two seats on the board and the board chooses its head, who then becomes the chief administrator. The chief administrator gives up any Color to take that position and holds their position until they die, or until the board, in its infinite wisdom, votes no confidence and replaces them. For all practical purposes, the chief administrator continues in their office until they become too feeble to do the job, and excepting a couple of sudden deaths, they have been able to pick their successor. Christian's father was chief administrator before him, and he selected Christian. That was the first time it went parent to child, and there has been grumbling about it for years.

"Then the signal came in and it was *made* into an issue, because the Greens aren't happy with Christian. You should note that it is base security and Sydney Yaeger who are not happy with Christian, but they dominate the Greens today, just as the scouts are identified with Blue. In fact, one Green director is always from base security and one Blue director is always a scout.

"I know Sydney's plan," he continued. "Red made it easy for her. She has been playing on the concerns in Red—fears about what the signal means, even if fears of alien invasions are ludicrous. She will move for a vote to replace Landrieu with the intention of taking his place. She also intends to keep her current seat for Green. That has never happened. We are going to oppose that, of course. Blue versus Green. Nothing new there, so the key comes down to Red. They fear the stars, anything beyond this world, and as I said, Sydney has played on that. At the same time, that fear has created among them an awe of starfolk. And a deference to starfolk. You've seen our starfolk, though. They are old; they are not impressive when you actually see them or hear them. You, on the other hand, could be important in swaying the Red votes. I need you to do that at this meeting. Can you? Will you?"

How do I get myself into these situations?

"I've heard that *you* made the signal an issue, because turning the response to the stars into a project would be an excuse to replace Landrieu with a Blue."

"That would be a natural outcome," he said, as though it were the most logical conclusion in the world.

"Then it's not about the stars," I said. "It's not about a signal from another intelligence. That's nothing but a convenient lever in a political game the bunch of you are playing here. I'm nothing but a tool you're trying to use, and I can't say I like that very much.

"I came here because someone around another star, a whole different type of being, wants to talk to us. This is more than a once-in-a-lifetime opportunity; it's a once-in-human-history opportunity. That's why I thought it was worth coming here. I didn't leave what I had to play politics." The clouds of breath I was blowing out in the cold air were nothing compared with the heat in my voice. For all that any of their politics mattered to me, I could be at home with Charity and the kids. Yes, I did think of that as home.

"That's not quite correct." Mario was still facing the hangar. "I said I had something to show you, and I do. I said it was politics and the stars, and it is both. You've had the politics part. Humor me a little longer." With that, he flicked his reins and started his horse toward the hangar he had been watching.

When we reached the open hangar doors, I could see that the interior was vast, as vast as a building that housed spaceplanes should be. I saw two of those, along with three regular airplanes. That was where normal stopped and weirdness began. Wooden panels had been hung from the wings and fuselages of the planes. These were nailed to wooden beams laid along the floor. More panels and beams were connected to make an open framework of wood along the walls. The effect was to transform the hangar into a huge barn, complete with separate pens for different livestock and bins to store feed, water, and tools.

"The spaceplane ramps are down, as you see," Mario said. "We use the cargo area for smaller animals. The planes are all dead. So is all the motorized equipment you can see around the periphery. At least this way we get some use out of it."

"It's all outside your wall, though," I said. "Looking at this from a defensive perspective, that's a risk. Is that what has Yaeger upset?"

"In part. We could drive livestock inside the wall, and we did hold them there during the Die-off. But we have far more people to feed now, and correspondingly, more animals and supplies. This is one reason base security fears too many from the East moving out this way."

"Wishing something won't happen usually doesn't keep it from happening," I said. "By now, people should know that. You need a better plan for the future."

"Maybe it will help to hear it from you," Mario said. "From someone out of the past, when wishful thinking failed."

Again, this was about their internal politics, about me as a magic way to get a point across. None of it had to do with the signal from the stars, which was the reason I had come. I said that and he grunted.

"I wanted you to see how we use the equipment from the past. This is how most people, even my scouts, think of spaceplanes. They see them as nothing more than part of the barn structure. Please come with me again."

We rode in silence from the hangar across the old landing field and headed away from the bustling scouts, out toward the featureless plains.

Concrete clacked under the horses' hooves again. We had come onto another runway. This one began to slope down as we followed it. Below ground level, I could see a door. An underground hangar?

Mario rode down the slope, with me beside him, to what did look like a hangar door. At the bottom, he dismounted and so did I. A regular human-sized door was set into the hangar door near the left-hand edge. Mario pulled a set of old-fashioned keys—actual metal, with a stripe that looked like magnetic tape along one side. He had three keys, and there were three locks in the door. He inserted a key into each lock and turned them to match marks on the circle of the locks. The door swung open to his push.

Mario stepped into the darkness beyond. When I joined him, he shut the door behind us. It was pitch black.

"Lights," Mario said.

White lights in the ceiling and the walls came on in response. They were actually pretty feeble, and many of them flickered, but after the total dark they made me squint.

"You have power in here." I was stating the obvious.

"Minimal," Mario said. "Enough, though, for now, although if we lose much more of our generating capacity—well, I don't know. What do you think?"

What I saw in front of me was a spaceplane. Not a large one; not like the one on the *Dauntless*. It was about the size of the old commercial spaceplane that had taken me up to what was then the New International Space Station prior to the first starshot. Small as it was, it and its equipment filled the hangar as though the hangar had been built specifically to house this spaceplane. Its paint was shiny, the markings sharp. This spaceplane had never flown.

"You have a brand-new spaceplane in a hangar taking power you can barely afford to spare. Scratch that. You can't afford to spare the power. What are you going to do with it? Drop leaflets on people moving west, telling them to stay on the other side of the Mississippi?"

"No." I think he took my last sentence seriously. He walked to the nose of the spaceplane, his footsteps echoing hollowly off the walls. "This is a part of our history that we are not proud of." He pointed up at the spaceplane. "The history we tell is that even before the final wars, there were many threats against Earthbase. We were hated, although no one now knows why. That's why the wall was built and its guns mounted. It was years before the wars. The wall was not built to protect us from the starving mobs during the Die-off; it was built to shield us from whatever caused the hatreds before it.

"This spaceplane was a secret; at least, its purpose was. It was here to take our leadership out if the survival of Earthbase might be at risk. After the wars, after the mobs were beaten off and died, this spaceplane was kept ready for our leaders, and they debated among themselves whether they should use it to flee. What stopped them were those twelve who came back.

"They denounced the leadership as cowards. Then they took some regular airplanes that could still fly, went out to what was left of this continent, and became saints to the people there, the foundation of the church.

"Here, well, their action set off a revolution. Leaders who are prepared to fly away and leave their people to a miserable fate are not something to be proud of. We disposed of them and have forgotten them. This spaceplane has remained, also forgotten—a secret in the custody of the leader of the scouts."

My mind reeled. Too many parts of his fable didn't make sense. "Where could these leaders have gone after the wars and the Die-off?" I asked. "Let's just call it the Tribulation, like everyone else does. Where would they go? There was no place this spaceplane could have taken them. It can't go beyond orbit. I know that, even if you do not. The space station was dead. Hell, the moon, Mars—every settlement in the solar system was dead. They had to have known that. Maybe they were cowards, but they had no place to run and that's why they stayed."

"Not so." Mario shoved his hands into the pockets of his coat. "The last starship ever built was never launched. Nobody really knows why, but we can guess. No support for it. That ship is still in orbit. That was the escape plan our magnificent leaders had. That knowledge is passed down through the leaders of the scouts, along with the keys to this hangar."

"What are you trying to tell me?" I had a suspicion I knew, and I wasn't sure I wanted to hear it.

"This is the reason I sent Caleb to find the crew of the starship that came back last year. Not so we could send a signal. If we could find a new crew, one that had just returned to find the world as it is, I thought they would be willing to take this ship out. Go to that starship and fly it to where the signal came from. Greet whoever is out there as no less than equals."

My first impulse was to retch. If we had landed at Earthbase when the *Dauntless* returned to the solar system, we could have learned of the signal and of this ship. I knew Yong would not have hesitated. She would have gone. And I would have flown that mission with her. All the casualties would have been avoided. Probably our whole crew would have gone with us. But now, Yong was gone. Decisions made could not be unmade. One year can make all the difference in the world.

"Caleb didn't know, naturally, about any of this." I realized Mario was still speaking. "He didn't know why we needed a full crew. He found you and you only, and brought you here, thinking that was best. You are not a pilot, are you?"

"No."

Mario bent his head to stare at the floor. In that instant, he looked and sounded like an old man. "Leif, please believe me when I say I am serious about answering the message from the stars. I will plead guilty, if you wish, to political machinations, and if answering the message makes a Blue chief administrator, I would say that is good. But I am serious about the stars. I must ask you what you think. Can our old starfolk do this? Can they fly back to the stars and meet this race?"

I stared at the spaceplane and thought of a starship in orbit, readied for a starshot that had never been made. Adrenaline roared in my blood, and my stomach lurched as though I were going through loops on a roller coaster. Not simply a signal to answer a signal, but to go there, meet these other beings, and learn more in a month than a millennium of messages would bring.

That was the high before the crash, and the emotional crash was a hard one. The starfolk here now were elderly; they weren't Yong and the crew I had flown with in the *Dauntless*, and the ship up there wasn't the *Dauntless*.

"Mario, I … I … it won't work. God, I wish it could, but it won't."

"Why not?" His tone was soft, his voice measured.

"Because … because," I spluttered, "you don't even know where the problems are, because you've never done anything like this. The *Invincible* crew hasn't trained for a mission in close to thirty-five years. This is not something you just pick up again. And this starship? Systems don't stay fresh for a century. We, my pilot and I, were going to fly out again, but it would have been in our ship, where we knew all the systems were functioning well.

"To be honest, I'm not sure even our crew could have done it with the ship you're talking about, because I don't know that it's still ready to fly." I threw my hands up in the air, a kid whose lollipop has been yanked away. "What we can do with the ship is to ask Mikhail if he can get enough power out of it to boost a signal someone will pick up. I'm afraid that's the best we can do."

That feeling of wanting to retch was back. It occurred to me, as I stared at the spaceplane and thought of landing from a starship in front of an alien species, that preparing to launch a starshot could leave Mario issuing directives for some time, probably with a broad interpretation of that authority. Of course, why should it matter to me who ran Earthbase?

Mario let out a long sigh. "If that's truly what you think, I don't know who would be able to say otherwise. Will you come to the meeting, though, and give us your support? Bischoff and Red will never vote to back Yaeger. It would mean the end of their trade. If you are strong enough in your support, you could tip them to us despite their fears. If Blue is leading when this is over, I will promise you the stars, however you think we can do it. Can I ask that much?"

Back to the politics. *Vote for me and I will give you the stars.* Other than having a leftover starship available—maybe—was Mario's offer all that different from Yaeger's? Who could I trust? Probably no one.

"I'm going to back whoever I think will truly support a reply to that signal," I said. "And after it's done, I'm headed home."

CHAPTER THIRTEEN

By the time I returned to the Starfolk's Home, I was ready to scream. From the day I had arrived at Earthbase until this morning, I had spent my time beating my head against the brick wall of people's indifference to the greatest opportunity humanity had ever had. All people could think about were their petty political maneuvers and advantages and their personal grudges. And then Mario had offered me the stars on a plate, and I had to be the one telling him it wouldn't work. Was something wrong with me? Had finding a family done something to the way I saw opportunity and risk? When I went to find the other starfolk, they were gathered in the caf playing a game they called checklist. This consisted of crafting questions on the checklists and mission plans from their starshot. Whoever was asked the question had to pull up the checklist or plan from their chip and solve the problem that was posed within a time limit. I actually knew the hib routines better than Max. In fairness, I had been working on hibs for years and was much closer to doing it than he was, but he still didn't appreciate it. I didn't want to play checklist.

·　　·　　·　　·

I walked out with the need for fresh air. Listening to Shane, Max, and the other starfolk even for a little while had reinforced my conviction that nothing was wrong with my judgment. Flying a starshot was not playing a game of checklist. For once, it would be nice to be wrong, but I wasn't.

Waiting for me outside the caf was Ramón Ugarte, minus his M8c. "Yaeger wants to see you," he said. "Do you have time?"

I had nothing but time, so I went along with him. Yaeger was waiting for me in the slight shelter offered by the entrance to another old and vacant building, wrapped in her coat against the chill. I glimpsed two other Greens not far away, as a perimeter of sorts.

"I see you did not take my advice about the party," Yaeger said as soon as Ugarte withdrew. As before, her eyes were the same temperature as the air.

"I've been known to take my own advice as opposed to what's given me," I said. I wasn't entirely surprised I had been spied on, but it still annoyed me.

"So I gather," Yaeger said. "You spend a lot of time with Blue. Your young friend is also spending time around Caleb, and I have heard enough to believe that Caleb, young as he is, is being prepared to be Mario's successor, even if Mario hasn't said it yet."

Yes, Yaeger was spying on me and wanted me to know it. She wanted me to know her network was extensive. I wondered if she knew only that I had spent time with Mario—or did she know about Mario's underground hangar? The reporting she'd received, however, wasn't entirely accurate. No Nonsense may have been around Caleb, but that was because he was hanging around Sho, and Caleb was keeping an eye, probably both eyes, on him.

"What is your point?" It was too cold to stand around outside and listen to a recitation of my activities. "I don't care about your politics. I want to reply to whoever sent us that message from another star. That's what matters to me. It should matter to all of you, but if it doesn't, that's okay—as long as the reply is sent."

"You are being played for a fool," she said. "Mario will get your influence at the board and then his promises will disappear like vapor. He is playing Red, too, dangling regular escorted caravans. Bischoff is so hungry for the trade, she will take the bait. Red sees danger from the stars, but not the danger in front of their nose. Landrieu will then put his thumb on the scale, but on the wrong side, as he often does."

"You are telling me this for a reason," I said. "What do you want from me?"

She favored me with a cold smile. "Direct and to the point. All I need is for you to express your distrust of Mario. Say that you cannot trust his promises. Bischoff is not an idiot. If *you* say it, and say it more than once, that will make her think about the promises he is making to *her*, and she will pull back from Mario. Then, when this is over, I will see to it that we send your reply signal."

Sure. Assuming that I could trust her. Yaeger might know we had gone into an underground hangar or bunker, but clearly she did not know what was in it. If she did, she would have given me a reason to disregard the spaceplane. "I'll make my own decisions about what I think and whom I trust," I said.

If Yaeger's face could have grown colder, it would have formed icicles. "I am going to ask Landrieu to postpone the meeting for a few days," she said. "If you are going to do as I now think, I will need some time to figure out how I will safeguard this town afterward." With that, she snapped her fingers at Ugarte and strode away, accompanied by him and the other Greens.

God, do I hate politics. If forced to choose, I would rather be in combat, and that is saying something.

I stayed where I was until Yaeger was out of sight. By that time, I was thoroughly disgusted. This should have been a simple matter. Oh, the technical aspects of it weren't simple, not in the postapocalyptic remains of the world, but the fundamental principle of "send a reply" was straightforward. At least, to me it was. I wasn't fantasizing that we might be missing an invitation to join some galactic federation, but still … how could we elevate chairing a board of directors for a few years over making contact with other beings in the universe? Easily, I suppose. All the people at Earthbase wanted from me was to swing a vote one way or another.

I had to admit that Yaeger could be right; Mario might be playing me. He had wanted my political support first, and he might not care if that spaceplane could ever leave the ground or if Mikhail could boost a signal. Was caring about connecting with the universe beyond Earth a luxury, one that only a technologically advanced and stable culture could afford? And was I the idiot for wanting something people concerned with day-to-day survival saw as frivolous? Should I give up and go home? What difference would it make, in the grand scheme of the universe?

I sighed. I did not want to go back to the Starfolk's Home right away. For sure, I did not want to play checklist. I didn't even want to talk to Ruth at that moment. I wanted to be alone.

I did make a quick stop at the Starfolk's Home to buckle on my pistol. If I was going to be alone, I would rather be armed. Politics had a way of getting nasty.

·　　·　　·

THE MARKET WAS MODERATELY BUSY. SMALL SHOPS LIKE MIKHAIL'S HAD A TRICKLE OF customers for everything from clothing to pots, while open-air stalls did a brisker business for barbecued chicken on skewers and other meats I chose not to examine closely. I thought of the small apple orchard behind Charity's farmhouse and would have bought an apple, but I didn't see any fruit on offer. I attracted a number of stares, but no one bothered to stop me, and I wasn't in the mood for a random conversation. The whole of the Earthbase market was only a rough square of about three blocks confined by streets that had been planned in the heyday of the ISC programs but never built up. I walked out of the market and past the crossball field, now empty and quiet. I kept going in the direction of the wall, an area I had never explored.

A long stretch of ground was covered not with buildings but with heaped-up masses of material under canvas. Curiosity got the better of me. I picked one at random and pulled up a corner of canvas. Underneath were steel rods and concrete blocks. I remembered the way Shane had mentioned the abrupt halt to construction at Earthbase. These mounds were built of old construction materials, gathered here for building and then left when the work was shut down. Burial mounds for ambition.

A large structure loomed up beyond the piles of old construction material. Two long, one-story wings projected off toward the wall from a central building that was square and three stories high, all of concrete blocks and brick. From the irregular way the building blocks had been mortared together, I deduced that this was postapocalypse construction, not part of the original Earthbase.

Plumes of smoke rose from multiple chimneys in the central building and the wings. Stripes of blue paint from eaves to ground along the length of the building told me, before I could even see the sign at the front, that this was scout headquarters and barracks. Sho and No Nonsense were probably out wrestling cows and sheep. I had nothing to say to Caleb—nothing I was going to allow myself to say— and I did not want to run into Mario. I wondered if one of the people I saw around the building worked for Yaeger on the side. I steered away from the entrance, walked past one of the barracks wings, and continued on toward the wall.

I had no idea what I would do when I reached the wall except, probably, turn around. When I made it there, though, what I saw alerted me that I was hungry. It didn't look like much; it was on the order of a long, low shack, half of it brick and the other half concrete block. Earthbase's wall, several feet higher than its roof, served as the building's back wall. That roof slanted sharply down from the Earthbase wall, a mélange of mismatched shingles and tarps on top of plywood sheets. Smoke poured from two chimneys at either end that listed in opposite directions more than the tower of Pisa ever had. At least that meant the interior would be warm. As I inspected the place, a steady flow of customers went in and out of the front door. What won me over was the name painted in black on a plank nailed over that door: THE STARSHOT TAVERN.

Inside, the light was dim, dependent on sunlight that came in through two partially opaque windows and on lanterns that hung from fixtures in the walls and ceiling. Fires roared in each hearth, generating additional light as well as smoke that mostly went up the chimneys. The fires, plus pots bubbling on two stoves in an open kitchen at one end, behind a bar, made the interior pleasantly warm, if a bit smoky. Tables were a mixture of metal and plastic from before and nailed-together wood with plywood tops from now, standing unevenly on a floor of packed earth.

The place was nearly full, but one table, a small one, was empty. Directly past that table and close to one hearth was another small table occupied by two women. One of them gave me a smile and raised a tankard of beer in salute. I gave the barest nod in return, and she resumed her conversation with her companion. When no one else paid any attention to me, I took a seat at the empty table. It was pleasant to absorb the warmth, stare at the fire, and try to turn off my brain. After a while, and after seeing that I made no move toward the bar, a middle-aged woman came over and I was able to order a chicken pot pie.

The food arrived promptly, and it was good—plenty of meat in it to go with chunks of potato and carrot. I lost interest, though, after a few spoonfuls and went back to gazing at the fire. My brain refused to shut down. Images of the Earthbase I remembered kept circulating through my head.

Along with the images was a growing conviction that coming here had been a mistake. The Earthbase of now did not fit with the Earthbase of before. It was, as Sydney Yaeger had said, a provincial small town a long way from anywhere. Was this where humanity's pretensions of ranging across the stars had come to die?

I wasn't paying attention to anyone else in the tavern. It was only from the corner of my eye and by listening to an internal sentry from my army days that I became aware of two men at a table by the back wall. Their eyes were fixed on me. One of them had a knife out and was using it to chop little Vs into the edge of the plywood tabletop. From the cuts and gouges I saw in the top of my table, I guessed that the proprietor didn't care as long as only wood was chopped. When I focused on the two of them, they stood up, walked over, and planted themselves at my table.

One was pole-thin, his loosely woven, poorly manufactured shirt draped across narrow shoulders. An equally thin pink face sported a sparse blond beard. The other, who still held the knife, appeared thickset by contrast, his hands dense with muscle. A dark brown beard covered most of his white face and a scar split his forehead diagonally. The hair on both of them could have used a trim. Red shields were pinned to each shirt.

"Did I invite you to join me?" I may not have used the nicest of tones.

"You didn't," said the man with the scar. "We invited us. Want to have a word with you." He started to cut a V into the edge of my table with his knife.

From the gust he blew across the table, he had drunk more than one beer while readying himself to have a word. I looked from one to the other and again at the knife chiseling itself into the edge of my table. How was this going to end? Probably not well. The question was, for whom? My pistol was on my belt. It was hidden from the two of them by the table, but I had one hand on a bowl of pot pie and the other held a spoon. It wasn't a big table.

"Is it going to be one word?" I asked. "Or more?"

"Hah," said scarface. "You're the starman who rode in the other day. Guess you don't come from the sky anymore. We all know about you. Everyone does."

"So? I'm a stranger in a small town," I said. "I'm not surprised everyone knows I'm here by now. So what?"

"We know that damned stupid scout brought you here because of that signal," he said. "Green and Blue have already been at you about it. I'm damned sure of that. But you damned well need to listen to Red too. More of us than Green or Blue and we do honest work, most of us anyway. The thing is—" He stopped. He took the knife away from the table edge and held it up. Firelight glinted off the blade.

I tensed and put the spoon down. I slid that hand toward the edge of the table. "If you're going to trim your nails, do it over the floor, not the table."

"What's that supposed to mean?" he asked. The knife came down and carved another V.

I took the opportunity to drop my hand off the table down to my hip. I wondered if the people here were as nonchalant about the occasional gunplay as they had been in Eastview. I doubted it.

"You said you wanted a word," I said. "Is it a word or a fight?"

He made the V deeper. "I'm trying to tell you about that signal," he said. "Abe here"—now he pointed the knife at the other man—"will tell you the same. Somebody sends a signal no one can understand, they're just lookin' to see if someone is dumb enough to stick their head up and show themselves. We answer that, we show ourselves, and they'll be right here with an army and that's the end of us. We gotta play dumb. Keep our heads down. Let 'em go fish somewhere else."

I managed to avoid smiling. "Listen," I said, "that's not the way these things work. It took years, a lot of years, for that message to get here. If we send a reply, it's going to be the same number of years for them to get it and even more years for anything they do."

His eyes narrowed, hardened. "That's bullshit!" he shouted loud enough to stop other conversations. "I can send a message by rider across the Mississippi and it'll get there in less than a year. And these signals are electronics. You do something electronic, it happens right then. Immediately. Everybody knows that."

You can't have a battle of wits with an unarmed man.

"I'm not going to get into details," I said. "I'm only telling you that's not how the science of these things works. I know the science."

"Science!" he exploded. "Don't tell me to follow the science! That's what all the before-people did, and you can see what that got 'em. Bricks and stones! We all know what we know, what's obvious. Don't give me that science crap."

With that, he pointed the knife across the table at my face. My hand went to the grip of my pistol. In the instant between that moment and disaster, a tankard swept in from the side and hit his knife hand. The knife flew away, bounced on the floor, and slid under another table, where someone put a foot on it. Immediately, the tankard backhanded him across the face. The man gasped and clutched at his cheek. Blood dripped from one nostril.

"Bert Colangelo, you're an asshole and an idiot." Standing next to the table was the woman who had raised a tankard when I came in. The handle of the tankard was still gripped in one fist. She glared down at the man, who stayed in his seat. "You were pretty damned happy about science when you came to my clinic dripping pus and screaming how it killed you every time you had to piss. We can also talk about how you got that way. That's science, too, if you want me to go into it."

"For God's sake, Doc!" He did not get up. Laughter was erupting around the room.

"You go home and sober up, Bert," she said. "Take Abe with you. Next time you come by the clinic, you can thank me. This man is wearing a gun, which you obviously didn't notice. Now, get going."

Like a couple of boys caught doing mischief in someone else's yard, the two of them scrambled for the door and vanished. The knife stayed under the other table.

I took a closer look at who had intervened. She wasn't tall; I doubt she topped five feet. She was slim, maybe in her late thirties, with thin lines spreading out from her eyes and a rough hand on the tankard handle. Those eyes were partially rounded over high cheekbones, suggesting a mix of Asian and Caucasian in her ancestry. Dark hair was chopped off at her jawline and appeared black in the low light of the tavern.

She seated herself in the chair Bert had vacated. "Dr. Hannah Jin," she said.

"Leif Grettison. You have one hell of a bedside manner."

She smiled. "Sometimes you have to be direct. And it's not as though that business with him was a secret. Not in a town like this."

"I guess not," I said. "You're not wearing a color."

"The docs don't. By tradition, we don't take sides and nobody will raise a hand to any of us. Sensible, I think you'll agree."

I nodded.

"I do want to say something to you. Just for a minute. I heard what Bert was spouting. Impossible not to have heard it. There are a lot of people like Bert. Not necessarily bad people, but they are ignorant, and they're scared of what they don't know. Can't see past the cows they're milking or the field they're sowing, and you can't blame them. It's a hard life.

"I can remember, though, when I was a girl, my pa would take me out at night and show me the constellations. I know we went to space and to the stars from here. I've walked the Avenue of Heroes and looked at the statues. If there's somebody out there we could talk to, who wants to talk to us, we've got to do it. Somehow. Someway. If I could send a message back, I would, even knowing I'd never live to hear what they said in return.

"If I could give Landrieu and everyone on the board a slap across the face and make them see that this is what's important, not their petty Colors and their petty politics, I'd do it. I can't. Maybe, though, maybe *you* can. I thought when you came in that it was a lucky sign. That's all I wanted to say. Can you do it?"

I looked into an earnest face across the table. Dr. Hannah Jin was the first person I had spoken with who had the same vision I did. Where there was one, there would be others. "You may have restored my faith in humanity," I said.

That earned me a puzzled look.

"I'll get it done," I said before the moment could get awkward. "That's my promise."

"Thank you." She went back to the table with the other woman, and neither of them looked my way again.

I finished my pot pie and walked back to the Starfolk's Home. I kept one hand near my pistol as I walked through the chilly night, but there was no sign of Bert or Abe, and no one else bothered me. That is, no person bothered me. I looked at the sky and my eyes saw what was beyond. I knew what Yong would say. All of this was on me. How was I going to make it happen?

.   .   .

HAVING MIKHAIL FIGURE OUT HOW TO SEND A SIGNAL WAS PROBABLY THE BEST BET I had. If that was what I was going to propose in front of Landrieu's board, and if Shane and the other starfolk were going to be there, it would be a good idea to understand their relationship with Mikhail a bit better. That didn't mean I was going to join the reminiscing about a New Golden Age I hadn't lived in, nor did I intend to play checklist. I had noted that Magda moved a lot slower than the others and was usually the last one to leave the caf in the evening. I arranged to "just happen by" when she was alone.

"Sure, I have a minute," she said when I asked. "That's the one thing I still have plenty of."

"What's the story with Shane and Mikhail? Or is it with all of you and Mikhail?"

"I knew that would come up, as soon as Shane said he was taking you to see him." She started to limp over to where I stood, her right leg swinging around in a stiff circular motion. "Sorry, the hip is bad tonight."

I crossed over to her immediately and offered to sit with her at the closest table, but she shook her head and said that sitting would hurt more. She forced herself to straighten and tried for a smile. Magda was an old tree, gnarled and bent with the storms of the years, but the strength in the wood was still evident.

"You wanted to know about the problem with Mikhail," she said. "He is Russian."

When nothing more was forthcoming, I had to ask, "And?"

She sighed. "After more than thirty years, you could say it sounds silly, but with the results of the wars out there"—she waved her arm at the ceiling—"maybe it's not so silly. He was a very late swap into the crew. I have no idea what ISC was thinking. Shane said, when the crew was first announced, that they gave him final approval on the list. Not on Mikhail, obviously. Maybe ISC had to do something for Roscosmos, put a Russian on the ship. I don't think Mikhail had any particular pull. Maybe Roscosmos was trying to get rid of him. None of us know. Shane demanded an explanation from ISC and never got one. He and Mikhail started off badly almost immediately."

"Where did the Mickey stuff come from?"

"Right at the start," Magda said. "When Mikhail introduced himself, Shane said we'd call him Mickey and we could pretend we had an Irishman instead of a Russian on the ship. Shane swears it was a joke, but Mikhail didn't think so, and pretty soon, it wasn't a joke at all. He and Kwame almost came to blows because Mikhail would say Kwame couldn't follow the official procedures and Kwame said Mikhail couldn't do anything *but* follow procedure. Mikhail seemed to find a bone to pick with each one of us." Magda's voice was weary.

"Would I be right that all of you gave him reasons to find a bone to pick?"

"Yeah." She looked down at the floor. "Not something I'm particularly proud of."

The *Invincible* had needed a kindergarten teacher more than a pilot-in-command. "I'm surprised you launched with that situation on the ship. I would have thought Shane or Mikhail or the whole damn crew would have demanded a crew change."

"No." Her voice firmed at that. "You don't know what it was like then. Things hadn't come apart yet, but we all could see it coming. Knew it was coming soon; we just didn't know how soon. If the starshot was delayed, we feared it would never go. If we weren't on the *Invincible*, we feared we would never have another ship. We were pretty much right about that." She forced a small laugh. "We thought we'd go away for a century, come back, and find the world had been patched up again with the problems solved. Pretty much dead wrong about that."

"If I'm telling the board to have Mikhail work on a reply and Shane is there, do you think Shane will keep the peace, or am I going to have a problem?"

"If you're doing the talking," she said, "I don't think there will be a problem, but I can't be sure. Now, if you don't mind, I need to lie down. That's the only way I can be close to comfortable, and I do have to climb the stairs."

She declined my offer of help with the stairs. I watched her go, thinking that the Colors might not be the biggest problem with the board meeting.

•   •   •

I WAS ABLE TO PUT THE DAYS YAEGER DELAYED THE BOARD MEETING—AND I ASSUMED she was the reason for the passage of time—to good use, even if I fretted about the time passing. I put the question I had asked Magda directly to Shane. He shrugged it off with a comment that it was Mickey who had the problem. I then went to Mikhail, in case Landrieu decided to have *both* of them at the meeting.

Mikhail took a moment before answering. "As long as he can keep his mouth shut and not start something, there won't be a problem from me."

I figured that was the best I could do to cover the bases. As long as Shane and Mikhail did not get into a pissing contest, I could probably grab control of that meeting, and I might decide which Color I trusted more when we were in the room.

I spent more time with Mikhail as he checked the hangars and the spaceplanes. He was able to send power to the systems in the hangars but was noncommittal about the comm systems on the spaceplanes. He muttered more than once that he had a different option, but he dodged any attempt to press him on it. He also let me satisfy my curiosity and listen to the audio rendition of the message we had received that the Earthbase system played through a speaker. Not surprisingly, it was unintelligible, nothing more than a twittering noise, even though I could tell that it repeated itself with regularity.

"Whatever it says, it's short," Mikhail said. "Fifty-three minutes, to be exact. After an hour and fifty-six minutes, it repeats. It seems to always be the same. It's probably some sort of digital code, but I have no idea what. Could be anything from binary to hexadecimal, or something completely strange. Even if I can get one of those space-planes functioning, their computers won't have the ability to decipher it. Maybe the AI on a starship could, but even then, I'm not certain."

I also decided I would use those days for a little politics of my own. I took Landrieu up on his offer from the day I arrived. I had one of the ever-rotating group of kids around the Starfolk's Home take a message to him. It said that, in fact, I had a plan.

That led to a brief meeting at the administration building, where I gave him a thumbnail sketch of what Mikhail would do and said that I would be happy to stand up in front of his board and make the proposal.

Landrieu's face lit up with delight. "I'll set the rules for the meeting," he said. "I'll limit it to your proposal, a proposal from the starfolk, and then I'll turn it over to you to speak. None of them are going to interrupt you. We'll go to a vote immediately after that and I can keep the rest of their damned agendas out of it."

There was real enthusiasm in his handshake.

It all sounded good to me.

·　　·　　·

ON THE MORNING OF THE FOURTH DAY AFTER MY DISCUSSIONS WITH MARIO AND then with Sydney, a squad of three, each wearing a red, blue, or green brassard, showed up at the Starfolk's Home and announced they were my escort to the board meeting.

This was it! After all the talk, after all the politics, we were going to orchestrate humanity's response to the beings around a distant star who had contacted us. I spent the walk to the old administration building mentally rehearsing what I was going to say and whom I wanted to focus on when I said each part. I had never met the Red director, Bischoff, so I would need to figure out fast how to read her. Plenty of times I had briefed senior officers I didn't know, but the difference here was that I intended to end up as the decision-maker.

A group of Greens wearing the gray wool of base security stood in the lobby of the administration building. They weren't doing anything other than standing around in their heavy serge coats. They brought to mind a bunch of grunts taking advantage of no superiors being present to shelter in the heated lobby instead of outside, where the cold was intense. I ignored them and went up the stairs with my escort.

The boardroom was on the same floor as Landrieu's office but at the other end of the building. The entry was impressive. Ten-foot-high, ornately carved doors of dark wood separated the room from the corridor. Next to the doors was a black granite slab on the wall, with BOARDROOM carved into it above the gloved hand clutching a star. The directors of Earthbase must have met in this room back in the starflight days. My escort pushed the right-hand door open and stood aside for me to enter. Silently, the door swung closed behind me.

The interior could have come out of the late twenty-first century. A large octagonal table of cherrywood dominated the center of the room. Its top was polished to gleaming and an inlaid strip of darker wood ran around the perimeter, two inches in from the edge. Heavy wooden chairs with thick cushions were set around the table. In front of each chair, a small individual screen was mounted on a black tabletop pedestal. Larger screens were mounted on the two side walls and angled for easy viewing from the table.

The illusion of the past lasted only seconds. All the screens were blank. The lights in the ceiling were out. The light in the room came through the windows in the wall opposite the door and from lanterns that hung from hooks screwed into the old paneling on the walls.

Of fifteen chairs around the table, only seven were occupied. Six of the people wore brassards: two green, two blue, and two red. Of the ones with colors, I recognized Mario and Sydney. The seventh person was Landrieu. All of them stood when I entered. Neither Shane nor any of the other old starfolk were present.

Landrieu came around from his seat in front of the windows to greet me. He wore a black gown over his clothes, I guess to distinguish himself from the Colors. It looked like the graduation gowns I remembered from school. When he came close, I could see that it was moth-eaten.

"Leif, on behalf of the Board of Directors of Earthbase and all of Earthbase, let me congratulate you on your return from Starshot Fifteen and thank you for coming here to contribute to what will be, possibly, the most important decision we ever make." He extended a hand in the direction of one of the vacant chairs. "Please have a seat. We will review for you all the information that we have, and each of the Colors will provide their position. After that, you will have as much time as you wish to give us your thinking."

I hadn't gotten any farther than putting my hand on the back of the chair when loud noise erupted from the corridor beyond the boardroom doors. I heard running feet. There were shouts, but no distinct words. Landrieu turned toward the doors, surprised. I turned with him. The doors were flung open and I heard the shout, "Red says no to the stars!"

A group of three men burst in, two wearing the gray of base security with green armbands. In front of them was a young man who wore a coarsely woven, homespun shirt and pants. His eyes were wide, his face contorted in a lopsided grimace. His right hand came up. A pistol was in that hand.

"No to the stars! Death to the starman!" he screamed.

He fired three times. I saw the muzzle flashes. The crack of the shots filled the boardroom. I heard screams behind me and more tumult in the hallway. Despite being shot at from point-blank range, I was not hit.

Training took over. Two steps covered the ground between us even as the third shot was firing. I launched myself at him, got my right hand on his gun hand, and pushed the pistol off-line. A split second more and I smashed my left forearm into his gun arm, above the elbow. I used the leverage and drove him down, and we both went to the floor, with me on top. I smashed his gun hand against the floor twice. He lost his grip on the pistol and it skittered away across the floor. I gathered my legs under me to stand and started to pull him up with me. That was when something smashed into the back of my head and the world went white.

PART II

The Banshee's wild voice sings the death-dirge before me,
The pall of the dead for a mantle hangs o'er me;
But my heart shall not flag, and my nerves shall not shiver
Though devoted I go—to return again never!

Sir Walter Scott, "MacKrimmon's Lament"

CHAPTER FOURTEEN

I must have been out briefly and then dazed, because when I next realized what I was doing, I was on my hands and knees, trying without success to stand up. People were yelling and screaming all around me, but only snippets came through the roaring in my ears.

"… shoot him now …" Who? Me?

"No! … need … later … in charge …" Was that Yaeger screaming?

"… lying … we vote …" Female voice, not Yaeger?

"… got away …"

"Security here … go … him back … shoot him!" Him who?

I heard gunshots. At least three.

I wasn't processing any of this. They were words without meaning, without reference. Rough hands grabbed me under my armpits, pulled me to my feet. Then I was walking between two men, my arms over their shoulders. Walking, hell! I was shambling, at best. My feet didn't understand where to go and my brain couldn't figure out where to put them. I had a splitting headache, and my ears were ringing. The fog in my mind was as bad as the worst post-hib blur I'd ever had.

Through the mental clouds I heard, "You have to come with us."

"Wha—? Where?" I croaked.

"Yaeger said to put you someplace safe." That voice came from the other side of me.

I didn't recognize either voice. I did realize that we were going down a flight of stairs. Which stairs, and where they led, I couldn't tell. I held on to that pair of shoulders. I don't think I could have negotiated the stairs without support.

Then we were outside. I felt the cold. The glare from the sun hurt my eyes. I could see the starshot memorial in front of me. I knew where I was again. Somehow, we had left the administration building. We walked past the memorial and kept going. I wasn't sure how far we went. It felt like miles, but it couldn't have been too far, because I couldn't have made it any great distance.

The two of them walked me to the ground floor entrance of a four-story concrete building. By that time, my brain was processing what passed in front of my eyes. A man and a woman were stationed at that door. Both of them wore green and held rifles, the lever-action Winchester type, not M8cs. The two of them fell in behind us as we went through the door. More stairs. I was able to count that we went up three flights. By the time we left the staircase on the third floor, I was walking okay, but neither of the men with me showed any inclination to let go. They walked me down a short corridor to a door at the back of the building. There was a bar across that door that hadn't been part of the original structure. The man on my right let go of me and fished in a pocket. He came out with a key that fit into a lock in the bar. I heard a click. He pulled the bar up and pushed the door open. The two of them gave me a shove that sent me through the door and stumbling to my hands and knees.

"This will be plenty safe." He laughed. "You stay here until we come for you."

I heard the door close behind me, a clank as the bar came down, and then a click.

"Leif! What happened to you?" That was Caleb's voice.

I looked up. Saw Caleb. Saw puzzlement, but no wounds or bruising.

I sat back on my butt, arms on my knees, and stared at him. "I'm not sure. Took a hit to my head. Give me a sec."

I knew I was concussed. I wasn't sure how bad. I thought my mind was clearing, although my head still hurt and I still heard the ringing in my ears. For the first time ever, I wanted one of those personal health apps from my chip. I'd deleted all of them, intrusive annoyances that they were, and now, when I could have used one, I didn't have any of them. It probably didn't matter. I'd had meds for this sort of thing in my medikit, but that was long gone with the *Dauntless*. Part of my mind—the army part—told me I was going to have to get up and function, no matter what.

"Ask me some questions," I said. "Where I am, what year it is, simple arithmetic."

Caleb fired off a series of questions that made me think he had done this before. When he told me my score was perfect, I nodded and immediately regretted the movement. I used one hand to help me push off the floor and get to my feet. I wobbled a bit.

"What the fuck is going on here?" I asked. "What does any of this have to do with a decision on communicating with the stars?"

"No idea," Caleb said. "Runner came to the barracks early this morning, said one of the Greens had something important I had to see. Something urgent. When I got where I was told to go, there were two Greens with guns. Brought me here and locked me in. What happened to you?"

My head throbbed but my mind was working again. I told him about the man who had burst into the board meeting shouting, "Death to the starman!" and something about Red saying no to the stars. "He fired three shots," I said. "I remember that. I can still see the muzzle flashes. I don't know how he could have missed me. I mean, I saw ridiculously bad shooting in Eastview, but I don't think this guy was drunk. Even if he was, I don't see how he could miss with all three. I tackled him and then something hit me, and he didn't do that."

I explored the back of my head with the fingers of one hand and wished I hadn't. I probed the tender area anyway and decided I was going to have quite a goose egg there but did not think I had a fracture. When I brought my hand down, there was no blood on it. I guess I have a thick skull.

"It doesn't make sense," I said.

"No." Caleb agreed. "Plenty of Reds are scared of the stars, but I hadn't heard they wanted to kill you. Nobody has ever bothered the old starfolk. And I don't know where Sho is. No Nonsense said he was going with her but I didn't see either of them this morning. If anybody's hurt her, I swear I'll kill them. If they try to run, I'll leave a trail of blood from here to the Mississippi."

"Let's save the rhetoric." I put a hand up in case he planned to say more. "There's no point talking vengeance until you know you need it. Any guess why someone wants us out of the way, or for how long? This doesn't feel like safekeeping."

"No answers," Caleb said. "This building is in the old part of Earthbase; people don't live here. There's no food or bedding, which argues it's not going to be too long, but there's a bucket in the corner for a chamber pot that could argue the opposite."

My eyes followed his hand and saw a large rusted bucket almost the size of a washtub. Shit, I thought. Literally. Starting from there, I took stock of what might as well have been our jail cell. A hundred-plus years ago, this had been someone's office. An important someone, because it occupied a corner of the building and had windows set into the corner. The floor was carpeted in a neutral gray. Time rather than tread had flattened it. A large desk with a chair behind it occupied the corner with the windows. Another window let light in on a coffee table with a couch and two chairs on either side. I checked the windows. They were not the kind that opened. Naturally. The glass hadn't been cleaned in forever, and taller buildings blocked some of the view, but I could see plains and hangars in the distance. We were facing the back side of Earthbase, away from the administration building and the Avenue of Heroes.

While I was assessing the office, I heard the rattle of distant gunfire. It wasn't concentrated, didn't come from only one location.

I wasn't sure I was ready to trust my senses, but Caleb confirmed my impression. I went to the door. The handle turned but the door wouldn't open. Yes, there was a bar on the other side. And guards. Somewhere.

"Okay," I said. "We need to get out of here. How?"

"Pound on the door. Make a lot of noise," Caleb said. "When one of the guards opens it to see what's happening, we jump him and take his gun. Maybe take a shit in the bucket first and toss it at him when the door opens. That'll distract anybody."

I sighed. Caleb couldn't have seen any of the superspy vids I'd enjoyed when I was growing up, but he sounded as though he expected real life to follow one of those scripts.

"Listen," I said, "what you're not taking into account is that they may not be stupid enough to have only one person there when they open the door. If there's two of them, well, lever-action rifles don't fire on automatic, but they can be fired rapidly. That ends badly. For us."

"Yeah." Caleb let out a long breath and seemed to deflate. "I'm sure you're right. Anyway, I don't think they're outside the door or even on the floor. I didn't hear anything out there until they brought you. The guards are probably at the building entrances. We could pound as much as we want and I'm not sure they'd even hear it."

That brought up another option, though. "That door swings. It's not a slider, which makes sense because in a building without power, the sliding doors won't work. It swings inward; the hinges are on our side." I walked to the door and ran my fingers across the hinges. "If we can find some kind of tool to get the hinges off, maybe we can create an opening despite the crossbar they put on the outside. If we can get out, they won't be expecting us downstairs. Surprise can give us a chance of taking both of them without getting shot."

It sounded good when I said it. Unfortunately, there wasn't anything in that office we could use to dig into the wall and unhinge the door. I guess there was no reason for a chisel to be in an office desk drawer, although it would have been convenient.

I was still engaged in the fruitless search for a usable tool when

I was interrupted by a knocking on one of the windows. I can be forgiven for thinking I was still dazed when I looked over at the window and saw Sho. She was *outside* the window, holding on to a rope. Two M8cs were slung across her back.

WTF?

She rapped her knuckles on the window again. Caleb and I stared at her, then ran to the window. The surprise on Caleb's face convinced me this was real.

The rope she was holding ran up to somewhere on the roof. She was talking but I couldn't hear anything through the glass and the persistent ringing in my ears. I can't lip-read.

I put my mouth next to the window and yelled, "These don't open!"

When I want to project, you can probably hear me through the armor on a tank with the motor running. Well, maybe not that. Sho did hear me through the window. She gave a thumbs-up and mouthed what might have been, "Got it."

With one hand holding the rope, she braced herself with her feet against the side of the building. Her free hand was fiddling with the rest of the rope. She grabbed something I couldn't see. Then, somehow, she took one foot off the building, bent herself forward into a bit of a pretzel, and made a loop with the loose rope around her boot. How she did that without falling, I wasn't sure—and this was the kind of stuff I did. Then I saw what she had fastened to her boot. It was a crude climbing anchor. Those things have spikes that can be driven into rock. How did she have that? What could you climb in Kansas? I left those questions for later.

Sho squatted down low with both feet now against the window, then thrust herself backward away from the building and let the rope swing her in again. The spike hit the window dead center. The glass shattered. She flew through the shards of falling glass to land on the office's coffee table.

"Oof!" She picked herself up gingerly and stood. Blood leaked from a cut across one cheek and from another on the back of her right hand.

"My God! Are you all right?" Caleb wrapped her in a hug, even with the rifles across her back. Then he tried to stanch the flow of blood from the slice in her cheek with his shirt. "Why didn't you just shoot the window out?"

She pushed his hand away from her face. "Unslinging one of the rifles seemed harder," she said. "I didn't want to take a chance on dropping one. And for sure, the guards would hear a gunshot and know we had at least one."

She stepped back, hands on hips. "So my valiant big brother is in here along with the big, strong starman, but it's left to the girl to do the hard work."

I could see Caleb focused on Sho, revving up for a retort. They were kids playing a game. I might not know what was going on, but I knew this was not a game.

"Enough of that," I said. "Even without shooting out the window, it's likely someone heard your grand entrance. I'll bet we're going to have visitors. Give me one of the rifles. Now!"

Sho visibly startled at the snapped-out *now*. Without a word, she unslung one of the rifles and handed it to me.

I had no way of knowing what made this M8c different from the M8s that I'd carried in Central Asia and Mindanao—other than that the barrel looked an inch longer—but it set for full automatic, the way I was accustomed to. At a quick glance, it looked ready for use. Should I be starting hostilities? Well, we were locked in a room and there were Green guards around the building. That qualified as being held against my will. Possibly, those guards weren't hostile. Tough shit. By similar reasoning, it was Green that had locked me up, and Blue was the enemy of Green. The enemy of my enemy is my friend. Anyway, I liked the Peterson sibs.

The sound of footsteps pounding up the last flight of the stairwell told me I was right about Sho's arrival having attracted attention. That door wasn't reinforced. It was nothing more than an old-time office door. I'd bet that the walls weren't anything more substantial than wood sheathing and maybe particleboard.

"You two." I pointed at them. "In that far corner, out of line with the door. Sho, train your rifle on where the door would swing open in case anyone starts to come through it."

That was all the time I had before the feet stopped outside the door. More than one person? Definitely. More than two? Probably not.

A voice yelled out, "Hey, what's going on in there?" A fist pounded.

I heard the lock click and what sounded like the crossbar being raised. I squeezed the trigger. The ancient M8c responded by spitting out a nearly continuous stream of flames. I lit up the door and the walls on both sides of it. The blast of bullets being fired and blowing holes in the door and walls made an earsplitting racket in the office. Screams came from the hall. Those didn't last long. I could barely make out the thuds of bodies hitting the floor.

I released the trigger. There was no sound, no movement outside the door. Acrid smoke filled the room. The door swung inward a few inches, but no one was pushing it. It was only the impacts of the bullets that had filled it with holes that opened it, and the crossbar was no longer in place. I pulled the door completely open, checked the corridor, and stepped out. The others crowded behind me.

Two bodies, riddled with bullets, lay on the floor. Bullet holes, splashes of blood, and chunks of tissue adorned the opposite wall. I turned to Caleb and Sho. If their eyes grew any bigger, their faces would disappear. I hoped neither one would get sick.

"Did you bring extra magazines?" I asked Sho.

She couldn't get words out, only gave a little back-and-forth twist of her head.

I sighed. I wasn't out of ammunition, but I was going to have to be careful.

"Is there any way down besides that staircase?" I asked.

"There might be another staircase, but I don't know," Caleb said quickly.

"Okay. Any building like this and built when it was built has to have more than one exit, and that means at least one more set of guards. If they have any brains at all, they'll set up to shoot us when we come down the stairs. So, we don't." I turned back to Sho. "How did you get to the roof?"

Her eyes were still fastened on the bodies, but she did find her voice. "The building next to this one. It's the same height and pretty close. Nobody's watching over there. The only Greens in this area since the shooting started are the guards on this building. I went up to the roof and jumped across. There's piping on the top of this roof. I tied the rope to it."

I wondered how she knew about other Greens, but that had to wait. "And no guards below on that side of the building?"

She shook her head. "I had to look in a number of windows. The street below has been clear. We checked. The shooting is all in the new part of town."

We? Did she mean No Nonsense? I decided to table that until the three of us were away from this building.

"Will the rope reach the ground?"

"Almost," she said. "I think."

"Let's go look."

Given a choice, I wanted to get down to the ground and away from this area as fast as I could. That argued for going down the rope, even if neither of them had ever tried rappelling, rather than climbing up to the roof and retracing Sho's steps.

We retreated into the office and retrieved the rope from where it lay across the coffee table and floor among the shards of glass. I dropped it out the vacant window frame and looked down. The end hung close to the ground. About six feet short. Close enough. I ran back to the stairwell and heard no noise from below. Maybe the only guards who had stayed here were the ones I had shot. I wasn't going to make that bet. The others could be hoping we would come running down the stairs and make it easy for them to shoot us. I doubted any of them were eager to *climb* the stairs, not after that barrage of fire. Our opportunity wasn't going to improve.

"All right," I said, "I'm going down first. I'll keep guard at the bottom while you come down one at a time. Anything happens on the ground, go up the rope and across the roof to the other building. Sho, you've got the other rifle, so you're last. Anybody comes to that door, shoot first. Then get out the window. I'll shoot anybody who sticks their head out when you're on the rope."

"I understand," she said. Her voice was back to normal.

With that, I slung the rifle, leaned out the window, grabbed the rope, and pulled myself against the side of the building. Quickly, I passed the rope under my down-building leg and looped it up over my opposite shoulder. I rappelled down until I ran out of rope. Then I stopped myself and went hand over hand until only a short drop was left. Even from only a few feet up, I rolled when I hit the ground. My right knee had been rebuilt after I was wounded on Mindanao in 2062, and it did not do well anymore with big jumps. It had taken nearly two weeks for the swelling to go down after the parachute landing on my return to Earth. This time, I felt nothing beyond a slight twinge when I put weight on it. I was much more bothered by the dizziness from the roll. My head wasn't right, but it would have to do.

The others came down more slowly than I would have liked, but they didn't know the technique. Once Sho's boots hit the ground, she waved us away from the direction of the administration building and took off in the direction of her wave. Perforce, we followed. Once we were well screened from where we had been held, I caught Sho's arm.

"Sho, do you know what the fuck is going on?" Sporadic gunfire continued to sound in the distance. My head ached and my stomach was queasy, both of which I blamed on the concussion. It did not do wonders for my mood.

"I don't know, not really." She shook her head, which sent curls flying on both sides. "They've still got me on livestock duty, so I had to be outside the wall before daylight this morning, and No Nonsense went with me. Maybe that was a good thing."

Caleb was emphatic in his agreement. I shut him up. I needed to hear more from Sho.

"Mario often has cadets—that's the group younger than juniors— watch areas, because people don't pay attention to kids playing around.

I used to take that kind of duty, so I know. They were posted near the old administration building and in this area. One of the cadets saw Caleb brought to that building under guard. The senior cadet sent one of the young ones to find me. Nobody bothers with a crying little girl who's running away. Hah!

"Anyway, there's plenty of rope in the hangars where we keep animals. Scouts have climbing competitions going up the wall, so we also have those spikes. I wasn't going to chance the gate, so No Nonsense and I went over the wall. That rusted old wire on top just crumbles. We could hear shooting by then.

"Two Greens had a guard post not too far from the wall. They were playing cards, not paying attention. We jumped them and knocked one out; the other ran. I took the rifles when I came for you."

"You took the rifles," I said. "What happened to No Nonsense?"

"He's with the others. They told me you were with Caleb. No Nonsense said he's been in fights and I haven't, but I went to get you because I'm better with ropes and climbing. He barely got over the wall."

"Who are the 'others,' and what made you think going alone when you had support was a good idea?"

Sho flushed. "One is less likely to be seen. And it worked. Come with me. You'll see."

She led us deeper into old Earthbase to an open square amid a cluster of empty buildings. She whistled twice. Four armed men and women emerged, in no particular order, from a doorway across the square from us. No, not men and women. These were mid-teens at best. Another low whistle came from my right. No Nonsense stood up so I could see him. He held a rifle and had taken a sheltered position that allowed him to cover the entire square. I walked to a place on the side of the square where No Nonsense could keep watch on the open area and buildings across from it and waited for the four of them to meet me there.

"I'm Aurora, Aurora Chisolm," said the girl who led the other three over. "I'm the senior cadet. I'll be in juniors in two months." She had lank brown hair that draped down the sides of her face to her shoulders. The rest of her was as malnourished as her hair. The death grip she had on the stock of her rifle turned her knuckles white and looked tight enough to squeeze a round out of the muzzle without the trigger being pulled.

I stared at her. Two months shy of juniors meant she wasn't even fifteen. And she was the senior. "Do *you* know what is going on?"

She recoiled from the harshness in my voice—but I had to give her credit: her own voice stayed firm. "No. Except that the world has gone crazy. Leadership told us to watch the area all around the administration building until the meeting was over. That's usual. But one of the cadets told me about Caleb being brought under guard, so I sent Emily to get Sho. Then we heard shooting in the building, and Greens brought you to where Caleb was. We heard more shooting start up; it seemed like it was everywhere. I sent a cadet to Blue HQ. That one didn't come back, so I sent another. They did and said they couldn't get through. Green was attacking us! With guns! At HQ!"

She took a breath to steady herself. "That's when Sho got here. She brought him." Aurora indicated No Nonsense with her rifle. "It's insane! Greens are running around saying Yaeger had to take over because there's been a revolt by Red, and Chief Administrator Landrieu is dead. Greens, Blues, and Reds are shooting at each other here and there. We haven't seen any seniors, not even juniors till Sho. I've only got three of my cadets. I don't know where the others went. We don't know what's going on." She was fighting not to cry. "I knew Sho would get Caleb and she did; he's leadership."

"Mario is in that ISC administration building," Caleb said. "If Green is saying Yaeger is taking over, then she's holding him prisoner there, just like they locked me up. We have to get him out. That's what we're going to do."

"I'm with you," Sho said.

"The four of us will go with you," Aurora said. "We can help. We know how to shoot."

"Wait a minute. Just hold on. Please!" I had the feeling the world had slipped its moorings. I had taught Elvy to use a rifle at twelve, and she had saved my life with it by gunning down a raider when the ranch was attacked. But that had been her home under attack. They were talking about assaulting a defended position. "You don't know how many Greens are in that building. There could be a dozen, and some will be armed with M8cs. You try to break in, all you'll do is get yourselves killed."

"We can't leave Mario in there," Caleb said, as though that were all the explanation needed. "Help us get him out, Leif. I promise, we'll do whatever you need to send your reply to the stars when this is over."

"Don't say that, Caleb," No Nonsense said, "You can't promise what you can't make happen. Yaeger will make the same promise. You know that." Then he turned to me. "Leif, I can understand this isn't your fight. You can stay out. But Sho is going and I'm going with her. That's enough for me."

Sho gave No Nonsense a quick peck on the cheek, which turned him bright pink where his beard didn't cover his face.

Oh my God. Had I ever been like that? I'll deny it under oath.

There are some people who inspire loyalty, and maybe Mario was one of them. I looked at the seven of them, all grim determination mixed with fear, off to do what they said they would do. No Nonsense had been trained to fight as part of a team, but he had no training or experience in leading one. The others had no idea what they were doing. All they had was grit and more loyalty than sense. I couldn't let them go on their own. I couldn't.

The French revolutionary Ledru-Rollin's line, which had been a standing joke in my battalion in Central Asia, flashed through my head: "I must follow them. I am their leader." I've been told he never said it, but if he didn't, he should have. It fit. You don't do crazy, stupid things for abstract ideas like the stars. You do crazy, stupid things for people. These people.

"Goddammit. God-fucking-dammit. If you're all so fucking determined, we'll do this together. But you follow my orders. Every damned one of you and every damned order. We'll get Mario out; we'll find out what happened to Landrieu, and we'll stop whatever Yaeger is doing. Got it?"

Seven yeses followed.

I guess I had chosen my side.

All I had to do was extract a rival faction leader held in an isolated building from under the noses of a coup leader and her guards, and do it with a completely untrained crew, half of whom would barely have been in high school in my day. Sure. Why not?

CHAPTER FIFTEEN

I WOULDN'T CALL US MUCH OF A SQUAD WHEN WE MOVED OUT FOR THE ISC ADMIN-istration building. More like a random group of refugees who had picked up a bunch of rifles. I was on point with one of the M8cs and No Nonsense was at the rear. The rest bunched up in the middle. No Nonsense understood how a team worked from his time in the Army of the Northeast last winter, but neither Sho nor Caleb had any experience in a combat team and the cadets were … kids. I improvised. When we reached a cross street, I brought all of them to a stop by whatever cover would let me take a quick look down the other road. Then I would sprint across and, from the other side, hope to cover them.

The first street went fine. Not the second. I heard the crack of a rifle while I was in the middle of the crossing. I dived, rolled, and prayed. Emphasis on the last. The next shot came from where Sho was positioned. It was followed by a cry from down the cross street. There were no more shots.

Sho and I advanced cautiously, rifles at the ready, down opposite sides of that cross street. I could hear crying, and a couple of times, "Ma, please, Ma" came from a place ahead of us. I didn't see any movement.

Halfway down the block was a dumpster that had probably stood there since the day my world ended. A foot, toes up, projected out on the ground past the dumpster. The gunman had used that dumpster for cover when they fired on us but must have exposed themselves enough for Sho to have a shot. When I reached the dumpster, I saw his body lying on its back behind it. Sho's return shot had taken him high in the chest. Blood soaked his shirt and puddled on the ground next to him. His eyes were open, his chest motionless.

Sho came up next to me. "Oh God," she said. "Oh God, he's one of the juniors."

I looked at the dead gunman's face. Beardless. He was younger than Sho. Maybe fifteen, I thought; not much older than our cadets.

She knelt next to him and stretched her hand out, stopping with her fingers just short of the entry wound through his shirt.

"His name was Nathaniel," she whispered. "He played against us that day in the challenge game. Not a bad kid. Not at all."

"Oh no." That was Aurora's voice. She had come up behind us. "You killed Nathaniel. He just made juniors."

"He fired on us," I said. "Keep that thought in your head."

Sho straightened up and faced me. Her eyes looked wet. By that time, all the others had clustered behind us.

"Does this get any easier?" Sho asked.

"Sadly and unfortunately, yes," I said. "Maybe that's what's wrong with humans." I looked down at the weapon he had used. It was a lever-action rifle, the type the armies in the East had used. "Caleb, take the rifle and his ammo." I looked over the unorganized group around me, no one with eyes anywhere except on the body. If this Nathaniel had had support, we'd all be casualties. "Let's move," I said none too pleasantly. "Standing around like this is a good way to get killed."

·   ·   ·

WE MOVED WITH GREATER CAUTION FROM THAT POINT ON, AT THE COST OF MOVING slower. We did not, however, encounter anyone else on our way. Perhaps Nathaniel had been the only one who had stayed at his post and not run off to where the other shooting was coming from. Possibly, he was only a young boy playing at soldier. Maybe it was pure luck. I don't know the truth.

·   ·   ·

It had reached twilight of the short fall day by the time I approached the administration building with my makeshift squad. Heavy clouds cut the light down further and cast a gloomy gray over everything. It was freezing, a reminder that it was late fall on the Great Plains, and the raw cold warned of snow coming. I shivered in a gust of wind and missed my winter clothing every bit as much as my night vision combat visor.

While I thought about how to organize this crew, I could hear Petey commenting in my mind. *Sarge, what're you doin' goin' in with these irregulars? Take us. We'll get it done ASAP.*

Yeah, Petey, I thought. *You would, and I wish I had you, but you guys died on Mindanao. And even if you hadn't, it's been a couple of centuries. I've got to go with what I've got.*

What I had, in addition, was a throbbing headache and nausea, reminders that I needed rest and sleep. That wasn't possible, unfortunately. As long as I could fight, I told myself, I wasn't going to worry about it. I wasn't going to have a future to worry about if I didn't take care of the present. I had a tactical problem to solve.

The administration building stood by itself at the end of the Avenue of Heroes, with open ground all around it. This wasn't the manicured lawn of a century ago, but forests didn't sprout on the Great Plains. It was mostly high grass and weeds, now brown and limp as winter neared. The only cover close to the building was the Starshot I monument that sat on its own circle of overgrown grass and shrubbery at the front. Despite the cold wind, I held my troop where we were until the light faded. Thank God for the grandiosity of the old ISC. Along with the gathering dark, that monument, with its huge base and its statues, screened us from the front of the building and let us shelter behind it.

"Here's what we're going to do," I said. "Aurora, you and the other cadets, this monument is your station. Take positions that give you cover and let you fire at the front of the building." I had to take the time to position them. "When you start shooting at the front, that will make them think we're going to rush the door, and it will bring all of them to the front. That's when the four of us are going to circle around and break in from the back. Whatever you do, don't leave your positions. Keep firing at the front, but don't burn through your ammo. I need you to keep up the shooting."

"We can do that," Aurora said. "We will do that. Count on us."

The other cadets all nodded, although their faces said that they were realizing what they had bought into.

It wasn't a great plan. I didn't know the internal layout of the building; I didn't know where Mario or Sydney would be. If Sydney's Greens were able to keep watch all around the building, even after the shooting started, we would be in trouble. Its merits were that it was better than trying to rush the front door, and raw troops who were scared—the cadets—would do best in covered positions, where they did not need to move.

Of course, a problem surfaced immediately. No Nonsense, Caleb, and Sho all wanted to break in with me and find Mario.

"No, no, and no," I said. "Caleb, we need someone to guard the spot we go in so we don't get trapped in there. Same reason, since we will probably have to go upstairs, someone guards the staircase we use. No Nonsense, that's you. You have to keep our line of retreat open. Sho and I will get to the top floor and work our way down."

"It should be me going with you on that, not Sho," said Caleb.

"I've got the M8c," Sho said.

"We can swap."

"No." By moonlight, I could see Sho's face set and tense, her lips squeezed into a thin line.

Caleb made the mistake of starting with "You're still my little sister—"

Sho shoved him away hard enough that the sentence ended with an "oof."

We were in proximity to the enemy. I didn't need them fighting with each other or indulging in fratricide. Right then, I did wish I had Petey and my old squad. I was a little afraid that Sho was trying to prove something—maybe to herself. However, the fact was that she had shot straight before, when it mattered. Caleb might be fine, but he hadn't proved it.

"Sho, you're the hunter with me." I made a point of glaring at each of them. "Any more argument, and I'm doing this solo. Understood?"

I wish I could say they looked chastened.

.   .   .

It started out promisingly. Aurora and her cadets opened fire, spraying bullets across the front of the administration building, while my team went around the other side of the monument and headed for the side of the building. It took a couple of minutes, but then a fusillade of oaths and shots erupted from inside. While that was happening, we made it to the side of the building without incident. A century's worth of grass and brush gave us some cover there. I kept us moving past the far corner of the building and around to its back. A continuous crackle of automatic rifle fire erupted from the front, punctuated by a scream.

I expected a building like this one would have an emergency exit, and in fact there was a door in the rear wall; the original had been replaced with a wooden frame and hinged wood door like the front. More than that, the door was ajar. No light showed from inside.

"We'd have run into anybody they sent from here toward our position," No Nonsense said.

"Yeah," I said. "Or it doesn't close and there's a guard on the other side. It could have been this way for weeks."

Scattered shots came from the front. We had no time to speculate. My chip gave me limited, very limited, night vision. I flattened myself against the wall next to the door, then flung it completely open and burst through the entrance. I swept my M8c across the vestibule. No one was there.

"Caleb, guard the door. Watch for anyone coming, outside or inside. Anybody with a weapon is a hostile." My voice stayed at a whisper. "We want to avoid detection, but if someone comes here and would block our way out, shoot to kill."

Dim light coming through another window was enough to see the stairs going up a little farther down the inside corridor. I posted No Nonsense at the second-floor landing, in a place where the moonlight didn't reach. Sho and I went up.

My plan was to start with both the boardroom and Landrieu's office. The top floor made sense as a place to put a prisoner, and those rooms were at the ends of the hallway. Sydney might be there as well, since those rooms would seem secure and away from the shooting. In fact, when we came out from the staircase, flickering light greeted us. Candles or lanterns. A quick peek showed an empty corridor in both directions. I reached out and touched Sho's arm to get her attention. With hand signals, I directed her toward Landrieu's office.

I followed the corridor the other way, to its end at the grand doors to the boardroom. A flicker of yellow in the space between door and floor said there was light inside. Time to kick it in and see what happened.

Before I could bring my knee up, more shots and yells came from the side of the building facing the monument. They had not died away before two shots rang out from the staircase. Noise, possibly furniture being moved, emanated from inside the boardroom. I shrank back into the minimal space offered by a doorframe with a closed door in it. Someone pulled open the boardroom doors.

The silhouetted figure in the opening held a weapon. I opened fire.

The body my bullets hit fell into the doorway in front of me. I had a vague glimpse of movement through the open door.

"Mario! Get down!" I yelled. Then I fired. A cry followed. I heard doors open behind me, then more shots. Sho was firing, too, at the other end of the hall. Screams and thuds. Then quiet.

In a rush and staying low, I reached the side of the boardroom doors and did not draw fire. I bolted through the opening and swept my rifle across the room, ready to shoot. A form on the floor reached for a rifle that had been dropped. I fired into the body. Somebody in a dark corner was whimpering for me not to shoot. There was no other movement. More shooting came from the direction of the staircase.

"Sho, go help No Nonsense!" I shouted down the corridor. "I've got it up here." I hoped I did. Without voice or message channels, communication was limited.

I checked the boardroom quickly. Mario was not there. Three bodies lay on the floor. Two of them were base security, still holding M8cs with full magazines. I did not recognize the third. I snapped out the magazines and took them with me.

I ran back down the hall to where the door to Landrieu's office stood open. Sho had killed two in there. One of them was Sydney, who had been sitting behind Landrieu's desk.

The gunfire from the direction of the staircase was ratcheting up into a mini battle of its own. Sho and No Nonsense were firing downward. At a break in the shooting, I yelled out, "Greens, you are surrounded! Sydney Yaeger is dead. Drop your weapons and put your hands up or we'll kill all of you!"

The sounds after that were rifles hitting the floor.

· · ·

THE FIGHTING AT THE ISC ADMINISTRATION BUILDING COULD BE CONSIDERED TO HAVE turned out well for us. The Greens in the building never realized how few were shooting at them from the monument. Our sudden appearance inside the building unnerved them and made them fear our numbers were many times greater than they were. That's what happens when people are surprised in the dark. They were almost eager to surrender when I demanded it. Yes, there was luck involved, but there is luck involved in simply surviving any battle.

Six Greens on the ground floor surrendered. We put them under guard in a second-floor office while we swept through the building looking for survivors, other casualties, and Mario.

All our shooting at the front of the building hadn't caused a single Green casualty, but inside was another matter. Sho and I had killed four Greens, including Sydney, on the top floor. Sho and No Nonsense killed another two Greens on the staircase. The third body in the boardroom was one of the Red directors, who died when I fired through the doorway. Landrieu's body was in a separate office on the top floor, but his was cold and stiff. However Christian Landrieu had died, it was long before we attacked. Our only loss was Aurora, who now would never make juniors. One of the boys who had been at the monument with her was wounded in the leg. I was reasonably sure he would heal okay.

There was only one reason the battle did not qualify as a success: we couldn't find Mario.

CHAPTER SIXTEEN

"GODDAMMIT, WHERE'S MARIO?" I SAID WHEN WE HAD BEEN THROUGH the building twice and it was obvious that he was not there, neither alive nor dead. With all the lives risked and lost to extract him, I was not pleased with this state of affairs.

We questioned everyone still alive in the building and all we could get was that the bullets fired after the shout of "Death to the starman!" had hit Landrieu, and that in the chaos after I tackled the shooter, he himself had been shot. Two of the base security Greens claimed Mario had been shot at on Yaeger's order, but none admitted to firing at him or knew if he had been hit.

"Somehow he got out of here. Out through that back door. He must have gone to scout headquarters," Caleb said. "If Yaeger was trying to take over and he got away, that's where he would go to lead the Blues."

"Mario was here," I said, "which is a long way from your HQ. Assume he's not dead in the dark out there. The cadets said there was fighting around your headquarters, that it was under attack. Let's give him credit for knowing where *not* to go. Trying to sneak into your HQ like that is a recipe for getting captured or killed."

"Then where would he be?" Sho asked.

Good question. I tried to ignore my headache and my stomach and *think*. I hardly knew Mario, but he seemed like a man of action who held the loyalty of people. Where would he go? He wouldn't hide in a corner. Only one place presented itself to me.

"He's with the old starfolk," I said. "That's where we have to go."

"How do you know that?" Caleb demanded.

"It's the only thing that makes sense." I was more than a little irritable. "That building is away from where all of you live, away from the fighting, and not far from the administration building. I'll bet he's had a kid or two posted there, the way he had Aurora's cadets out here. And if he was hit, he knows they have a doc from before."

Caleb didn't look ready to agree, but I cut him off before he could speak.

"Listen to me. Right now, I'm in command and you'll follow my orders. Either that or I'll do what I need to do, and you can go find an empty room and diddle yourself. Got it?"

Caleb subsided with a meek yes.

•   •   •

I left No Nonsense and the cadets to keep control at the administration building and took Caleb and Sho with me. I didn't see a guard in front of the Old Starfolk's Home when we arrived. I supposed that made sense. If a contest for control of Earthbase was underway, putting guards around a bunch of elderly people who stayed aloof from the community would be a waste of resources. Unless someone else figured that Mario would run there.

Caleb put a hand on my arm as I was gauging the open ground to the front door. "Here, I'm going first," he said.

"How do you figure that?"

"If Mario is here, he will have someone watching the front. They see you with a rifle, they might shoot. I'm going unarmed and any watcher will know me."

"You're not going without me," Sho said. "Anybody with Mario will be a scout. Even the cadets all know me."

Caleb tossed his hands in the air. "Come on, then."

I didn't say anything. Smart move or not, arguing with Sho would only waste time.

Brother and sister ran across the open ground before the door, then disappeared through it. I heard no shots. I set a timer on my field. As the timer reached a minute and a half with no sign of anything, I wondered how long I was going to wait before I assumed trouble and rushed the door. At two minutes and four seconds—which is an eternity when you're expecting trouble—Sho stuck her head out the door and waved for me to come. It was a frantic wave.

As soon as I reached the doorway and passed a cadet-age boy who was watching the outside, Sho grabbed my arm and yanked. "Come with me!"

Our destination was the caf, and the lantern-lit scene inside was chaos. Mario was lying on top of one of the tables, holding his left shoulder. A young man was slumped against the wall behind Mario, his right arm in a sling. Both the sling and the blue band on his arm were soaked with blood. Max, the starfolk's doc—who should have been taking care of those two—was slumped in a chair near Mario's table and looked worse than either patient. Sweat stood out on his face. His breaths were quick and shallow. A woman was squatting in front of him, taking his pulse, her back to me.

"Do you need help?" That seemed like the best way of announcing my presence.

The woman stood and turned around. Hannah Jin. Her loose shirt and pants were liberally stained with blood.

She wasted no time on pleasantries. "This man is having a heart attack," she said. "Acute angina. Came on while we were helping the others." She snapped her fingers at Shane, who stood with the other *Invincible* crew in a corner, looking lost. "Drag a mattress down here so he can lie down and at least be more comfortable."

There are people whose voice and posture project calm and organization even in the midst of swirling disaster. That was Hannah Jin. I liked her immensely.

"She's right," Max said. "My chip is showing ST elevation. I'm having an MI. A bad one. I'm only sixty-six, bio age, but it's my family genetics. Shouldn't be a problem, of course. Going on meds at bio age forty would reduce the risk to four percent; easily dealt with if it happens. I figured there'd be even better options when we came back." He tried to laugh but couldn't. "Of course, now there're no meds for this at all, no usable equipment even for a stent. It's not fair."

Life isn't fair.

Hannah put a hand on his shoulder. "When I can reach the clinic, I'll get you aspirin. We'll take care of you. Let you rest. We'll have to see over the next couple of days."

"Aspirin by itself is not enough. It's nothing," Max said.

"Rest is important and aspirin is the best we can do. I know we don't have the other old drugs." She straightened and spoke to me. "Sometimes I think it was better in the real old days, when doctors would make poultices or mixtures of berries and leaves and they could tell their patients and themselves they were doing something that worked. Now we know better, but we don't have the meds that used to be effective either. You're not a doc, are you?"

"No," I said. "I was what we used to call a paramedic. I've also taken care of all sorts of injuries on battlefields." There wasn't much else we could do for Max. Part of his heart muscle was going to die. Either he would have enough functional heart afterward to survive, or he would die. It was that simple. "Do we have more wounded here?" I pointed at the bloodstains on her.

"No. I was taking care of wounded at scout headquarters. A runner got through and asked me to come here and take care of Mario. My escort"—she inclined her head to the injured man at the wall—"was shot when we left, but he stayed with me. Mario's shoulder is dislocated, but I had to attend to the others first."

"Leif, I need to talk to you." Mario broke into the conversation.

I walked over to the table where Mario lay. They had taken his shirt off, so it took only a glance to know Hannah's diagnosis was correct.

"How did it happen?" I asked.

"Talking about it and fixing it can wait. Listen, the shooter was a Red. His name was Gavin Rice; he killed Landrieu. Gavin is a simple person, in a way. Follows instructions well, really doesn't think for himself. He's done odd jobs for base security. He was yelling about shooting you, but all three of those shots hit Landrieu. That's who he was aiming at."

Mario's face wore something between a grin and a grimace. "Everybody was looking for cover or hitting the floor. Bischoff bashed her face on the table trying to get down, but I stayed up and saw what happened. One of the Greens pulled a pistol. Ramón Ugarte. He had time to shoot Gavin, but he waited to be sure Landrieu was killed. I'm sure the plan was that he shoots Gavin after Gavin kills Landrieu.

"You messed it up when you took Gavin down. You moved so damned fast, Gavin wasn't shot then. He went down under you. When they clubbed you and then had to pull you off him, Gavin was screaming that he'd only done what they told him to do and he wasn't going to hurt you. Knowing Gavin, I'm sure that's the truth.

"Ugarte shot him, all right, but too late. We all heard Gavin. It was lunacy in there. You were on the ground. Sydney was yelling that Red killed Landrieu because of the signal and she had to take charge, but after we heard Gavin, that didn't work, so she called for more base security."

"I've heard some of what happened, but not all of what you said. I'm not surprised stories are confused, but some of this doesn't make sense. Why would Yaeger do this? It can't be because of a decision about replying to the message."

"Actually, I think it was you," Mario said.

"What?" I stared at him. That did not make any sense.

"Yes. I think you spooked her, Leif. She thought you would get the board to back me on the signal. Either a Blue would take the chief administrator position to manage the response to the stars, or Landrieu might keep his spot, but his directives would be what Blue wanted. You made her think she would lose her chance at power, so she delayed the meeting a few days to give herself time to put a plan together.

"When you had that meeting with Landrieu—she knew about it; we all knew about it—I think she panicked and decided on a violent overthrow. But she was improvising, without a lot of time. She'd blame Red for the assassination—she did—and would use that to arrest the Red directors and block their caravans, which she hates. She would take charge in the crisis. Temporarily, of course. She'd have me under her thumb, or maybe they'd shoot me too. There would be no chief administrator, and she would be the only senior director. She had base security go to scout headquarters to have them give up their weapons and accept Green as being in charge during the emergency. I heard that from a runner who came here."

"Then why didn't they shoot me?" I asked.

Mario laughed, then grabbed his shoulder. "You're valuable. A newly returned starman. Plenty of people will respect what you say, especially Reds. She'd promise you what you wanted in return for your support to make her control permanent. When it all went crazy, she wanted you out of the way but alive, I'm sure. She got you out of there. Probably figured that the signal was important enough to you that you would still make a deal with her later.

"I made a run for it while her people were busy with you and trying to keep the others under control. Someone did take a shot at me as I got to the bottom of the stairs. I ducked, missed a step in the bad light in the stairwell. That's how this shoulder happened. I got out the back. Fortunately, I'm a suspicious man. I thought that delay meant she was up to something, though I didn't know what.

"That's why I had the cadets around the area. They can carry messages and they can shoot. One of them found me a hiding place for a while, then helped me get here. When the shooting happened in the administration building, apparently one of them went to scout HQ to let them know. And when Green made their demand, Blue fought back. Between you and that messenger, Sydney's plan fell apart almost as fast as it started."

It occurred to me that Mario was not only suspicious but also ruthless. Using the cadets that way had worked, yes, but Aurora had paid the price for it.

"First casualty in any battle is the plan," I said. "That's a very old line. It doesn't sound like there was any contingency plan."

"Too true," Mario said. "I'm sure very few in Green knew what was happening. Not Sydney's style, anyway. She liked control and keeping secrets. The fact that I was able to escape shows that even among those base security guards, only a few knew about her plan."

I stopped him and told him what we had done and learned.

"So you killed Yaeger," he said.

"I did that," Sho said.

Mario looked past me at her. "Yes, I always thought you could be cold when it was needed." His nod was one of approval. "That's important for a scout and a leader."

"What happens now? Do you know who controls what in Earthbase?" I asked.

"I'm not sure," Mario said. "Sydney did not plan a war, I'm sure of that. There are no armies here! Not nearly enough people and not that kind of organization. This was supposed to be a quick coup. She takes control and sorts it out after. Now? Don't know who controls the power out of the solar panels; also don't know if anybody has thought about the livestock outside the walls. Can't see how this can last to the point where that becomes important. At least I haven't heard any shooting for a while."

"It's night now. Without electronics and without night vision, armies rarely fight at night. In the morning, though, once the sun is up, it may come down to how much ammunition people have."

"We need to stop this," Mario said. "I need to be more functional. Can you fix this?" He pointed first to his shoulder, then to Hannah, who'd moved to the table while Mario was summarizing the situation.

"Yes," Hannah said. "Leif, you're much bigger. Can you put counter-traction across his chest while I put traction on the arm and rotate it?"

"No problem," I said.

She was expert at handling the arm. The shoulder popped right back into place. We sat him up and improvised a sling. I looked back over at Max. Shane and Kwame had brought a mattress down, so Max at least had that to lie on. He was staring off to his right and didn't look good. I knew he was looking at the electrocardiogram and vitals his chip was projecting on his field. I'm sure they looked bad, and he knew what all of it meant. It was watching yourself die step-by-step. Sometimes it's better to know less.

Mario pushed off from the table and stood up. "It's time to stop this insanity. Caleb, as soon as it's light, go down to base security under a white flag. Tell them about Yaeger, all of it."

"What about me?" Sho asked.

"You stay here until this settles down. Word will get out that you shot Yaeger. I don't need anybody trying to settle scores. Leif, can I ask your support? We need to go to the administration building and talk to the remaining directors. I will owe you, and you can feel free to remind me of it."

The stars had waited fifteen years for us to answer; they could wait a little longer. My head ached. "I'm with you. Let's make peace."

CHAPTER SEVENTEEN

BY DAYLIGHT, EVERYBODY IN EARTHBASE HAD WORD OF WHAT HAD HAPPENED. Caleb had no difficulty convincing base security to accept a truce. With Sydney dead, the Greens showed no interest in continuing the fight. Similarly, the surviving directors at the administration building were happy to agree with me and Mario that the fighting had to end.

We spent the day after the fighting stopped burying the dead, while Hannah and the two other town docs tried to keep more from dying. The starfolk buried Max outside the Starfolk's Home in a small cemetery that held other starfolk who had come back to Earth and lived out their lives at Earthbase. He had not made it through the night.

Having pacified the town with relative ease, the Colors were all left with a bigger problem. They had to put their society back together. Too many people in a small town had killed or wounded each other, and everybody knew everybody who had been involved. It's easy to break something into pieces. Reassembling it so you can't see the cracks is a different order of magnitude. Just ask Humpty-Dumpty.

· · ·

Earthbase's board of directors was missing its chief. The remaining board members could all agree that a chief was needed, but even after the Reds and Greens replaced their directors who had been killed, the board could not come to agreement on a chief. Trust was gone.

I could see the lack of trust in the market area. The boisterous back-and-forth barter over clothing, food, tools, and weapons had vanished. I had hoped people might quit wearing colors, might make a show of unity after the shock of neighbors shooting at each other. The opposite happened. Everyone wore colors and they even pinned them on little children. People were subdued. The first look they gave each other was for the Color pinned to the clothing, as if that were a statement about the character of whoever was wearing it.

I had my own issue.

"We need to talk." I had parleyed a concern about Mario's shoulder into an entrance to the scout headquarters. He was in a ground-floor room whose walls were mostly chalkboard filled in with the names of scouts and assignments. I still had a headache, but I didn't think I could give in to it. At least the nausea was gone. "It's time to deal with sending our reply. It can't be part of political games anymore. I want Mikhail to have what he needs to get it done. To be blunt, you owe me."

"It's so nice you were concerned about my shoulder." Mario pushed up his chin, as though he were trying to make it meet his nose. I hadn't actually checked his shoulder once I reached him. "I and Blue have survived. That does not mean I am a dictator or accepted as any kind of ruler. You may have noticed that we have some problems, and I would say those are the priority. Feelings are bad now. There were two brothers, but different Colors, and one of them actually killed the other. What would you say about that? Seeing as you come from the people who actually did destroy civilization."

"Dammit." I wound up gritting my teeth. That was a low blow, but I had to concede that he had pressing problems to deal with. "This is what happens in civil war. It won't get better overnight. I'm here to deal with the stars and I can't stay here forever."

"Fine," he said. "You help me with my situation, I will get people to support what you want."

I wasn't comfortable with that, but I didn't see a choice. "I'm not a politician," I said. Truer words were never spoken. "What I can tell you is that pulling apart, emphasizing the different groups, is *not* the answer. You've got to get people together."

One side of Mario's face twisted up in a wry grin. "It probably shouldn't be a crossball round-robin. We'd be carrying bodies off the field."

"Then get together with the other directors and talk it out. Put some chairs in the middle of the market area, where everybody can see you, and talk."

"And what if some hothead takes a shot at us?"

"What? You want a risk-free life?"

At that, Mario laughed.

·　　·　　·

THEY ACTUALLY DID PUT SIX CHAIRS IN A CIRCLE, WITHOUT A TABLE, IN THE MIDDLE OF the market the next afternoon. People clustered around until they had a sizable audience, drawn by curiosity at seeing Blue, Green, and Red directors talking about what to do. It wasn't perfect. They didn't come up with a new chief. They did, however, work out an approach to managing trade with the East, the water flow from the wells, and the declining electricity production from the solar panels. That got them applause from the crowd. I think they liked the positive feedback. They decided not to schedule any crossball games for two weeks, which brought laughter, but voted in favor of holding an after-party, as though there had been a game. That drew the most applause.

They did not mention the signal from the stars.

As the meeting broke up, Mario slipped away and disappeared into the crowd. I couldn't find him afterward, either. Had I been double-crossed? I figured he would have to show himself at the party, which was scheduled for the following afternoon. Large signs were posted on each road into the market: WELCOME. NO WEAPONS. NO COLORS. It seemed like almost all of Earthbase came.

I drifted through the crowd, keeping an eye out for both trouble and Mario. People were following the rules. The only colors were people's natural ones, from pale white to near black. God knows, that alone had caused enough trouble in the past, but right now, those weren't the colors I worried about. I saw no weapons either. Also good. If an argument led to a busted nose or missing teeth, those were consequences Hannah Jin and her partners could deal with. The banjo players made a small stand out of plywood on top of concrete blocks and between them and the gyrating dancers, we had enough heat to banish the chill of the day. No Mario, however.

I bought a skewer of chicken chunks roasted on a brazier and stood to the side of the dancing mass. Also on the periphery, I saw Sho. Unlike the previous party, she wasn't cutting a path through the crowd surrounded by a cluster of boys. She was by herself, arms loose at her sides and her curls equally limp against her face. The focus of her eyes seemed to be far beyond the crowd. I had an idea of what was going on behind those eyes. This was something I could relate to. I walked toward her, but a woman of perhaps forty years wearing a crude homespun blouse beat me there. She planted herself in front of Sho and jabbed an index finger like a rapier at Sho's chest.

"You killed my boy," I heard the woman say as I walked up. "I want to hear you say it. Want to hear you admit it. He was barely in juniors and you shot him down. And for what?"

Sho was looking past the woman. She said nothing. The woman's finger jabbed again, this time into Sho's chest.

"Say it, goddamn you. Say you're a killer. None of us are going to forget. Not as long as you live. Bricks and stones will hide the bones first, little girl."

I moved forward to stop this, but No Nonsense was there even faster. He shoved the woman's arm to the side and interposed himself between the two.

"Your son's name was Nathaniel," No Nonsense said. "People have been talking all over town that you were going to make a scene at this party. I was there when it happened. He took a shot at us. I don't care what his age was. He fired at us; he got what he earned."

Nathaniel's mother stepped back. She had to look up at No Nonsense. No further words came.

"If you have something to say, you say it to me." No Nonsense's tone was harsh.

The woman only shook her head and walked away.

"She lost her son, No Nonsense," Sho said, "and I did kill him. I don't know what I feel right now."

"What you feel is that you're alive, which is better than you being dead." No Nonsense had his hands on her shoulders and turned her so she was looking at him. "I was with Mendenhall's army in Pennsie. I saw enough killing and did enough killing to last me the rest of my life. And then, like the other day, a time comes when killing is necessary again. I know what it feels like." No Nonsense saw me standing there. "Leif tried to tell me about it before I left home. I didn't listen. How many men and women have you killed, Leif?"

"I have no idea." That was the only truthful answer.

"You adjust to it. I did. Right, Leif?"

"It's true," I said.

Sho tried to smile. "I'll be all right."

"Of course you'll be all right." No Nonsense put a very light kiss against her curls. "Let me get you something to eat." He moved one of his arms completely around her shoulders and walked her in the direction of the food stalls.

I watched them go. No Nonsense was all of seventeen. How could he do that so naturally? I had planned to say something, well, reasonable, but I couldn't have done that.

"I never was a soldier, never in combat, never killed anyone," said a voice right behind me, "so I don't know how it must feel." It was Hannah. "I know you get past it, get used to it, because so many did. That's what we learn about the past. I worry about her, though. I don't like the way she looks."

"Usually, you don't have the mother of an enemy soldier in your face right afterward," I said. "You're with your buddies. That gives you support." I saw Mikhail nearby as well, and I could see that he had heard the conversation. When he walked over, I said, "That's also why we find names to call our enemies that make them seem less than human. That makes the killing easier. We used to call Russians some interesting names."

"Our soldiers had names for Americans too," Mikhail said. "Our media used them all the time. I don't think we need to repeat them here."

"No." I let out a sigh. "Sometimes I think the world would be better if we couldn't make this easy, couldn't get used to it."

"I'm sure you're right," Hannah said. "It would be hard for it to be any worse."

When she looked away to the banjo players, Mikhail spoke again. "I was looking for you," he said to me. "Mario spoke to me. He's arranging a public board meeting. The only topic is the signal from the stars. He's going to use the old ISC auditorium. I can get the power on in there. He wants to have all the old starfolk there."

This wasn't quite what I thought I had bargained for with Mario. Was this his way of making sure he had support? Or was it to give him an out? "Are you ready with what we talked about before?"

"I am. I have the details worked out and I want to be the one to present it. Understand, though, I'm not going to let Shane make it all about him, and I'm not having him hear about it beforehand. This will be my plan, my way to settle this. Back me on this."

CHAPTER EIGHTEEN

THE OLD AUDITORIUM BUILDING WAS ONE OF THE PLACES IN EARTHBASE THAT HAD been designed to use the solar panel backup power in case the main power grid ever went out. That made it simple for Mikhail to power it up, although, given the anemic state of Earthbase's energy generation, it meant shutting down other functions for the duration of the meeting. I guess Mario thought it lent a certain gravitas to the occasion.

Turning on the power did not mean everything went smoothly. The exterior door was one of those powered sliding doors. The panel lit up and the door responded, but it ground to a halt after making an opening of only three inches. It had not been designed to work after a century with no lubrication. Eventually, four people with crowbars were able to pull it back far enough in its track for people to walk in.

Most of the lights in the auditorium worked. That lit the place more brilliantly than any other room in Earthbase that did not have the sun shining into it. I stood at the back wall while people gathered and looked at the semicircular rows of seats, the stage, and the massive screen behind the stage. I had been in this auditorium once, 183 years ago, for the press conference before ISC shot me into space for the first starshot. The auditorium was rather worse for its age than I was. Puffs of dust arose from the seat cushions when people sat down. The big screen that, during my press conference, had shown the ISC symbol of the hand clutching a star, was dark and blank.

Mikhail could supply juice to the building, but the computer connected to that screen was as dead as every other computer on the planet. Six chairs facing the audience were placed on the stage, without any table or desks. The directors filed in, two for each Color, and took them. I noticed they had eschewed wearing their colors. Probably, they assumed that what worked in the market would work in the auditorium. I wondered if we would have been better back in the market, rather than staging the discussion about the star signal amid the trappings of old ISC. The auditorium was dusty and dank, suggesting decay, not power.

The *Invincible* crew took seats together in the front row. That is, they were together except for Mikhail, who sat in the last seat at the opposite end of the row behind them. Rosann was next to him and I could see her anxiety from where I stood at the back. Mikhail's face was grim and he was watching Shane. Old Ruth tottered in with a junior scout helping to support her. She sat in the front row, but in front of Mikhail, not near the *Invincible* crew.

A steady stream of people came in through the door, and I saw Blues, Reds, and Greens. The colors that had vanished for the party in the market were back. As a concession to superficial bonhomie, people were not sitting in any order. Other than wearing colors, it was a random crowd. They filled all the seats and kept coming until the auditorium was packed with people in the aisles and at the back with me. Sho sat in one of the middle rows, with Caleb on one side and No Nonsense on the other. I remembered how petrified No Nonsense had been of wires and electricity. His face was so pale under these lights as to appear almost bloodless, but his eyes were on Sho and nowhere else. I smiled to myself. Maybe they were good for each other.

I didn't try to take a seat, although I was in the auditorium well before it filled up. Instead, I stayed where I was and leaned against the back wall. I could support Mikhail's plan from where I was as easily as from anywhere else. It was also a good vantage point to watch how this show was going to unfold. I wasn't sure I trusted Mario.

Mario stood up to start the meeting. Nobody paid attention to him, and the conversations buzzing through the populace continued unabated. After a short period of this, he sat down. Then he stood up again when it was obvious the other directors were looking at him. His hands fluttered around in front of him, as though he didn't know what to do with them. The others kept silent, as if in trances.

Mario cleared his throat and started to talk. He did not have a microphone, and it was impossible to hear what he was saying above the other conversations. Finally, he raised one hand and roared, "All right, goddammit. Shut up!"

That brought quiet. It also brought Mario back to himself. "All right," he said again, this time in his usual gravelly voice. "Thank you for coming. We don't have a chief administrator now and it may be a while before one is chosen. We also have an issue that has nothing to do with Colors, an issue we've been putting off for a long time. That's the signal we all know we received. It's time to make a decision on what to do about it. We have all the old starfolk here." He swept his hand across the *Invincible* crew and Ruth, then pointed at Mikhail separately.

"We also have Leif Grettison, who came back to Earth a little over a year ago." He found me at the back and pointed me out. I saw the crowd twist in their seats as though they needed to confirm I was there. "Those are the only starfolk there are. They all come from before, when we were going to the stars, so it makes sense to have their advice. We also decided to do this openly, the way we had the discussion in the market. I know that's not the way we've done things in the past, but it's been a bad several days and maybe it's better if everyone who wants to can hear what's said and what's decided."

The silence from the crowd, along with Mario's words, acted as a tonic for the other directors. A woman in the chair next to Mario was on her feet even as Mario was finishing his last sentence. This had to be Paula Bischoff, the senior Red director who had survived the short firefight in the boardroom. I had heard her name several times, but she was the only one of the original senior directors who had not come to speak with me. She had shoulder-length brown hair, turning gray, and a huge black eye on her right side. The expression on her face was as pleasant as that eye.

"I've said this before. I'll say it again. There is nothing to do about this business except to forget it. Yaeger said that maybe there was a way to do this carefully, but we know—oh, we certainly know now—that anything *she* said was nothing more than part of her schemes for taking power. We all need to realize that even if we can find a way to reply, doing so will only make us a target. Let's say this never happened and move on with our lives. We have enough trouble as it is without stirring up aliens." She sat down to murmurs of agreement through the auditorium.

Alex Barttleby, who was now the senior Green director, stood up next. He was a tall, thin reed of a man whose stem had bent forward near the top. His voice was high-pitched, but it projected well. "I'm not Sydney," he said, "and probably that's just as well." That brought applause, and he waited to allow it to wash over the crowd. It had been a calculated statement. "I'm not going to try and justify what she did. I think most of that was about Sydney and not about anything to do with Green."

Another pause came with more applause. "But I will tell you that when it comes to this signal, she was right. We can't afford to spend resources on it. We need those resources for our security here. If someone knows a way to answer this without spending much, maybe we can do it and not worry about monsters under our beds." He turned to smile at Bischoff. "But consider."

He pointed to the ceiling. "Just to have power on in this building, we had to shut down other machinery we need. Ask Mikhail." He shifted his arm to point at Mikhail. "If some group of creatures is going to show up in a hundred years or whenever because we never answered their message that we can't even understand, well"—he threw both hands up in the air—"then whoever is here when they show up will have to figure out what to do. If we don't take care of ourselves now, there won't be anyone here in a hundred years."

Was this the time for me to break in? No. Let those two take their opening positions. Wait for Mikhail to speak. Think of it as a negotiation. I'm not great at negotiation.

Someone in the crowd I didn't recognize stood up and yelled, "What if they're already coming? What if that signal was just to give us a little warning and they'll be here in a year and they want us to have something ready for them? What do we do if that's true?"

"Then there's really nothing to do," Barttleby snapped. "If they're going to show up in two years, or next year, or next month, there is *nothing* we can do. Beg for help when they get here, maybe."

"Don't be fools!" Mario shouted from his seat. "Whoever sent that message spent fifteen years sending it over and over. You don't give someone a little warning for fifteen years."

"All the more reason not to bother with it," Paula said. "Don't take the bait."

The buzz around the auditorium started again, and I think it was mostly in agreement with Barttleby and Bischoff. People worried about food through the winter, not what might show up in the sky a year or a century from now. I couldn't blame them. Charity and the kids had crept into my mind while I was listening, and I remembered how careful Charity had been in planning the food. I could see how the mood was going, but told myself again to wait for Mario to speak, and for Mikhail.

"No!" The exclamation lacked force, but the crowd fell silent again nonetheless. Ruth had gotten to her feet with the help of the young scout next to her. She turned around so that she was facing the bulk of the audience, one hand clenched in a fist. She shook that fist at them. "Listen to me. I've gone to the stars. I'm old now and I'll never go again, but I've been there. Most of you have never been as far as the Mississippi."

She was shaking on her feet as she looked around the room. The only strength she had was in her voice. "I have gone. It was all about finding someone else out there. All our lives, all our treasure. That's what it was for. And now we can make contact. Keep faith with those of us from before. We must make contact. Whatever it takes." She held on to the chair in order to sit back down.

Her words sent a chill straight into my bones. Yes, I knew the truth about the ISC and the interstellar program, as so few did even back then. It had not been about making contact with another intelligent species. It was nothing more than a cynical attempt to keep the peace by channeling resources into space instead of into armies, and it had—obviously—failed. But Ruth didn't know that, and neither had nearly all the other starshot participants, men and women who gave their lives and their sanity pursuing a role for humans in the universe, and looking for someone else doing the same.

Even knowing all of that, I had dreamed about being the first to meet other intelligent beings back when I thought of flying the starways forever with Yong. The myth of first contact was a powerful one. After Ruth sat, I heard it whispered in conversations around me. Here at Earthbase, it had survived the apocalypse.

Mikhail chose that moment to jump to his feet. I tensed.

"Barttleby said, 'Ask Mikhail,' and you should. First, let me thank Starwoman Ruth." Mikhail made that into a title. "We do have a way to respond, one that does not involve diverting precious resources from caring for ourselves. Believe me, I know about our resources. When it comes to power, I'm the one who keeps working to fix everything when it fails. So, listen to me for a little bit."

An expectant hush fell over the auditorium. Everyone looked at Mikhail, who drew himself up as much as his height would permit. Mario gestured for him to continue. Had Mikhail let Mario in on the plan he had developed?

"The truth is that we have a fully powered, maintained spaceplane that has been kept in a special hangar." Mario's visible startle on the stage told me he hadn't expected this. Mikhail had not confided in him.

"I know about that spaceplane, Mario. Who do you think keeps the power on in your precious hangar?" Mikhail smiled. He was obviously enjoying being the focal point of the assemblage.

"Now, it's a fact that using it to route a signal through any of the old orbiting starships won't do any good. I've spent enough time checking, and they were powered down. Also, I doubt anything on GSY Station can be made to work. But there is a broadcast antenna on our tech center building. I can send the signal from the spaceplane out that way.

"Yes, that transmitter is not designed to power a signal over interstellar distances, but any radio signal will continue to propagate outward. That's the way radio waves work. As long as the star that signaled us is in the sky when I send it, our signal will go there. Yes, the inverse square law will weaken our signal as it goes. I know this. However, *nothing* else is going into space from Earth now.

"If these aliens are advanced enough to be contacting others, they must have receivers sensitive enough to pluck a very weak signal from space. And they did send us a signal, so they will be watching for a reply. I can do this. This is *my* way to put humanity back among the stars."

Mario smiled the smile of a man who has found the moment for his reveal. "There's a starship that goes with that spaceplane." He spoke to Mikhail, but he made sure everyone heard it. "Not one of the old ones that have little or no power left. This one is functional, fully powered. It's been in orbit, waiting."

It was Mikhail's turn to startle. He almost tripped as he turned from his audience back to Mario. "A starship with full power available?" His voice almost squeaked. "Yes, I can connect the spaceplane to the starship and use that to boost the signal. It will still be weak over interstellar distances—not nearly as powerful as the one they sent here—but that will improve the likelihood of detection. Yes, I can do this. I can send the reply. I *will* send humanity's reply."

"No, you can't." Shane was up, and the two glared at each other as though no one else were in the auditorium. "What frequency are you going to use? Do you think the aliens are watching the spectrum reserved for the ISC? Typical hidebound, bureaucratic Russian thinking, which is why you people could never manage anything truly new."

Mikhail startled again, but it was only an instant before he had his composure back. "I'll send back on the same frequency they used. They will certainly watch that. Even an American who prides himself on thinking of infinite possibilities and problems, to the extent that you actually think, should realize that."

"If Russians actually thought, you would realize that won't work," Shane said. "It's the hydrogen twenty-one-centimeter frequency. That was a forbidden frequency even before the ISC existed, because it was reserved for radio astronomy and the old SETI program. A spaceplane can't broadcast on that frequency; the transmitter is designed with that in mind."

"Then I'll rig it so it will!" Mikhail's voice rose into a scream. "It will take some supplies from our stores, maybe, and some work by me, but I will do it. If you actually did any work, you'd think of that, but you don't. You can't even land a damned spaceplane without crashing it and practically killing all of us."

Shane's complexion started to resemble a beet. His mouth worked but nothing came out.

"Wait a minute!" Barttleby cried out from the stage. "If you're starting to talk about needing resources and putting your work into this instead of what our community needs, I have a problem."

"Never mind your problem!" Now Bischoff was shouting. "If you want to send a weak signal nobody will hear so we can tell ourselves we replied, that's fine, but if you're going to boost the power so these aliens might actually notice it, I think that's dangerous."

"Paula, you should shut up. You sound like an idiot," Mario said.

The byplay gave Shane a chance to recover his poise.

"We're not going to do anything stupid like you're talking about, Mickey." Shane opened his arms to the audience. "We're going to take that starship and go there."

There was an audible gasp throughout the auditorium. Even on the stage, Barttleby and Bischoff closed their mouths and stared at Shane. If Shane had left out the scorn and the nickname, that single statement probably would have carried the day. But Shane and Mikhail were from before, from my age, and they wouldn't let go of their hatreds.

Mikhail flushed so deeply that I could see it from where I stood. Rosann grabbed one of his arms and tried to pull him back to his seat.

Mikhail pulled free of her. "Nice fantasy to solve your temporal alienation," Mikhail said. "It's your fault you never tried to fit in here. What do you think you're going to do? Fly a nursing home starshot? You folks can barely get out of bed in the morning as it is, much less walk to the market. Old folks don't go to the stars."

"That's why we have scouts!" The words rang out across the room.

Sho had leaped to her feet. I stood up straight and stared.

"If you're going to the stars, you need a scout. I'm not old; I can work, and I'm going."

"I'm going with my sister." Caleb stood and put an arm around her shoulders, which, naturally, she shrugged off.

"Also me." No Nonsense smiled at Sho as he stood up.

What the fuck was going on here?

"And now the starship is a day care?" Mikhail asked. "You don't take children with no training on interstellar missions."

"We've got *practical* training!" Sho shouted. No Nonsense nodded vigorously.

"Maybe it's a good idea if *she* goes!" Barttleby yelled from the stage.

"We'll take them," Shane said. "This isn't ISC rules anymore. They could be important when we land on this planet."

I don't know if Shane thought about what he was saying before he said it or was merely taking the opportunity to contradict Mikhail.

"It's nice to trot the children out so someone can look vital, but they can't help you run the ship," Mikhail said. "Be assured, I am not going with you."

"As if you were ever essential," Shane spat out.

"I don't need a piece of Russki shit to manage the ship systems,"

Kwame said, "and I am quite capable of doing it. You were never any good with comm systems, which is why you missed the whole issue with the frequency. Anyway, if that system is as far away as we think, the signal you want to send will disappear into noise by the time it arrives."

"Oh, please!" Mikhail's laugh was as nasty as any pejorative he could have come up with. Rosann had her face in her hands. "Look at the drones standing up for the greater glory of Shane. As if *you* were ever accepted as a real American. You never understood my job anyway; you just checked a box.

"I doubt any of you even remember your own jobs, for all you sit and recite your old checklists and drill to each other. And for whatever you may remember, you don't even have a doc. Not at all. Max is dead."

"I'm a doctor." Hannah was up on her feet now. She was on the other side of the auditorium, but it was impossible to miss the anger in her face and voice. The woman sitting next to her might have been the same one I had seen at the table with her in the tavern, and she put her fingers over her eyes. "We should be looking for ways to do this, not coming up with one excuse after another for why we won't. I may have a life here, but I will fly to the stars in this ship. Now we have a physician."

"You may be a physician, Hannah Jin," Mikhail said, and at least his tone toward her was respectful, "but you know nothing about hib, about hibernation. We manage the time that passes on ship—and it's less than the time that passes on Earth, but it's still years—by being in hib. The ship's physician needs to handle that. It's essential and you can't do it."

"We all know how to put ourselves into hib," Shane said. "It's part of the training we all go through. Even as determined as you are to ruin this mission, I'm sure you remember that."

Mikhail's nasty laugh was back. "Sure. And I know how little I remember, and you won't know it any better even if you can still pull up the steps on your field. You've never put yourself into hib for real, and our training was what, thirty-five years ago bio-time? You won't do it even as well as you landed our spaceplane, and you damned near killed us all doing that. You'll fail, which is about what I'd expect from you."

For all the ugliness and obvious desire to settle old personal scores between Mikhail and Shane, Mikhail had a point. None of the *Invincible*'s crew had touched the controls of a starship—they had not even used a computer—in thirty-three years. I had basically told Mario the same thing, in more polite terms. All Hannah's bravery couldn't compensate for not knowing the techniques that were needed.

The venom and vitriol that poured out had stunned the crowded auditorium into wordlessness. No one moved. Even the whispers were gone. They were hearing a lifetime of hate distilled into voice and expression, the same hate that had laid waste to the world. In that frozen tableau, Ruth struggled back to her feet, pushing aside the helping hand the scout offered.

"We can't just give up," she said. "That's not what starfolk do. We've gone where we've been alone and beyond help and where a mistake could cost our lives. How can we give up a dream because it's difficult?" And then her eyes found me. "Leif, you haven't said anything. What do you think? You've been out twice, and you went out first. Will you lead the way here?"

Her words were a battering ram against my gut. Rangers lead the way was the motto of the US Army Rangers; RLTW was tattooed on my shoulder. In my mind, I saw Yong that day when she stood up and said she would fly any mission. Then she did it in a ship she had trained for only on a simulator, and that, only the day before. I had flown with her. And here I was. The last Ranger. This might be humanity's only chance for a first contact. The moment for me to speak, that I had been thinking about for so long, arrived with a jarring suddenness.

Thoughts flashed through my mind as I searched for the right words. Mikhail said he could send a reply signal, but could he do it for real? And if he did, was Kwame right that no one that far away would be able to distinguish it from background noise? Was this merely a way of pretending we'd answered—nothing more than a salve for our consciences and a chance for Mikhail to preen as the hero? Taking the starship would mean making contact for certain; we would learn so much, so much more than we would ever manage with radio signals. But neither spaceplane nor starship might be able to fly. The crew was unready at best and could not make the journey at all with no one to manage the hibs. The last point stuck in my mind. It was the deal-breaker.

I could feel every set of eyes on me; I could feel the silence as they waited for me. This was that special moment in time the Greeks called *kairos.* I remembered Petey touching my shoulder one grim day as we were pinned down in a merciless firefight. *Leif, what do we do about that machine gun?* I had known what to do, and I'd done it without thinking about the risk I took.

"It has to be the damned starship, and we have to make the damned flight," I said abruptly. "I'll handle the hibs. I've put myself into hib more than anyone else ever, and I was in charge of the hib deck coming home on the *No Name.* Now it's time to shut up and fly the damned mission."

Sometimes I think I would be better off if I learned to keep my mouth shut. However, I knew that Yong approved. I knew it.

CHAPTER NINETEEN

Once I'd shot my mouth off, Mikhail couldn't find anything else to say. He stood where he was and gaped at me. Rosann finally got a grip he couldn't shake and pulled him down. Barttleby and Bischoff on the stage did much the same.

Mario seized the moment. "Blue proposes that we agree to have our starfolk and Earthbase volunteers take the old spaceplane and starship and fly to the star the signal came from. In the absence of a chief administrator, I ask to be authorized to issue the directives I see as necessary for this. Let's vote now."

This was a board meeting and it should have been a board vote, but Mario had gauged the mood in the auditorium, and by gesture, he included everyone in the call to vote. Hands started to go up throughout the crowd with the call for ayes, and more hands followed the first wave of them. The directors sitting on the stage could see where the vote was going, and they voted yes. Just like that, we had a starshot and Mario had the authority to issue directives.

The voting done, the crowd stood, milled around, and then began to filter out. I stayed where I was at the back wall. I was a bit stunned, partly at what had been done and partly by what I had done. I had no idea if this crazy mission could actually work. I knew far too much about what was involved in starflight, both the going out and the coming back. The implications both ways were daunting. Still, I knew I had made the right choice. Yong would have done the same.

However, Yong was not going to be the pilot on this mission. Had my superannuated collection of starfolk thought through the problems of making this flight and bought into it, or had they been swept up in the moment when Shane and Mikhail had regenerated the Troubles and the old Cold War before that? To answer that question, I needed to find them.

I couldn't reach them in the auditorium; I couldn't even see if they were still in the room. A solid wall of people had me trapped at the back wall. By the time I freed myself from the mob, the starfolk were nowhere to be seen. The auditorium was mostly empty. I could not find them outside either. The Starfolk's Home was the logical place to look, but the only people in the caf when I got there were Kwame and Hope, hunched over a table in animated conversation, arms and hands moving every bit as fast as they were talking.

"Ahem," I said loud enough to break in. "Where are Shane and Magda?"

"With Mario," Hope said.

That figured. "Did Mario set the whole thing up? I noticed that he ended up being authorized to issue directives."

Yes, I was still processing that point. Mario had ended up with most of what he wanted at the start. In fact, he was close to having what Sydney Yaeger had been aiming at. Had I been the one to hand it to him at the end? Not only do I hate politics; I'm a lousy politician.

"I don't know that he set it up," Hope said slowly while I tried to digest my own role in what happened. "I mean, he did tell Shane about the starship, because Shane talked to us."

So Mario had planned it, if not in the precise way it had evolved. "And Shane is all gung ho to resuscitate this ancient ship and take flight. Right?"

"You need to understand, Leif," Kwame said. "Shane, he'll always start off with the problems, but he wants to do this. You could see a switch click in his head while he was talking, that we could leave this time and place and come back to a better time for us. That's what he said. Magda was 'Hell yeah, let's do this!' from the first. She saw it right away. Then you saw Mikhail put a roman candle up Shane's ass. From that point, he would have taken any chance to make the flight and rub it in Mikhail's face. Hell, he agreed to the three scouts. He and Magda are off with Mario, talking about how soon we can get to work."

"And what about the two of you?"

Kwame's features hardened. "It's good for us. All we're doing in this time is sitting in this building, wondering how many years we'll live to sit here. Coming back to another time will be better."

"We know our work," Hope said. "In a way, we've been practicing for thirty years."

Mentally reviewing your mission plan and checklist from a mission past is far from carrying out a spur-of-the-moment mission under different and not ideal circumstances. However, Kwame had a point that would be hard to argue with. "And what does Ian think?" I asked. "You haven't mentioned him."

"He went upstairs," Hope said. "He said he's in, same as us. Changing times will take care of a lot of problems."

Listening to them was almost the same as listening to my father. Whenever he was fired because of his drinking, he'd swear that he would stop. The next thing we'd do was move to another city or another state where he said he'd be able to start over, leave his drinking behind and stay sober. These people wanted one more trip on relativity's time machine that would take them to a time when they would fit in better. I suspected that the relativity cure for temporal alienation would prove as illusory as the geographic cure for alcoholism. They were set on trying it, though, and I had committed myself. Publicly.

Kwame and Hope went back to discussing how they would manage their areas and wanted me to join in. I told them that I was sorry I had interrupted and left.

I had barely cleared the doorway when I saw Shane coming up

to the entrance. I hit him with the same questions I'd had for Kwame and Hope.

Shane's big smile could have sufficed for the answers, but he gave me the words also. "A starshot to their planet is the definitive answer to their signal, and yeah, coming back in a different year is the best way to go for us. I saw that immediately, the moment Mario told me about the ship, and that's what I told the crew. I know you had some concerns. Mario told me about what you said. You don't need to worry. When ISC reviewed the possible pilots for *Invincible*, I was the best of the best. That's out of a pool of space test pilots and ones with interplanetary experience. They said they'd never seen a record like mine. I'll grant it's been some years and my eyes aren't what they used to be, but here and here"—he tapped his head and over his heart—"is what counts. You don't have to worry at all." He started whistling as he passed me to enter the Starfolk's Home.

I wasn't sure what to think about that speech. I knew the best of the best. The name wasn't Shane Crystal.

The starfolk might have made a decision and walked into this with their eyes open, but we had four others who had not done that; could not have done that. That was something I intended to rectify. As I thought about what they had done, I found myself getting angry. *Angry* is too weak a word. I was furious. I wanted to grab the four idiots—I mean volunteers—and shake them until their brains scrambled. I understood what we had signed up for just as certainly as they did not. I wanted to talk to them about it. *Talk* is too mild a term. They each needed a new orifice ripped in their ass.

Sho, Caleb, No Nonsense, and Hannah were nowhere in the old part of Earthbase. This was neither surprising nor a major problem. Earthbase wasn't very big and I doubted that they were trying to hide from me. I'd find them. Call it search and slightly destroy.

It didn't take me very long. They had acquired sufficient notoriety that people on the street and in the market were glad to give me directions when I asked.

The Starshot Tavern was full when I arrived, with people seated at tables clustered near the fire or the stove. The four of them had a table next to the fire, a mug of beer in front of each. I swiped an empty chair from another table, slammed it down at theirs, and dropped onto the seat.

"What the fuck did you think you were doing?" I asked.

They looked surprised.

"What do you mean, Leif?" Caleb asked.

"Volunteering for this crazy thing," I said. "Do any of you have any idea what you've gotten yourselves into?"

 Four heads nodded.

"You should have a drink, Leif," Caleb said.

"You know I don't drink! The subject is you, not me having a drink."

"We understand," Caleb said slowly. "We understand the risk, the danger."

"You do not. You don't know what you've done. You don't have a clue." I fixed each one in turn with a glare that would have had any soldier in my old platoon fumbling to come up with some duty that had to be immediately attended to. It made no impression on them. They really didn't understand.

"Look," I said, "it's not about going into danger, or risking death. What you need to understand is that from the moment you leave on a starflight, as far as everyone you know here is concerned, you have *died.*" How could I explain relativity to people who didn't even know algebra? "A starship travels almost as fast as the speed of light. Time is, well, strange when you do that. Inside the ship, what we call ship frame of reference or SFOR, time slows down. Several years will pass, but that's all. You won't even age that much, because we'll be in hib. But this star isn't close. We don't know how many light-years, but it has to be a lot, and here on Earth, what we call Earth frame of reference or EFOR, time will move normally.

"Many, many more years will pass. Even if we survive the mission, I'll bet at least two centuries will have passed by the time we come back. Everyone you've ever known, all of them, and their children and their grandchildren, and probably their great-grandchildren, will be long dead. A starshot is a time machine, a one-way time machine. Once you go, you can't come back. Not ever."

They were quiet for a moment.

"It doesn't matter," Hannah said. "I have a life here with my partner, as I said before. I also just finished forming a cooperative clinic with the other two physicians in Earthbase. We will treat patients and train new doctors. However, some things are more important than what happens to any one person. This is one of them. I am willing to accept whatever happens to me, and I am proud of my choice." She looked at me across the table, her face calm and relaxed. She knew the choice she had made and she was comfortable with it.

What she said was too close to the code I had lived by for so many years. It was the sort of choice I had to respect. It shut down whatever I might have said next and gave Sho a chance to speak.

"I also understand what you're saying." Sho's voice was as soft as I had ever heard it. "That's why you starfolk are all from before." She sipped at her beer, then met my eyes. "It's okay. There's nothing left for me here. No one will ever forget what I did the other day. I did what I had to do, but no one will forget, they will not forgive, and they won't let me forget. This is good for me."

This was different, very different from what Hannah had said. "That's not true, Sho," I said. "For God's sake, you're only seventeen. I know everything feels like it's permanent, will never change, but it's not true. Time heals. People get perspective. They will understand what you did, and why, and they will respect you for it."

"No," she said. "I could see it in Nathaniel's mother's eyes. I heard what Barttleby said too. I have no future here. Not one I would want."

I tried again. "Sho, one person is not everyone."

She didn't say anything in response, but she set her jaw and gave me a mulish look that could only mean no. Of course, I thought, they had just seen Shane and Mikhail give a demonstration of how long enmity could last.

Caleb put a hand on Sho's shoulder. "What you said is all the more reason I'm going with my sister. You should know that."

I guess I did. I turned to No Nonsense. "What about you? What's your reason?"

No Nonsense took a deliberate gulp of beer. "How old were you, Leif, when you left home?"

"Seventeen," I said, "but that was a different situation!"

That brought a chortle from Caleb. "My pa always said exactly that whenever he'd tell me what I'd done was dumb and I'd tell him how I'd heard he did the same thing at my age."

"So, why is it different, Leif?" No Nonsense asked.

I had no intention of going into the details of my father. "There was a war on. I joined the army. I needed to go. None of that is true now. You've got a home. If you go, you'll never see your ma or the other kids again."

"I've always said I was heading out for adventure." No Nonsense took another big swallow of beer. Then he wiped off foam from his mustache. "I'm not the one who promised he would come back."

CHAPTER TWENTY

N o Nonsense's comment hit me as hard as any concussion from a howitzer ever had. Abruptly, I left them to their beers and walked outside, where I hoped a gust of chill air would clear my head. I realized I wasn't angry at them for not understanding what they were doing. I was angry at myself because I knew exactly what I was doing and I was taking it out on them. I was leaving Charity. All the way to Earthbase, and for all the days at Earthbase, I had been telling myself about going back to Charity and the kids and the farm, and I wasn't going to be doing that. I was going back to the stars.

Why was I being like this? The mission was important. It might well be the most important in the history of humanity to this point, and it would certainly be the most important Earth would have for a long time to come. I carried out my missions. That's who I was and what I did. I did not become attached to people, Yong excepted, and she was the same as me. Rissi, the Harvard psychologist I'd had a fling with in 2097 and who had worked out temporal alienation, told me that from my profile, I could walk through the sands of time without leaving footprints. Seems she was wrong about that. Going to this star was the right decision. Why did I feel like shit?

Obvious, I suppose. I'd fallen in love with Charity; I'd come to think of Elvy and the others as my kids. I was breaking my promise to them. This was a disaster for a starman. Even at the time of the first starshot, ISC had known enough to prohibit people who were married or had children from becoming starfolk.

I couldn't go back to Mario and say, "Never mind what I said in that auditorium. I'm not going. Oops, my mistake." Even if I could be a coward and bail out of a mission after I took it on, the sad fact was that if I wasn't on that ship to manage the hib deck, the likelihood of mission success would plummet close to zero. People who have never done it and whose only experience of hib is in a vid or a book think it's simple: climb into the bath, put the port on your arm, pull the mask on your face, and go to sleep. It's a lot more complicated than that. Not as complex as launching a starship, but complicated enough that someone who knew what they were doing had to check everything. Only one doc had come back with the *Invincible*, and he was dead of a heart attack. I was the only one who could pull this off.

What was I going to do about Charity and the kids? I could do nothing, slink off to the stars, and never need to face the consequences of my actions. This wasn't going to be like the first starshot, when we returned after twenty-eight years EFOR and most of the people we left were still around, allowing for reunions, albeit awkward ones. From what little we knew, this would be at least a century out and then another century back. As I had told them in the tavern, effectively this journey was forever. To simply leave—a thief in the night who had stolen a family's affections—was a coward's move. I'd been many things in my life: foolish, impulsive, downright reckless. I was no coward.

I had to go back to the farm to tell them what I was doing and why I was doing it. I had to do it. We could have the scene face-to-face. They could hate me to my face.

I left the Starshot Tavern to find Mario and tell him there needed to be a delay in the launch date. Unfortunately, when I found him at scout headquarters, he stared right through me and said, "That's impossible."

"Why is it impossible?" I asked. "With all the time that's already gone by, what's another few months?"

Mario smoothed down the sides of his mustache. "The most obvious reason is that trying to cross the Empty Lands at this time of year is foolhardy. Even if I sent a well-equipped party with wagons, the risk of losing them in a blizzard is too high. I'm not going to send an expedition like that. However, even if you made it and returned, it would take too long. The support for this expedition is tenuous. I don't care what it looked like in that auditorium. The Greens and the Reds will start to pull away, especially ones who weren't there to see the show.

"I'm already starting to hear it and it hasn't even been a day. If you ride east, the support will collapse. I will lose the vote that follows and the authority I have to issue directives will go with it. This mission will be canceled, and do not expect that I will support any other proposal. Is that what you want to do?"

Yeah. I heard the messages in what he said. All of them. I knew what the answer had to be. I hate it when I can't think of a way to win an argument.

I walked all over Earthbase. Then I walked up the Avenue of Heroes and stood in front of the Apollo 1 monument. I thought not only about the men who had been willing to risk and lose their lives but also their families. I stayed out there in the cold until dark.

I didn't feel any better when I reached my room in the Starfolk's Home. I had promised Charity and the kids I would come back, and that wasn't going to happen. Elvy had screamed at me that I was lying about coming back, and she would be right. Were the children going to grow up hating my memory?

Trying to sleep was useless. I cursed in the dark. I got off the bed, found a candle and lit it. Then I found paper and a pen, and using ink on paper, I wrote a letter to the family that could have been mine.

It was time for me to put my feelings on paper. I'm not good with feelings under the best of circumstances, and these were far from the best. I don't think I'd ever tried to write them down before.

I wrote to Charity how much she and the children meant to me. I told her how much I looked forward to seeing her smile and hearing her voice. I wrote about how I felt at story time in the evening, with the children gathered around and listening, and I said how simply being around all of them made me feel relaxed and at home in a way I had never had before. I wrote down how I imagined Elvy all grown, strong and independent and making her own life. I went ahead after that and wrote something about each of the children, how I could visualize their growth and what they would do. I told her that I loved her. Then I paused.

When you write by putting pixels on a screen, no one can see afterward where you had to stop and consider. This was ink on paper. I thought and stalled long enough that a blot formed on the page. When Charity read this, she would know I had delayed writing the rest of it. I had to go on, however.

I wrote about duty and honor. I wrote about obligations, those that I had taken on and had to fulfill. I told her that I had to go to the stars. I wrote that I would not be coming back. I said that it would be best if they all thought of me as having died.

And a bit of me did die when I wrote that.

When I was finished, I found Mario and woke him up. Yes, come springtime he would have a scout deliver the letter according to my instructions. I wrote those down for him as well.

I think that was the best I could do, although it's possible that the person I was trying to convince was me.

CHAPTER TWENTY-ONE

IT WAS ONE THING TO SAY WE WERE GOING TO LAUNCH A STARSHOT. IT WAS another thing entirely to do it. None of the infrastructure the ISC had assembled for the purpose of building and launching starships existed anymore, at least not in any functional way. Could we do it?

I spent a long day on too little sleep with Shane, Magda, and Mario, discussing the problem across a table in the caf of the Starfolk's Home. We knew we had a spaceplane that had been set aside to be ready for an emergency departure. It had sat there, ready for that departure, for more than a century. Would it fly to space? Would it even leave the ground?

Shane and Magda had been practicing their takeoff checklists for three decades. If the electronic systems could be turned on, they would be able to tell if the spaceplane could go. Presumably, the hangar held enough fuel and had the pumps to transfer it. Since this spaceplane would take off from a runway rather than the ground of a new planet, it had wheels and tires instead of landing skids. The hangar needed to have pumps to inflate the tires properly, and hopefully those tires would hold the pressure. Speaking of hope, we were hoping the pumps worked. These were only at the top of a list of myriad details involved in making certain the spaceplane would reach orbit.

Assuming the spaceplane would fly, the next problem was the starship. Where was it? We didn't know. Oh, it was in orbit around Earth, but that covered a lot of space. This wasn't like looking down the block and spotting your car. Supposedly, the spaceplane had in its computer the access codes, the frequency, and the orbital parameters to allow it to find the starship and communicate with it. Once that communication was established, we could check from the ground the starship's supply of antimatter fuel.

Again, that would be only the beginning of the work necessary to make sure the starship was capable of making a flight at relativistic velocities after floating in orbit for a century. As we worked through the list, it became apparent that a lot of what had to be done would need to happen on the ship. We were going to have to work on the assumption that all those things would check out okay when we got up there. There were an awful lot of items that could either stop us from ever leaving the ground or, once on the starship, force us to come down in the spaceplane and admit defeat.

I picked up on one point that was conspicuous by its absence from the checklists. "You haven't mentioned suits," I said.

"That would be part of the ship's inventory," Shane said. "We can probably check that they are present once we have communications, but like a lot of these things, we'll have to check functionality when we get to the ship."

"Although," Magda said, "we would only need them if we had to go EVA from the ship. We can fly without them and accept the risk."

"It's not the ship," I said. "We need them on the spaceplane. If we don't have them, it's finished. We can't go."

That earned me hard looks from Shane and Magda. Mario, of course, had no idea what I was talking about.

"Listen," I said, "when I went out in 2098, people went into space either up the elevator or by spaceplane to GSY Station or the old NISS. We transferred to the *Dauntless* by people-pusher from the station.

Was it the same when you left nineteen years later?"

They nodded.

"Yeah. Spaceplanes from Earth don't dock with starships. The starship bay already has a spaceplane in it that is designed for a new planet. However, there aren't any people-pushers up there for us to ride over in. I left a small transport docked at the space elevator station, but after all the booby traps and malware we found when the *Dauntless* came back, we don't dare turn on that ship's computer and use its main engine.

"In fact, it wouldn't do us any good even if we could use it. The spaceplane we have in the hangar can't dock at the elevator station or with that transport. We'll have to rendezvous with the starship, then suit up, go EVA, and gain access through the starship's air lock."

Shane frowned. "Even if we have suits here, no one except you has trained on them in thirty-five years, and the four Earthbase people never have." He paused. "I don't like the idea, but we could dock at GSY Station. I can match the rotation at the docking port. There are probably people-pushers there we could still take."

"No, no, and no," I said. "I've been on GSY Station. It's a death trap. The air isn't breathable, any bot we come across is probably infected with malware that will cause it to attack us, and if there is any interface with the station computers, they'll download malware into our systems that will cause a crash. That's what happened to the *Dauntless*."

Shane's eyebrows pulled together, forming a deep V in his forehead. "We can open the starship bay and lift out the spaceplane there by remote. Then I can dock this one in the bay. Afterward, we can do the process in reverse so we have the correct spaceplane for the voyage. Cumbersome, but we can do it."

"Also a bad bet," I said. "The clamps in those bays are designed for the specific spaceplane, and they engage with skids and struts as well as wings. On the *No Name*, the clamps didn't engage properly, because we had jettisoned the spaceplane's cargo bay housing to save weight. Something in the clamp mechanism blew. Killed one of the crew. Maybe they remedied that, but maybe not. We can keep the idea, but only as a last resort."

"Then we have to hope that the people at Earthbase during the wars put suits in the spaceplane," Magda said, "and we will have to manage with them. They would have thought about the same transfer issues you just brought up. At least it's easy to check."

Before we could even make that check, another issue in the way of our departure reared its head. Heavy gray clouds rolled in and blanketed the sky from horizon to horizon. They dumped a foot of snow on Earthbase.

I'd become accustomed to snow piling up at Charity's farm and in the town of Eastview. I knew how it drove people indoors and brought a stop to most of daily life. Somehow, however, my brain assumed that runways and landing strips at Earthbase would be kept clear because that's what the air bases that I remembered did. Not anymore.

Earthbase had plenty of snow removal equipment in some hangar somewhere, but I had no idea when it was last used. Would any of it work, even if Mikhail could charge up some of the machinery? I thought it was worth a try.

Shane wasn't having any of that. "I'm not asking that man for anything," he said.

"I'll ask," I said. "You don't have to come within a mile of him."

"He'll know it's for the spaceplane. That's obvious. So, he'll know it's for me."

I put a hand on Shane's shoulder and turned him so he was facing me. "This starshot is supposed to be about our first contact with another intelligent species. It's not about you. He should realize that."

"It won't matter," Shane said. "And where the spaceplane and starship are concerned, I am in command."

"Don't you think the two of you should sit down together and clear the air?" I asked.

"There's no point," Shane said. "Anyway, once we leave, whenever that is, it won't matter. I'm going; he's staying behind. At that point, it's over."

I could have ignored Shane and gone to Mikhail anyway, but I was afraid the row that would precipitate would be harder to clear than the snow. I slogged through snow over the tops of my boots and drifts up to my knees to find Mario at scout HQ in his chalkboard war room.

He grunted after my recitation of the problem and began to erase assignments. Once the snow stopped falling, he rounded up scouts and passed out shovels and brooms. The runway for the spaceplane would be cleared by hand.

Our intrepid crew of scouts, laboring and sweating in the wind that blew snow back right where they had shoveled it from, finally managed to clear the hangar door and the runway. This being Kansas in the winter, naturally, it snowed again. Mario paid no attention to the curses and sent them back to shoveling as soon as the snow was down to flurries.

· · ·

THE SCOUTS MIGHT BE OUT CLEARING THE RUNWAYS, BUT NO ONE BOTHERED WITH THE streets of Earthbase during that time. Shopkeepers dug out around their shops, which kept the market open for business, but otherwise people relied on tromping on the snow to pound out paths.

A couple of days into this, I was having a meal at a Starshot Tavern packed with scouts who had been assigned to Mario's snow-shovel brigade, when Sho came there to find me. I had my back to the fireplace—I had acquired the habit of never sitting with my back to a door in Eastview—so I saw her come in. Heads turned to look at her, but she paid no attention. She went straight for my table. It was more of a stomp or a stalk than a walk. She dropped into a vacant chair without so much as a hi.

"I need you to do something for me," she said abruptly. Her fingers twisted with one another on the tabletop.

"You have to tell me what it is first," I said.

"I want you to tell Caleb not to go with us." The words came out one on top of the other.

"I think I already told all of you not to go."

She was shaking her head before I even finished the sentence. "I have to go. Caleb doesn't. He shouldn't."

"You don't have to go either, Sho."

"Yes, I do. Everybody here hates me now."

"Sho, you are overreacting to what one woman said."

"It's not just her!" She ducked her head as she realized half the tavern had heard her. Then she bit at a fingernail already down to the quick and drew blood. "I see the way people look at me. I hear what people say. 'Better not cross Sho. She'll blow your head off.' That's even Blues, even scouts. I'm not the only one who killed people that day, but all people can say is that I killed more than anyone else, or I shoot little boys. I need to go. No Nonsense wants to come with me, and that's fine. I like that. But Caleb should stay."

"Have you told him that?"

"He won't listen to me. He never does. He thinks he has to be my pa and my ma, and he can't do that anymore." She leaned forward on the table. Blood from the bitten fingertip made a smear on the tabletop. Her eyes were as wide as they could go. "Caleb's already certified; he's respected. Mario trusts him, that's why he was the one sent to find you. He'll be the senior administrator for scouts after Mario. That's what he wants to be. I want him to have what I know he's always wanted. It's not to be a starman. I can take care of myself, and I have No Nonsense also."

I leaned back in my chair and waited. The energy leaked out of Sho. Her shoulders slumped. The stubborn set of her jaw did not change, however.

"Please," she said.

I sighed. "I'll talk to Caleb, but that's all I'll promise. If he doesn't change his mind, that's the end of it. I can't make him stay. I can't seem to make any of you stay."

I checked scout headquarters first. Mario wasn't in his war room, but I could see that almost all the assignments for scouts had been rubbed off and replaced with SNOW REMOVAL. A scout came by while I was looking at the boards and told me I could find Caleb at the stable.

He proved to be finalizing a deal with another scout to have that man take his horse after Caleb left. I brought up Sho's request.

Caleb stared at me when I finished, his eyes gone as hard as Sho's had been. This was a sternness I had never seen in him before. "She is my sister," he said with the finality of a judge passing a life sentence. "From the stories, starfolk never cared about families. That's what is said, and looking at you now, I guess it's true. I'm not like that. I'm going with her, and I don't want to discuss it anymore."

I wanted to tell him that I wasn't like that either, not really, but the words wouldn't come out.

.   .   .

THE RUNWAYS WERE FINALLY CLEARED, BUT NOTHING ELSE HAPPENED. WELL, IT WASN'T that nothing happened. We continued to discuss what was *going* to happen. For all that Shane had triggered the decision to make the starshot, he had a nearly infinite list of items we needed to review before we *did* anything. I found it exasperating, but maybe that was because I had never been responsible for launching a spaceship. The others from the *Invincible*, when I complained, would shrug and tell me it was "Shane being careful Shane." At a certain point, careful becomes procrastination, but if that was in their thought bubbles, none of them voiced it.

A bigger concern than Shane's dilatory approach to launch was that the more days that passed from that emotional vote, the more the fragile political unity of Earthbase frayed. I didn't need Mario to point it out to me. The board had still not agreed on a new chief administrator and the uncertainty around that position added to the tension among the Colors. The fact that Mario was the one with the authority to issue directives didn't help.

I made a point of walking through the market area a few times a day, almost the way I had walked around Eastview when I was marshal there, to pick up on trouble before it erupted. The stress was palpable. Shops posted colors on doorposts or hung them on the dividers between stalls, and almost all their customers wore colors that matched.

Where the Colors had to mix, like in the streets, it took little more than a wrong-way glance to lead to harsh words, and I saw those words more than once lead to pushing, shoving, and punches. The only saving grace in all of it was that people didn't carry pistols all the time the way they did back East, so the scuffling did not lead to gunfire. My mind put a *yet* at the end of that thought. Sooner or later, something was bound to happen. If it involved one of the M8cs, we would have an awful mess.

I joined Mario one afternoon in his chalkboard room, and in between rubbing out names and assignments with a rag and rewriting them, he told me that the tension on the streets was mirrored in the board, which had reverted to meeting behind closed doors.

"I have committed to our course, to sending the starship, and my authority is tied to it. They all know it," he said. "That allows all of them to push me to support their pet ideas in return for not opposing the launch. The only good thing is that Green and Red can't agree on the concessions they want to force from me."

I didn't know what Mario's limit on concessions was. How much would he give up before he decided his current position and the starshot weren't worth it? He wouldn't tell me, of course, but the risk of the mission being canceled was real and growing.

The smile—more of a smirk—I saw on Mikhail's face when I ran into him in the market told me that he was making the same assessment. I knew that he would enjoy seeing the news delivered to Shane if we were scrubbed. The fact that he would put that satisfaction ahead of humanity making contact with an alien species was a sad commentary on what motivated people.

Then more ranks of dark gray clouds rolled in like waves of bombers loaded with snow. Our laboriously cleared runways were buried again. It took more days of shoveling to re-excavate the hangar and the runway. By the time the snow finally stopped and the skies cleared, the calendar had rolled into January of 2253. I celebrated my second New Year's Day on Earth postapocalypse with stew at the Starshot Tavern.

The place was packed with both scouts and others who preferred a different kind of toast. That was a lot more celebration than I'd seen in Eastview, where the only marker of the New Year had been the fireworks my chip displayed on my field. It gave me the same display this year, a reminder that for all our talk, we were no closer to launch than we had been weeks before.

Mario was there as well and made a point of giving me the same reminder. That pushed me to demand that we start the real, physical preflight checks.

It was a bitter cold January 3 under a polished blue sky whose brilliant sunshine did nothing to improve the temperature. I rode out to the hangar with Mario, Shane, and Magda.

The cold turned Magda into misery incarnate inside a shapeless bundle of many sweaters and coats. Two knit hats covered her head as well as most of her face. All her limbs and her back were stiff. Each arthritic joint ached in the cold. She needed help to mount and dismount from the horse. As I watched her movements, I thought about what it was like to come out of hib after an interstellar voyage.

At best, joints were stiff and moved only with pain. Muscles shuddered under load and threatened to give way when you stood up. She'd had the experience, she knew what was coming, but she said not a word about it.

How bad would it be for her this time? Would the reconditioning regimen I had designed work for her at all? For all my experience, I had never put a geriatric starperson into hib. Old folks did not fly to the stars. Until now.

Before I could worry about Magda coming out of hib, we had to be able to open the main hangar door. It didn't open.

"I don't understand what's wrong," Shane said after we stood in front of it for a minute. "I can't chip in."

"What do you mean?" Mario asked.

"I understand," I said quickly. "The computer systems are kaput.

There's nothing to chip in to."

Like me, Shane and the *Invincible* crew came from an era when almost everyone had an implanted chip that, among other things, allowed a direct interface to computer system networks.

Along with our phones, they were the foundation of our chip-and-phone civilization. Now no computers existed for our chips to interface with. Our chips were useless.

"Okay, yeah. Of course." Shane rubbed his forehead with one hand. "What about the spaceplane itself? I mean, I can pilot it without chipping in, but it would make things a lot easier if I could."

"We'll find out when we power up the spaceplane," Magda said. "If this was part of a secret escape plan," she turned to Mario, who nodded, "I would assume they kept the computer isolated, probably shut off, during the cyberwar. It ought to be okay."

"Let's get inside first," Shane said. "I would assume we can open the hangar door from the inside."

More assumptions. I hate assumptions.

•   •   •

WE ENTERED THE HANGAR THROUGH THE SAME DOOR MARIO HAD USED WHEN HE showed me the spaceplane. The air inside was chilly but it felt like a summer day compared to outdoors. We all pulled off a layer or two of clothing. The spaceplane loomed over us. I imagined it was eager to be on its way. Shane went immediately to a control panel set into one wall.

"Still can't chip in," he said.

"Try voice and eye," I told him. "That worked for me on GSY Station. ISC kept the access in the system for starfolk."

"Got it." Shane seated himself on the bench in front of the panel so he could look into the retinal detector. Then he spoke his name and gave his position as pilot-in-command of the *Invincible*.

"You are recognized," said a synthetic voice in English devoid of any regional, ethnic, or gender identifiers. No one had personalized this system.

Multiple areas of the board came alight in front of Shane. "This is good," he said. "The hangar door shows as operational. I wonder if we should test it."

"I wouldn't," Magda said. "We don't want to freeze everything in here, and the fact that the door works once doesn't mean it will work twice."

"Good point," Shane said. "We do need to check—" His fingers tapped at controls.

Lights came on in the spaceplane. With a loud pop, the hatch to the pilot's compartment cracked open. Then it swung up, and a ramp extended to the floor of the hangar. We all stared at the brightly lit opening.

"I feel like a girl at school again," Magda said. "When we went sneaking into places at night where we weren't supposed to be."

"Do you mean the boys' dorm?" I asked.

Magda's face colored. "You don't have to ruin the moment with a bad joke, Leif."

I guess I have a knack for that.

Magda and I followed Shane up the ramp into the pilot's cabin. Those cockpits were designed for two: pilot-in-command in the left-hand seat, copilot on the right. Three of us made it a bit cramped, so I was glad Mario had stayed behind.

The layout, to me, was the same as other spaceplane cockpits I had been in with Yong the times I had sat in the copilot seat because we didn't have a copilot. I could feel her presence in the cabin even though she had never been in this spaceplane. It was a sign that I belonged here too.

Shane slid into the pilot-in-command seat. He studied the panels in front of him and tapped. They came alive, and mostly, I saw green.

"The tires definitely need pressure," he said, "but we can do that, either by bot or with a bunch of people." He frowned. "I'll bet on them for takeoff. Let's hope we don't have to come back down in this, because I don't think they'd survive a landing."

"What about fuel?" Magda asked.

"Needs to be fueled," Shane said. "No surprise there, and the system to do it shows operational." He spent more time studying his panels. "Yes, computer is up now. I'm chipped in."

As he said that, I saw a notification flash NETWORK AVAILABLE on my field.

"My God," Shane said. "I feel like I've been reborn. It's been so long."

"Let's not have a religious experience," I said.

"Yeah, I know." Shane sounded annoyed. "But it's been thirty-three years with no connection for me."

I'd never liked being chipped in, going all the way back to boot camp, where the chip gave away everything about me to the DI.

After communing with the computer a bit, Shane said, "This ship is operational. I think this spaceplane will fly."

"Good," I said. "What about suits?"

"We have them," he said. "In the locker."

"Not good enough," I said. "We have to check them. Our eyes on them. You can probably trust the computer to tell you the ship can fly, but it can't tell you the status of the suits. I'm not trusting anything that has sat around for a century if I can't check it."

"Christ," Shane said. "How long do we need to be out here to check each one?"

"As long as it takes."

I went through the door into the passenger cabin and found the suit locker. The life-support pack on the first one I checked was dead. That got everyone's attention. We pulled them all out of the locker and started checking. When we were finished, we had eight suits I would bet my life on—which is, in fact, what the matter came down to.

"These aren't individually fitted suits," Magda said. "The inner layer will adapt to the person wearing it across a pretty good range of body types and we don't have any outliers in size. So, that's okay, but we don't have enough functional suits. We have five people from *Invincible*. Then we have you, Leif, and the four from Earthbase. That's ten. We have to have you and the doc, but I think if we try to leave out two of the Earthbasers, we'll have a fight. We may need all the young ones anyway, for physical reasons."

"We send eight across to the ship, get out of the suits and bring suits back over for the others," I said. "Pain in the ass, but we can do it. Our four Earthbase people need to be in that first group."

"Why?" Shane asked.

"You want them trying to suit up in zero gee?"

"No." That was both of them and emphatic.

Yeah, I thought. It was going to be bad enough with people who hadn't trained on it in thirty-five years and had probably only ever done it in drills. There wasn't much reason to go EVA from a starship. The more we looked into the details, the more this trip was looking like the longest shot of all time.

CHAPTER TWENTY-TWO

THE NEXT DETAIL WE ARGUED OVER WAS ABOUT A VERY SPECIFIC SUPPLY. I WANTED weapons.

"You're being idiotic," Shane said when I brought it up in the caf of the Old Starfolk's Home, where I was having coffee with the *Invincible* crew.

"Why don't you tell me how you really feel?" I shot back. "I'm telling you they're necessary." Maybe I sounded petulant.

"Look, Leif," Magda said, "if this is going to be anything more than a gymnasium shouting match between children, you need to give us your reasoning. We are traveling to meet a civilization that sent us a message across many light-years. Don't you think our first contact will go better if we tell them we are coming in peace?"

"Coming in peace is fine, and telling them that is also fine," I said. "Going back home again in one piece may be more likely if we're not helpless. We have no idea what we're walking into. For all we know, that message is a warning not to come."

"Now you're sounding like one of the Reds," Kwame said.

"I doubt it's a warning." Shane ran his fingers through his hair. "But suppose for a second that you're right. We show up in a solar system that turns out to be armed to the teeth and hostile. What are we going to bring? It's not as though we could mount missiles on a starship. Think about what you are saying."

"I am thinking. I'm remembering that if we hadn't had an M8 on the first starshot, a lot more of us would have died than did, and quite possibly, the whole expedition might not have come back. What would have happened to some peaceful, unarmed aliens who arrived here during the wars or right before them?"

"Nothing good," Hope said.

Shane grunted and scowled. "Okay. Why don't you go ask your friend Mario to write a directive to give us something more effective than those versions of nineteenth-century rifles they make. See how far you get."

. . .

I THINK THE STRAIN OF KEEPING THE BOARD AND THE PEOPLE OF EARTHBASE AT PEACE with one another was starting to tell on Mario. When I found him in at his HQ, if the bags under his eyes got any fuller, they would be swollen shut. I don't think he was sleeping much.

"Any directive I issue is public," he said. "The M8cs are precious. I don't need to give Green and Red another reason to undermine my authority."

I understood his position. Somewhat. As with the crew, anything that went on this venture was gone forever. That didn't stop me from arguing. We went around and around, essentially restating our positions.

Finally, I said, "It's simple, Mario. I'm going armed, and I don't mean the rifle and pistol I rode in with. Otherwise, I'm not going, and if I don't go, this whole scheme falls. How will that do for undermining your authority if there's no starshot to tie it to? That's the choice you have."

Mario's eyebrows drew together and his eyes narrowed until his face was mostly a nose surrounded by hair. He threw a piece of chalk against his assignment board.

"This is blackmail," he said.

I agreed.

He found another piece of chalk and threw it. That hit a corner and splintered, with one fragment caroming past my head. I don't think it was intentional.

"You have two scouts, your friend, and yourself who are trained to use weapons. I will make four M8cs and a supply of ammunition disappear from our stores. There will be no directive. That's all I can do and all I am willing to do. I hope you are satisfied, and I hope this is not the start of another endless round of talk. People notice that too. I am becoming surprised Earthbase ever launched anything."

After I said, "I'll take it," he told me to meet him outside the Starshot Tavern after lunch the next day. He showed up as promised with a heavy canvas bag slung over his shoulders. Inside were four M8cs and ammunition.

I wasn't going to make a show of pulling out assault rifles next to a busy tavern. I did take out one of the magazines. I stared at the bullets.

"Hollow point," I said. "Where did these come from? They were prohibited in militaries even before the twentieth century. Even during the Troubles, even when we were using chem weapons on the battlefields, we didn't use these."

"I don't know anything about the Troubles or military history," Mario said. "These were used during the Tribulation. Nasty things. There are magazines with armor-piercing rounds as well. You'll take them. Right?"

"Yeah, I'll take them."

Shane thought it was crazy when I told him. "Do you honestly think, Leif, that four rifles are worth the ill will you've caused here?"

I grinned at him. "What was it you told me about Mikhail? Whatever ill will is here, we're going to leave it behind forever."

Examined rationally, I would have to admit the scene I'd caused was childish. Or so it seemed at the time.

.   .   .

After I left Shane, I decided it was time for me to take hands-on preparation into my own hands. I took our four Earthbase volunteers to the hangar to teach them about space suits, starting with how to put one on. Strictly speaking, this wasn't my job, and nobody had ever trained me in how to teach others.

However, nobody else was stepping up to do it, and this wasn't the first time I had done things that weren't my job. I remembered a parachute drop into contested territory when one of the troopers had frozen at the door. He had made a combat jump before, but this time he froze, couldn't move. I had to get him to jump. I know I didn't do that by the book, but out he went. He survived the jump, anyway.

I enjoyed seeing the faces of my fearless four when we stepped through the door of the underground hangar. Eyes widened to the point where they were at risk of falling out. Mouths dropped open. This reaction wasn't due to the presence of the spaceplane. They had all seen the wrecked spaceplane from the *Invincible* out on the field, and they had also seen spaceplanes in hangars used for livestock.

This was different. This hangar was *alive*, brightly lit with artificial light. The control panel was on, status lights all green. They could hear a soft background hum of motors, noise that my ears tuned out but that they could not ignore. I touched a control, and the interior lights of the spaceplane turned on.

"Shit." The word came out of Caleb in a long breath.

None of the others said anything. No Nonsense's pale skin shaded toward green. Sho was there, though, and I would have bet money that No Nonsense would keep moving no matter what happened. Hannah and Sho looked grim but determined.

"C'mon," I said. "Let's pull out some suits and practice."

I took a suit we had tagged as functional from the locker for each one of them and also one for myself. The mechanics of putting a suit on went rapidly. All of them were agile, and all of them, including Hannah, had handled tools and done mechanical work since they were little. They were also motivated to show me how well they could do this.

These were soft suits, easy to manipulate, not the hard-shell ones used in space construction or for long periods in space, which were more like getting into medieval armor. The looks of awe on their faces as they felt the material of the suits and looked at each other wearing them told me that the biggest problem they would have with the equipment might be psychological, not physical. Fortunately, a space suit is designed to work while making minimal demands on its occupant to manipulate it.

"Close the helmet and seal it like this." I demonstrated the technique. "As soon as the helmet is closed, the oxygen will come on. Also, you'll see a green light just to the right of your chin. That shows that your comm channel is open." I realized as I said it that those words meant nothing to them.

"Comm channel is how we talk to each other in the suits. The general ship channel is on automatically. Don't worry about any other settings. You won't need them." Just that much might be enough for our purposes. All they'd have to do would be to clip to a line and go, one after another, from air lock to air lock. I had no way to train them on jetpacks, and frankly, I didn't consider myself expert with them either. "It feels like we've gone back in time to before." No Nonsense's voice sounded shaky. It was weird hearing him on a comm channel.

"You okay?" I asked.

"I will be," he said. "Takes some getting used to."

"I'd love to get used to this," Sho said. "Imagine having this all the time. Imagine what we could do."

"You have too much imagination," Caleb said. "We know what people did with all of this. Just follow Leif's directions."

"We will." The words came in duplicate from Sho and No Nonsense.

I decided it would be best to move quickly into some exercises. The big problem surfaced with them suited up when I tried to check their statuses. I couldn't.

"I need you to—" I chopped off the sentence before I could finish it. I had started to tell them to chip in so that I could see the readouts, but none of them had chips. Or phones.

"You know," I said, "staying in the suits to practice problem-solving drills isn't going to be that useful and it will use up life-support resources we can't replace."

I had them open up the suits to shut down the systems. Then we practiced putting on and taking off the suits a few times before I called it a day. As we put them back in the locker, Hannah touched me lightly on my arm to get my attention.

"Leif, the starship will have a medical clinic, am I correct?"

"Yes, of course. We call it the Med Unit."

Her lips pressed together and her eyes narrowed. "I'm thinking of what will be in it. All the medicines and tools they had before. On one hand, it will be marvelous to see that, but it is also going to show me how little I really know, how little we have to work with here. The youngsters, they look like they were given a roomful of toys—well, maybe not Caleb, but Sho and No Nonsense for sure. I'm afraid what I see is going to make me embarrassed to call myself a doctor. I'm not sure … not sure how I'll handle it."

"You'll be fine," I said. "I mean, I'm not a doc and we need you. I'll show you everything I can and I'll show you how to find information on everything else. Okay?"

"Thank you," she said. "Now, I'd like to get out of here for a while. I'm glad we practiced, but it's a little overwhelming."

.   .   .

It turned out to be a good thing we had even that much practice with the suits because two days later, Mario came by the Starshot Tavern in the morning while all our crew were having breakfast together. "You need to leave now," Mario said. "Whatever you have in that spaceplane, whatever you have with you, take it and go." He dropped the keys to the hangar's small door on the table.

"Are you serious?" Shane looked at him over the rim of his bowl with disbelief obvious in his voice. "We haven't completed the real prep. We don't have our flight plan finished; it's not final. Not yet. We haven't planned for what we do on arrival. This is not a formula for success."

We could have done it in the time we'd had, I thought, but we hadn't. Now, Mario was making it happen. Now. There had been plenty of times—far too many—that I had been given orders amounting to *Go from here to there, and somehow, make X, Y, and Z happen.* Sometimes it worked. Other times, not so well.

"It doesn't matter." Mario's manner would brook no further delay. "I have word a group of Greens and Reds are coming to block the spaceplane, maybe try to destroy the hangar, maybe attack you. Even if we stop this attempt, there could be another tomorrow, or the day after, and eventually they will succeed. The weather is good today. If we have another snow, you may never get out."

"Mickey is behind this," Shane said, and he stood up. "Goddamn untrustworthy Russian bastard. This is his doing."

"If Mikhail were going to do something," I said, "all he'd have to do is cut the power to the hangar. Let's leave the Russia–America crap behind. That's all in the past and we don't need to deal with it anymore."

Prescience is not my strong suit, but Mario did agree with me.

"Mikhail will be living here with us," Mario said. "I have a good memory, and he will be careful of me. It's more likely Bischoff is behind it. Bischoff has been saying that the scouts are going to take the spaceplane, go pick up some old space colony, bring them back here, and set up a dictatorship."

"That's nuts!" I said.

"Doesn't mean people don't believe it," Mario said. "In the end, it does not matter. You must go now. Whatever you may have thought about me," and he was looking at me when he said that, "I have always been serious about a reply to the stars and about the starship. Know that. I and my people have committed too much to this. We cannot afford, will not allow, a failure. I will deal with the situation here after you leave." His voice turned brusque and impatient. "I have horses for all of you. My scouts will block whatever rabble they put together. Get outside the wall and go. Go now."

I stood up. Mario was already gone by the time I was standing. "Forget preparation, then. We have to know where we're going, though." I looked at Shane. "Do we, and can we go?"

"I have the communication frequency for the starship, and the access codes. The orbital parameters are in the spaceplane computer. I can fly the spaceplane. It's not as though we need air traffic control. I'm the one to do what needs to be done and I'm always ready." His face, however, belied his strong words. "I can't imagine you've got a lot to pack," he said to me.

I've always traveled light through life. The weapons I had argued for were already stowed in the spaceplane. The old printed pic of me and Yong in the Shadowland meadow on High Noon with the red star's frozen sunset behind us was the only other item I cared about. Its edges were beginning to fray a bit, and it was creased in one place, but the image was still clear. It never left the special pocket in my pants. That was all I needed to take with me.

"I'm good to go," I said. "Let's do it."

.   .   .

LESS THAN TWO HOURS LATER BY MY CHIP'S CLOCK, WE ALL STOOD IN FRONT OF THE hangar door. Scattered gunshots back inside the Earthbase wall while we rode told us that Mario's worry was real and that he did have our backs. For the moment. The skies were clear above us, but a wind from the north and a line of dark gray clouds at that horizon suggested they might not stay that way. No one else was around: no crowd of well-wishers, no marching band. It felt like we were a bunch of refugees trying to catch the last flight out of a besieged city. A burst of gunfire from the direction of Earthbase said that image wasn't far from the truth.

"I guess it's time to find out if this is going to work at all," Shane said.

He led the way through the human-sized door. Magda, moving stiffly, almost shuffling in the cold, couldn't lift her leg high enough to clear the framing at the bottom of the door opening. Her foot hit the frame. She tripped, gasped, and grabbed at her knee in pain. Fortunately, Sho was close to her and caught her before she fell.

"Thank you," Magda murmured.

Shane was halfway to the control panel but turned around at Magda's near fall. "When we get up to the ship, there'll be some stuff in the Med Unit that should work," he said.

"I hope so," Magda replied. "We haven't seen any records of what the ship's carrying. We've all been guessing at what we'll find."

"Yeah," Shane said. "No point worrying about that, though, until we get up there. The ship was supposed to be ready for flight. There's no other way to know except to go."

Abruptly, he spun on his heel and went to the control panel.

"Let's see if we can get out of here," he said. "This place feels like a damned underground tomb." I found his sudden resolution interesting. He stabbed at a panel with an index finger. The beat of pumps echoed through the hangar. "Fueling system has engaged," Shane said. He clicked another control.

A loud crack sounded through the hangar, followed by a jolt that shook the floor. A thin line of light shone through a gap that had appeared between the ceiling and the top of the hangar door. Slowly, to the accompaniment of the screech of a thousand nails on chalkboard, the hangar door sank into a recess in the floor. A ridge about an inch high stuck up when the movement stopped. Shane walked over and kicked it. Of course, that made no difference at all.

"It's stuck," Kwame said, looking at the panel.

"We can roll over it," Shane said. "Won't even notice the bump. Let's get going."

I pulled suits out from the compartment in the passenger cabin. I suited up first, then watched my four Earthbasers put theirs on. Hannah was all business. Caleb looked worried, but no more so than usual. The excitement on the faces of No Nonsense and Sho could not be missed. Kids climbing into costumes for their first Halloween party. The little practice we had been able to do paid off. They were ready quickly.

"Leave the helmets off until I tell you to put them on," I said. "I want to preserve as much suit time as we can. I've set all your systems to automatic. Your comm will go automatically to the ship channel. Don't play with any of it. You can't control any of it electronically, and I can't access your system once you're on the suit systems.

"Once we're in space, both in the spaceplane and when we get inside the starship, you'll be weightless. I can talk about it all day, but until you feel it, you won't really understand. You'll see blue strips on the walking areas. Those are called StickStrips, and the bottoms of your boots will grip them.

"Anchor yourselves so I can help you out of the suits, because I'll need to take two suits back to the spaceplane for others. There will be foot coverings and boots on the ship that will also grip the StickStrips after you're out of the suit. Let me help you. Do not try to be heroes. Got it?"

I had heard that line plenty of times on my first deployment, and I had used it myself when I became a noncom. The four of them nodded, but I wondered if any of them meant it any more than I had in the past. No time to worry about it.

I walked forward and through the door into the cockpit. Shane and Magda were there, both in suits, going through their checks. They stopped at my entrance and looked around at me.

"When we reach the starship, I'll need you to bring us to rest relative to its air lock. We also need to be close enough that I can get a tether from the spaceplane lock to it. No drift, no rotation. I know there's no way we could practice, but that's what I need."

"That's not a problem," Shane said. "I understand you're concerned about our ages and my eyes. About how many years it's been. You don't need to worry. I can fly this spaceplane, Leif. So can Magda. We know what is needed."

In fact, I was worried, but it was because neither of them was Yong.

"Good enough" was what I said.

I went back to the passenger cabin, took a seat by myself, and stared out the window. I tried to tell myself that I felt tense only because I had become accustomed to sitting in the cockpit with Yong. We hadn't had a copilot in the spaceplane on the ascent from High Noon, and neither up nor down at Heaven, so I had sat next to her. I had no real business in the cockpit, of course, and Magda was hardly going to give me her seat. Even so, being relegated to the passenger cabin made me feel shunted aside. Other feelings, ones I refused to think about, might have been driving my mood as well.

"Engines on," said Shane over the comm. "This is it."

A roar built up in the hangar, followed by a jolt from the spaceplane. I could see the walls slide back as the spaceplane began to roll forward. Normally, a bot-tractor would have latched to the front strut of the spaceplane and pulled us forward, with the SuperSabre engines igniting only when we were clear of the hangar. We had no charged bot-tractors, however, so all the motive power had to come from our engines. This would leave the hangar a shambles, but I didn't think anyone would be needing it again.

The spaceplane bounced as it rolled over the ridge left by the stuck hangar door. Then we were past that. We rolled up the ramp and onto the runway the scouts had cleared so laboriously.

I stared morosely at the line of clouds that already took up more of the sky than when we had come out to the hangar. I waited to feel better.

"I see riders coming toward us," Shane said on the comm. The sound of the engines died down.

"Blast the engines and let's go!" I yelled. "They're not going to block us with a few horses."

"It could damage the landing gear if we hit them. The spaceplane has no armor," Shane said. "If they fire at us, if we take any damage ... I don't know ... this could be dicey."

I did not like the way his voice sounded, and that wasn't only because he wasn't Yong. I unbuckled from the seat, ran to the storage locker, and gave thanks that I had not stored the M8cs in the cargo bay. We were stationary on the runway. I grabbed one of the rifles, snapped in a magazine, and ran for the air lock from the passenger cabin.

"Open the inner and outer doors," I said into the comm channel. "Do not put the ramp down."

Both doors were open by the time I positioned myself in the lock. I could see riders on horseback in the distance. Not many; a half dozen perhaps. I hoped they would stick to the area the scouts had cleared, but my field of vision was too restricted to be certain.

An M8 could be effective at half a mile. I didn't know if the M8c had greater effective range. I didn't care. I opened up with a long burst at the riders I could see. I was gratified to see them slew around, although I didn't see anyone fall.

"Engines!" I shouted into the comm. "Get us out of here while we can!"

Nothing happened. We sat there. The riders backed off. I saw a couple more. I fired again. The only visible effect was that they did not come closer.

"Do it now!" I yelled. "*Now* as in now!"

"On it." Magda's voice.

The howl of the engines ratcheted up from the rear of the space-plane, and a jolt knocked me to the deck. Past the open door, I could see the ground sliding past.

"Close the damn door!" I rolled back through the inner door into the passenger cabin. I had no intention of imitating a waist gunner on an ancient attack helicopter. This was a spaceplane headed for space.

The engine roar increased. We hurtled past banks of snow on either side of the runway. I scrambled for a seat and was pressed into it as I felt the wheels leave the runway. A quick glance at the others told me that everyone was secured.

The spaceplane rose into the air. Details of the land below shrank away quickly as we gained altitude. I could not help thinking about rising past the clouds on Heaven as Yong took us up.

I remembered thinking that we would never see the friends below again. I would never see any of the people on Earth again either. The finality of being committed, of having passed the point of no return, should have made me feel better.

For the record, it did not.

CHAPTER TWENTY-THREE

I LISTENED ON THE SHIP'S COMM CHANNEL AS WE FLEW, BUT THERE WAS LITTLE TO hear. Shane and Magda were mostly quiet as the sky darkened toward black.

At one point, Shane said, "Rocket mode."

That was followed by another jolt to the spaceplane. The acceleration pushed me deeper into the seat cushion. The stars came out.

We continued to climb. This was the first time our Earthbasers had seen the view of Earth from space, and nothing had prepared them for that.

"Oh my God," Hannah said in little more than a whisper. "It's so beautiful, so, so beautiful." Her face was as close to the window as the suit would allow.

"It is, isn't it," Kwame said to her from across the aisle. "It's a view worth making a fuss over."

No Nonsense was staring out in the same way, his arm around Sho in the next seat, who was leaning across his lap. Only Caleb sat apparently unmoved, his eyes fixed to the interior of the spaceplane.

"I have a response from the transponder on the starship," Magda said. "Our approach is on target. We are go for rendezvous."

"Good," Shane said. "That's another problem down."

I could have said that I was not impressed with the way he'd faced the previous problem, but I kept quiet. Maybe he needed to readjust to a risk environment.

We flew in silence for a little while as Shane matched the orbit of the starship and began to bring us close. I mentally rehearsed my jump from our air lock to the outer door of the starship air lock. In particular, I thought through the checklist steps for the jetpack on my suit. I had experience with those devices, but they were touchy and I wanted to conserve as much of the pack as I could in case one of the others needed help.

Magda came onto the comm channel. "There's another ship close to the starship. A small one. Transport, maybe."

"Any reason that should be there?" Shane asked.

"Not that I know of," Magda replied.

I went on the comm. "Is it going to obstruct my line to the air lock? Can you give me a clear approach so I don't have to go around it?"

I didn't get an answer. The spaceplane vibrated. Then I felt a bump. A dull gong sounded inside the cabin.

"Attitude thrusters, reverse thrust!" Simultaneous with Shane's words, my body pressed against the seat harness. Shane was screaming into the comm channel. "Helmets on and locked! On suit systems! That other ship fired on us!"

"We don't have suits!" That came from both Hope and Ian.

"What the fuck! What's going on?" I wanted an answer fast.

"Don't know," Magda said. Her voice stayed cool.

"I'm coming forward," I said.

I unbuckled and pulled myself into the air over the seat. It took a wave of my free hand and an emphatic command to stop Sho and No Nonsense from unbuckling. I did *not* want either of them loose in the cabin. Hannah and Caleb, thankfully, were wise enough to watch our other starfolk and sit tight. Using the seat back as a launcher, I flew the short distance to the cockpit door, grabbed the handhold there, and anchored on the StickStrips. As I entered the cockpit, foreign words filled my helmet.

"What the fuck is that?" Shane asked.

"Sounds Russian," I said, "but I don't speak it."

"Translate!" Shane demanded of the computer.

Without inflection, the computer said, "This ship is Russian property. If you continue to approach, you will be destroyed. If you do not depart, you will be destroyed."

"How is this possible?" Magda asked. "How can we be facing a Russian force here? Now?"

So, a century and an apocalypse notwithstanding, we still weren't quits with the Russians. It didn't make sense.

"It's not possible," I said. "When we returned to Earth on the *Dauntless*, we did see evidence of some populated areas in the old Russian sphere, but no evidence of any tech civilization beyond what we have in North America."

"*We* are here," Shane said. "Could a group of Russians have done the same?"

In the back of my mind, I thought it would be a whopper of a coincidence, but that could wait for later. "How do you know we were fired on?"

"Look at the vid we caught on one of the cameras." Magda brought up an image on one of the screens. She enlarged it, and a small dot in the center grew into an image of a transport ship.

As I watched the screen, that ship fired thrusters to change its orientation. I saw a flash from one side of the ship, a flash to the front and to the rear. Seconds later, another pair of flashes.

"Right after the flashes, we were hit," Shane said. "Damage to one of the hydraulics in the left wing. We have redundant systems and we weren't planning on landing this spaceplane anyway. The other impact was in the fuselage. That's designed for stopping micrometeorites, and I guess a bullet qualifies."

"You're telling me they attached some sort of improvised recoilless rifle to a transport spaceship?" I said. "And those were the only shots?"

"Wouldn't need a rifle in space. Could be some kind of smooth bore. Doesn't matter. Since I fired our thrusters, our vector is away from them. Not with any great velocity, but it is away and not toward. So maybe that complies with their warning. We're not approaching. We're going away."

"It's still odd," I said. "The traps we ran into with the *Dauntless* were simply murderous. They were designed to kill without warning or conditions."

"How does that help us?" Magda asked. "We still have to reach the starship. Unless those were the last shots they had and they're out of ammunition."

"I wouldn't bet my life on that," I said. "I also wouldn't bet that the next bullet won't penetrate something vital. We don't have enough functional suits to have everyone suited up."

"So, what are you proposing to do?" Shane asked.

The obvious implication of his question was that I was going to be doing whatever it was that I proposed. That did make a certain amount of sense.

I decided to discard the idea that some group in what used to be Russia was pulling the same stunt we were trying. The likelihood was so low as to be preposterous. My tactical problem was how to stop a homicidal transport ship from ruining our day. The spaceplane had no armament and, essentially, no armor. That meant I would have to go over to the transport and do … something.

From that point, my mind churned through a series of ideas that all had my death as the most likely end result. If I was going to survive this escapade, I needed to create a distraction. I left the cockpit.

"Kwame and Hope," I called out on the comm and suit speaker as I walked back into the passenger cabin, "I want four of the suits we can't use. Pick ones that will at least power on, so I can assess the jetpack controls." Hope was one of the ones without a suit, but I needed someone who could navigate in zero gee.

"What do you want them for?" Kwame asked.

"Don't ask. Just do." It was a tone my old platoon would have recognized. Both of them got out of their seats and did.

It took longer than I wanted, but I ended up in the air lock with the two of them and four empty suits that had their power on but were not pressurized.

Hey, Sarge, Petey said in my mind, *what idiot thought up this shit-ass maneuver?*

I did.

I told Hope and Kwame to go back inside the passenger compartment. I shut the inner air lock door and started the depressurization.

"Shane," I said, "orient the spaceplane so that the lock is facing that transport. Once you do, I'm going to open the outer door and send four suits out under jetpack thrust toward the starship. Then I'm going out, but not with them. Once I'm out of the lock, get the spaceplane out of the line of fire from that transport. Got it?"

"Yes, but—"

"No *buts*, please. We don't have time."

Talk about not looking before I leap!

Anchored to the StickStrips in the lock, I could feel the ship rotate as Shane applied the thrusters. The outer door slid open. I could see the transport. It looked only a million miles away.

I set up the four empty suits so that their controls were on my field. I aimed each one in sequence at the starship, past the transport, and sent them on their ways with a puff from their jetpacks. Then I broke my own contact with the StickStrips and flew out of the opening with a thrust from my pack, but at an angle away from the vector I had given the others.

I could see the transport rotate so that its weapon aimed at the empty suits. I hoped Shane had the spaceplane out of the way. I hoped *I* was out of the way.

The transport's weapon flashed, front and rear. The suits kept flying. It might have hit one of them, for all I know, but there was nothing inside them, and a high-velocity shot could zip right through without transferring much kinetic energy.

My problem now was to change my direction of flight so that I was headed directly at the transport. It's not as simple as it sounds. In space and zero gee, put a mass—me—in motion, and it will keep going along the same line. Apply a thrust in a different direction, and you'll go in the direction of the sum of the vectors. It's simple math and physics, but I was having to do it by eye.

I hate math and physics anyway.

Three more shots from the Russian. A flash from one suit told me its pack had been hit. A suit vanished from my field. I could see that I was slightly off-target as I headed to the transport. I used the jetpack to change my vector again. Another one of the empty suits flashed and disappeared from my field. I nudged my vector again as the transport grew in front of me. I still seemed a touch off-line. I had no tether. If I missed and didn't have enough left in the jetpack to stop myself and come back, I was going to be a very lonely corpse.

The Russian fired again and again. Another empty suit blew up. I had to reach my target before that stupid bot destroyed my last decoy and decided to aim at me.

Flash and flash again. How much ammo did it have?

The side of the transport loomed in front of me. Its outer air lock door appeared to be open. That was odd, but I had no time to think about it—I was closing too fast. I triggered a reverse thrust with the jetpack. Not enough. I banged into the ship and rebounded. The controls for the last empty suit vanished from my field. The transport began to rotate. I triggered another push from my jetpack. A little push, enough to stop my rebound and a little more. The transport continued to rotate. I was sweaty inside my suit.

I grazed the surface of the transport. Magnetic soles and palms held me fast. I blew out a loud gust of air into my helmet. I was safe from the gun, if nothing else.

Careful to keep magnetic contact, I worked my way over to the air lock. The outer door was open. The lock was dark. I anchored on the StickStrips in the lock and shined a light on its interior. The inner door was also open.

My gut wanted a weapon in my hand, but all I had was the flash. I moved forward into the ship. The interior picked out by my beam was a virtual copy of the one that had been set as a trap at the antimatter production plant. The pilot-in-command seat was occupied.

I worked my way forward to stand next to the pilot. Her helmet was open. I assumed from the hair I could see that the pilot had been a woman. My light picked out the white-blue-red Russian flag on the shoulder of her suit. The control panels in front of her still showed lights, some of them green. She was long dead, however.

I summarized the situation over the comm for everyone in the spaceplane. "The transport is mostly powered down. I guess that conserved enough power to keep certain systems functioning. I don't know, really, what happened. I'm guessing there was a mission to take over the starship. Something went wrong. Don't know what and don't know where the others went, but the pilot never got picked up. At the end, she set this up as best she could to kill anyone who came here and then she killed herself. Don't know why she didn't dock the transport with the starship."

"I can tell you that," Shane said. "The access codes to the starship are in the spaceplane, and I'm in the system. The docking port is set to refuse connection. That Russian couldn't dock. Wait a sec."

I did, and there was a long pause.

"I've unsealed it," Shane said. "What do you think about me talking you through a dock? That way, we have the transport and its gun out of the way, and you don't need to jetpack to the air lock without a tether."

I almost laughed, but I was able to shut it down before it came out. I had docked a transport with Yong talking me through it. I'd done it three times, in fact, and had figured I could do it myself in a pinch. However, it had been over a year since I had done that and Shane hadn't even done it himself in a lot longer. Naturally, I said, "Sure."

I pulled the dead cosmonaut out of the pilot-in-command chair and belted her into a seat behind to keep her out of the way. I sat down as pilot-in-command and surveyed the screens and panels. That's when I realized what I should have already known. Every label, every readout was in Russian. Talking to the computer on the transport did not help the situation. Obviously.

"Bit of an issue," I said, and explained the language situation to Shane.

"Shouldn't be a problem," he said. "You're going to have your camera on the panels and screens anyway, so I can see them. Our computer will translate."

That was great for Shane, but I was looking through my faceplate, not at the camera feed. I needed the computer output sent back to me so I could see on my field what everything looked like in English. Shane wasn't seeing my side of the problem. Literally.

"Let's give it a try," he said.

"Shane, I need a minute to adjust to switching views." Then I added, "You're rushin' me, y'know," and grinned.

"Was that supposed to be a joke, Leif?" Shane sounded annoyed. "This isn't the time."

People never seemed to think it was time for one of my jokes, but in this case, he may have been right.

"Sorry," I said. "Let's see if we can get this ship oriented toward the dock."

When I had done this before with Yong, the human–human circuit had often been too slow, and Yong and I were accustomed to working together and relying on each other. The way it went with Shane, especially with the additional translation issue, was much too cumbersome. I had the feeling I would have to do the actual docking myself.

First order of business, though, was to get close enough to worry about it. My suit life support wasn't going to last forever. Shane gave me a combination of thruster settings. I tapped them in. Alarms went off.

"Leif! Shift your camera," Shane said. "I can't see where the problem is."

I did, and the translation on my field showed me the problem as he was saying it. "Two thrusters out on the same side."

"You're spinning," Shane said.

I could tell that by watching the stars rotate past. "What now?"

"Try this," Shane said.

Another thruster combination stopped the spin. Pretty much, anyway.

"Let's try to use the main engine to get closer," Shane said.

The previous times with Yong, I had never fired the main engine. I had to hunt around for the controls. When I had them, the engine wouldn't fire.

"Do you want to try chipping in?" Shane asked.

"No. No way. I won't have access rights, and from everything we saw up here about the way those wars went, it's probably rigged to blow up if anyone tries."

"Okay, okay," Shane said. "Take it easy."

Excuse me? Take it easy? There was nothing in my voice but taking it easy.

"I'm going to try to jetpack to the EVA air lock on the starship. You need to bring the spaceplane in close so we can link a tether the way we originally planned."

"If we can't dock the transport, we have to shut it down so it won't fire again as we move in," Shane said. "I can't take a chance with the spaceplane."

That took a little more work. The computers that run spaceships don't have a single on–off button. First, we checked trajectories and made sure the transport was not going to run into the starship. Then we shut it down, piece by piece, until it was totally closed. I went to the open air lock and looked out. The curve of the huge cylinder that was the starship rose before me like a wall.

"Show me where the air lock is," I said to Shane.

On my field, he projected an image of the starship with the air lock highlighted. Naturally, it wasn't in my line of sight. With a few puffs out of the jetpack, I flew across the space in between. Once there, I had to work my way up and around the curve of the ship.

"How are you doing?" Shane asked when I didn't say anything for a while.

"Getting stuffy in here." It wasn't, of course, but I could see my oxygen and carbon dioxide levels on my field along with my pulse, which was up, and my imagination supplied the "stuffy" sensation. I hid the pulse readout. I'd know if it stopped.

The air lock was outlined in brilliant orange. Large touch pads on either side were there to make entry easy for a panicked or hypoxic individual. I put one hand in the center of a touch pad. Nothing happened.

"Hang on," Shane said. "It seems to be locked. I'm checking, and there's no pressure in the lock. This is odd. I'm changing the settings through my access to the ship."

A moment later, the outer door to the air lock slid open. Inside the lock, glued to the StickStrips, were four motionless space-suited figures. A small Russian flag showed on the shoulder of each one.

"What the fuck?" I said.

"Inner door is locked too," Shane said.

"It was a trap," I said. "Another damned trap. They got into the air lock but didn't have a specific access code for the inner door, and the air lock didn't pressurize. Who would expect that in an air lock in space? You're supposed to be able to enter easy and fast. Instead, the inner door locked and then the outer door locked. They were stuck until their air ran out."

"I'm chipped in to the ship," Shane said. "I can release the inner door."

"I need the access too," I said. "I'm not closing the outer door until I'm chipped in and can see the door settings."

"Trusting soul you are." Shane chuckled as the codes appeared on my field.

"I'm not. That's why I'm alive."

CHAPTER TWENTY-FOUR

THE CORRECT ACCESS CODES WERE MAGIC. THE AIR LOCK WENT BACK TO BEING an air lock instead of a diabolical death trap, although I will admit to a moment of tension when the outer door closed and I waited to see if the ship would pump air into the lock. Once the inner door had opened so that I had access to the ship, I wasted no more time going farther in. One starship looks like any other, and I had no time for sightseeing. I needed to arrange the transfer of our crew from the spaceplane.

I left the four dead Russians standing on the StickStrips in the lock. This may have made for a macabre welcome to the ship, but it felt wrong to cycle the air lock and shove them out without any ceremony. I also had no time to take them to a storage bin, and pulling them through the inner door to float in the corridor in zero gee wasn't going to help the situation. We could give them a formal burial in space later.

Our transfer to the ship went smoothly. Shane parked the spaceplane close enough to the lock that I could run a tether from lock to lock. I wanted the Earthbasers across first, in case we had any difficulties, but they adapted to zero gee very well. With the exception of Hannah, they were young and adventurous. I helped them out of their suits, found SureGrip slippers in the locker room for their feet, and then installed them in the caf. Readouts showed ReadyMeals were available, and those things are immortal, so I showed them how to get something to eat and told them not to explore. I took suits back to the spaceplane for our nuclear engineers, Ian and Hope, and did not wait for them to suit up. I turned around and went right back to the ship. I had work to do.

Once out of my suit, the first place I headed was the caf, not to eat but to orient the Earthbase folks. I found them where I had left them. Caleb, No Nonsense, and Hannah were seated at a table, staring up. Sho, not surprisingly, was floating in the air upside down relative to the table, anchored by only a thumb and forefinger grip to the back of a chair. The ReadyMeals were half-eaten and being ignored, but Sho was not the focus of attention.

"This is crazy," No Nonsense said when he saw me come in. "Why are there tables and chairs up there also?" He pointed above his head.

"It's not really up," Sho said. "I could give a little push and I'd float up there and I could sit there, and I'm thinking it would be fun, but what's the point?"

I took a few seconds before answering. It was dawning on me how many things about starships I took for granted that I would have to explain to people who rode horses for transportation. "The ship flies by having the engine push from the back. That force will make it feel like normal gravity in here, so where you're sitting now will be the floor. When we're coming into the other star and need to slow down, the force will go in the other direction, so that—" I pointed above them—"will be the floor. You'll see the same in your quarters. Get used to sleeping with another bed on the ceiling."

"Why not turn the ship around?" Hannah asked. "Seems like that would be easier."

I grinned. "That would mean flipping around a ship traveling at almost the speed of light. Trust me, that's not a simple thing."

Sho laughed and gave herself a little push. She floated to our ceiling, where she stuck to the StickStrips, upside down relative to us. "And what are we supposed to do when the ship does that? Jump from the chairs you three are on to the ones up here?" For the first time since the fighting at Earthbase, her face was relaxed and smiling.

"No," I said. "We'll be in hib, the hibernation units. They adjust to the direction. You'll never notice. Those units also keep you from aging. Most of the reason you don't age is relativity, but the hib keeps the rest down to about one month of aging for each year in hib. You don't need to worry about that either. I'll handle the hibs, and Hannah, I'll show you everything we need to do."

I folded my arms across my chest. I needed to get to work, but I also needed to get them settled and oriented. The ship, as I went over it with them, could be thought of as a fusion-ramjet-powered layer cake, with the flame shooting out the bottom. The top layer—deck—was the bridge.

"The next two decks down are the crew quarters," I said. "This ship was originally designed to carry a colony, so there are rooms for probably two hundred people. You'll have plenty of choice. We'll set them up for you. We have to do that because the doors are designed to open when you look in a little detector and speak, but your eyes and voices aren't in the system yet. That's not a problem, we'll put them in.

"Right now, we're on the deck below those rooms, and the other side of this deck is the gym. That's where you can exercise. You'll feel crappy when you come out of hib. I'll give you a routine for the gym to get you feeling better. The next two decks down are the hib units and the Medical Unit. Below that are storage decks, then the bay that holds the spaceplane, and finally the reactors.

"You don't need to worry about any of those. Now, unless you've got some burning questions, let me find Kwame so we can get you into rooms. Then I'm going down to start checking the hibs and medical. Hannah, you should probably come with me."

·   ·   ·

Before I could take a step toward the exit from the caf, a notification flashed on my field: JOIN ME ON THE BRIDGE. Shane's voice repeated the message over the speakers a moment later.

Even with all of us on the bridge, it wasn't crowded. One of the screens had a starfield with a highlighted yellow circle around one of the stars.

"We haven't done any checking of the systems yet," Shane said. "This was the first thing we wanted to do and we wanted to show all of you now. That's the source of the signal Earthbase picked up. We input the NGL number into the ship's computer, and the ISC database has some information on it."

"How far?" Kwame asked.

"Two hundred thirty-six light-years." It was Magda who answered, her voice soft.

Her words made my gut clench. Any starflight pulled you out of the time you lived in, but this flight out and back was going to last as long as the Western Roman Empire.

"So what else have we got?" I asked quickly, to avoid thinking about the number of years. "Is there something special about it that we knew before the wars?"

"It's a binary system," Shane said.

That surprised me. I could see from the reactions of the starfolk—other than Magda, who had also seen the results—that it surprised them also.

"Binary means 'two,'" Hannah said. "Two what?"

"Two stars in that system," I said. "Does that mean there's a mistake?" I asked Shane. "Is it possible there's a habitable planet there?"

"We can be sure this signal did not come from anywhere else," Magda said. "Well, as sure as we can be about anything, given the state of the equipment we have."

"And there is a planet in the habitable zone," Shane went on. "The system has two G-type stars in a close orbit around their center of mass. The planet is approximately ninety-one percent the mass of Earth, and the database says there's oxygen in the atmosphere. It was intriguing enough that it went on the ISC mission list. It didn't get priority, though, because of the distance. As you know, Leif, your ship and the *Daredevil* had the longest missions. By the time we flew, they only wanted short flights. They even argued it would take us too long to return."

I stared at the screen and wanted to kick something. The whole ISC bureaucracy, for a start. We could have sent a mission to this world. One that would have arrived as emissaries of an interstellar civilization. What a wonder that would have been.

"I wanted all of you here," Shane said, "because this validates our target. We need to get this ship in shape to launch."

.   .   .

BEFORE WE DID ANY FLYING TO THE STARS, WE NEEDED TO BE SURE WE HAD A SHIP that could do it. The crew always carried out a thorough preflight check of the ship's contents and systems—that was part of the checklists the *Invincible* crew kept quizzing themselves on—even after ISC completed their own check and cleared the starshot for launch.

This time we didn't have the benefit of that ISC clearance, although I've always believed that expecting some other group to catch mistakes makes people more careless and increases the likelihood of error. When your life depends on your equipment functioning—from your rifle in the field to your parachute before a jump—you damned well better rely on yourself and pay attention. We had no idea what condition the ship had been left in, and a century in space was not going to improve anything.

Did we have enough food? All of us gathered on the first storage deck for this check. The ship status readings we had checked from the spaceplane when it was in the hangar had shown adequate food present. A readout was one thing, but did the reality match it? If we had nothing more than a few ReadyMeals in the caf, the flight was going to come to an ignominious end.

Those lockers were full! A general sigh of relief went up once that was obvious. The ship had originally been planned to carry a colonizing mission. We had food for two hundred. We could eat our way across the galaxy.

The next question was clothing. This was more nice-to-have than need-to-have; however, all we had with us was what we were wearing when Mario told us to run for the hangar. Without more clothing, we would be a very bedraggled and threadbare bunch of starfolk in front of whatever civilization we met.

We were in luck on this as well. The storage deck held bins full of clothing packages, each package bearing the ISC seal of the suited hand clutching a star and the label CLOTHING ALLOWANCE, ONE PERSON. STARSHIP RANGER along with a size.

The ship's name was the *Ranger*. That brought a smile to my face. It was time for a good omen on this mission.

Inside the packages were standard blue polos, NASA symbol over the left breast, ISC hand clutching a star over the right along with STARSHOT XXIV embroidered under it. I puzzled over the shirts for a moment, trying to figure out what felt wrong. Then I got it. I had always seen individualized polos with the person's name under their agency badge on the left. These had no names, and every polo we looked at had a NASA emblem.

I would never know the truth, but I guessed that at the end of the starflight program, they didn't have a crew selected and politics restricted the ship to Americans. In addition to the polos were pants, underwear, socks, and boots. We were all glad to trade the clothes we were wearing for new ship's clothing. I would say our Earthbasers were pleased with their appearance. Sho, in particular, admired the fit and I saw her showing it off to No Nonsense.

All the time this took brought me to the first critical system that had to be checked: toilets. Our Earthbasers had grown up in a world of outhouses and chamber pots. They had seen flush toilets in the old buildings, but never used one. A zero-gravity toilet was something from another dimension. A starship has both kinds of toilets, of course. When the ship is at one gee, either accelerating or decelerating, we use flush toilets that look and work much like typical toilets on Earth.

This won't do, however, in zero gee. Toilets for that environment are similar to the ones NASA sent up on missions as far back as the early space stations and still used as recently as two or three decades before the Troubles. They all use a flexible tube topped by a funnel for urination and have a small circular seat where you can sit and shit. Sitting properly on one of those is an art form. It takes a little getting used to.

I could talk all I wanted about the mechanics of keeping your feet on the StickStrips and keeping your butt in close contact with the little seat while properly positioning the tube and funnel so that nothing floated away, but a demonstration proved necessary. Sho developed a severe case of the giggles and, for the first time since I had known her, came across as a self-conscious, awkward teenage girl.

In any case, there was an urgency behind the reason I had gone for the toilets right after food and clothing. Discussion and demonstration had to be followed by actual use.

The toilets did not work.

This may sound humorous. It was not. Consider that a starshot basically consists of sealing a bunch of people in a can and flinging it across space for years. Every system in that sealed can has to work properly if the people are going to come out alive, healthy, and happy. *Every system* means more than the oxygen and heat. It means toilets. You can't dump a chamber pot out of an air lock as the ramjet is pushing the ship to the speed of light. (Maybe it would be possible, but it would be inelegant in the extreme.)

I messaged Shane that we had a minor crisis. Then Kwame and I got to work on it. Our plumbing systems, as we found, had developed an air lock. I was able to squeeze into a crawlspace under the decking to reach the piping and clear it. That gave us one working toilet.

"I wonder if each one of these has to be cleared individually, and if the regular toilets are going to have the same problems," I said as we finished up.

"Probably," Kwame answered. "Won't know until we accelerate, though." He chuckled.

Yes, I was glad for plenty of new clothing.

. . .

Having acquired my space explorer's plumbing badge, I took Hannah to the hib decks and the Medical Unit. Fortunately for me, and therefore for all of us, starflight hib hadn't changed much in the sixty-eight EFOR years between the time I had been Prof. Chiang's tech in Miami and the apocalyptic wars that ended our civilization.

The names of the selective telomerase activators, the drugs that slowed aging while we were in hib, were different. New and improved, with supposedly even less bio aging, but they were used the same way, according to the documentation in the system. Same with the hib bath, the nutrition, and the process. The principles were the same, and thankfully, so was the actual machinery of the unit. I read through the details until my eyes were ready to fall out. Again, some good luck. I was used to being Prof. Chiang's guinea pig—or lab rat, if you prefer—so I was accustomed to having the process tinkered with from one time to the next. That's what had led me to design the port that connected to the vessels in your arm. I had needed to make it easy to put myself into hib. I was proud to see that the port with these hibs was almost the same as the original one we used on the *No Name* for the first starshot. Sixty-eight years of starflight, I thought, and they couldn't improve on what I had done. Okay, I got a little carried away with that.

We had plenty of extra hib units for the same reason we had extra rooms. I disassembled one completely, down to the nuts and bolts. Then I put it back together and made sure that it cycled properly. I did that in front of Hannah, explaining everything as I did it. Then I told her to do it while I watched. That startled her so much she actually lost her anchor on the StickStrips and floated for a bit. So I offered to do it again. She wanted a pencil and a pad of paper to make notes, but starships don't have that kind of equipment. I gave her an electronic pad, but she couldn't type and found the electronic stylus clumsy.

"Take your time with this one, Leif," she said. "Go slow. I'll watch you and memorize the damned thing."

In the end, she took apart three units and put them back together. The results of the last one were satisfactory. It's always good to have backup.

After I satisfied myself that the hib units would be okay, my next stop was the Medical Unit. I worried about the meds there—everything from simple antibiotics to fancy biologicals. The fact that half of our crew were now sexagenarians created its own set of missing supplies.

A starship's Medical Unit was designed with young, healthy adults in mind. Starships did not even stock drugs for heart disease or enlarged prostates. Even for the meds we had, none of them had traditional expiration dates on their labels, because a month, day, and year made no sense in the face of relativity. Instead, they were marked as "expected good for twenty years SFOR from the date stamped below." The problem was that those dates were 117 years ago. How could I tell if they would work or even be safe to use? We did have instruments to check drugs that were used for the hibs, like the selective telomerase activators. I knew how to run those tests, and the hib agents passed. For the rest?

"No way to be sure," I told Hannah. "You can check on the screens if a drug turns into something dangerous if it's too old, and those we won't touch." She couldn't chip in, of course, but I showed her how to tap her way through the system on-screen to see the information. "None of this will tell you if they'll work, though."

Hannah held her hand up to stop me. "Maybe there is a way to make a reasonable guess," she said. "We can make some medications at Earthbase. We store everything we can in solid form because solids keep their activity longer than liquids. Not universally, but most of the time. I don't recognize the names of these medicines—almost all of them are strange—but the same principle should apply. If it's liquid, we should assume it's useless unless we can actually test it."

"Thank you. That makes sense," I said. "It fits what I remember about drugs. Let's work on that assumption. Then there's this." I pulled out an ampoule that held a small amount of freeze-dried white powder. "This is the sleeper, the med that puts you to sleep for hib. It's the last one we shoot in before we close the lid. We have to dissolve it right before we use it. According to the checks I ran for the hib meds, it's lost some potency, so I'm not going to exactly follow the directions; I'm going to increase the dose. People can have panic attacks if the lid closes and they're not going to sleep." I showed her how to do it and put a note in the system she could bring up. Of course, if Hannah had to do this herself, we would likely have other problems.

"I've got it," she said, her face set in a grim mask. "We don't really have other choices, do we?"

"No," I said. "I guess that makes some decisions easy."

I didn't worry about expiration on the food we would eat during the awake time. Whether ReadyMeals, Hi-Cal bars, or regular food, it had all been irradiated, vacuum-packed, and stored at the temperature of space. I would bet it was still good—or at least safe to eat—despite the years that had gone by.

·　　·　　·

At the same time Hannah and I went off to immerse ourselves in the hib deck and the Medical Unit, our pilots and engineers began to inspect the rest of the ship. The same type of questions I had about the hib units and medicines, they were asking about the ship's critical systems.

Had we lost fuel for the antimatter rockets to space over time? What would happen when we tried to fire those rockets after they had sat unused for so long? Would the ramscoop field work? Did a century of exposure to radiation in space cause any change to the radiation shielding in our hull? Nobody had ever done anything like we were about to attempt, and there was no one we could ask to run a simulation or even ask for an opinion. Other systems on the ship had their own surprises for us.

"The computer is functional," Shane said when we met in the caf for coffee during a short break. "We've run all the scans we can and a variety of simulations, the type that ought to trigger malware if it's there. The system is clean—at least, as clean as I can tell without actually operating the ship. So, that's good. What's missing, though—"

"What do you mean 'missing'?" I asked. "Are you talking about modules pulled out of consoles and dangling wires?" I have a literal mind sometimes.

"Nothing so melodramatic," Shane said. He sucked at the zero gee nipple on his coffee before he continued. "The database has huge gaps. The technical stuff is there; what we need to operate the ship and navigate. That's all okay. But little else is.

"There are some books and vids in the library, all fiction and mostly old. Nothing from any newsfeeds. No Community at all. I mean, I know there's no Community to connect to, but there's no archive. Most links, damn near all links outside the technical ship operations, are broken. The AI is gone. I don't mean reduced functionality. It's totally gone." He stopped and regarded me with a rueful smile.

"They were afraid of malware and booby traps," I said. "That's consistent with what we've seen from the war years that's still floating out here. Can we fly? Can we do the mission?"

"Yeah." Shane stretched that into the equivalent of two syllables. "This ship was set up for a star mission, and I think the computer still has the capabilities for that. Of course, from what we were told, the plan for the ship was probably to run to a world with a settlement already there, not to make first contact with an alien species. We may not realize we're missing something we need until we need it."

He squeezed his empty coffee flextainer into a ball, and a little remaining coffee sprayed out the nipple and floated off into the caf. "That's how we found the AI, or lack thereof. We figured we'd have it take a shot at translating that message Earthbase got. Well, we can't get the message out of that isolated receiver at Earthbase—didn't think of that beforehand—but we also found there's no AI on the ship."

I thought about that while he went for another coffee.

"That may make speaking to the people on the other end of this trip difficult," I said. "Are any of the crew linguists on the side or quick to pick up other languages?"

"No." Shane shook his head, then stared at his flextainer. "We'll have to rely on the aliens learning English fast. That and we'd better come up with some plausible reason why we're having trouble with their language."

"Great," I said. "Wasn't that the old nasty crack about Americans? That we assumed everyone in the world spoke English? Now it's the universe."

"It may not seem so funny when we meet whoever they are," Shane said. "It's not even that funny now."

He left to go back to the bridge. I got another coffee.

·　　·　　·

THE ONE GROUP OF PEOPLE WHO WERE NOT HARD AT WORK WAS THE THREESOME OF Caleb, No Nonsense, and Sho. There was no work they could do. I gave them a physical training regimen for the gym to keep them busy, which they liked, but there was a limit to how much of the day they could spend at that. No Nonsense and Sho amused themselves sightseeing around the ship. They enjoyed doors that slid open at the touch of a hand or a spoken command, and they were intrigued by screens that lit up in response to a touch, with displays that changed depending on which symbol or box was tapped. I came across them once when they were shoulder to shoulder, with faces almost against the screen, slowly trying to sound out words that referred to nothing in their combined experience. No Nonsense saw my reflection in the screen and turned around, almost losing his adhesion to the Stick-Strips.

"Hi, Leif," he said in the tone of a child caught raiding the kitchen at night. "We didn't do anything. I think." He sighed. "I'm wishing now I had paid more attention when Ma wanted me to work on my reading. I just never thought I'd be anyplace like this."

"Maybe," I said, "when this business is over and we have the time, we'll all work on it together."

"I'd like that, Leif. I really would. Sho would too." A silent nod from Sho confirmed that.

I looked at two eager faces and found myself in a little daydream about what we would do when we returned to Earth. With all the years that would have passed, maybe civilization would have recovered and would have a new starflight program. I could put up a sign: LEIF & SON, EXOPLANETARY SCOUTS. NO PLANET TOO STRANGE. Maybe it should be Leif & Son & Daughter-in-Law. That would be a family of sorts.

Daydreams needed to wait, and I needed to find another pastime for them, since random taps on screens could lead to consequences. I also wanted some release for Caleb, who was spending much of his time sitting morosely in the caf. I think I knew what was bothering him, but if he didn't want to talk about it, I wasn't going to intrude.

I tried showing them the library, even as depleted as Shane said it was, but their marginal literacy ruled out the available books. Most of the vids that were still in the library were of no interest to any of them because they couldn't relate to the settings or the dialogue. What I finally hit on were Westerns. It worked. When they weren't in the gym or eating, they sprawled across the furniture of one room or another, watching fanciful stories of the nineteenth-century American West. Thank God for John Wayne and Clint Eastwood!

I was relating the story of this fortuitous, and fortunate, discovery to Hannah after we pronounced our review of the hibs and the Medical Unit complete. She gave me a funny little smile and held up a hand to stop me. The little bit of smile vanished almost immediately. The work must have been exhausting for her—not only doing the work but having to memorize parts of it because she couldn't easily access it in the system.

"I'm sorry," I said. "I can see you're tired. I should let you get finished and get out of here."

"That's not it," she said. "Can we sit down for a minute so I can talk to you?"

Her voice was as weary as her face. I anchored a chair to one side of a diagnostic bed and sat in it. She did the same on the other side.

"Look," Hannah said, "you've been really nice about teaching me and showing me everything, and I know you could have done this many times faster if you didn't have to take time to teach me what I don't know." She propped her elbows on the diagnostic bed and held her head in her hands.

"Statements like that usually come with a 'but' at the end," I said. "Can you tell me what the problem is? You've gotten a decent grasp of the hib units faster than anybody I've ever seen. And I'm the one thanking you for your insight on which meds to trust. What's wrong?"

"In my experience," she said slowly and carefully, "men don't take that kind of time with a woman, put in that kind of effort, without expecting something in return." She stopped speaking and watched me warily from across the table.

I guess I'm dense. I stared at her for what had to be a minute before the light went on in my head. "Wait a minute. Just wait a minute. You think that in my mind this makes you obligated to have sex with me?"

"It's fairly typical male behavior." The words came out very slowly. Her face was flushed, forehead to chin.

From the heat I felt in my cheeks, I was probably just as red. I grew up in a very straitlaced era, a reaction, or overreaction, to the issues of the early twenty-first century. It is an established fact that I miss all kinds of signals from women. "Are you saying this so that I won't ask, or are you upset that I haven't asked?"

"I'm not interested in relationships or sex. With men."

"I—" I wasn't sure what to say. The truth was that my mind had been so wrapped up for so long in thoughts of Yong and Charity that this had never even occurred to me. I tried to explain that and couldn't get a coherent sentence out.

Finally, I settled for saying, "Can we say that I taught you what I did out of self-interest, because the ship needs a backup to me, that I'm impressed with your work, and we're teammates. Maybe friends. Can we leave it at that?"

"That works for me." She held out a hand across the diagnostic bed and I shook it.

CHAPTER TWENTY-FIVE

Eventually, we had to say we were finished. Ian and Hope believed our engines and the nuclear catalytic cycle in the ramjet would work and that our shielding would keep deep space radiation from frying us. Kwame certified the internal ship systems. I signed off on the hibs. There was no one to check our work. The *Ranger* was as ready to fly as we could make her, and the only thing left to do was try. Shane called a meeting in the caf to announce this and to review the flight plan.

"We're basically ready to start the antimatter rockets and leave Earth orbit," he said. "We're going to monitor all ship functions closely. If anything fails, or even looks like it is going to fail, I'll abort and return us to orbit. If we can fix the problem and we haven't used too much fuel, we'll try again. If not, we do have a fueled and functional spaceplane in the ship's bay. I can take us back to Earthbase in that. No guarantee, of course, but that's what we signed up for. If all goes well, we'll reach six percent cee in three weeks and light the fire on the ramjet. Again, if that doesn't light, we'll abort. However, there is something I want to do first." He paused, looking at his hands resting on the table as if he was uncertain about how his next words would be received. "I want Leif,

Magda, and the nuke engineers awake with me until ramjet ignition. Leif, I'd like you to put the others into hib right away, before we even fire the rockets, and make sure those units function properly."

"Basically, you want to do a live fire test of the hib units on the crew," I said.

"Yes. Like the ship itself, that's the only way we're going to know if they'll work. If you see a problem, wake everybody up and we'll abort. The more time we have to check these units before ramjet ignition, the better."

"It's easier, and there's a lot less risk, if I do this at one gee, not zero gee," I said.

My observation did not make Shane happy. "Maybe easier for you," he said, "but that means I have to use up fuel and take a chance on the rockets before we even know about the hibs."

"Yes, it does." I stopped there and waited. There was a protocol for putting someone into hib in zero gee—there was a protocol for damned near everything—but it added dimensions to a complex undertaking. Hib involved too many liquids, and those behaved better under one gee.

"If Leif can put them in quickly, it should be okay," Magda said.

A look passed between Shane and Magda. He said, "If you can do it in zero gee, that's how I want it. I need to decide on which risks we run, and this is my call."

"Got it," I said. There was nothing else to say. He was in command. "This whole business is a live fire drill. I'll want Dr. Jin to assist with the hib work. Sho, No Nonsense, and Caleb, you three will go first." Shane signaled agreement with a tip of his head. "Good. Might as well get started."

. . .

Before I put anyone into hib, we had one duty left to attend to that I wanted everyone to be awake for: the dead Russians whom we had left in the air lock. We all gathered in front of the air lock inner door, and among

Shane, Magda, and me, we came up with a brief service for them. We didn't know their names or anything about them beyond the fact that, a century ago, they would have been our enemies. The time for that enmity was long past. After the service, I suited up, went into the lock, and detached them from the StickStrips. Then we triggered the outer door and gave them to space.

Everyone was still in the locker room, anchored to StickStrips, and waited as I got out of my suit. They continued to wait while I stowed my suit. I couldn't understand why they were standing there.

Magda cleared her throat. "Leif, you're the oldest of us—well, what I mean is you were born the longest time ago. You lived through the Troubles. You know what people were like when there was fighting, open warfare. So I brought this up while you were in the airlock and all of us thought we should ask you.

"In five years or so, SFOR, we're going to show up in front of some other species. These are creatures who are already reaching out through space to contact others. They are probably more intelligent, more rational, certainly more peaceful than we are. What do you think they're going to make of us?"

I turned to look back at the door to the air lock and thought about the question. "Well," I said finally. "We don't have to tell them the truth."

.   .   .

By the time I made it to the hib deck, Hannah had already activated units for the three who would go in first. I found her standing with a forefinger to her lips, contemplating one of the units as the bath was filling it, the fluid guards for zero gee in place. The materials and testing equipment we would use were laid out on trays. These were zero gee trays with a tacky surface designed to adhere to a strip on each piece of equipment. This was sticky enough to prevent an inadvertent bump from launching instruments into the air while we were working, but not so adhesive as to interfere with our using them.

"Looks daunting, doesn't it?" I asked.

It's not possible to spin around when you're surprised on StickStrips. She partially tangled her feet and laughed softly as she recovered. "In the stories about this, it's so simple. You take your clothes off and get in. Even with all the setup work we were doing, I still have that image in my head."

"It should only be that easy." I gave her a smile. "It is complex to put someone into hib for five years, which is going to be our ship time, especially if you want them to come out of it alive. I thought we would have plenty of time to do dummy runs on the routine and do it under one gee, but Shane wants people in hib right away, so I'll take you through it now.

"The temperature of this bath"—I pointed at the one in front of us, now nearly full—"needs to be as close to freezing as the human body will tolerate. Forget your Goldilocks story! We need to check its composition, from antibacterials to electrolytes, not assume it's fine because we set up the unit properly.

"Same reason, we need to check that the lines supplying nutrition, vitamins, fluids, and oxygen to the port and mask are doing what they should. Then we double-check them. Some of them will be familiar to you from the work we did checking the units. The person going in needs to be checked as well. That, you haven't had any practice at. First, we get some of their blood and check their blood counts and chemistries."

By this point, Hannah had that glazed but determined expression I had seen before. "What do we do if their blood doesn't look right?"

"Good point." I ran a hand through my hair. "In the situation we've got, not much we can do. I mean, we can make some adjustments to what the hib unit infuses, but we certainly can't send anyone back down to Earth and get a replacement."

"Then maybe we can shorten the list."

I liked the way Hannah thought. "I agree with you. Let's run a check on my blood first and see what we get."

I guess the reagents that the instruments used for analyzing our blood didn't last a century. My results were incompatible with life.

"I'd say that settles it," I said as I looked at the string of red flags on the analyzer screen. "I'm going to go with standard doses and concentrations for everything in the hib infusions. Forget any individual adjustments. It ought to be okay, although I might miss something important because of how old our old starfolk are." After staring at the machinery for a few more seconds, I said, "Fuck it. They all have to go. We have no choices. I'm not going to start making guesses at adjustments. We'll be okay, or we won't."

"What's next?"

"Sterility," I said. "People need to do a clean scrub to bring their bacterial counts down to a level the bath can handle. We need to check that and double-check it before they go in. They swallow meds to knock down the bacteria in the gut also. Those were some of the ones we were able to check for potency. And we might as well get started on it if we're skipping the blood work, because the sterility checks always take time. A clean scrub doesn't actually make your skin sterile. We've got to check from multiple places on the body, and the more hair someone has, the more problems you and I could have. That's why starfolk usually cut their hair short starting out."

Hannah ran her fingers through her hair where it came down past her ears.

"Yours will be okay," I said. "Most women I flew with wore their hair that length or even a bit longer. We can manage." Yong wore her hair as short as or shorter than mine. I could see it as I was speaking to Hannah: soft brown hair, every strand in place, almost invisible when she had that hat on. I missed what Hannah said and had to ask her to repeat it.

"I don't know why hair has you staring off into space," she said. "Mine isn't all that remarkable, for sure, and if it needs to come off, it comes off. Our young friends, on the other hand … we need to have a conversation."

Indeed. The beard on No Nonsense was a forest of dense undergrowth. It jutted off his cheeks and chin like a sturdy boot. Caleb's wasn't as bad, but it was still long. Both of them had unruly mops that extended down the backs of their necks to go with the beards. We put a message out on the speakers calling the three of them to the Medical Unit, where I decreed that the beards and hair were coming off. From the arched eyebrows, wide eyes, and open mouths, you would think I was planning to cut something else off and emasculate them. I held out shaving cream and a razor and told them it was that or being shaved with my knife.

Sho was greatly amused by all of this. She giggled and laughed and made jokes. That is, she did until I pointed out that her mass of bouncy curls was going to follow the beards into the disposal. Hannah responded to the horrified and unprintable response by going to the Med Unit and coming back with a clipper. I was thankful she had grabbed the zero gee unit, the one with the suction that pulled in the clipped hairs. She proceeded to give herself a close buzz cut, which was an accomplishment for someone who'd never used an electric clipper before. Then she offered Sho the choice between a short bob or down to the scalp. When we were done, they were a trio of embarrassed, plucked chickens, assuming a plucked chicken can look embarrassed.

"How about that for a 'hair-razing' adventure?" I said to them with a wicked smile.

No one liked my line.

Hannah managed to sit cross-legged in the air over an examining table with her arms folded across her chest and opined that if that was what passed for humor before, she understood why the world had destroyed itself.

I thought it was funny. And clever.

·   ·   ·

THE TIME REQUIRED FOR THE SCRUB AND THE CHECKS PROVIDED A BUFFER BEFORE THEY went in. That proved useful. Sho, No Nonsense, and Caleb had done well facing the high tech of the ship, a totally alien environment for them. However, going into hib meant risking their lives in that tech.

I thought it might be a little intimidating, so Hannah and I gave each of them a close-up tour of the units and let them ask questions before they went in. No Nonsense was tense, I could see that, but he did not ask any questions.

When it was his turn to go in, I asked, "Are you okay with this? It's a lot of electronics and wires. I know that."

"I know I have to do it," No Nonsense said. "I trust you."

"Thank you," I said. "I'll be here when you wake. You won't notice any time between now and then."

   .   .   .

With the three young Earthbasers in hib and the systems working properly, Shane sent a notice by message and speaker that we would be leaving orbit. please make certain you are anchored and also be certain of your orientation relative to the axis of thrust. the ship interior will be returning to one gee, read the notification on my field.

I found myself a seat at a small table in the gym and planted myself there. Other than me, the gym was deserted. I realized only after I sat there that I had been sitting at an almost identical table when the *No Name* launched toward High Noon on the first starshot. This time was different. On the first flight, I was sitting and chatting with Laurence Moreau, who had been the ship's doc when we left the solar system. The wall-mounted monitors had been on then. Those had shown crowds in Beijing's Tiananmen Square, Moscow's Red Square, and the Mall in Washington, all cheering and dancing to celebrate the launch. The monitors in the gym of the *Ranger* were dark. Those three cities were ruined and deserted. The optimism of that first launch was gone. Other than at Earthbase, no one would even know this launch was occurring. Even at Earthbase, they would not know it was happening now, and most would not care. The only sign in the gym that anything was going on was a window in one of the otherwise dark monitors counting down the minutes and seconds to our departure.

"Ignition sequence started." Shane's voice came across the comm channel.

Would the rockets fire? I wondered. Would they explode? Did I care?

"Ten, nine," Shane counted off the final seconds over the comm.

I remembered Yong doing the final countdown in Chinese. I wished that I were hearing her voice saying those unfamiliar words again.

"Ignition," Shane said.

I heard the familiar hum through the ship of the antimatter rockets. Weight returned. They had fired and had not exploded.

"We are leaving orbit," Shane said.

I don't need a blow-by-blow description, I thought. It's pretty obvious. I sat and watched the counter on the monitor, now showing time since ignition. It had reached eight minutes and thirty-two seconds when my isolation was broken by Hannah Jin.

"You can be a hard man to find. Mind if I join you?" She was already in the chair. "It actually feels weird to have weight and be walking normally again."

"Were you looking for me to ask me about that?"

"No." She ran her hands over the stubble that was left of her hair, then placed the palms down on the table. "I wanted to ask if you were okay."

"Huh?" That pulled me away from the monitor and its timer. "Of course I'm okay. Why would you ask that?"

"I'm worried that you're depressed. So I wanted to ask how you are feeling and also if something is bothering you."

"Depressed? Why would you think that? Because I wasn't chasing after you to have sex, even though that's not something you wanted?"

Calm brown eyes held mine in a mutual gaze. "No. Although lack of interest in sex can be a symptom. However, you've hardly been eating. You're practically living on coffee. You look exhausted all the time, and I'll bet you're not sleeping much, because there are times when we're working together, you're repeating things you've already told me, or not paying attention. And you're making snide remarks for no reason."

"And you're putting this together and thinking I'm depressed?"

Her eyes were still on me. "I am a doctor, you know. I may not have all the training or understanding of the medications from before, but I do know about patients. Something is troubling you, and it's not the risk we are taking on this flight."

Yes, she was a doctor. I knew that *doctor* tone in her voice. That didn't mean she was right. "Hannah, I'm not depressed. I don't get depressed. If I'm short on meals and sleep, it's because we've got a lot to do and no margin of error. And I've had plenty of comments in the past about my sense of humor. Does that address your concern?"

"No. It really doesn't." She pushed her chair back from the table and stood up. "Leif, you're important to this expedition, more than you realize, I think. I know what you did at Earthbase; I've heard No Nonsense talk about what you've done before. You're good under pressure and in strange situations. We need that. But something is eating at you. I'd like to help with whatever it is, but that only works if you want me to. Just remember that I'm here. As a teammate and friend, if you don't want a doctor."

I sat in the gym for several more minutes after she left. The last thing I needed in the middle of all of this was for Dr. Hannah Jin to be putting diagnoses on me. Depression! This was ridiculous. I had too much to do to even think about that.

.   .   .

THE ROCKETS DID PERFORM PROPERLY. THEY PUSHED THE *RANGER* AWAY FROM EARTH and toward the outskirts of the solar system. Hannah and I put Kwame into hib a few days after we left orbit, so that gave us four functioning hibs, one of which contained a man in his biological sixties.

I spent my time watching the readouts from those hib units, praying that everything stayed within normal limits. Around the orbit of Saturn, Magda made a private call to ask about the hib units.

"They're fine," I said. "All four of our crew look good and Kwame's readouts are as good as the others."

"Good. Listen, Shane is on a rest break, so I am pilot-in-command. I want you to know that I'm disabling the abort sequence that's tied to hib failure."

"Why are you doing that? It's all fine now, but we've got a long way to go, and six of us aren't in hib yet."

"You had a death in hib on Starshot One. We've all studied that case. How the computer triggered a mission abort." Her voice was terse.

I hadn't studied it. I had lived it. Yong had overridden the abort and I had worked out what had happened so that the mission continued. "That wasn't a hib failure, not really," I told her. "The unit was fine."

"Exactly my point," Magda said. "Except for you and the Earth-basers, we're all on the elderly side. Nobody our bio ages has ever flown before, and it's going to be five years SFOR in hib. I know my medical condition, in particular. If something happens to one of us, it happens. We're not aborting."

Yong would have approved of her attitude. "Just do me a favor, Magda. If something does happen, it can't be both you and Shane. I can fly a transport ship with thrusters. I don't have my starship pilot's license yet." I tried to leave her with a chuckle.

I kept an even closer watch on the hib units after that. I may have skipped some additional meals in the process, and I had the impression that Hannah was keeping a watch on me.

·   ·   ·

Aside from the hours on the hib deck, I kept mostly to myself, which wasn't hard with so few awake. The pilots and nuclear engineers had plenty of their own work, and I knew Hannah wasn't looking for male companionship, so there was no reason for me to spend time with her. I thought a lot about Yong, about how I missed her. I had wanted to fly the universe with her forever, but I had lost her. When I was alone, I could sometimes feel her presence. I could imagine that I would go to the bridge and see her in the pilot-in-command chair. I knew it was dangerous to dwell on those thoughts, but I indulged in them anyway. Indulged might be the wrong word. Wallowed may be better.

I also thought about Charity and her kids. Those thoughts had a bitterness that thoughts of Yong did not. I had accepted that what happened to Yong was neither my fault nor my doing. Leaving Charity and the family had been entirely my choice. I would have to live with that.

I was recycling those thoughts one morning in the caf, having one in a series of coffees—it might have been my fourth or fifth, not that my conversation with Hannah had me keeping count—when a message popped up on my field. PLEASE COME TO THE BRIDGE. I read it, deleted it, and finished my coffee before I moved. It gave me another few minutes to think about what I had lost and what I had given up.

Shane, Magda, Hope, and Ian were there when I arrived. Pilots and nuclear engineers.

"We've reached six percent cee," Shane said. "I need a final word on the hibs."

"Working fine to this point," I said.

"Got it." Shane turned back to his control panels and spent a few minutes inputting commands.

The low background hum I associated with the antimatter rockets died away. I felt a little drop in my stomach, then a thump, and then my weight felt normal again.

"The fire is lit," Shane said with satisfaction. "We're running on ramjet."

I nodded. When Yong did it, the transition had been smoother. "Let's talk about the rest of us getting into hib. Ian and Hope, Hannah and I will put you in next. Then Hannah, and I'll do Magda and then you, Shane. I go last and put myself in." That was a perfectly reasonable sequence. It also ensured that Hannah and I would not be the last two awake.

·　　·　　·

WHEN THE OTHERS WERE ALL TAKEN CARE OF, THE LID ON SHANE'S UNIT CLOSED, AND the lights on all the units green, I could have put myself in right away. I've done that drill so often it's almost automatic. I should have done it, but I held off. I went back up to the caf instead.

I've been the only person awake on a starship before. It's a spooky sensation. It's not totally quiet, of course. The machinery of the ship makes noises. There are no human sounds, however, and it's different from being up in the middle of the night when everyone else is asleep. When everyone else is in hib, no one else *can* get up. No intrusion is possible.

You feel totally alone, and knowing that you're sitting in a thin-walled can in the middle of infinite nowhere, being propelled by the flame out of a fusion ramjet, you feel very insignificant and vulnerable. I wanted to let that wash over me for a little while and continue my daydreams about flying with Yong. I wanted to feel her hand resting on mine. I wanted to hear her voice.

It didn't work. My mind couldn't conjure up Yong's ghost. Instead, my thoughts went elsewhere, to Charity and a houseful of kids.

I shook myself and ordered my mind to shut down all the recriminations. I marched myself back to the hib deck, my sense of purpose reasserting itself. I had made the choices I had made. I had done what I had done. No possibility of doing it any differently existed. I had only one way to go, and that was forward. We had a mission, and we were going to carry it out.

Humanity was headed back to the stars. We were on our way to meet other intelligent beings whose civilization was probably more advanced than ours. I wondered if this would be the first time such a meeting had happened in the history of the universe.

I thought about the meaning of such an event, the downright magnificence of it. I thought about how we were going to this appointment with fate and found myself laughing. It was a long, loud laugh and it drowned out the faint hum of the hib units around me. Yes, we were on our way to this momentous meeting. We were headed there in a ship that had been mothballed in space for over a century. Its computer had been lobotomized and had a severe memory deficit. The toilets were clogged. Our pilot-in-command needed cataract surgery. Our geriatric crew were doing their jobs by rote, and our youthful crew could barely read.

What could possibly go wrong?

HELL
AD 2489, EFOR

PART III

Look on my Works, ye Mighty, and despair!
Nothing beside remains. Round the decay
Of that colossal Wreck, boundless and bare
The lone and level sands stretch far away.

Percy Bysshe Shelley, "Ozymandias"

CHAPTER TWENTY-SIX

SAT IN THE COPILOT'S CHAIR, ALONE ON THE BRIDGE. AS THE PERSON IN CHARGE OF the hib deck, I had set my unit to wake me first. On the screen labeled FORE, a bright yellowish star shone in the center of the starfield, brighter than all the others. Our target.

At the current magnification, it was a single point of light not resolved into the components of the binary. That didn't matter. It was only an image. What did matter to me was that the stars looked like normal stars. Without looking at any of the instruments, that told me the *Ranger* had successfully switched the ramscoop field from funneling interstellar hydrogen into the ramjet to braking. The fusion ramjet had been shut off.

If that changeover had not worked, we would be pushing ever closer to cee. The stars ahead of us would be shifted to blue light and would appear condensed into a tight cluster. I had seen that once. With what Shane had said about the state of the ship's computer, I hadn't entirely trusted that it would work properly until I saw the starfield.

My hand, where it rested on the console next to a half-eaten energy bar, shook slightly. I had come directly from my first post-hib workout in the gym and the quivering in my muscles wasn't limited to my hand. I should have gone to my quarters and taken a nap, but I had to see the starfield before I could think of closing my eyes.

I think the only reason I had managed to have my sugared OJ, energy bar, and the start of my workout before rushing to see the stars was that it had taken that long for the thought of the critical ramscoop shift to braking to penetrate my post-hib blur, a dense fog in the brain that always accompanied coming out of hib.

I watched the little tremor in my hand, felt the aches in every muscle and the pain in my right knee, and I had to grin. It was at the memory of the way Hollywood had portrayed star travelers, back when there was a Hollywood to make vids. Starfolk would bound lithely out of their hib units, certain body parts discreetly out of view—my era—or full frontal—New Golden Age—and dash off to save the universe from some catastrophe. Hah! I had to laugh, even though it hurt my ribs and my belly.

Forget lithe and forget dashing anywhere. You hobbled when you came out of hib, muscles quaking as they tried to hold your weight, and you prayed you would make it to the bathroom without leaving a puddle on the deck. While you were in that bathroom, you prayed the laxative pack would work, as your bowels tried to shit out the brick wall that constipation from years of hib had built. Throughout the whole experience, you fought the post-hib blur that constipated your brain and turned simple arithmetic into a challenge. There was nothing heroic about coming out of hib.

My solution to the problem of emerging from multiyear starflight hib had been a graduated set of workouts along with careful stretching. Those routines were agony in themselves, but they did speed the return of muscles to normal and they helped with the blur. Interspersing workouts with naps was best. Nothing helped the constipation, though, except the laxatives. That and prayer.

I told myself that since the universe looked normal, I should return to my workout routine. Before I got out of the chair, I glanced at the chronometer: AD 2489 EFOR. I struggled to remember our mission plan, such as it was. The date seemed correct. More thoughts spilled through my head. I saw Charity in her rocker after dinner, Elvy and the other kids grouped around her, listening to a story. At that date on Earth, they would be so long gone that not even their descendants would remember them. Had I stayed on Earth with them, my life would be over, too, but maybe it would have been a better life.

Stop that thinking! You know better.

I pried myself out of the chair, stood, and tested my knee. In the brief time I had sat on the bridge, the joint had stiffened again. Pain shot through it as I tried to flex it. Every time I came out of hib, that knee was worse than the time before. What was it going to be like bringing my geriatric crew out of hib? I wanted to feel normal and have a clear mind before I tried that. Back to the gym.

.   .   .

I WOKE SHANE NEXT. HE CAME AWAKE EASILY ENOUGH, BUT WALKING TURNED OUT to be problematic. I helped support him from the hib deck to the caf, where I took time getting calories and protein into him. He knew the workout plan, as it had become part of the starflight mission protocol, but I worked with him through the first couple of sets. We had to reduce the number of repetitions and the weight he was lifting.

That experience made me decide to wake Hannah after Shane. She came out of hib as well as I did—I would say as well as I did on my first flight. After one day of recovery, she was in shape to help, and I was glad of it when we woke Magda.

Magda's condition was fine as far as the monitoring system was concerned. All lights were green. However, when the bath drained, she did not sit up.

"I can't," she said. "I don't know what it is. Everything feels fused. I've got no strength. Any part of me I try to move, the pain is ten out of ten."

I suppose it would be better if hib units were designed so that a person could be slid out of them. As it is, the side of the unit comes up to the sternum of someone standing next to it. We had to lean over the side and scoop her out of the unit, and we had to have Hannah stand on a supply crate to help because she was so short.

Once we had Magda out of there, Hannah toweled her off and we dressed her in ship clothing. She gasped in pain almost every time we had to move her, apologized over and over for complaining, and bit down on her lip hard enough to draw blood. We could move her limbs. They weren't fused; her joints hurt and she was weak. We gave her sugared OJ and then I carried her to her room. There was no question of going to the gym.

"I'll stay with her and try some warm compresses for now," Hannah said as she positioned Magda in bed. "Then I'll start some passive stretching."

"We can also try some of the old-style anti-inflammatory pills," I said. "I'll bring them from the Med Unit. Then I'd better talk to Shane. It may be best to wait another day before we try to wake anybody else."

I found Shane on the bridge, seated in the pilot-in-command chair. His right elbow was braced on the console, that hand cupping his head. He gave no sign that he had noticed my entrance.

"How's it going?" I asked.

"What?" He pulled his head back from his hand and swiveled to face me. From the grimace on his face, his sinuses might have been bothering him.

"I asked how it's going." I pointed to the FORE screen. "I mean, I don't see three ranks of space cruisers firing missiles at us, so I guess it could be worse."

He eyed me, his face cold. "Leif, your sense of humor leaves a lot to be desired."

I smiled. "I think you've told me that before, and I may have heard it from one or two others over the years."

"I wish you had listened to them." Shane grunted and turned back to the screens. "You can see our target resolved into the components of the binary." He increased the magnification and I saw two yellow dots, side by side. "Parameters match what's in the database. Stellar masses are about equal; they rotate around the center of mass with a semi-major axis of 0.19 AU. The planet is where it's supposed to be. Circumbinary, about 1.1 AU from the center of mass. The measurements confirm the estimate in the database of surface gravity about 90 percent of Earth's. Can't confirm the atmosphere composition yet."

"Are we receiving anything?"

Shane slumped in his chair. "There's plenty of activity on radio frequencies coming from the planet. Most of it's weak and we can't decipher any of it, but it's there, and it has to be a product of civilization, not some natural phenomenon. There's also a repeating broadcast from the planet, like a beacon. I used the frequency it's on and sent the first contact signal that ISC put together, never mind how many years ago, in case a ship came on another civilization. It has pictures of us, a key to English, voice recording, math. The beacon signal stopped almost immediately, allowing for distance and time to the planet. What's come back since is like the signal we picked up at Earthbase. Naturally, we can't decipher it with no AI."

"Great." I stared at the twin dots. I wished we were ready to make orbit around the planet already. I wished we were in orbit. "We can't understand them, because our computer was partially disabled from fear of a malware takeover, and for some reason, they can't figure us out either. Is it possible they're at a stage where they have the ability to beam signals to other stars but never developed the computing ability to decode signals that would be alien to them?"

"Doesn't seem reasonable, does it?" Shane stretched in his seat. "My blur has cleared enough that I know it's the situation that doesn't make sense, not my thinking." He turned back to me. "I'll send our signal again and see if anything changes. If not, maybe we wait until we're in orbit and can get a good look at the surface. I'll be sharper with more time out of hib." He paused and rubbed his chin. "You know, I hadn't realized that the torture routine in the gym was your invention."

I took a bow. "Came up with it on Starshot One when we had a problem and I had to figure a way to be functional fast. It does get you loosened up and helps the blur fade."

"Being broken on the rack might produce the same loosening, and

I think it's the pain that breaks through the blur. This was much worse than coming out of hib on the *Invincible*."

"My impression is that each flight I've taken has been a bit worse than the one before," I said. "Of course, each starshot has been farther, too, so even with the time slowing, the SFOR time in hib has been a bit longer. Maybe I don't want to try flying across the galaxy." I laughed, but he didn't. "More importantly, you aged thirty-three years at Earthbase."

"Yeah. Starflight is for the young." He paused again and watched my face. "How's Magda? That routine is only good if you can use the gym."

"Not so good." I gave him a brief rundown on her condition. "Hannah is working with her. The Med Unit inventory doesn't have the right drugs, although even if it did, they probably wouldn't be good anymore. I'm trying old anti-inflammatory stuff. She has to loosen up sooner or later."

"I hope so," Shane said. "She has rheumatoid arthritis." I nodded. "It got really bad over the last ten years or so, and there wasn't anything we could do about it. It's in her family. I guess inflamed joints don't do well in starflight hib. It's not something anyone would have thought of."

I was accustomed to having things happen that no one thought of and having to deal with them. "I'm going to space out the wake-up cycles for the rest of your old crew. Won't start Kwame until tomorrow and then at least a day between each so we can work with them. I'll wake our young scouts last. There's nothing for them to do until and unless we go down to the surface, and they should recover fast."

"Makes sense," Shane said.

.   .   .

OF THE REMAINING THREE FROM THE *INVINCIBLE*, ONLY HOPE BLANCO CAME OUT OF hib with no more than the usual difficulty. Hannah spent days doing physical therapy with Magda to bring her to the point that she could hobble around the ship. Three people had frozen shoulders. One was

Magda, which was not really a surprise. She would do better, I figured, when we were in zero gee, but we were still decelerating and would be for a while. The others were Kwame and Ian, both of whom I thought were in good shape for their bio ages. However, it turned out that both of them had torn rotator cuffs playing sports in college (football and rugby). One had had surgery, the other not, but both were now stuck trying futilely and in pain to mobilize their arms. Granted, those sports injuries were not recent, but I had to wonder if they had something to do with why the shoulders froze up in hib.

Their problem sent me into an unexpected spiral. I could not help thinking about what would have happened to my knee if my old and lost dream of flying the universe forever with Yong had been able to come true. That started me thinking about Yong again, and that led, in a quick segue, to thoughts of Charity. Once I started down that path, I couldn't get off it. We needed to work on those shoulders, but I needed some time to myself. I had to clear my head, but it didn't want to clear. This wasn't post-hib blur. I didn't want to think, couldn't find the motivation to do anything.

My personal pity party ended with a banging on the door to my quarters the next morning. I wasn't still *in* bed. I was sitting *on* the bed, which, in the dubious interest of honesty, was where I had ended up when my thoughts had turned into an endless loop. "What is it and who is it?" I yelled without getting up. "Why are you pounding on the door?"

"How else am I going to get you?" It was Hannah. Of course. We had no phones and she didn't have a chip to chip in with. Once back on the *Ranger*, I had reverted to my old expectations. "Is something wrong with you?"

"I'm fine. Nothing's wrong."

"Got it!" she yelled through the door. "If it's the same problem that you don't want to talk about because it isn't a problem, I understand, but I don't have time for you to be feeling sorry for yourself and not talk about it. We have patients to take care of."

That got me pissed off, and that was enough to get me off my bunk.

I think Hannah understood me better than I wanted to believe, and she certainly understood which buttons to push. I was grateful she was around. Most of the time.

Our three patients were seated in the Med Unit, waiting for us. Kwame was rubbing his sore shoulder with one hand, Ian was rigid upright in his chair, and Magda kept shifting around, trying to find a comfortable position.

"I've worked with them on stretching and exercises," Hannah said. "They know how to do them on their own, and I can keep working with them and adjusting them."

"But that doesn't solve the problem," Ian said abruptly. "She told us this can take months to resolve, and we don't have that kind of time. We have to be fully functional by the time we make contact, certainly by the time we make orbit, and that means I have to be able to use this arm. Kwame's in the same boat. Magda can get by with limited mobility, we can't. She can't get it done." He pointed at Hannah and thrust his chin forward to add emphasis.

I was immediately sorry for the time I had wasted in my room. "First things first," I said. "This," I indicated Hannah, "is Dr. Jin. Hannah is also okay. 'She' is not. Do we all understand the word 'respect'?"

Ian gave a one-shouldered shrug. "Yeah."

"The correct answer is 'Yes, sir.'" I was in no mood for bullshit, and seven years of army was coming through. "Now we're going to see what we can do, but while we do that, you're going to behave properly."

I fixed him with a glare that lasted until he said, "Yes, sir."

After that, I started searching through the Med Unit database. Frozen shoulders happen after shoulder injuries when the shoulder is immobile for too long. For a crew exploring the unknown, it was a good assumption that the Medical Unit would be prepared for this problem. In fact, during the New Golden Age, a drug had been developed precisely to loosen up the shoulder capsule. Our ship had it. The packaging came with a quick analytic test and readout so that the doc could be sure the drug was potent. Every vial in our unit was dead. It makes sense that drugs with a potency check built into the packaging don't age well, but it was discouraging nevertheless.

One way to release a frozen shoulder is surgery, and we had surgi-bots. That's not a procedure a paramedic is trained to do, however, and Hannah couldn't use a surgi-bot.

"That's not the issue here," Hannah said. "I'm a good enough surgeon on my own, and I've done this procedure a few times. However, recovery can still take months. I don't think that's what we want."

It wasn't. What I could do with a surgi-bot was a steroid injection, which according to our limited database was a quicker approach to solving the problem. The unit had plenty of powdered steroid that I could use to make up the injections. Unfortunately, when I powered up the surgi-bot, I found it was a new model. At least it was new relative to the year I'd left Earth in the *Dauntless*. The interface and controls were different from the model I had been trained on. I chipped in and searched for the manual and a demonstration vid. I came up with a broken link and a message: REMOVED DUE TO POTENTIAL INFECTION.

"Okay." I held up a needle and syringe. "I'll put the anatomy and a description up on the screens, and we'll do the injections ourselves.

"I'm comfortable with that," Hannah said. She smiled at Ian.

Ian's face was now a study in fright. I would say he deserved whatever was coming. It all went smoothly, however.

.   .   .

I WAITED TO WAKE OUR THREE YOUNGSTERS FROM EARTHBASE—AND THEY DID recover from hib very rapidly and had even regrown much of their hair—so we could spend more time reconditioning our elderly crew, at least to as good a physical condition as possible. As good as possible was far from perfect. While Ian recovered full motion in his shoulder without any pain, Kwane continued to be limited. He could not raise his arm above the shoulder. He was able to do his work on the ship, particularly once the deceleration stopped and we were in zero gee again, but we ruled him out for any trip to the surface, even with the expected lower gravity there. Magda's arthritis was worse than it had been on Earth. Although she made some progress with her strength and mobility, she hit a plateau after a week or so. She was fine on the ship, where she could chip in and most controls needed only a tap for physical effort.

"Magda's not going to be able to manage the spaceplane," Shane told me as he prepared the course change that would take us into orbit around the planet. "Assuming we're going to go down to meet these whatever-they-ares, I'll have to take the spaceplane. We have fuel for two trips, and it will have to be me for both, if we do that."

"Maybe they'll have enough medical sophistication to help with this, even though I'm an alien species to them," Magda said. "We can ask when we make contact."

I know wishful thinking when I hear it. I could also think of a different problem with that approach. "I would think very carefully about asking for anything like that," I said from where I was standing behind Shane's pilot-in-command chair. "One of the arguments for making this trip, if you remember, was to project the image of a competent star-faring people. Do we really want to show up begging for help?"

"It's a question." Magda took her eyes from the screens to look at me. "We don't have to beg. You're letting your military macho interfere with your thinking. We can say we've had some unanticipated issues due to aging on the flight. They contacted us over two centuries ago. It's not unreasonable to think they're advanced enough to solve it."

"Which gets into the question of why half the crew is so old," I replied. "Which starts getting into other issues we don't want to discuss. I don't care about looking macho. There is a risk in looking weak in a totally unknown situation. We still don't have a real reply to *our* signals, and I don't like the way they're acting."

"You're assuming they even think the way we do," Shane said. He leaned back in his chair, his work done for the moment. "In fact, the little information we've got says they probably don't. We've sent the

ISC greeting and friendship message three times now. Each time we send it, we get the same signal back. If you factor in the time for our signal to reach the planet and for their signal to reach us, they are responding almost immediately. They know we're here. Yet this is all we get. If a starship showed up in our solar system, this isn't the way *we* would act. What they are doing makes sense to them, so they think differently."

"We'll find out when we make orbit," Magda said. "This will have to resolve itself at that point, and I'm betting they turn out to be helpful."

"I hope you're right," I said. "Because if we make orbit without mutual communication and they think like we do, what they will send up is likely to be a missile."

Shane gave me one of his stares.

I stared back. "I wasn't joking."

CHAPTER TWENTY-SEVEN

"I NEED EVERYONE ON THE BRIDGE." SHANE'S VOICE CAME OVER THE PHYSICAL speakers in addition to the notification that popped up on my field. "You all should all see this together." I wasn't imagining the strain I heard in his voice.

I don't think it took more than two minutes before the entire crew of the *Ranger* was on the bridge, anchored to the StickStrips. We congregated close behind the pilot-in-command and copilot seats occupied by Shane and Magda. Neither of them spoke until all of us were present.

The large screen showed a hemisphere of the planet below as white clouds and blue oceans, landmasses in ocher, brown, rust, and some green. The green was mostly along coasts. Small areas of bright light—it had to be electric light—shone against the night on the dark side. Above the upper limb of the planet's curve were two partially merged circles of yellow light as one of the stars began to pass behind the other. It was beautiful; it was strange. It was a bit eerie.

"Okay," Shane said after the silence on the bridge had reached the point of being suffocating. "I'm going to show you images of a large island; it's really more of a subcontinent. I'm not going to say anything until you've had a chance to look."

The image on the screen was replaced by one of a landmass all in various hues of brown and surrounded by ocean. Then the screen began to show close-ups of various parts of the land. A collective gasp went up from the crew. I know I contributed to it.

What we saw were craters. Craters and obvious blast zones. Craters inside other craters. Craters on top of the walls of older craters. Craters everywhere. Magda tapped at her control panel and other parts of the globe came on-screen. When those were magnified, we saw more craters and more blast zones.

"Oh my God," Kwame said. "This is worse than what we saw when we came back to Earth. Much worse."

"Wait. Wait." Hope had both hands up. "Is it possible that this is natural? That somehow this planet was hit by a shower of meteors? Could that be?"

"No," Shane said. "There is radiation associated with many of the craters. Different levels. As though what was in one place had been blown up, rebuilt in another place, and blown up again. Maybe more than one or two times; I can't be sure. Look at these." High-magnification images popped up as windows and filled the ship's screens. Some showed built-up areas around small blast circles. "These could represent enhanced radiation release warheads that left minimal structural damage in some places. I don't know." Other images showed destroyed areas that had been partially rebuilt and then destroyed again.

"When did this happen?" Hope asked.

"Again, I don't know," Shane said. "Our computer has no AI capability. It's too limited in general. The best I can do with the computer capability we've got is come up with an estimate based on weathering around some of the bigger craters. Some of this goes back more than a thousand years; much farther back."

My eyes were on the screen, but I could hear the rustle of people moving and SureGrip soles going off and then back onto StickStrips. The question, "What?" came from multiple voices.

"That's long before they sent the first signal Earthbase picked up," Hope said. "How is that possible? How could they have blown themselves up first and *then* sent an interstellar signal? And how is anyone even alive down there?"

"No answers," Shane said. "Not yet. What we can tell is that there is still a technological civilization down there. You can see the lights."

"I don't know if I'm ready to call that civilization," I said. "Between what we did on Earth and what we're seeing here, I'm starting to wonder if intelligence is an adverse marker for the survival of a species. Maybe intelligence is actually an evolutionary dead end." I paused to look at craters on the subcontinent, a land with no signs of life. "You said there's a technological civilization still there. Where is the signal coming from? Is someone sending it, or did the last person to die forget to turn off the lights?"

"I don't think we need the sarcasm right now," Shane said.

"I wasn't being sarcastic. What's the story with the signal?"

Shane shook his head and blew out a long breath. "The source is here." The image on the screen shifted to show a different continent and zoomed in on two long, arcing bays on either side of a peninsula. A flashing red triangle was superimposed on the shoreline. "At least, the signal that's responding to our ship is coming only from this spot, but it doesn't have the power that would let us pick it up on Earth with the equipment we had. The interstellar signal could have been sent from someplace else."

The coastal region was green on both sides of the marker. Inland stretched the same shades of brown we had seen on the subcontinent, albeit with fewer craters.

"There is a city at the marker," Shane said. He increased the magnification and I could see structures tucked up close to where mountains separated a coastal plain from the cratered brown lands.

"There's a wall around it," I said. "Looks more like a fortress. A fortified city, anyway."

"Yeah," Shane said. "There are others, also sending emissions on radio frequencies. I'm going to show you areas along the coast, away from this city on either side. Tell me what you think."

The screen windowed in two. I saw zigzag scars across the green, running from shore to the mountains inland.

"Trench lines," I said. "Defense in depth."

"I was afraid you were going to say that," Shane said.

I scrutinized the images carefully. "I'd say something is camouflaged behind those lines. Can't tell what. Maybe they still have air capability, but I'll bet not a whole lot, and they're probably not throwing missiles at each other anymore. But somehow, they're still fighting."

"Yeah," said Shane.

"What does this mean for us?" Hannah asked.

"I don't know," Shane said.

CHAPTER TWENTY-EIGHT

WE REASSEMBLED IN THE CAF A COUPLE OF HOURS LATER, BECAUSE WHILE Shane's *I don't know* might have finished the conversation on the bridge, it wasn't a plan for what to do next. The old crew loosely sat or floated around one of the tables. Caleb, No Nonsense, Sho, and Hannah took seats at the table, not because they didn't enjoy flying around in zero gee but because this was a serious discussion, and their upbringings were that one sat properly at a table for a serious discussion. I stood on the StickStrips by a wall monitor that showed the source of the signal.

The scene in the caf reminded me of the one on the *Dauntless* after Yong had shown us images of the destruction on Earth. We had left the bridge and gathered in the caf then, as well, when we hatched our ill-fated plan. The similarity ended there, however.

On the *Dauntless*, the destruction in the solar system had shaken all of us, hit us at our emotional core. Those feelings were missing now. Yes, what had happened here was bad—awful, really—but it hadn't happened to *us*. It felt like times I'd been through with my old platoon. The mission was a fubar, the mission plan was out the window, and it was up to us to figure out what to do next.

"So, now what?" Hannah asked the question we were all thinking. "We're not going to meet some great, advanced civilization. We don't need to bluff them about how great we are. They're not going to help us here or in rebuilding Earth."

"What it means is this whole expedition has been useless," Ian said. "We could have ignored the signal, and it wouldn't have made any difference."

"Are you trying to say we should just go home?" Hannah asked.

"We can't do that," I said. That drew all the faces to me, where I stood at the wall. "We can't go home, because we don't have a home to go to. All of you from the *Invincible* should know that. The four of you who grew up at Earthbase, we talked about it before we left. Now it's real. Maybe I'm the one who really understands because I've been out to the stars twice before and the voyage to Heaven was the longest until this one." I made a point of looking into each set of eyes in turn. "Whatever we do now, by the time we return to Earth, 472 years EFOR will have passed since we left. I don't know what we'll find there. I will guarantee it won't be anything that feels like home. For anyone who was at Earthbase when we left, we might as well have died. All of them are dead now. Relativity is a one-way time machine."

"What are you getting at, Leif?" Shane sounded testy. "Speaking for the *Invincible* crew, one of the reasons to make this voyage was that we would come back to a different time. Ian, you had agreed on that too. This voyage hasn't been useless. We've learned about the situation here, and Earth will have changed when we return. Leif, we understand the relativity time-machine analogy. It works for us. This is mission accomplished."

"And what if we go back to Earth and it's like … this?" I pointed at the screen on the wall. Hannah had her stoic look in place, but Sho, Caleb, and No Nonsense were grim-faced.

Shane looked not at me but at his *Invincible* crew. "Sure, there's some risk it could be worse than when we left, but what we had there wasn't so great."

Yeah. I had more in common with the four from Earthbase. I had given up a home. It would be gone. It was already gone.

I searched for words, again felt like I was leading a squad in an action when everything had gone to shit. "We came here to find out what that signal meant. Why it was sent. To make first contact with another intelligent species. That was the mission we accepted. This is not mission accomplished. Not yet."

"We know what we need to know," Shane said. "They blew themselves up. Worse than we did. Whatever was in that signal doesn't matter anymore. What matters is that we can go back to an Earth that will have changed from what we left."

"Wait." I pointed at Shane. "From what you said about the age of some of those craters, they were already blowing themselves up when the signal was sent."

Shane took a moment to digest that. "Are you trying to say they want to send refugees? Or maybe warn us of an invasion? That doesn't make sense. You don't wait four and a half centuries for an answer. Not in the middle of a war that is destroying your planet. If they were going to do either of those things, they would have simply shown up at Earth."

"You mean like we did here?" Magda said. "They're likely to think we're hostile."

"I think we've already learned what we need to know," Kwame said.

"Goddammit! Wait a minute!" Hannah broke into the conversation. Startled faces all around the table turned to her. Her voice was harsh, her eyes blazing. "Are you saying you don't care what was in their message or why they sent it? You're not even curious? There will be somebody back at Earth when we get back, and it doesn't matter who they are. What are we going to tell them? That we took Earth's last starship and came all this way and couldn't be bothered to finish the job?"

Magda and Kwame flushed and turned away.

"Hannah's right," Sho said. "We have to finish what we started."

Shane snapped, "You are a seventeen-year-old girl. What do you know about any of this?"

"I am a seventeen-year-old girl and I run toward trouble. Not away from it."

That had the *Invincible* crew looking at their hands, at the table, anyplace except at Sho.

"All right," Shane said without looking at anyone. "What are you suggesting we do?"

"What we came for. What Leif said," Sho told him. "We know where the signal comes from. Let's go down there and find the answers."

"My sister is right," Caleb said. "I'm with her."

"Me too," said No Nonsense.

"Please stop this," Shane said. He had his hands on his head as though it were about to split. "You don't know what you're talking about. The three of you are nothing more than children. This isn't the Empty Lands or even the states east of the Mississippi. This is another planet around another star—two of them, in fact. None of you is trained for this."

"I am," I said. Hannah's words, her vehemence, had broken through the lassitude gumming up my mind. With all I had given up to be here, I wasn't leaving without answers either. "They are my team and they are right. We are going to complete the mission."

"You can't go down there," Kwame said. "We need you for the hibs."

"All the more reason to wait for me to get back," I said.

I saw red on faces. Lips pressed together on some of them and jaws bunched on others. I didn't care.

"I can't land the spaceplane near that city." Shane enlarged the image on the monitor and walked over to where I was standing. "The land along the coast looks like farms and buildings. There is no place to put down a spaceplane. Even if there were, everything we see says this is a war zone. We don't even know what they use for weapons. We can't take that kind of chance."

Yong would have found a way to land us there. But I didn't have Yong.

I blocked out the voices that babbled over one another at the table and scrutinized the image. I had studied aerial recon photos of plenty of sites, and I had done it in situations where my life, and the lives of my teammates, depended on how well I understood the information those photos conveyed. The fortress—city, if that's what it was—that the signal emanated from was on a promontory from which the two broad, scalloped bays stretched away on either side. The mountains and the brown interior behind them came down close to the water where the city stood. In fact, the city took up almost all the remaining space between the mountains and the shore. It was almost as if the city and its walls had been constructed to back up to the cliffs.

That would make sense if one was designing a defensive position, and from the looks of the shattered world below us, the inhabitants had plenty of reason to do that. The coastal plain, where Shane claimed he couldn't land, only broadened out and turned green outside the city walls and a distance away. I wished I had a drone that could give us a different angle, instead of only the overhead view of a satellite. No use wishing for what I couldn't have.

"Shane, I need this section enlarged." I stepped next to the image and traced a rough rectangle in the air with my fingers that took in a portion of the city wall, a dark brown band of ground behind and past the wall, and then some of the ocher interior beyond that.

The image zoomed, blurred, and then sharpened again. A thin line of lighter brown stood out against the dark brown band.

"Enlarge more. Then pan the image from coast to the interior." Again I used my fingers to define the area I wanted.

After Shane did that, I was certain it was not my imagination.

"Here." I tapped my finger on the screen on top of the light brown line. "This is a trail. Maybe a road. If you put up sections from the coast to the interior, you can see that it runs from this interior region down to the land the city sits on and not very far from the city wall." As the image shifted, I traced the line for everyone. "Now look at where it goes through a pass and ends in the interior. Enlarge again."

When I had the magnification where I wanted it, I stabbed my finger at a gray object that was the interior terminus of the light brown track. It was an octagonal structure.

"This is not a natural feature," I said. "Each side is a perfectly straight line, all the same length. All the angles are the same. Given everything else we've seen, I'd guess this is a redoubt guarding the pass and the road to the coast. Call it the Octagon. I don't see weapon emplacements, but that may be because they're underground or because the weapons here look very different. Doesn't matter. If we can't land on the coast, we can land up here and go down to the coast."

Shane rubbed at his facial tattoos, shaking his head. "If I bring the spaceplane down and you're sure there are weapons that you're not seeing, why don't you think they would use those weapons and shoot us down?"

"I think it would be obvious we're alien. Why should they shoot before even trying to talk? If a flying saucer suddenly showed up at Earthbase, we wouldn't start off by opening fire."

"Are you sure of that?" Kwame asked. "Mario wouldn't, maybe, but if some of those Greens or Reds were in charge … who knows."

"Maybe whoever lives here would shoot first," Shane said. "I mean, the only thing we know about them is that they've blown up their world."

"And we haven't?" Magda put in.

Everyone started talking at once. Sho looked at me with eyes that asked me to do something.

"Enough!" I said loudly to overwhelm the jabber around the table. "We're here to make contact, and that's what we are going to do. There are no guarantees, but I'm going down in that spaceplane."

"Well, we can't land where you're pointing at anyway," Shane said.

"Why not?"

"Look." He panned the view around the area of the redoubt. "There are ruins here. That's probably what these are. Look at the shadow patterns. Now look between the ruins and the structure. The ground is irregular and slopes up toward this Octagon of yours. At the bottom of the slope are the ruins, and they're extensive. Leaving aside whatever the reaction of the natives in that structure might be, we can't land a spaceplane near it."

"Is there any place you think you can land the spaceplane, Shane, that's a little closer than Earthbase?"

"Goddammit! If you weren't—"

"If I wasn't what?" I cut him off. "Find me an LZ, Shane. Find me an LZ, and then we'll plan it from there."

"We'll find a place to land," Magda said. "Just give us a few minutes. We should go back to the bridge and use the screens there. The resolution is better, and we can have more windows."

The change of venue didn't shut off the argument. We went back and forth over more potential locations than I can remember. Every one of them had some apparent unevenness or possible ruins, or something that could pose a risk to the spaceplane. Finally, Magda found an area that looked flatter than the Bonneville Salt Flats. Shane was still grumbling that there could be issues on the ground that we couldn't pick up from space, but Magda shut him down.

"This area will do," she said. "If I were cleared to fly, I would take it down here. If you feel that strongly, we can call this an emergency that overrides my fitness issue and I'll do it."

"No, no," Shane said, his hands up in front of his face. "There's no need for that. I can do it. But the place you've picked is too far from Leif's target."

Magda turned to me. "Leif? Your call."

I checked the grid superimposed on the image, then backed off the magnification so I could see all the way to the Octagon. "This ship carries an exploratory rover. Correct?"

"Yes, of course," Magda said.

"Yeah," I continued, "it's not ideal, but we can do it in the rover. I make it about three planetary days from the LZ to the target. A day here is about twenty-five hours. What are we expecting for conditions on the surface?"

"Pretty extreme in that area," Kwame said. "Hot during the day when both suns are in the sky. Modest temperature drops when one of them eclipses the other, and subfreezing at night. That barren surface will lose heat fast."

"Do we need suits?" I asked.

"I don't think so," Kwame answered. "It's an oxy-nitrogen atmosphere, almost identical ratio to Earth. Carbon dioxide is a bit low, if anything. Atmospheric pressure at the proposed landing site is equivalent to a mile up on Earth, say like in what used to be Denver."

"But you don't know for sure it's breathable," Shane said. "Could be allergens, trace gases we haven't detected. We're not set up to make a full habitability check, and it's not like we can ask them."

"I can do a lot of that work once we're down," Kwame said. "I'll suit up to do it."

"If your initial assessment at the LZ is okay, we'll just take chances on what we can't check," I added. I had played guinea pig on High Noon, and I wasn't concerned about doing it again here. I think my perception of risk had changed a bit over time. "We can sleep in the rover if it's cold at night. Not comfortable, but acceptable for three days."

"You don't have phones, though," Shane said.

"I've noticed," I said. My temper was starting to fray. "The Vikings managed to sail to North America without them, if I remember correctly. An exploratory rover will have a built-in phone that can connect to the ship. Power comes from the engine and the photovoltaic skin. Should be good even after a century. We'll test all of that before we go. We can put a small hab at the LZ with an uplink to the ship as a backup. Once we make contact, we'll figure how to connect if we have to leave the rover. Now we need to pull our gear together and plan out how we're doing this—not come up with one argument after another *not* to do it."

"I'm not objecting," Shane said, "just pointing out what we need to consider. Is anyone going in the rover with Leif, or is this a solo expedition? The rover can hold a maximum of six."

"We are, obviously." That came from Caleb, Sho, and No Nonsense all at the same time.

No surprise there, I thought. This was their adventure. They were young, fit, and accustomed to coping without fancy tech. They weren't my old squad, but there was no reason I needed a bunch of battle-hardened soldiers.

"I'll go down to the landing site," Kwame said. "You'll need me to run the checks on the surface. But my arm still isn't very good. I won't go farther than that."

"Do you need me?" Hannah asked. "I'll go if you want."

I considered that offer, but not for too long. Hannah was neither as fit as the others nor as familiar with living rough. She was volunteering because she thought it was her duty.

"No," I said. "I'm comfortable dealing with injuries in the field in case anything happens, and I have a lot of experience doing it. I'm not comfortable leaving the ship without a doctor."

The away team was set. Now we had to make it happen.

CHAPTER TWENTY-NINE

READYING THE SPACEPLANE FOR THE DESCENT WAS A SIMPLER JOB THAN PICKING the LZ. All the spaceplane systems had lit up green before we left Earth orbit, and it had passed the simulation checks we were able to run. Our recheck now showed that nothing had changed. Of course, the true test was going to be when we took it out of the bay and tried to land it on the planet in real life. There was no point worrying about that in advance. We had done what we could do.

I may have felt that way, but to my eyes, Shane looked a lot tenser than any pilot had a right to be. Yong never looked tense, no matter what crisis was blowing up around us. The only way I could ever spot any tension in her was her occasional tug at two fingers, or when we were both chipped in and her chip gave away a rise in her pulse rate. I tried to talk to Shane, but he blew me off.

"We're landing on an alien world that seems bent on suicide," he said. "I have no idea what the surrounding area is really like or what traps might be there that we can't see."

"The LZ and the area around it look like the emptiest desert I've seen," I said.

"The operative words are 'look like,'" he responded. "I need to make sure this ancient spaceplane is in perfect working order, and that's what I'm doing. I would think you have a checklist to work through yourself, instead of bugging me and wasting my time."

I considered that the mental state of the pilot was on my checklist, but saying that to Shane would not have been useful. Instead, I bent Magda's ear about it, since she was our copilot.

"I'm sure what happened at Earthbase is still in his mind," she said. "The runway hadn't been maintained, and a block of concrete had heaved up. That's how the landing turned into a crash. He talked about it for years. He's going to check everything three times and want perfection. He knows we're very alone out here."

I have no problem with checking three times or wanting perfection. "I've been very alone with no possibility of help," I said. "I've also been in situations when people were actively trying to kill me. It's the way he looks that bothers me. Little stuff. In his face, in his posture."

Magda gave me a wry grin. "Yes, you were a soldier. An elite unit too. All your pilots on Starshot One were ex-military, but we moved away from that as a standard in the New Golden Age. Shane was never in the military, but he'll be fine. He was picked as pilot-in-command of the *Invincible* because he's good."

When I didn't immediately smile and say that made me feel better, she said, "Look, I'd be happy to fly the spaceplane, but the way my hands are …" She held them up in front of her. I could have seen the swollen joints and lumps at her wrists from across the room. "Now the shoulder is bad too. I shouldn't be cleared to fly. Never mind who is making that decision." She winced. "The neck isn't too good either." The wince was replaced with a quick smile. "Shane will be fine once you get going."

Nothing she said made me feel more confident; however, standing around bitching never improved a situation. I mumbled a thank-you and went off to check what we would need on the ground.

The *Ranger* had originally been built for a colonizing expedition, and its spaceplane was appropriate for that purpose. The ship was huge, even bigger than the one the *Dauntless* carried. It was far more ship than we needed for an exploratory mission. Most of its cargo area, however, was empty.

I guess the flow of money to the ISC had dried up after the ship was built, but before all the supplies needed for a colony had been stocked. Shortly after that, reality would have set in at Earthbase. There would be no more starshots; the Powers were putting all their resources back into their armies. The *Ranger* would have swung in orbit, partially stocked, until it was obvious the apocalypse was coming and the Earthbase leaders wanted an escape hatch.

They made sure the *Ranger* was ready to fly, but the story was they wanted to flee to an existing colony, not try to start a new one. A lot of inventory wouldn't have been necessary. By the time those leaders decided on the *Ranger* as their emergency exit, they may not have had the capability to make trips to the ship to add supplies to what it already carried. I thought of Magda's comment and smiled. Yes, I was going to personally triple-check what I would want on the surface against what we had, but I intended to be in good humor and whistle while I worked.

The rover the spaceplane carried was in good shape. Its surface was covered with a skin of photovoltaic cells so that the light from the twin suns would keep the battery charged. The battery itself had been disconnected and the connectors were stored separately. Once I located them in the bay, I found No Nonsense and had him help me install the battery. We might be in zero gee, but some parts had to be moved in order to get the battery connected, and they had substantial mass. It was clumsy moving the pieces around.

"No problems with electricity now?" I asked No Nonsense with a smile. "Sho's cured it?"

He grinned broadly enough to show through his partially regrown beard. "I've flown in a starship, Leif. I'm an actual starman. Maybe I'll bring luck back with me, like the stories everybody used to believe. This"—he whacked the battery—"is nothing." Then his expression changed and his eyes narrowed. "Stuff I said about wires and electricity, you know, back at the farm, stuff from the past you warned us not to talk about anymore, that all seems silly. Like it was somebody else who felt that way or said those things. You haven't … you won't tell Sho any of that … will you?"

"I actually forgot all of it," I said with a laugh. "Don't worry."

"Thanks," he said. "Look, Leif, would you do something for me?" He floated and twisted in the air so that he was facing the rover.

"Name it," I said.

"Could you show me how the electronics work on this? I mean, what controls what and what it will do. I want to show it to Sho."

"Sure. Why don't you bring her down and I can go over it with both of you together?"

"Uh, Leif …" From his voice I thought he was turning red, even though I couldn't see it because he was still facing away. "I'd like to be able to show it to her myself."

"Ah." I got the point. No Nonsense was a nice guy, a good guy. I daydreamed, briefly, again about our return to Earth, a different Earth than we had left. Maybe there would be no renewed space program to need exoplanetary scouts, but there should still be places on Earth for adventuring. No Nonsense would be a good companion. He would bring Sho, and she was all right too. Maybe Caleb would come. He was okay; he only needed to quit looking worried. The Three Musketeers and D'Artagnan had been a family, in a way. We could be as well. I refocused on the rover. "Why don't we do a quick tutorial now?"

·   ·   ·

AFTER I FINISHED WITH NO NONSENSE AND HE LEFT, I CHECKED ALL THE CONNECtions myself anyway and then checked the current flow. I shut it all down, left it for a day, and checked it again. It worked. I repeated the shutdown and checked over another two days. It still worked. In between those checks, I went over the motors that powered each wheel, checked the air filtration system, the comm link to the *Ranger*, and the internal controls.

Somewhere in that sequence, No Nonsense brought Sho to the

rover and went over with her what I had shown him. I made sure I was not around while they were there together,

When I was done with all my work, I pulled up the official checklist for the rover and ran through that while having No Nonsense and Sho sit in the bay, each one checking me as I did the work. I had to go through the words on each item with them instead of leaving them to read the list, but they listened closely and repeated back verbatim what was being checked. I guess when you can't rely on reading, you pay very close attention to what you are told. If the two of them had sat any closer together, the fabric of their ship's pants and polo would have been squeezed into a thin film, but they did check me in duplicate.

At the end, I figured the rover was as good as it could be without taking it for a test drive on the planet. I set about stocking it for the trip. I estimated three days to the octagonal redoubt, three days back, and then doubled everything in case we took the rover down the trail to the city. Again, No Nonsense and Sho double- and triple-checked my tallies. Finally, I stored the ammunition and the M8cs in the rover. I included the illegal bullets Mario had given me. If I needed to blow a hole in someone, it was going to be a big hole. No earthly laws of war were going to matter if I needed to use one of the rifles here.

     ·   ·   ·

IT TOOK US SEVERAL DAYS TO COMPLETE ALL THE CHECKS AND RECHECKS AND REACH the stage where I was satisfied that we were ready to go. Left to himself, I'm not sure Shane would ever have reached that point, but faced with a united front of me, Magda, and Kwame, he declared that we were cleared to attempt the landing. Throughout this period, we received no communication from the surface. As a last step before we launched, we sent our message one more time. Once again, there was an almost immediate transmission from the same city as before. Again, whatever it said, the contents were unchanged.

"It's almost like an auto-reply," I said. "You know, 'Your call is very important to us. Please hold."'

Shane glared at me. Actually, they all glared at me except for the four Earthbasers, who could not know the reference.

"While you're trying to be funny," Shane said, "the situation on the planet is deteriorating. Look at this."

He brought up images of our target city and the coastal plain on each side. Cloud cover blocked the view in places, but on the western coast, where we had seen trench lines, a haze hung over the lines. The line farthest west was partially obliterated; the ground looked cratered, and there were multiple sprays of dark earth.

"Somebody tried to assault those lines," I said. "They held, though. Whoever tried, retreated."

"Yeah. But look on the ocean." The view shifted. Far out from the coast, there were ships on the water.

Somehow, I doubted those boats were there for a fishing contest.

"Setting up a blockade or an invasion," Shane said. "Going down there is looking riskier by the day. Maybe too risky."

"I'm not discounting the risk," I said. "But I would say this makes it even more imperative we go now. That city is where the signal is coming from; the only place a signal is coming from. If that place falls, we may lose any chance of finding someone here to talk to and any chance of learning about the original transmission."

"You could be driving into a city under assault," Shane said.

"Shane, I'm doing the driving. Not you."

He reddened, and I saw his eyes dart from face to face around the room. "As you say, you're doing the driving," he said slowly. "However, I'm not going to take a chance on these hostilities expanding or on us becoming a target. Once you drive off, I'm bringing the spaceplane back up to the *Ranger*. When you return to the landing site, I'll come back down and get you. We're going to need this spaceplane to land on Earth at the end of all of this. With the size of the spaceplane and the little mass it will carry compared to a fully loaded one for a colony, there will be adequate fuel for the landing on Earth even after two landings here. Doing it this way is a lot safer than sitting on the landing site like a big, fat target."

I thought there was a mountain range and a lot of desert between what was happening at the coast and our LZ, but I decided that this would be a bad time to point it out. "Good enough," I said. "Let's get going."

CHAPTER THIRTY

SINCE EVERYTHING WE NEEDED HAD ALREADY BEEN LOADED, WE WENT DIRECTLY from the argument to the spaceplane bay and up the ramps to the craft. I asked Shane if he wanted me to strap into the vacant copilot seat in the cockpit. He didn't exactly slam the cockpit door in my face, but I can take a hint and retreated to the passenger cabin. No Nonsense and Sho sat glued together. That is, they had adjoining seats at the front on one side. Caleb and Kwame sat next to each other in the front seats on the other side. I walked all the way to the rear and took a window seat. I doubt anyone who scripted humanity's ambassadors on their way to first contact with another intelligent species had ever imagined this.

Magda's voice came over the comm channel. "You are go for departure."

"Depressurizing bay," Shane said.

I repressed an urge to chip into the spaceplane system and peek at Shane's pulse and blood pressure. He probably had them blocked anyway.

It was quiet for a few minutes. Then the spaceplane shuddered, and its structure groaned as the wing and landing gear clamps released. I felt a slight push into my seat as Shane used the attitude thrusters to lift us out of the bay. Through the window by my seat, I could see the open bay doors as we rose past them. The brightly lit bay was below, with black, star-speckled sky above. The stars swung past the window as Shane oriented the spaceplane for the rocket deceleration that would take us out of orbit. I caught a glimpse of the world below and the boundary between night and day down there. It crossed my mind that this might be where I left my bones. Then the shutters slid closed and blocked the view.

"All systems are go," Shane said.

"Cleared for atmospheric entry," Magda replied.

A hard shove pushed me deep into the seat as the rockets fired. We fell toward the ground, a cloud of flame beyond the shuttered window. If they had air defenses, we had to have lit up every system on the planet. We might well look like a missile on reentry. They had, obviously, plenty of experience with those. Would we even know an interceptor was coming before it hit us?

The fireball outside dissipated, and the shielding over the windows retracted as our velocity slowed. We were intact. So far. The sky was dark, although the stars were gone. Gradually, the blue lightened. Clouds met us and we fell through them toward the land below. I searched through the window for the contrail of a missile fired at us. When I didn't see one, my mind insisted that was because I could only see to one side. The missile was on the other side, or at our tail, or coming straight on our nose. I sat there unmoving, externally peaceful, for multiple hour-long minutes.

We dropped lower, until we were almost skimming the surface. I wiggled in my seat to try to loosen my muscles. We were not going to be shot down.

The land I saw through the window looked empty. I couldn't believe anyone was even there to see us. In some areas, the ground rose and fell in lines: squares and rectangles, circles and smooth areas. Structures, or remnants of structures, were there under the otherwise featureless surface. Then even those features vanished. The land was a vast pan of salt.

"Brace for landing," came Shane's voice.

I watched as we dropped the last few feet. A jarring shudder rocked the cabin when our landing skids hit. I heard a bang as the final parachutes deployed and then a roar as the engines helped to brake. The friction skids bit into the ground. I could feel the vibration of the spaceplane through my seat. Outside my window, the ground stopped sliding past.

"We have landed," Shane said. "Kwame, set up your habitability tests. Nobody goes through the air lock except in a suit, and on suit systems, until we have clearance from the testing."

I got out of my seat to give Kwame a hand. I had been through a first landing on a strange world and, having been a lab tech in the past, could follow directions for setting up scientific equipment. I could see his shoulder was bothering him, and working beat sitting in my seat with nothing to do.

We pulled two planetside suits out of the spaceplane locker. These weren't pressurized space suits; they were more like hazmat suits with a sealed helmet and life-support systems. I helped Kwame into his suit and then carried most of the equipment through the air lock and down the ramp to the surface, where we set it up.

"It's pretty basic," Kwame said. He worked with some of the instruments while telling me how to handle others. "I think a few hours will provide what we need. That will give us an analysis of any trace gases or aerosols that might be a problem. We'll also see if there are any microorganisms floating in the air that might be a problem for us to inhale. I'd like to do a large organism biotest for a twenty-four-hour period, but we can't do that."

"What do you mean by that?" I asked.

He laughed. "Fancy name for putting out a cage of rodents and letting them sit out here for a day and see if anything happens. It's a last check, in case we've somehow missed something lethal. If the tests are negative and the mice are okay, we assume we will be okay, at least for being outside and breathing the air. Unfortunately, after more than a century of storage, the embryos wouldn't grow. No mice."

"So, we'll be the lab rats," I said. "I'm familiar with that role."

Kwame laughed again. Then we went back into the spaceplane to wait.

It took until the next morning, because by the time the instruments had enough data, the suns had set. Not only was it night but the temperature outside plummeted to nearly freezing. I couldn't think of any reason to start unloading the rover in the cold. It was pitch dark too. I couldn't see a spark of light anywhere on that desert until the first of the planet's two moons rose. Well, if there was one thing army life had taught me, it was to sleep when you had the chance. I reclined my seat and was out before they shut off the ceiling lights.

Kwame was outside by himself at first light, checking to see what his filters had captured and examining the readouts on the instruments. I watched on-screen as he trudged back up the ramp.

"We should be fine," he said when he was standing in the corridor of the spaceplane, his suit still on but his helmet off. "It's not a guarantee, but it's the best we can do with the time and equipment we have."

"Thanks," I said. "Has it at least warmed up?"

"Some. Still a bit chilly."

"Okay. My turn."

I walked into the spaceplane's air lock and closed the inner door. Then I opened the outer hatch and walked down the ramp to the ground clad only in my ship's polo and pants. I had been the first to remove my helmet after our landing on High Noon, but that had been a typical spur-of-the-moment Leif move. This time, it was a considered decision. Kwame had done the best he could; we would have no greater surety. Ahead of us, we still had the journey to the Octagon, the city beyond, and hopefully, the trip back. We weren't going to be able to do that in those suits.

From the moment we agreed on the LZ, I had known at some level of my consciousness that it would come down to this. As I had said to Kwame, we would need to be the lab rats. More specifically, me. Rangers lead the way, like it says on my shoulder.

The air did hold some of the night's chill. It also held an electric tingle, as though there had been a thunder-and-lightning storm, but there was no humidity, and the sky had not even a fragment of a cloud. In the distance, over a far mountain range, I could see the twin suns, each one above a separate peak. The sands stretched away, twinkling and sparkling in the light and absolutely barren. It was an eldritch scene.

Footsteps sounded on the ramp behind me, then crunched into the sand on both sides of me. Caleb, No Nonsense, and Sho had joined me.

"It didn't seem right to sit up in that plane and wait to see if you were going to die," No Nonsense said.

"What No Nonsense means is that we're all going together. However it goes," Sho said.

"I will say," Caleb added, "that the Empty Lands never looked this empty, and I've been riding across them for years."

I bent down and scooped up a handful of dirt. It was loose and pebbly. Mixed in were tiny, hard grains. Those were brownish and translucent.

"This is what's catching the light," I said. "Like glass of some kind."

"How does that get made here?" No Nonsense asked.

"I don't know," I said. "Really high heat on sand would do it. Some kind of thermobaric weapon, maybe, and then different explosive weapons later to pulverize it."

"My God," Caleb said. "What did they do to this world?"

"We know what they did to this world," I said. "I want to know why they contacted ours, and I want to see what kind of beings they are. Then I'm going to pray that when we return to Earth, we don't find that we've done the same. Let's get the rover unloaded and get started."

CHAPTER THIRTY-ONE

W E HAD ONE MORE CHORE BEFORE WE SET OUT ON OUR JOURNEY. WE
put up a small hab to shelter a transmitter that could
connect to the *Ranger*. This shouldn't have been necessary.
However, Shane was adamant about returning the spaceplane to the
Ranger while we were on the mission to the city. I guessed that having
become comfortable with landing the spaceplane on that site, he could
focus on his anxiety about the turmoil on the planet. I thought that; I
didn't say it.

The communication system and antenna in the rover were
adequate to reach the orbiting starship and alert the crew that we had
returned and were waiting for pickup. However, the risk I wasn't going
to take was that the old equipment in the rover might have a failure,
which would leave us trying to scratch letters in the desert sand to
tell the *Ranger* to send the spaceplane. I wanted a backup plan. The
other transmitter was just as old as the rover's, but one of them ought
to work. Having a hab there would shelter the transmitter from the
elements and increase the likelihood that it would continue to work.

The bots that we should have been able to use to construct the hab
were missing from the spaceplane. They had probably never been put

on board. Our young Earthbasers, however, had no problems with the lift and carry work to bring all the materials out. On a planet with only 90 percent of Earth's gravity, our Earth-bred-muscles were more than up to the task. The positioning of the materials went quickly. After that, it was simple. The hab was designed for self-assembly, and Kwame and I were able to set up the transmitter. Aside from stashing some food and water, we didn't bother with any other interior components. This was the hab version of a shack.

"All right, then," I said to Shane as we stood by the rover, "we will be in constant contact until we reach the Octagon. From there, if we do go to the city, we may have interruptions until we get back, either if we lose line of sight or get involved with locals. Comm failure in the rover—well, that's why we've got this." I pointed to the new hab. "Worst case, we'll head back here and signal."

"Good luck with the contact." Shane held out his hand and I shook it.

"Thanks." I gave him a little grin. "I'll try not to start a war."

He didn't laugh. "I don't think we need to worry about that."

The rover behaved fine as I drove it away from the LZ. The barren plain was featureless on all sides, save for the tread marks we left behind us. As we drove, one sun moved behind the other. The light dropped noticeably and the wind picked up enough to push loose granules around. Those began to fill in our tracks. It wouldn't take too long before there was no evidence we had been there.

Caleb sat up front with me and watched what I was doing. I gave him a running commentary, as though I were preparing him to be my backup. Sho and No Nonsense sat in back. I think they were holding hands. That made me smile, and I told myself not to make it obvious when I took a look.

Night fell before we reached any of the rectilinear formations. Two moons rose overhead, bathing the plain in a ghostly white light. I doubted there was anything living on that sand that could bother us; nevertheless, we reclined our seats and slept in the rover. It was cold outside anyway.

We were up with the suns and resumed our drive. After a couple of hours, I saw the first of the formations rise in the distance. From ground level, it did look like a low wall ahead of us. I brought up the images of the area that we had taken from space and let the rover's nav system plot the most direct route to the Octagon through the gaps and passages.

The formations came up to about half the height of the rover. The sand covered them and fell down their sides in an arc to the floor of the passage where I drove the rover through. In some places, I could see a hard grayish material in the formations where sand had fallen away or blown free.

"These do look like walls, or what's left of them," Caleb said. "Do you think this used to be a city?"

"All the ruins I've seen from before are full of junk," No Nonsense said. "Even where it was all built up and paved, there was junk and plants growing over it. There's nothing here. Not even any bones."

"We don't know how deep this gravelly sand is," I said. "Maybe it's all buried and we're driving over the top of it. Maybe here, bricks and stones do hide the bones."

I was rewarded with three nervous laughs. If this was the partially buried skeleton of an old city, it was a spooky place to be.

"Hi, Leif," Magda's voice came out of the rover's comm. "There's a funny landmark not far from the route you're taking. It could be worth a few minutes to drive by and see what it is."

"Sure," I said. "We're not doing anything more interesting than a walk through a corn maze now. What are you looking at?"

"It's a curved area that's free of the lines, what you're calling low walls. From the shadows, it's raised above ground level. Past it on both sides, the ground slopes away, facing in the direction of the Octagon. Beyond that is an open area, flat plain like where we landed, and then the lines begin again."

"Okay," I said. "We'll take a look."

The line on our nav system shifted. I steered the rover through the warren of mostly buried walls so we followed that line, although it was impossible to tell from looking out the windows that our direction had changed. One passage between walls was identical to every other one.

We passed an intersection, again unremarkable, and suddenly, the ground in front of us was open. Indeed there was a low rise ahead of us, with blond sand on top and more open land to either side. I stopped the rover to look at it. Featureless. I decided it would be a bad idea to drive over the top of it, so I steered to the side, past where the rise began.

Just as Magda had said, the ground fell away in a steep slope in front of us. The rover slid as much as it rolled down the loose sand and gravel, making me think that we might need a different route back. The land leveled out again. In the distance, as Magda had described, I could see the low walls start again. I drove out onto the flats and turned the rover to have a look at the other side of the rise. What I saw made me hit the brakes suddenly enough to snap our heads forward.

The rise was, in fact, a half dome. An arc of dark gray material, the same as had been exposed in some of the walls, rose maybe thirty feet from the sand in front and supported the sand on top. The side of the half dome we were facing was open, and in the opening, illuminated by the rays of the twin suns that slanted in and sheltered from the sands by the dome, was a statue.

"We've got to get a look at this!"

I was out the door of the rover before I had finished speaking, the others fractions of a second behind me. It was a slog to the front of the opening, with our boots sinking a half inch into the sand with each step. Then we stood and stared up at the figure, which was a good twenty feet tall and mounted on a pedestal.

"What is that?" Sho's voice was pitched low. Were it not for the dead silence around us, she might not have been audible.

"Not what," Caleb said. "Who?"

"Yeah," I said. "That's who used to live here."

At first glance, the figure suggested a bird, with a crest of feathers across the top of its head that definitely grew from the head and was not a headdress. The face tapered forward like a bird's, too, with etchings on the surface suggesting feathers. The eyes were binocular, however, and the flattened nose and mouth, open as if in a howl and showing omnivore teeth, resembled a primate. Broad shoulders below a short neck upheld a flowing robe and reinforced the primate concept; however, the arms ended in hands that had three long fingers forward and one to the rear, again similar to a bird, although the nails were blunt. The right hand brandished a long tube that had odd protuberances and a grip. I took that as a weapon, and I would bet it was a weapon that fired something, although what or how I couldn't tell. Incongruously, two tiny feathered wings projected up behind the shoulders. They were far too small to lift a figure that size into the air. Thick thighs tapered rapidly to thin, tubular lower legs, each ending in a booted foot. Perhaps a gloved foot would be more accurate. As with the hands, each foot had three long toes forward and one to the rear. The toes of the right foot circled around the neck of a similar figure that was prostrate on the ground, its face being smashed into sculptured rocks.

"Are they giants here?" Sho asked. Her head was tipped back to look up at the head of the figure.

"I don't think so," I said. "Look at the proportions of the figure. I think if they were really that size, the legs would need to be shorter, or at least thicker at the bottom. Anyway, some of our images from orbit show what are probably these beings outside in and around that city. We can't see any kind of detail, certainly not like this, but I doubt they're any bigger than we are."

"But what's it here for?" No Nonsense asked. "Why put this here?"

I turned around to look in the direction the statue was facing. "There are more of these ruins in the direction where we're headed. If you came from there, you'd have to see this as you approached. Maybe it's a warning or a sign of how great this place was or how mighty a particular king was. It reminds me of an old poem a teacher made me memorize in high school. It was about finding a wrecked statue of some ancient king out in the desert and all that was left of his kingdom was the statue." I paused. "Maybe they are like us." What I didn't say was that I would be afraid for us if we were too like them.

"Something moved," Sho said, breaking into my morbid reverie. "Out on the sand." She was pointing in the direction of the ruins on the far side of the open land ahead of us.

"I don't see anything," No Nonsense said, shielding his eyes with one hand against the glare of the suns.

"Sho has the keenest eyes of anybody at Earthbase," Caleb said. "If there was anything moving on the Empty Lands or a stray out there, she'd be the one to spot it."

"It was black," Sho said. "Not large. I just saw it at a corner because everything else here is so bright and there's nothing else moving. It's gone now."

I scanned the area and also saw nothing. Sho might have keen eyes, but my chip gave me some magnification on my field. "If there was something there and it wanted to get back under cover, it could have done it. Particularly if it was *someone* there." Amid the deserted ruins and under the gaze of that statue, the idea gave me a chill.

"Back to the rover," I said. "Rifles ready at all times. We've got another day of travel before we reach that Octagon, but I'd rather spend the night on open ground, where we can see around us, rather than push into the next field of ruins. We'll set a watch through the night."

CHAPTER THIRTY-TWO

THE OPEN SANDS BETWEEN THE STATUE AND THE FAR RUINS WERE GHOSTLY WHITE under the double moons as I took my turn on watch. I had parked the rover around the midpoint between the two sets of ruins, figuring that was as safe as I could manage in a universe where safety was a child's fantasy. The moons, each of them near half-full, were bright enough to blot out all but a few stars. The moonlight shone on wisps of clouds that floated across the sky, none of them more substantial than tissue.

Was any danger out in the desert, any living creature at all? For most of my watch, I thought not. But then I saw in the distance a brief flick of black across sand where I was certain I had seen smooth white a moment before. I focused on that area of ground. Saw another black cloud across the sand. I stiffened, adjusted the position of my M8c.

"What's wrong? Did you see something?" Caleb's voice was a whisper. I hadn't realized he was awake.

"Out there." I pointed at the windshield and then tapped the screen that showed the forward view from the rover to enlarge it. "Nothing much. Like a shadow on the ground. There!" I kept my voice down, although I doubted anything short of a yell would have woken Sho and No Nonsense.

"I see it," Caleb said. "What are you thinking? Could be nothing more than some nocturnal animal."

"It could be," I said, "but I'm not betting on that." I'd spent enough time in the wild on enough combat missions to have a sixth sense about things that moved in the dark. Call it superstition if you want, but I was still alive after all those missions. Something was out there. "We're being watched," I said. "No idea by whom and no idea why, but the safe thing is to assume they're not friendly and their purpose isn't one we would appreciate."

"No argument from me," Caleb said.

I could see him strain his eyes, looking through the windshield to spot another movement. That was where he focused first, not the screen, even though the screen offered magnification and some night vision. Like No Nonsense and Sho, he didn't think to use tech unless it was pointed out to him. For me, it was second nature, an extension of myself.

"I've been out in the Empty Lands by myself plenty of times," Caleb said. "We call them empty for a reason, but there's always *something* there. Even if it's nothing more than grass blowing in the wind or a field mouse scooting into a burrow. This place ... there's *nothing*."

I had to agree. This was the most desolate land I had ever seen. It hadn't always been this way. The ruins and the statue proved that. What had it been like when that signal was sent to Earth? Could it have been changed to this in less than five centuries?

"Do you think we'll leave this world alive?" Caleb asked abruptly. "I mean, I've made my peace with dying as best any man can, I think. You have to do that if you ride across the Empty Lands. But I want Sho to be okay. I wish she hadn't said she was coming, and afterward there was no talking her out of it. What she did ... I know she'd never shot anyone before, but it's not like they weren't shooting at us. So, what do you think? You've been in wars, in bad situations. What do you think?"

"We're armed and we're alert. We'll come through," I told him. "We're going to complete our mission and then go back to the LZ for spaceplane pickup. Those shadows may watch, but they'll keep their distance. We'll be fine."

That was the same line I had always given my squad and then my platoon when that question came up. I could hear Petey saying to some FNG after my back was turned, *Listen, if Sarge says it's gonna be okay, it's gonna be okay.*

It had always been true, too, at least for most of them. That is, it was true until that day when it wasn't.

.	.	.

I NEVER REALLY WENT TO SLEEP, EVEN THOUGH CALEB TOOK THE WATCH FOR THE remainder of the night. I blinked at the growing light as the suns peeked over the horizon behind us. My head felt full of congealed mud. I dug into a pocket with one hand, reaching for the stim pills I had pulled from the Med Unit. One now and one in two hours, per the old US Army protocol. As with almost everything else in the Med Unit, I had no idea if they were any good. Mentally, I shrugged. They would work or they wouldn't, and if they didn't, I'd be no more tired than I would without them. Of course, they might have deteriorated into something harmful, but I doubted they would do me as much harm as dozing off at the wrong moment would do.

"Up and at 'em, kids," I said, waking Sho and No Nonsense. "It's Octagon or bust today."

The two of them came awake fast without so much as a groan. When had I gotten old?

I angled the rover northwest across the sand and gravel. Something about the ruins ahead was foreboding, probably because of those black shapes I had glimpsed in the night. I had no way to reach the Octagon without driving through these ruins, but I didn't want to go straight through the widest part of them. They thinned out to the north and west. I could make a loop and still reach the Octagon with plenty of daylight. I gave the *Ranger* a terse summary of the night and my current plan, as I drove.

We were closing in on a low ridge of sand, all that remained of the ruined structure that had stood in that place—when I saw something black flap near the opening between it and the next low ridge. Instinctively, I swerved away from that route and turned parallel to the wall to go to the opening beyond it. As we went past, I saw a figure in black crouched by the end of the wall. They held a long tubular object that reminded me of the one the statue had. The end of the tube blinked blue. Simultaneously, I heard a popping sound from the rear window. There was a hole in the window; the glass glowed red around it. There was a black char in the top of the rover, and a whiff of smoke came from the char.

"We're under fire!" I yelled. "Return fire! Assume anyone you see is hostile."

I hit the control to lower the windows. They were no protection, and it was easier to shoot back with them out of the way. No Nonsense had his rifle out the open window and was scanning the area for a target.

"They're gone," No Nonsense said. "Just gone. Like they dropped into a hole in the ground."

"Might have done exactly that," I said.

"What did they use?" Sho asked. She made a quick tap with a forefinger against the char in the top. "Hot," she said.

"Don't know what it is," I said. "You can call it a laser, but it probably isn't. Maybe just call it a death ray. It doesn't matter. It's a lethal weapon. I don't know how much protection the rover will give us."

Probably not much, I thought. The vehicle was not designed for a battlefield. It had no armor. It was made for exploration and, like all gear for starshots, to be as light as possible, to reduce the mass that had to be carried by the starship and the spaceplane.

"Each of you watch a quadrant," I ordered. "Shoot on sight. No friendlies here."

That was a minor blessing. Any built-up area was fertile ground for setting ambushes and planting IEDs. I occasionally had nightmares about street scenes turning into blazing hell and chaos. At least here we had no risk of a mother and her children being in our line of fire.

I eyed an upcoming passage with suspicion. Sooner or later, I had to turn into the ruins. The rover might be able to climb the little ridge where a wall had been. Some of them were low enough. That might surprise someone trying to set an ambush—but the surprise would be temporary, and I didn't know what might be in the central area of these walls. Maybe the surprise would be ours. More risk. Not enough gain.

"I'm going in there." I pointed to the opening beyond the next passage, which seemed a bit wider. "Be ready."

"Got it," Caleb said.

This wasn't my old team, but they were okay. No Nonsense had been through vicious fighting at Gettysburg, and I had seen Caleb and Sho handle themselves well under fire. It was time. I turned the rover into the ruins.

We passed through the first set of walls without difficulty. Then suddenly, a figure wrapped in black was in front of the rover. Their weapon was aimed. It blinked blue. Nothing happened. The attacker barely had time to look at their weapon before Caleb fired from the front seat. No Nonsense leaned far out of his window and fired from the rear.

The crack of the M8cs split the graveyard silence of the ruins. The bullets hit our erstwhile ambusher and knocked them back against the wall that formed one side of the passage. I floored the accelerator—as much as it's possible to do that with a rover—and the vehicle lurched, then shot ahead. From the corner of my eye, I caught movement on the other side. Sho cut loose with her M8c. I heard a cry and we were past the danger point.

"My God, look what they're doing!" No Nonsense had his head out the window, twisted to see behind us.

I glanced at the rearview screen. Several figures in black had clustered around the body of the one Caleb and No Nonsense had shot. They had knives out. As we drove away, they were butchering the fallen one. And eating as they watched us drive off.

"I do not like this," Caleb said. "I do not like this at all."

"Neither do I," I said.

I didn't, not even if their weapons were unreliable, which must be what had happened with that attack, and not even if killing one of them could provoke a feeding frenzy from the others.

"This is a bad place to be," I said. "Let's just hope that there aren't many of them and that we can get through this area before another group organizes an attack."

CHAPTER THIRTY-THREE

OUR LUCK HELD ALMOST THE WHOLE WAY TO THE OTHER SIDE OF THE RUINS. I was watching the screens, figuring how much time until we cleared the ruins and reached the open ground in front of the Octagon, which I assumed was the fort guarding the trail down to the city. The rover was trundling down a passage between walls no different from all the others we had passed. Something caught my eye. A patch of sand at the base of a wall ahead wasn't quite so smooth as all the other sand around it. It might have been a gleam of sunlight reflected from an object in the sand that drew my attention.

Involuntarily, I yelled, "IED!" I jammed on the brakes, bringing the rover to a sudden stop.

The blast echoed off the walls around us. A cloud of sand and gravel hid the way in front of us and towered into the air. We all ducked as loose chunks of gravel flew through the open windows and pinged against the rover's surface.

When the rain of dirt and rock stopped, I picked up my head. Where the mine had been planted was a small crater, and the little ridge that marked the remainder of a wall under the sand had been blown away for a space of six to eight feet.

"Check the rear!" I shouted.

My eyes were scanning the ground ahead. I doubted this explosion had been set in isolation. Yes! There, in the clearing cloud on the other side of the passage, I saw a figure in black. It was carrying a tube and it looked like the sort of tube I was familiar with.

"Rocket! Out of the rover!"

I flung myself out the door and was gratified to see near simultaneous duplication by the others. As I landed on the ground, a flash came from ahead. A streak of smoke drew a line from the black figure's position to the rover. The thunderclap of an explosion rocked the front of the vehicle.

"Enemies behind us!" No Nonsense yelled.

I heard the staccato stutter of M8cs from behind the rover. I had no time to look in that direction, however. Two more black figures were coming through the hole in the wall created by the first explosive. One of them leveled that type of tube weapon we had seen, but the end of it only flickered blue. Nothing happened to me or around me. I fired. Arms flung back, those odd-fingered hands outlined against the sky, and the figure dropped. The one next to it fired at me with a hand weapon. I saw the flash and heard two slugs hit the rover next to where I crouched to get as much cover as I could. I fired a burst and the figure toppled.

Caleb's M8c was chattering from the other side of the rover. I heard No Nonsense cry, "Help!" from the rear. I dashed for the back of the rover. There were two down near Sho, but three had attacked No Nonsense. He had shot two of them, but the third had reached him and was on his back. I raised the M8c, but the wrestling figures twisted and I had to hold off shooting because the bullet would have drilled through both of them. Sho covered the short space between her and them in a fraction of a second. She clubbed the black-clad figure across its head with the stock of her rifle. It fell on its back, and before it could rise, she pumped five bullets into it.

With that, the fight was over. The same eerie silence that had pervaded the ruins before was back. If there were any enemies beyond the ones we had killed, they had vanished as silently as they had crept into position.

My first thought, after I saw Caleb coming around the rover, was No Nonsense. He was on both knees with Sho holding him at the shoulders. His back was bloody and there was a knife, liberally smeared with blood, on the ground next to him.

"Caleb, Sho, eyes on our surroundings. I'll take care of him."

I had No Nonsense lie prone so I could see what had happened. He had three wounds in his back. Two were superficial, but the third was a deep puncture below his rib cage. When I pulled his shirt away, some fabric came out of that wound. I got the little medikit the rover carried, but there wasn't much I could do beyond clean his wounds and bandage them. I put a pressure dressing on that puncture in his lower back. We'd need the Med Unit in the ship to do anything more.

"I'll be all right," No Nonsense said.

"That's what I'm planning," I replied.

Sho had a bloody gash across one cheek from a chunk of flying gravel at the start of the fight, but no other wounds. Caleb was unmarked.

The rover was in far worse shape. That rocket had blasted the front, wrecking the electric motors that powered the front two wheels. Even if I could fix them—and I couldn't—between the rocket and the initial blast, the photovoltaic skin on the rover that charged its battery was burned, scored, and pockmarked. Once the battery ran out of power, it would be done. For the moment, though, we did have power, and most of the internal systems on the rover worked.

"We were ambushed," I said on the comm channel to the *Ranger*. "We've got the bodies of nine attackers here. At least for now, we've beaten them off. No Nonsense has a knife wound that needs the Med Unit, and he needs to be evacuated."

"How do you think we're going to do that?" Shane asked.

That knocked my mind out of the groove it had fallen into, one worn into it by actions in long-ago wars. "Bring the spaceplane down" is what I said after a brief hesitation.

"The spaceplane can make only two trips. You know that," Shane said.

Right. All of this for nothing. I looked at the others. No Nonsense was trying to smile, trying to hold himself as though he had no pain. Sho had her hands on his shoulders, strain and worry carved into her face. Caleb's eyes were on the two of them.

"Bring the spaceplane down," I said. "Evacuate No Nonsense. Sho and Caleb go with him. I'll complete the mission."

"If you do that, Leif," Magda said, "it means you're not coming back."

I looked away from the others. I saw Yong as though she were standing on the sand next to me. Past Yong, I saw Charity. I saw Elvy and the other kids. All gone. All taken from me either by war or by my own choices. I won't say my eyes misted. I insist they did not.

"I know that," I said.

"Even if you're determined to be a damned suicidal hero," Shane said, "there's no place to land the spaceplane near you. The ground in front of the Octagon is unsuitable. The open ground closest to you is to the northwest, but the terrain looks irregular. It's too much of a risk."

Our medevac pilots during the Troubles had never hesitated to come in, regardless of terrain and regardless of risk, even in the middle of combat. Of course, a spaceplane wasn't a chopper. Still—

"I could land it, I think, back between the two sets of ruins where they were last night." A red dot showed on the image of the area as Magda spoke.

"I don't agree," Shane said. "On his previous call, Leif said something moved across those sands in the night. That area is not safe and you're in no condition to be flying anyway."

"It doesn't matter," I said, staring at the screen. "To get to that LZ would mean a long trek through the ruins or backtracking, again through the ruins, and then a long hike in the open desert. It would be on foot. The rover is out." I paused to think, then I said, "The quickest way out of these ruins is straight ahead to the Octagon, and that's also the least amount of open ground to cover afterward. If you won't put the spaceplane down in front of the Octagon, our best chance will be going to the Octagon and hoping for help there or in the city, if we can reach that. Whoever lives there is beaming signals into space. They ought to be willing to at least talk to us. There's only a short stretch of ruins we still have to get through if we go directly for it. There's not that much open ground in front of the Octagon."

"I can do it," No Nonsense said.

"I agree," Caleb added. Sho merely nodded.

"All right," I said. "That's the plan. Now, one thing you all need to realize," and I said that as much to the crew on the *Ranger* as to my team on the ground, "is that once we leave the rover, we're out of communication with the ship until we can get back to the hab at the LZ. That is, unless we can manage something from the city, which is unknown.

"I have no idea how long this is going to take. I mean, it won't take long to reach the city. What I can't tell is how long it will take us to establish communications or to convince them to help us get back to the LZ. If we assume we can get food in the city, to be safe, give us three months." I didn't add the words, *before you write us off*, but I was sure everyone heard them in their heads.

"No problem with that," Shane said. "We've got plenty of supplies up here, and we all know it makes no difference when we start back to Earth."

"That's it, then," I said. "Away team out."

CHAPTER THIRTY-FOUR

CHIPPED IN AND DOWNLOADED WHATEVER I COULD FROM THE ROVER TO MY CHIP, then shut down the rover's systems. After that, I walked over to take a look at the closest of the attackers' bodies. I used the toe of my boot to catch a flap of the black wrapping and kick it back.

The exposed head had a crest of black feathers. The rest resembled the statue, but it was narrower and more pointed in the jaw. The mouth, open in its last gasp, showed pointed teeth. From where I stood, I wasn't sure if they had been filed down or were naturally that way. I wasn't going to bend down for a close inspection.

Behind the shoulders, where I had kicked the wrap clear, an underlying robe was open to reveal two short stumps where the statue had wings. Amputation, or only vestigial wings? I couldn't tell. The body, what I could see of it, and the face were covered with tiny feathers, mostly black with a sprinkling of other colors.

"Where did they come from?" Caleb's voice came from behind my shoulder.

"Underground, maybe," I said. "Almost has to be. There's no place else in this desolation for them to be."

"I don't see any openings." Sho came to stand by her brother.

"I don't see any either," I said, "but I'm not going to go look for them. Even if I saw one, we don't have grenades to drop into it, and I'm for sure not going down myself." Fighting in someone else's underground tunnel was *not* what I wanted to do.

"And what do you think of them?" Caleb asked.

"They're different," I said. "This one and the statue. Related but different. Maybe a different species or subspecies. I'm not any kind of scientist; I don't know how that works. What I am sure of is that there hasn't been enough time, not nearly enough time, for the people of that statue to evolve—or devolve—into these.

"We may get the answer at the city, but it doesn't matter right now. What is important is that murderous as they are, they're not very good at tactics. That and they have a mélange of weapons, many of which don't work well. We were ambushed and outnumbered. If they knew their business, none of us should even be alive now, yet we killed all of them. So, they're dangerous, very dangerous, but we've got a chance. Let's get to the Octagon and the city, and then we'll take it from there."

"Damned right," said Sho. Blood from the gash on her cheek had run down below her jaw, and all of it had clotted. She had a wild look in her eyes.

No Nonsense gave me a weak smile and a nod.

We took as much food from the rover as we could stuff in our packs and filled our water bottles from the rover's supply. What we could carry would have to be enough to reach the city. After that, well, we were effectively making a bet that beings who had reached out to the stars would be willing to provide food and water.

We moved out in single file, alert to all sides. I took point, with No Nonsense behind me. Sho was next and Caleb had the rear. The twin suns stood high above us in a cloudless sky, as far apart as I could recall having seen them. Each of them blazed at us as though competing with the other to make us miserable. It made for a hot and sweaty march.

With the suns clear in the sky and the mountains behind the Octagon ahead of us, it was easy to keep on course even if the ruins all looked the same. The only time I needed the images of the ruins I had pulled from the rover was when walls blocked our route and we had to detour.

What slowed us down was No Nonsense. When I saw that he was having trouble keeping up, the first thing I did was to take his M8c and sling it over my shoulder. That meant we had only three rifles ready in case of trouble, but he couldn't manage both the rifle and his pack. In fact, that pack had to go next. I called a halt and we divvied up the contents among the three of us.

"I can do this, Leif," No Nonsense said. "I'm good. I swear it."

"I know you're good," I told him. "Being wounded gets you out of carrying the stuff, though. It's a tradition. Take a drink of water and we'll start up again."

Sho gave him her water bottle and a quick kiss. He rewarded her with a smile and tried to straighten up.

While this byplay was happening, I looked him over and didn't like what I saw. That knife had cut something inside that I couldn't see. No Nonsense was bleeding internally. I knew that even if I couldn't see it. I could tell his pulse was up with my fingers, but we couldn't chip in for me to check his blood pressure.

We had no other choices, however. The only way out of this was through it. In my mind, I damned Shane for being too much of a coward to land the spaceplane where we needed it. I damned Magda for not being able to fly the spaceplane. Most of all, I damned myself for being responsible for this cockamamie expedition and for ever letting No Nonsense leave Charity's farm.

It wasn't long before No Nonsense was in trouble even without the rifle and the pack. When I glanced behind me and saw his shambling gait, I dropped back and had him put one arm over my shoulder so I could help support him. That left me handling my rifle one-handed, not the best way to be if we walked into a fight. Again, there was no choice.

We did clear the ruins without being further molested. Beyond the last sand-covered walls was no more than a quarter mile of ground that sloped upward sharply. The sand and gravel gave way to bare, stony soil as the land rose. The Octagon, a mass of gray blocks ten feet high, stood in front of us at the top of the slope. Behind it would be the pass that led to the road down to the coast. I saw no movement at the Octagon, no windows, no lights, no evidence anyone was home.

No Nonsense couldn't manage the slope. His strength was ebbing fast. Unless there was help waiting for us at the Octagon or the other side of the pass—and I could guess the odds of that—I knew how this was going to end.

What I wasn't prepared to do was give up until it *was* the end. I told him to hold up while I slung my M8c as well. Then I stepped in front of him and lifted him in a fireman's carry. Going up that hill carrying him, two rifles, and a pack wasn't going to be easy, but I could do it. The lower gravity helped a little. No alternative, as the saying goes.

Because I had turned around to pick up No Nonsense, I was looking to the rear. A little behind Caleb, where the sand ended and the rocky slope began, a hole opened up. Out of the hole rose a head wrapped in black. Those creatures did have a tunnel network!

"Check behind you! They're coming out of the ground behind you!" I yelled.

Caleb spun around. He had just enough time for his face to register surprise before that figure had its weapon leveled and blue light flashed. Caleb screamed, hands clutched at his chest, black char bursting from the pack on his back. He collapsed where he was standing.

"Caleb!" Sho screamed.

I had both rifles over my shoulders because I was holding No Nonsense. Sho had her rifle ready. She fired. The head of the attacker who was rising from the hole exploded.

Sho ran to Caleb's side. She reached her hand down to his face. More holes were opening.

"Sho!" I yelled. "He's dead! Get to higher ground behind me. I'll cover you. Then you cover me while I bring No Nonsense."

"No! I can't leave my brother! I can't leave him to them to eat!"

Crap. Sometimes the world goes to shit very, very fast.

I put No Nonsense down on the ground. Unslung an M8c and dropped prone to make as much as I could out of the poor cover the ground afforded. I felt the earth rumbling under me. Disregarded that. Attackers were emerging from the holes. Sho shot down two. I swept the M8c across a cluster of them on full automatic and saw four fall.

"Sho! Get out of there! I'll cover you!"

"No! Take care of No Nonsense! I can't leave Caleb!"

She shot down another one, but as she did, a hole opened near her. An attacker in black leaped out and was on her with a knife before she could swing her rifle around. I fired and picked off that one, but she was down, two more were there, and my position was taking fire. Scorches appeared in the dirt in front of me. Bullets whistled past my head.

My time in the universe was coming to an end in the waste of a forsaken planet. The thinking, feeling part of my mind went far away. I picked a target. Fired. Picked another target. Fired. Again and again. Sooner or later, I would be hit. I kept shooting anyway.

Behind me, the Octagon awoke.

Flashes of blue scored the ground and dropped attackers in front of me all across the little battlefield. Blasts sounded behind me. Trailing streamers of smoke, missiles flew across my position and dived into the openings in the ground. Yellow-red flashes rose back into the air as thunder boomed. A large section of sand and dirt at the base of the slope dropped down as though the support underneath had been yanked away. And then it was silent.

Nothing moved on the battlefield save wisps of smoke rising from the openings in the ground and drifting across the hillside. With a muted crunch, another section of ground subsided. Whatever subterranean network had existed just collapsed. Staying flat on the ground, I twisted to look back at the Octagon. What had been plain gray blocks had swung open, revealing rows of weapon tubes and missile launchers.

I lifted my head. Nobody shot at it. Then I stood up because, well, at some point, you do need to get up. All was quiet.

I hustled down to the tangle of bodies where Caleb and Sho were. Both dead: Caleb with a burn through the middle of his chest, Sho with multiple stab wounds. I ran back to No Nonsense. When I squatted down to pick him up, his skin was cool and moist, his breathing fast and shallow. He moaned and said his belly hurt when I moved him. He was going into shock.

"C'mon, No Nonsense, hang in there. I'm going to boost you up again. We're going to go see the people in the fort who did the shooting. They'll help us."

I managed to run up the rest of the hill carrying him. My knee screamed at the abuse. I ignored it. By the time I reached the Octagon, the weapons and missile launchers were retracting. As they did, smooth gray panels slid in front of them until the fort looked like the massive blocks of stone we had first seen. In the center of the side facing the slope was a passage shadowed by the blocks on either side and above. I did not see a door, or a gate, or any kind of a barrier. I had no time to ponder the situation. I ran into the passage, shouting for all I was worth to attract attention.

The passageway ended at an interior octagon. It was empty, devoid of any person or object. On each side stood the same blank walls as the outside. They were illuminated only by the light coming through the way I had entered and through an identical passage on the opposite side that went out through the back. No one was in the fort. It was entirely automated and had fought automatically. There was no help here.

Carefully, I laid No Nonsense down on the floor next to one of the walls. His lips had gone bluish.

"I need to tell Sho I love her." His voice was soft, not much more than a whisper, broken up by quick breaths. "It's important. She needs to know how much I love her."

"She knows that, No Nonsense," I said. "She told me she knew and that she loves you. She told me before she went with Caleb to the city. You know that's where they went, right?"

"Yeah."

He closed his eyes, but only for a moment. Then they opened wide. "I think I'm going, Leif. I'm scared. I want Ma. Is Ma here?"

"Ma is a long way away," I said. "But I'm here with you."

"Please hold my hand."

I held his hand until his breathing stopped.

When I was certain, I put his hand on his chest, stood up, and looked down at his body. "Goddammit," I said, my voice thick with emotion. "Goddamn war, and warriors, and me along with all of it."

I walked back out the passageway and down the hill. I made two trips to pick up Sho and Caleb. I brought them back up to the fortress, which paid no attention to me, and laid them on the floor next to No Nonsense. I had nothing to dig graves with, and even if I did, I feared that anyone put into the dirt or sand might not stay there long. But inside the Octagon, I thought they would be safe from those desert marauders. If the three of them hadn't come along with me and done what they had done, our mission would be a failure and I would be dead. I owed them a debt I could never repay, but I could at least finish what we had started. When I was done laying them in a row, I came to attention in front of their bodies and saluted. Then I said goodbye.

With an M8c slung over my shoulder, another one at the ready, and a pack on my back, I turned and walked out the rear passage of the Octagon. The road through the pass and down to the coastal plain stretched out in front of me.

I had our mission to complete.

PART IV

WHOEVER FIGHTS MONSTERS SHOULD SEE TO IT THAT IN THE PROCESS HE DOES NOT BECOME A MONSTER. AND WHEN YOU LOOK LONG INTO AN ABYSS, THE ABYSS ALSO LOOKS INTO YOU.

FRIEDRICH NIETZSCHE, "BEYOND GOOD AND EVIL"

CHAPTER THIRTY-FIVE

Picture this: A lone American soldier, rifle at the ready, advances down a deserted road from a mountain pass to confront an entire alien and warlike civilization. Granted, I was wearing an ISC polo with starship cargo pants rather than camo and body armor, but if those twin suns were behind me and in your eyes, you might not notice the difference. Was this heroic? Idiotic? Too silly for words?

To be honest, I wasn't quite sure what I was doing. My odds of survival, while not zero, were very small. Salvaging food and water from the other packs would stretch my supplies for maybe two weeks, although if I cut my intake down that much, my physical condition would deteriorate. I had no idea if I could eat anything local.

My transportation was gone, which emphasized my food situation. My only chance of returning to the LZ would be to hitch a ride with a local or persuade them to give me transportation and hope I could operate it. In either case, I would have to run the gantlet of killers who lurked in the ruins, unless air transport was somehow available.

I supposed that if I found whoever controlled the signal we were receiving, I might be able to communicate with the *Ranger*, but the likelihood of Shane bringing the spaceplane down anywhere on the coastal plain was probably less than mine of surviving a trek across that hostile desert. Shane had lost his balls in that crash-landing at Earthbase. That was just one more factor to consider.

I didn't allow myself much in the way of emotion about any of this. Part of surviving years of combat and the losses that went with them had been learning to wall off any feelings, to simply not have them. That was how I dealt with marching down a road to likely death.

It was also how I dealt with the three I had left dead up at the Octagon. I had liked Sho and Caleb. They were good people; I enjoyed their company. No Nonsense had come close to making me think of him as the pain-in-the-ass teenage son I might have had in a different life. I was just about biologically old enough that he could have been my son.

None of that could matter. I had liked many of the men and women who had been killed in action fighting alongside me. I couldn't afford to have feelings about any of them. The only one who was different was Yong. Her loss hurt, and it hurt still. All the more reason not to have feelings about anyone else.

If I had no feelings, I can't say I had much of a plan either. I was going to be the first, and possibly only, human to meet another intelligent species face-to-face, but I couldn't think of what I should do when that happened. We had brought a video device packed with images and information—carefully curated, of course—but that had been lost with the rover. The only image I had left was the printed pic of me and Yong on High Noon, that was carefully sealed in a pants pocket. I doubted that would advance an interspecies communication.

The most obvious objects I had were the M8cs, but they might well start the wrong kind of communication. I guess I was figuring that when someone finally took notice of an alien tramping down the road, they would alert their authorities, and those worthies would figure out how to communicate with me. Assuming I wasn't killed in the process. This was probably not the most brilliant plan for first contact.

Precisely when someone might notice me was another interesting question. The road down from the Octagon was totally deserted. Its surface was smooth and hard, more like glass than concrete, but it had cracked like old concrete, and some brown vegetation with triangular leaves had grown into the cracks. I doubted that road had seen any traffic in a century. Maybe longer.

The slopes above and below the road were bare, brown dirt when I started out, dirt that would have looked at home on the Great Plains or in Central Asia. As I descended, clumps of a spiky green bush began to show up along the side of the road. Closer to the plain, taller plants that looked like trees shaded the road. Their trunks were wide at the base and tapered to a spike anywhere from twenty to thirty feet in the air. Those trunks were green and sprouted black branches from which bright green curlicues drooped.

At one point, the road went around a blind turn and the ground dropped away sharply on the seaward side, giving me a view out toward the bay. The water was deep blue, with wind-driven whitecaps. Large boats were out in the bay. Flashes and puffs of smoke told me those boats were shooting at something, even though the wind blew the sound away. I might have picked an improvident time to drop by to visit.

A little farther took me around the shoulder of a hill, and once I passed that, I could see the walls of the fortified city off to my left. Based on how the twin suns were sinking toward the horizon, I didn't think I would be able to reach the city before dark, although I should be able to make it to flat land. I decided that I would keep hiking even after darkness fell. If no one accosted me, I would walk all the way to the city wall, pound on whatever passed for a gate, yell, *Take me to your leader!* and see what happened. As a plan for first contact, it lacked finesse, but it had the virtue of being simple.

I did reach level ground as dusk was falling. The trees grew thickly once I was off the hillside, and the profusion of dangling green tendrils from the branches filled the space between the trees to create a green cloud for me to walk through. Low bushes that resembled giant puffballs in chartreuse grew under the trees and up to the road. With the light failing anyway, the vegetation left me a dim tunnel in the gloaming. Twin ten-foot-high blocks loomed up ahead of me. I was almost between them before I saw them; that's how cloaked the world was in green spray dangling from branches or large spheres of thin leaves that rose from the ground like smoke. I stopped at the sight of those blocks. The smooth gray surfaces looked the same as the ones I had seen at the Octagon, where they hid a massive array of weaponry. The Octagon had destroyed the killers in black but ignored me. Did I have any reason to believe the same would be true here?

Walking between those blocks could be a good way to commit suicide. I probed the eight-foot-tall puffball nearest me at the side of the road, using the barrel of the M8c to push the delicate green leaves to the side, trying to see the ground. Could it be mined? I was ready to believe anything, but I had to make a choice. Either off the road or between those blocks.

A snapping sound came from somewhere in the green-shrouded murk off the side of the road. The pathetically limited night vision capability my chip gave me showed the road ahead clearly enough but could not penetrate the darkness off the road. That decided me. I broke into a sprint down the road, hoping that I would make it past the blocks.

The world flashed white. Pain shot through every part of my body. Multicolored sparkles superimposed themselves on the white before my eyes. Then it all went black.

CHAPTER THIRTY-SIX

AWOKE TO FIND MYSELF LYING ON A SPRINGY MAT. THE MAT WAS IN A ROOM brightened by sunlight pouring in through a window and was supplemented with artificial light that emanated diffusely from the ceiling. Other than my mat, the room was devoid of furniture.

I had a headache. Headache! This was a railroad spike being driven into the top of my skull with a hammer. Every pound of the hammer vibrated out to my ears and triggered a wave of nausea. I levered myself up on one elbow in the hope that would improve the situation.

At that moment, the doorknob turned. It was actually in the shape of a small wheel with five indentations around its circumference. It was a logical shape to match the birdlike structure of the hands and feet I had seen. The door opened with a squeak, and one of the locals walked in.

They were not that big, possibly five and a half feet tall, although a forward-leaning posture took an inch or two away from their height. The face, with small black eyes that lacked any whites, flat nasal slits above a broad upper lip, mouth without a real chin, and a crest of black feathers sweeping back from the forehead, could have been a close cousin of the statue.

Except for the area around the mouth, the face, head, and all the visible body were covered with tiny feathers. Those were predominantly black with a scattering of pink, red, white, yellow, and blue. This individual wore an open-backed and short-sleeved coverall in light beige, embroidered with geometric patterns in red and blue. Small wings fluttered behind the shoulders. Nothing suggested either male or female.

For a couple of long minutes, I stared at them and they stared at me staring at them.

This was *it*. First contact with an alien, intelligent species. Desperately, I fought against the nausea to avoid commemorating the occasion by vomiting on the floor.

"I am glad to see you are awake and attentive," they said. "I was concerned about the combined effects of the stun and the machine learning because your neural network is so alien. From your anatomy, I thought you would like to lie flat. I hope that is acceptable." They pointed at the mat with the long middle finger of one hand.

Say something, Leif, I told myself. "I'm going to ask about what you said in a minute, but first, who are you, and where am I?" I stopped abruptly at that point because it penetrated my brain that this individual had spoken to me in a language I had never heard before. However, I had not only understood it but answered in the same language! "How am I speaking your language?"

"The machine learning has been successful" was the answer.

"What does that mean?"

"You have an interface. That was obvious when I examined you and scanned you."

I had an interface? My chip? I decided to play dumb and stared.

They waggled their wings. I continued to stare.

"Of course," they said. "You have a device that allows direct electronic interface of a computer network with your brain. We have many languages and therefore have programs that can imprint a language quickly. It is a form of machine learning. My computer system is very old and very sophisticated, one of a kind now.

"You must be from the starship that sent the transmissions—what else could you be?" The wings waggled rapidly. "And although the system flagged those transmissions as nonsense with major errors, it was able to create a map for the language. My system connected to your interface and allowed your brain to use a form of machine learning to acquire our language. You now speak our language. We also convey meaning through gestures of our wings.

"Our remote ancestors could fly short distances or use their wings for speed in chasing prey downhill. Some lines evolved to truly fly. In us, the wings are vestigial; they have no function beyond communication, although our skeletons retain the air sacs that reduce weight and assist flight.

"I cannot transfer wing language to you, as you have no such language of your own to map. By the same token, as I watch you, I observe tiny muscles in your face that I believe you are using to convey information. But I doubt I will ever be able to read it."

The last bit about wing gestures and facial expressions made sense. It was what came before it that bothered me. "Are you telling me you've reprogrammed my brain?"

"No." The wings waggled again in something I couldn't decipher. "I'm not sure that would be a good thing to do, even if I could. Please consider. You can think of a brain as no different from an artificial intelligence, one that runs on a biological neural network.

"When connected to my system, your brain learned, the same way an artificial intelligence would learn. That is why I said 'machine learning.' It is fast. I had judged the risk acceptable. Fortunately, it was successful, with no apparent damage."

No apparent damage. They had judged the risk acceptable. Okay. I would take that as a starting point.

"All right, I've got that," I said. "Now let's back up, shall we? My ship came here because of the transmission you sent, or your ancestors sent, hundreds of years ago. Right now, I'd like to know who you are, where I am, how I got here, what is going on, and what you meant by the word 'stun.'"

"Yes, it's natural that you would have many questions. I do as well, but let me try to answer some of yours first. We are unlikely to have as much time for this as either one of us would like." More wing waggling followed before they realized what they were doing.

"My name is Ru'andarko. I am a Watcher; that is, a member of the Society of Watchers, those tasked with watching for a response to the message that was sent out. We were a society that transcended all nests, nest-rings, clans, clan groups, and federations. I am, in fact, the last Watcher, the last of that society, and the last with this type of functioning tech.

"That is why, when your ship came to our system and transmitted, I was the only one to receive it. All return transmissions came from here." The wings stood out rigidly for an instant. "We call ourselves— that is, our species—the Jandi. You are in Gardiance City, named for the clan that is dominant here now.

"We are part of the Gowa clan federation, although the warships in the bay and the fighters attacking our western lines are also from that federation, so that federation is fiction and another war is fact.

"My tech works well enough that I detected your landing in the Bellaquo Plains, and it alerted me to the activation of the fort that guards the pass from there. Because of the history of the nu'Jandi, the road from the pass is guarded robotically in case nu'Jandi ever manage to pass the fort.

"As a Watcher, I have authority over dealing with any response to the transmission. I gave orders to the mechanicals to stun any creature coming down the road that is not nu'Jandi and bring them to me. Does that answer those questions?"

"Nu'Jandi? What is that?" My headache was subsiding, but my head certainly wasn't clear. That word was not in the vocabulary I had acquired.

"A derivative species. The Bellaquo Plains were once the most fertile and beautiful lands on all Sylvio." That last word seemed to mean "Earth" or "world" in my head, and Ru'andarko confirmed it. "We do not use that name much anymore. We prefer to say we live in Hell."

It was obvious in my mind what the Jandi word meant. I was among a species who saw their world as Hell. When I had my focus back on Ru'andarko, they were saying, "Incessant wars reduced those plains to the waste you saw. The nu'Jandi were engineered genetically during those wars to be single-minded murderers and terrorists. They are not very intelligent. Engineered and bred for aggression.

"When directed by Jandi, they are merciless and efficient killers. Without Jandi supervision, however, they cannot plan well or stick to a plan. While they remain murderous, they will swarm and rush a target even with knives and, so, can be killed themselves."

"They killed three of my party on our way here."

Wings fluttered. "We would have thought they all died out by now, but that fort was designed to detect and fight them specifically. So when it was activated, I knew otherwise. They live underground, and I guess they have found some source of food, although I doubt they will last much longer. Am I correct that you chose that route thinking a wasteland was safe—safer than landing near where war was active?"

I decided to avoid commenting on Shane's attitude. I also decided that being alone with the type of people the Jandi must be, I did not want to appear threatening. Definitely use the "we come in peace" concept, I told myself. "Yes. We are a peaceful people. We call ourselves humans, as I would think your system has already told you from our transmission. I am called Leif."

More wing movement. "You were carrying beautifully made weapons. The explosive rounds were designed to inflict great damage."

"We are peaceful unless severely provoked," I said. "We believe in defending ourselves."

"Naturally." A quiet period ensued.

"I would like to communicate with my ship. Can you show me how to use your equipment? You obviously know the frequency."

"Communication. Yes, we should discuss that as part of starting what you have come here to do. First, though, you should rest," Ru'andarko said. "But there is one question I must ask you."

I made a gesture for him to go ahead, realized he would not

understand it, and told him to do it.

"One of the major errors my system flagged in your transmissions, one of the ones that made it believe the translation was erroneous despite the language map, is that your planetary system has only one star. Is that really true? Your world circles only one sun?"

"Yes," I said. "Why would that invalidate your translation?"

"For millennia, we have debated the question of whether there is other intelligent life in the universe. In our study of the development of intelligence, we concluded that high intelligence can develop only on a planet that orbits a binary star system, as we do.

"The eclipse of one by the other, the predictable change in insolation and wind patterns; we determined those are key features in fostering the development of high intelligence. Schools of philosophy and poetry have grown up around these facts. This was one of the reasons my system concluded the translation of your transmission was unreliable. You are the ruination of it all."

I thought about that. My father had often claimed I was the ruination of his life, but even he had never accused me of destroying a school of philosophy. "I'm sorry," I said.

"Do not worry about it," Ru'andarko said. "For myself, I believe intelligent species are vanishingly rare in the universe because whenever a species becomes intelligent enough to make and use tools, it will go on to make and use weapons. From there, the path to warfare and extinction is inexorable. That is why I doubted there would ever be more than one intelligent species at a time, or a response to our message, although you have upset that line of thought as well."

"That's because we are peaceful," I said, while thinking that Ru'andarko's gloomy outlook on intelligence was closer to mine than I cared to believe. How alike were we? I pushed that away. "Tell me before you go," I said, "about your transmission. Why didn't you change what you were sending after our ship entered your system? Even if you thought your translation of ours was wrong, yours was always the same as your first transmission."

Ru'andarko backed up. Their wings spread wide. Their mouth

opened soundlessly for a moment. "Let me understand, without any possibility of mistake," they said at last. "You were unable to translate ours? You did not even translate the interstellar signal?"

I hated to admit it but saw no way to bluff my way past it. "No."

I thought the wing fluttering was agitated. "We must talk about that. About that and other things, after you have rested. In the meantime, I will compose myself and think. I will send my child when it is time to eat and you are awake again."

CHAPTER THIRTY-SEVEN

I DID SLEEP. IN FACT, ACCORDING TO MY CHIP, I SLEPT FOR TEN HOURS AND thirty-eight minutes Earth time, long enough that the planetary night had come and gone, pale light again streaming through the window.

My headache was gone, so if I was going to count whatever blessings I had, that would be number one. Did I have any others, aside from the simple fact of still being alive? I tried to figure out if Ru'andarko had hacked my chip in any way beyond using it, as they had said, as an interface to have my brain learn the Jandi language. I didn't feel any different. Would I notice anything at all until I started thinking or acting in some weird way? If I did, would I realize I was being weird?

It was a fruitless endeavor. My memories appeared to be intact—the good, the bad, and the ugly of what I had done—and my feelings about those memories felt right. Especially about Yong. Then I told myself that I would have no way to notice anything missing or feeling different, because the point of reference would be missing.

I shook my head and was simply glad it did not hurt. I had too many questions to think about to deal with a splitting headache. Why did Ru'andarko need to compose himself after I admitted we had not been able to translate their message?

It was also peculiar that Ru'andarko had not jumped at my request to communicate with the *Ranger*. His bosses or government, or whatever they had, probably wanted to talk to me first. Possibly, those individuals wanted to be part of any conversation with my ship. Or just as possibly, I was attributing a human reaction to a species I knew next to nothing about. In a way, it didn't matter at that moment. I was going to move forward with who I was and what I had, and whatever happened would happen. That was the beautiful thing about having no alternatives.

My stomach reminded me at that point that, unless I could reclaim my pack and the food in it, my timeline for whatever was to happen would be rather short. Even with my pack, I didn't have a lot of time unless I could eat the local food.

That thought pushed me to get off the mat and walk over to the window. It must be facing planetary east because the early morning suns were still near the horizon. Gray clouds over the water were broken by patches of blue. A large ship was standing out in the bay. It didn't matter that I was on another planet in the middle of an alien civilization. That was a warship, not a fishing vessel.

What should I do? I looked down and saw a substantial drop to the tops of nearby buildings. I wasn't going out this window. But was the door even locked? I chided myself for not having checked that first.

As I turned away from the window, the wall and the joins at the corners caught my eye. When I had first woken up, I thought the interior was the same smooth and seamless gray as the Octagon. I now realized I was wrong. The walls were some kind of thin board laid on top of other material. The corners were rough. I could see gaps. *Cheap construction* flashed through my mind. That was when the doorknob turned.

The person who bounced in with a jingle was not Ru'andarko but a smaller edition, not quite five feet tall. The black feathers visible past a similar coverall were the same, although the pattern of brightly colored feathers was different. The jingling came from a row of bells on the upper part of the boots that covered those long-toed feet.

"Good morning! I am D'Quilla. My parent sent me to bring you to where we are going to eat." Hands, arms, and wings all flapped along with the jingling bells. Yes, Ru'andarko had mentioned a child. Apparently, an enthusiastic one. More animated than me, for sure.

All parts of D'Quilla stilled momentarily. "What are you called? My parent didn't say. What's on your head? They don't look like feathers."

I had to smile. "I'm called Leif. And no, those aren't feathers." I searched my vocabulary for a word for hair and came up empty. I settled for stretching one to show them. "They're little strands. I'll find the right word, or your … parent will later. How old are you?"

"Thirteen. That's our years, of course. I know you're not from this world. Ru'andarko is the Watcher, which is why you're here, which is why I can talk to you and no one else can. I think that's fantastic!"

"You would be about thirteen by my years also," I said.

"How old are you?"

"Older." D'Quilla seemed ready to capitalize on being the only person in the world other than Ru'andarko who could talk to me, but I had too many questions of my own, starting with why my contact was limited to them. I needed Ru'andarko for those answers. "Aren't you supposed to be taking me somewhere?"

"Oh yes. Of course." Wings drooped. I knew disappointment when I saw it.

I followed D'Quilla out of the room and down a long heterogeneous corridor. Parts of the corridor wall were sheathed in the same gray material I had seen in the room. Other sections, though, looked like loose stone mortared together, or chunks of concrete block also anchored with cement. Still other sections looked like ordinary brick.

It reminded me of the way the buildings of Eastview had been put together with material salvaged from preapocalypse structures. The only difference, in fact, was the absence of plywood or other reused wood. The corridor was lit by the same ceiling glow as my room except for two sections where it was dim and one other where it flickered. D'Quilla made no comments and I held my questions.

The corridor ended in a steep staircase going up. The stairs were of varying height and of mortared stone. They were also quite narrow. D'Quilla took them easily on the tips of their three forward toes. I was more comfortable going up with my feet pointed sideways to put my whole foot on the stair. I made a mental note to take my time on the way down.

When we reached the top, D'Quilla led me into a small room with a clear dome for a ceiling. I had to stop and take in the view. The city below, enclosed by its wall, extended down the peninsula to the shore. On both sides, the coast swept away in broad bays. Beyond, water covered the world out to dark clouds at the horizon. Behind us, a cliff cloaked in green rose higher into the sky. Apparently, being the Watcher had perks.

"It's magnificent," I said.

"Thank you." That was Ru'andarko's voice, not D'Quilla's.

I had been so captivated by the view, I didn't even notice them in the room. They were seated at a small circular table in the center. The chair Ru'andarko sat in, like the one D'Quilla took, was contoured to their body and tipped forward in keeping with their usual posture. A three-legged stool without a back occupied the third place at the table.

"I apologize for what may be an uncomfortable seat," Ru'andarko said. "I do not think your anatomy would work well with our chairs, and this was the best I could manage. Please join us."

The table was also the wrong height for my knees. They banged against the edge, and I couldn't find any way to slide my legs under the tabletop while retaining my seat on the stool. I ended up sitting back from the table with my knees against the edge. Bowls of food with steam gently rising from them occupied the tabletop in front of Ru'andarko and D'Quilla. In front of me sat a mug of clear liquid with a cover and a straw.

"I must give you a second apology," Ru'andarko said. "With the little I could learn about your biochemistry, because we no longer have the technology we once did, I'm concerned that you would have difficulty with our food. To be frank, it might poison you, and I would not want to do that. Unless that was my intent, of course."

His wings gave a flick and I wondered if that meant he was joking. "The mug contains an emulsion of basic carbohydrates, amino acids, and fats. I think it is safe for you, and you can use it for calories and hydration while you are here with us. Like most complex organisms, I'm sure there are specific compounds you need that I cannot know or supply. I hope your stay with me will not extend until that becomes an issue."

Yes, vitamins would be an issue, if nothing else. "The food I had in my pack would cover any of those needs," I said.

"Of course. And we have kept that. But you will want it for your return journey unless you decide you can bring your craft down near the city."

"Probably not. Because of the fighting." I did not want to take the conversation in that direction, so I bought time by taking a sip. Rancid ranch dressing would have been tastier. I managed to avoid regurgitating it and searched for another topic.

I was going to ask about D'Quilla's comment that the two of them were the only ones who could talk to me, but got only to "Your—" before I came to a halt. Was D'Quilla a son or a daughter? For that matter, was Ru'andarko a father or a mother? Not only didn't I know, I couldn't even find the right words in my newly acquired vocabulary. I stumbled through a clumsy question about how reproduction worked. I hadn't felt this embarrassed about sex since fourth grade.

Both Ru'andarko and D'Quilla had their wings raised.

"Do I understand that your species has specific, specialized phenotypes that produce different gametes?" Ru'andarko asked. "This was another major error the system flagged in your transmission: Were there two different species on your ship? The system found too many inconsistencies stemming from that. There were, here on Hell, some lower animals with such differentiation in the past, but so many species have been lost, I do not think any such have existed for centuries. In any case, it would not seem possible that an intelligent species could have such a stark division."

I grew up in a very prudish period on Earth. I'm sure my face reddened. "Then, how do you, ah, do it?"

"Any adult can produce a gamete," Ru'andarko said, "and any adult can fertilize it."

I looked from one of them to the other. "Do you mean that you, ah, produced D'Quilla … yourself?"

That produced a wild flutter of wings from D'Quilla and a loud, "Oh!"

Both Ru'andarko and I looked at D'Quilla.

"I'm sorry. I'm sorry," D'Quilla said. "I know you didn't mean it that way. It's only that if you want to be very, very rude or nasty to someone, you tell them to go fertilize themselves."

So, in addition to ruinous wars, we and the Jandi had F-words in common, even if the word *fertilize* didn't start with an F-sound in their language.

This first contact wasn't going so well. Possibly, it could not be going worse. I wondered if they thought the same. I needed to talk about something other than sex.

"The hallway D'Quilla took me through to reach this room," I said in one of the most abrupt changes of conversation possible, "why does the building material vary so much? Is that your style, or is it something else?"

Both of them were quiet for a moment. They looked at each other.

"Will I have to leave now?" D'Quilla asked.

"No, child, not yet," Ru'andarko answered. "Some things can be serious but not secret." Ru'andarko shifted their eyes to me. Their wings were quite still. "Gardiance City was built out of the rubble of the city that was here before it. That city, too, was built from the rubble of a previous one. And so it has gone. With each rebuilding, it is less than it was before. We retain less of our technology, and what remains to us works less and less well. The only thing we retain in full measure is our habit of war." They paused. "You told me that you never translated our original message, that even when I sent the same content again and again here, you did not know what it said. Is that really the truth?"

"It is."

"Then why did you come here?"

"What?" Now I was startled. "We received a signal from the stars. In all the time we had searched and listened for one, this was the first. We wanted to make contact, to meet you, to see what you are like."

"Are you telling me that you launched an interstellar voyage simply out of *curiosity*?"

I did not need to understand the wing gestures to read the disbelief in that question.

"We had the resources we could spare," I said. That wasn't a complete lie. We weren't doing anything else with an old starship or a crew of old starfolk. I still wanted us as a species to appear competent and strong, as well as peaceful. "Why don't you tell me what that message of yours said?"

"It is a cry for help," Ru'andarko said. "A plea to save us and save our world."

Oh my God. "And when our ship appeared in your system and signaled, you thought someone had mounted an expedition to do that."

Yes, indeed, matters could get worse. They just had.

CHAPTER THIRTY-EIGHT

"D'QUILLA, YOU MAY STAY HERE AND FINISH YOUR MEAL. THEN YOU HAVE studies to attend to. We will be in my office."

Ru'andarko's statement was punctuated by a thud. The bowls moved on the table. The building itself shook.

"That was a significant impact," Ru'andarko said. "I think the sooner we have this conversation, the better."

We exited the domed room through a different door than the one I had entered by. It led to a steep staircase similar to the first. Ru'andarko led the way down. The rear-facing long toes of his feet gripped the stairs behind, helping to keep his balance despite the pitch. Lacking feet of that design, I again went sideways. Guardrails would have helped.

"Approximately five hundred years ago," Ru'andarko said as we descended, "a consensus arose that the unceasing warfare was leading to the destruction of our world and to our own demise. As obvious as that may seem to you, achieving any kind of consensus is rare among clans and confederations that are always at war amid shifting alliances."

"What surprises me," I said, "is that you have managed to carry on like this for as long as you have without wiping out all life on the planet. You have nuclear technology. There is evidence, let us say, that you have used it in weapons."

The wing waggle I saw and the sound that went with it might have meant a laugh. "We are clever, we Jandi. We do not use megaton weapons that create huge firestorms and block sunlight. At least, not after the first war, when we had such weapons. One continent has been uninhabitable since that time.

"But we have precision-enhanced radiation weapons, thermobaric weapons, chemical weapons, lasers, particle beams, and so on. Or, we had them. Much of our technology is lost or unworkable now, so we pummel ourselves and our remaining infrastructure with archaic explosives and simple poisons. It does not matter. A long, slow process instead of a short, quick one. The end will be the same."

We reached the bottom of the stairs, where three corridors led away. They pointed me to the right-hand one and then walked that way. I followed.

"What was even more surprising about that old consensus was that it led to a united action." Ru'andarko continued their recitation as we walked past more mismatched sections of wall. "It was decided that our only hope was to appeal for help, to send messages to the stars in the hope that there were beings around other stars; beings more intelligent than we, who would save us from ourselves.

"Forging that alliance was quite a spectacle. Many argued that since there were no binary systems nearby, such an intelligent race could not exist. Others argued that if such a species did exist, we would only be an amusement for them. I am sure there were clans, probably many of them, who secretly hoped that they would be able to steal military technology from anyone who did show up and then use that for conquest.

"I suspect it was the general level of disbelief that the scheme could work, coupled with those concealed selfish interests, that allowed the plan to move forward in the first place. A transmitter was built, powerful enough to send a signal that could be easily picked up hundreds of light-years away. The Society of Watchers was created—dedicated individuals who devoted their lives to watching for a response. Because of the suspicions and the infighting, the society was independent and was given complete charge of the contact if, or when, it occurred."

"I am surprised that we never detected your civilization," I said. "Somewhere around the time you say your people made that agreement, we searched for evidence of civilization around other stars. We should have detected broadcasting from here."

"Actually not," Ru'andarko said, "not with that time frame. We went away from broadcast transmissions far back in our history in favor of methods that are more secure. You would not have detected those. We use broadcast transmission today because, well, it is another evidence of the decline brought by war and destruction followed by more war and destruction."

Our walk ended at a closed door. Ru'andarko pulled out an old-style metal key from their coverall, inserted it in a slot in the door, and gave a twist. I heard a click, and they pulled the door open. Light flicked on inside.

"My office," Ru'andarko said. "I am certain it is the most sophisticated remaining on Hell."

It reminded me of a small command center. Ranks of screens three high covered the wall in front of a Jandi-style chair. A console on the desk before the chair could have passed for a combination of touchscreen and keyboard, from a distance.

"The consensus fell apart. Naturally." Ru'andarko was addressing the screens. "The transmitter was fought over like everything is fought over, and then it was destroyed. It lasted maybe a decade or two. The Watchers have dwindled as they were caught up in wars and Jandi lost interest in the plan until, as I have said, I am the last."

"Do you plan for D'Quilla to succeed you?"

"I doubt very much that will happen." Ru'andarko seated themself in front of the console. "There are some things I need to show you."

"A couple of questions first," I said. They swiveled the chair to face me. "Didn't your people, the Jandi, go out to the stars yourselves? I would think you had the technology to do it. Didn't you search the sky for other signals?"

"Space was never considered interesting," Ru'andarko said. "We cared about this world and its resources and who controlled them. Who would want to control vacuum and lifeless rocks? We did not search for signals, because we were sure, we knew, a binary system was necessary for higher intelligence. We are very sure of ourselves, we Jandi. There was no interest until desperation set in."

As they were speaking, I recalled that the whole purpose of the ISC and the starshot program had been a scheme to keep the peace by channeling money out into space instead of allowing it to be used by the various militaries. That had been quite the epic fail in the end also. I didn't want to tell Ru'andarko about our history. The Jandi reaction to another desperate species was not one I wanted to see.

"You said you needed to show me something."

"Yes."

Ru'andarko stretched out one long finger and made a single tap. A large screen first flickered out, then lit up again, showing an image of this world with the landmasses colored in green, tan, or gray. This presentation had obviously been preplanned.

"The color codes," Ru'andarko said, "are green for arable land, tan for nonarable. Gray is where I do not have good data, but I think it is reasonable that where good data are not available, we would not have arable land."

The map did not have very much green. They let me gaze at it for a minute, then made another tap. The image changed. All the green vanished. There was nothing but tan.

"This is a projection of the situation in seventy-five years. What do you see?"

"No arable land at all," I murmured.

"Correct. Now look at this one." Two more taps. "This is a bio-diversity map. The color key on the side shows the approximate range of species number for an area." I couldn't read the numbers, so he told me what the colors stood for. "I doubt you are an ecologist, so I will tell you that the numbers are rather limited even today. Here is the projection for seventy-five years from now." Another tap.

I had no trouble reading the projection. The numbers of species on all land areas projected to zero. Only in the oceans were any number of species expected to survive.

"The numbers for ocean dwellers are within the margin of error of the technique," Ru'andarko said. "I expect they will go to zero also."

"There's nothing you can do?" I asked.

"No. Not even if by some miracle we united to try. The land and water have been so severely poisoned and for so long by chemical weapons in our wars, and the poisons spread."

"Do your leaders know this?"

"Not yet." Ru'andarko was quiet for a moment. "The satellites that are key to collecting these data were a network under the auspices of the Society of Watchers. No one else would be trusted with them. The only remaining place these data can come and be analyzed is here. I doubt anyone else even knows that anymore. Since the outcome cannot be changed, I have seen no reason for a discussion. But then *you* arrived."

"And not with some magical means of rescue," I added, to finish their last sentence. "Surely some of your leaders must suspect what is happening, even if they don't have your data. They can't be blind. I'm surprised there wasn't a line of them outside the door to my room, waiting for me to wake up, especially with the machine learning trick you used to get my brain to understand your language."

"Never underestimate the blindness of leadership, particularly where power calculations are made." Ru'andarko's wings flared wide. "The Watcher is supposed to handle the initial contact. That is why you were brought to me without question. And no one, including me, had any idea if the machine learning would work. That risk would be mine to take. Also, our leaders are preoccupied with a war, which may eliminate this city seventy-five years before any deadline. They are waiting for me."

"What are you going to tell them?"

"You have not said which star you came from. Even if I now discard my system's rejection of your transmission, it was not in there either."

"That is correct." The exclusion from our information packet had been deliberate.

"May I assume your species has not found a way to travel faster than the speed of light?" Ru'andarko asked.

"That is a reasonable assumption."

The silence in Ru'andarko's office crackled with tension. We had not arrived equipped to save a world. Even without knowing which star was home to humans, Ru'andarko had to have deduced from the time it took us to arrive after their signal was sent that even if we flew back to a planet willing and able to undertake a Herculean rescue operation, by the time we returned, it would be too late. This planet would be dead.

Within the span of our conversation, my goals had undergone a dramatic shift. While I had learned what their signal to us meant and why they sent it, I had yet to learn much about the Jandi, from their culture to how they had created this hell for themselves. However— and this was a very big however—there might well be someone up the chain of command who was going to regard me as a massive disappointment when they realized we were not here as their deliverance. I needed to put extricating myself from this world ahead of acquiring knowledge about it.

"What are you going to tell your leaders?" I asked again.

"I don't know," said Ru'andarko.

CHAPTER THIRTY-NINE

I DIDN'T SEE RU'ANDARKO AT ALL FOR THE NEXT SEVERAL DAYS. THEY LEFT ME A message—via D'Quilla, since having learned to speak the language did not mean I could read the writing—that I should not leave the building, but otherwise could do as I pleased. I was not a prisoner, at least not in the sense of having guards or even anyone who would prevent me from leaving.

The first thing I did was to find the ground-floor exit. There was no one there. It was locked, but against the outside. I was able to open it and step outside to find a deserted street. No alarm sounded. No one came to check on me.

I could have made a run for it. If I were a real old Hollywood action-vid hero, that's what I would have done. I would hijack the first vehicle I saw, force the driver—of course, it would have a driver—to take me to the government center, where I would outfight and over-whelm twenty elite guards, capture the leadership, uncover and foil their nefarious plan to take over the starship *Ranger*, force them to open communications with the ship, and get myself rescued. Yeah. I have as much future as a screenwriter as I do as a stand-up comic.

The fact was that wandering around and poking my nose into

various places was far more likely to cause problems than do me any good. Yes, I could have made a run for the LZ. However, to do that, I would need to find my pack, or at least my food, then steal or hijack a vehicle, get it through the pass, and navigate my way across the waste. High risk, low likelihood of success.

As long as I wasn't being threatened or mistreated and there was any possibility of getting help from the powers that be, pulling a stunt like that was idiotic. There was a risk that Ru'andarko's conversation with the higher-ups would end with a squad of stormtroopers at my door, but it was a lesser risk than trying to outrun the nu'Jandi. I did the smart thing. I went back inside.

Most of the time, I hung around with D'Quilla. What else was I going to do? Play solitaire on my projection field with the app on my chip? Brood over my dead? D'Quilla, as it turned out, was happy to spend the time with me. Aside from the fact that I was the exotic creature from outer space, D'Quilla lived alone with Ru'andarko and was starved for companionship.

"This isn't typical," they told me. "Normally, six or maybe eight Jandi live together along with children. That's a nest. Then groups of nests are a nest-ring. A group of nest-rings is a subclan, and a group of subclans is a clan. That's obvious, isn't it? A clan governs an area, like this city. But my parent is a Watcher. They can't be part of a nest, or any structure above a nest, because they have to be independent in case the message is answered. Which it was! So it all makes sense.

"But that means I couldn't grow up in a nest. It's worth it because I'm able to meet someone from another star, but it is a bit lonely. I used to go to a group with a tutor, which is how we teach children—how do you teach children?—but we had to stop when the fighting started. I've never been past the walls; it's not really safe out there, although it's not so safe here when those ships are shooting, but going all the way to another star would be fabulous. Tell me what it's like!"

Yes, I was a welcome distraction. D'Quilla asked for stories so I told them, even though teller of tales has never been an avocation of mine. I was selective about my stories, since I had taken pains to portray humans as basically peaceful—and being among a warlike species looking to be saved from the destruction they had visited on themselves made me want to keep up that fiction—although a large part of my adult life had been anything but. Nevertheless, I could talk about the starshots to the planets we called High Noon and Heaven. Even if I did a little editing, there was plenty of adventure and strangeness to describe.

D'Quilla traded stories from Jandi history and folklore, mostly battles and heroes. These reached back, as they told it, a few millennia in time. The Jandi had been fighting each other since the dawn of their civilization, and only the fact that they had developed the sophistication to wreck their planet seemed likely to bring it to an end.

Before I judged the Jandi too harshly, though, I thought about Earth. About us, as a species. Hadn't humans been fighting with each other since we developed any kind of civilization? Was the only real difference between us and the Jandi that we had managed to destroy our civilization and kill most of the human population without eliminating all other life on our planet? True, we had only done the "destroy civilization" thing once, so far. The Jandi history was much longer, and they had done it numerous times. Were they our future, if we lasted long enough? Was intelligent life nothing more than a futile evolutionary dead end? This was depressing.

I wanted to get away from stories that made me think of self-immolating civilizations. Jandi, as it turned out, played games, including ball games. D'Quilla introduced me to one that resembled a mixture of basketball and cornhole.

The building Ru'andarko occupied as the city's Watcher had a cavernous space I would call a gymnasium. My mind's eye populated it with a raucous crowd watching college basketball or fifty ranks of people practicing tai chi. With only the two of us in it, the echoes were painful.

Indeed, the Society of Watchers had fallen on hard times. D'Quilla paid no attention to that while they explained the rules to me. I thought those were straightforward and D'Quilla made sure to point out how they were modifying them to account for the fact that my feet weren't designed to grip a ball the way Jandi could. I said I would manage. There was no way I was going to let a thirteen-year-old beat me.

I lost every game.

Losing aside, I liked D'Quilla. They were bouncy and mouthy, with an opinion about everything and a conviction that the most important part of my interstellar journey of 236 light-years was that the two of us got to shoot the breeze and play ball together. That got me thinking about different kids and a house full of them. I could believe that D'Quilla had a bit of Elvy—more than a bit—and some of a younger No Nonsense in them. They would have fit in well at Charity's farmhouse. My mind came to a sudden halt when that image materialized because that was one of the stupidest lines of thinking I could have had.

"Is something wrong?" D'Quilla asked. We were in the gym and they had the ball clutched in one foot, ready to start the next game.

"No, nothing," I said. "Why?"

"My parent said you use your face the way we use wings. I've been watching and they're right. That face on you then meant sad."

I had been learning a lot about wing expression, too, and D'Quilla's, at that moment, showed concern. "I was just thinking about people I used to know. How you remind me of them. One of the peculiarities of starflight is that whatever and whoever you leave behind, you leave behind permanently."

"I'm sorry," D'Quilla said. "Maybe you're not stuck. Maybe you can go back. I'll miss you, but maybe you can do that. We'll see when my parent is back."

"Maybe." I gave them a smile and figured the expression would pass for genuine. There was no point in discussing physics. I liked the image of D'Quilla at story time in Charity's farmhouse, with Elvy, no doubt, plotting some prank involving feathers. Relativity could go to hell.

CHAPTER FORTY

Ru'andarko was back the next day. They asked me to join them for a meal in the domed room at the top of the society building. This time, D'Quilla wasn't there. The view had also changed from our last meeting. In the intervening time, shells or missiles had struck the city below the Watcher's tower and turned a group of buildings into rubble, leaving a gash across the face of the city. I wondered how much longer this particular conflict would last.

The drink I was given as a meal was the same putrid concoction I had been drinking since I arrived. I wondered how much longer my situation could go on. From the way Ru'andarko was holding their wings, I thought the time would be brief.

"What did your leadership say?" I figured I might as well go straight to it. "Can I have access to your communication system? Do they want to meet with me? What do they want?"

"It is difficult." Ru'andarko's wings said they were uncomfortable. "Obviously, I could not tell them that, in answer to our transmission, you had brought a fleet of ships to repair our world. I thought it better to say there was difficulty with the machine learning and with communication, but that your people wanted to help us."

"And their response?"

"They are preoccupied with the fighting. The help they want is military. I will not pretend to be surprised. They want me to convince you to supply us with novel weapons. They want you to bombard our enemies from your ship and not to allow any other clan to know that you are here."

With all I had learned about the Jandi, I can't say that I was surprised either. I fell back on the position I had previously established. "I told you that we are a peaceful people. We don't carry any weapons beyond what you have seen."

"They cannot conceive of high intelligence without sophisticated weaponry. They are certain you have it, regardless of any claims you make about your purpose. They will not permit any access to our communication systems, because they fear you could call down the weapons on us. I am supposed to convince you, as I said. One possible way mentioned was vivisection."

If D'Quilla had said that, I would have taken it as a bad joke. I didn't think Ru'andarko had any sense of humor. Maybe I should have tried that action-vid idea when no one was watching me and I had the chance. "We are peaceful," I said, "unless we are unduly provoked. Then we become … unpleasant."

"Even if you are far less peaceful than you claim, you are one against many and cannot even eat the food you would find here."

All that was true. However, between the lesser gravity on Hell and the way Jandi evolution had gone, I packed a lot more muscle on my frame than they did. I was also skilled with a variety of weapons. I didn't intend to be a lamb to the slaughter.

"Please understand that I know you can kill me," I said. "Please also understand that I can kill as well and that I will take as many with me as I can. This is not bravado. In the end, if that is the way it ends, the Jandi will gain nothing."

Ru'andarko shifted in their seat. I watched wings flutter. "Yes, I'm sure that is true. I am also sure your peacefulness is a garment you can put on or take off as you choose. Underneath, I do not think you are very different from us. However, I mean you no harm and believe that there is a way out for you, a way to return to your ship. I would like to make a deal with you."

"A deal?" I asked. "What kind of a deal? Do you want me to take you and D'Quilla with me? I have to be honest; I do not think you can survive the starflight on our ship." Actually, that was a certainty. I could not think of how to put a Jandi into hib and keep them alive. I couldn't even think of how to feed them.

Ru'andarko half rose from their chair. Wings were outstretched and rigid. I had shocked them. "No," they said. "I am touched you would even think of that, but no. Even if you could do that, and even if you could figure out how to feed us on your world, I do not want to finish my life as a museum exhibit on an alien planet. Not I and not D'Quilla. What I want is that you take back with you a record of the Jandi: our history, who we were, our successes, and our failure. Promise that your people will translate it and keep us alive that way. I have built in the language map my system made for your learning. That should suffice for a proper connection. My mission as a Watcher is to save this world. Saving its memory is as close as I can come. Never come back here. Let a dead planet keep its dead."

Their request made a deep impression on me. It spoke of duty and commitment. "You have my promise."

"Good." Wings folded against their back. "There is one more thing we must do. It will improve your chance of returning to your ship, although it is not without its own risk."

"In my situation, there are risks everywhere. They are relative. What are you suggesting?"

"That we use your interface again for a different type of machine learning. This technology has all but vanished, but my system, the Society of Watchers' system, still has the capability. It is called the Warrior imprint. It will provide you great skill in fighting and with weapons."

"I am already very skilled."

"Yes. You have said enough for me to believe that. Having that base will improve the chance of success with this imprint. It will amplify your skills. All your reflexes and movements will be faster and stronger. Much more so. You will not miss a shot. Technique with any weapon, or anything that can be used as a weapon, will be perfect.

"As important, your brain will learn how to squeeze the last erg of energy and last bit of alertness from your endocrine and muscle systems. I do not need to know your physiology because it is your neural network, your brain, that will learn to do it. With the waste and the nu'Jandi between you and your goal, you should do this, regardless of the skills you already have."

"Can't we manage air transport to the landing area my ship used?" Flying to the LZ would give a higher chance of success than any warrior training Ru'andarko could add to what I already had.

"No." Wings said sorrow. "There are few craft left that can fly over Hell. Our authorities guard them jealously and will use them only in a military operation. I cannot access one for this purpose. I have already tried. I fear any further effort will give away my intent. That will have a bad outcome. For you. For the same reason, I am sending you alone. I would not trust the reactions of our authorities if they have you."

I considered what Ru'andarko had said. If air transport was out—and I had to take their word on it—this imprint might be my one chance of making it on the ground. That bit about managing my energy sounded like being able to generate my own stim pills internally. If I was going alone through the land beyond the pass, that ability could be the difference between success and failure, between life and death. Of course, there is no such thing as a free lunch.

"What is the downside?" I asked. "What can go wrong?"

Ru'andarko's shoulders made a gesture that, on a human, would have been a shrug. Maybe it meant the same on a Jandi.

"It is hard to say. Because mine is the only remaining system on Hell capable of creating this imprint, we have no current experience. I speak only of history. Your brain is alien, your physiology even more so. If you were a Jandi and did not already have substantial skills, it would probably kill you. Alien as you are, it still might. You might go insane, although since you learned our language through the system, I would say that is unlikely. There is one thing that was reported to happen to most Jandi, so it will probably happen to you." They stopped abruptly.

"What will happen?" I put an edge in my voice that I doubt they recognized.

"You will see ghosts."

"Excuse me?" This made no sense. "Do you mean I'm going to see random images of dead people? Human or Jandi?"

"Not random," Ru'andarko said. "Your mind will conjure images of those you knew. They will speak to you. Think of computer avatars. Fully three-dimensional. Drawing on your experience of them to speak and act. Almost like an AI-generated avatar of someone from a database. I understand it is very disturbing. They cannot physically harm you, however."

Again, I considered what they said. If this was going to be like Scrooge stuck with the ghost of Jacob Marley, I could see how that would be a problem. On the other hand, if I could see and hear Yong again, it would be worth it no matter what she said. I thought of those times I had imagined her standing near me or speaking to me.

"We all have our ghosts," I said to them, the same words Yong had said to me in what felt like a different lifetime.

They took that for my assent and led me down to the same office where they had shown me the maps of a dying world.

"I'm afraid I must ask you to sit in my chair," Ru'andarko said. "It will not be comfortable for you, but I have no other place to do this. It was never planned to do this kind of learning, and I must make do with what I have."

Their chair did not fit my anatomy. I could feel the strain in my lower back from the moment I sat down. My knees complained if I put my feet on the crossbar, but the edge of the seat cut into my thighs if I let my legs dangle.

"Please try to stay on the seat," they said. "Your interface does not allow a direct connection, so the orientation is important."

"Should I fasten my seat belt before departure?"

Ru'andarko did not get the joke. It wasn't one of my better ones, I suppose.

They opened a compartment in the desk and pulled up a device that reminded me of a dentist's X-ray machine. By pulling and twisting on the sliders that anchored it to a framework below the desk, Ru'andarko was able to aim the tapered end of the machine at my head. They reached past me to tap at controls on the console, then examined the squiggles of writing that appeared on one of the screens.

"I think this will work," Ru'andarko said. "I am sure the machine learning sequence will engage. What will happen after that, we will have to see."

"Do it," I said.

They tapped a control.

It was dark on Mindanao. Shadows moved in the dark. Gunfire flashed and boomed. I fired. I was on the line at Camp Schwarzkopf. Men and women fell around me. A wave of attackers surged at me. I fired, kept firing. I was on a dirt street in Eastview. A man reached for his gun. I fired. A monster rose up before me. Python heads with razor teeth. All I had was a knife. I cut and slashed. I fought Jandi. I fought with weapons I didn't know in a fortress I had never seen before. Combat after combat. Some familiar, some not. Again and again. Each time was deadlier, but each time I was faster and even deadlier myself. I ran across a desert all day and all night. Each time I ran faster. Each time I failed, I died, and each time I died, agony pulsed through my mind. But with each success, each time I killed, an elixir of pure joy coursed through me.

I screamed. I know I screamed.

I blinked. Light from the ceiling made me blink again. I was lying on my back on the floor, two feet from the chair. Ru'andarko was looking down at me. I checked, gave thanks my pants were clean and dry.

"How are you?" they asked.

"Like shit." My voice was a croak. Every muscle hurt. Every *part* of every muscle hurt. "How long?"

"Almost exactly one day." Wings stretched. "I have never run this before. I was not sure what to expect."

"Did it work?" I asked.

"I have no way of knowing that," Ru'andarko said. "You will know if you need it."

I looked around the office, saw only Ru'andarko amid his screens and consoles. "I don't see any ghosts."

"I didn't say you would see them all the time. They come and they go, and I am told the times are of their choosing and not yours. Can you stand?" They extended a hand.

I grasped their hand. It was warm and scaly. Then I got my feet under me and shoved myself up, being careful not to pull too hard on their hand. The Jandi frame looked slight, and I did not think they could hold my weight.

When I was standing, Ru'andarko released my hand, then pushed theirs into a pocket of their coverall. They withdrew a leather pouch, small and square.

"The record I spoke of is here," they said, and held it out to me.

"If I survive, I will keep my promise." I unsealed the hidden pocket in my pants that held my precious pic of me and Yong. I put the history of the Jandi in with it and resealed the pocket.

"A heavy rainstorm is coming down now," Ru'andarko said. "This would be a good time for you to go."

On the heels of their words, I heard a *crump* even through the walls. The building shook under my feet.

"That's not thunder from a rainstorm," I said.

"No. I fear our defenses are having difficulty in this weather."

Another blast hit. Not only did the building shake but I could *feel* the pressure change in my ears. A second later, the lights went out.

The yellow beam of a single-purpose handlight Ru'andarko held illuminated a swath of the office. All the screens had gone dark.

"That cannot have hit the reactor," they said. "It is too deeply buried. It must have disrupted the transmission system. This will create confusion in the dark and rain. We should take advantage of it. This building backs up against the cliff, as you have seen. Across a small open plaza by the cliff is a gate. I am known to the guards there. Past the gate, a trail runs along the cliff face and connects to the main road coming down from the fort. The defenses are set against nu'Jandi coming down, not anyone going up."

"Isn't this going to get you in trouble with those leaders of yours? Maybe serious trouble?"

"No. You will be cloaked in the dark and rain, and no one will know. Once you are through the gate, I will report that you died while I was trying to convince you to provide your advanced weapons."

Under the circumstances, that seemed to be as good a plan as any. I followed them through more corridors to a large room that swallowed Ru'andarko's light in its darkness. Another blast shook the structure as we walked. From what the beam showed me, we could have been in a garage that had been used to store junk for years.

"Here." Ru'andarko shined the light down. It picked out my pack and one of the M8cs. "I took only enough of your food to run analyses when you came. The rest is as you packed it. You will go farther on less food as a Warrior. I hope it will be enough. Take this also."

They shifted the light to reveal a narrow object that resembled half a canoe. Unlike a canoe, its sides were high to shield most of an occupant, and it had a two-handled stand at the front.

"This is what we call a floater. Few of them are left and even fewer function, but this one does. Blue button on the column starts the engine, steer by turning the handle at the top. I don't know how long it will continue to work, but whatever you can get from it will be useful."

"Thank you," I said. "I don't know if Jandi bury their dead, but if you have a shovel in here, I would bury my friends when I reach the fort."

"Some of us believe in burials." They walked away into the darkness and returned with a shovel.

"Thank you again." I hesitated. "Are you sure that you don't want to take D'Quilla and leave with me? Even if star travel isn't possible, I could maybe take you someplace safer."

"Thank you for your offer, but no. The floater can only take two, not three, and you are much heavier than a Jandi. In any case, D'Quilla and I do not have a home around another star we can go to. No location here would be safer than this. Within this city, I have status as the Watcher. We will hope the defenses hold. Now, it is time."

Ru'andarko's beam picked out a door in the far wall. As they walked to it, I experimented with the floater. Pressing the button caused a low hum to start, and the frame rose four inches from the ground. I stepped into it, and it sank an inch but then held steady. I pushed the column and it moved toward the door.

Ru'andarko pulled back on an old-fashioned crossbar and then pulled the door inward. Sheets of rain thrummed across the plaza beyond. I could barely see the wall past the plaza. I pulled on a cloak that was in the floater, hoping it would be enough to conceal my alien form. Ru'andarko put one on as well and walked beside the floater.

When we reached the gate, I could see a guard station to the side, but it was dark and deserted. Ru'andarko called out, but there was no response.

"The guards seem to have left their posts," Ru'andarko said. "That isn't good, but it makes it easier for you. All we have to do is open it ourselves."

The gate was held closed with a double-crossbar arrangement. It was heavy, but I could lift it clear by myself. Once I had done that, the door swung open.

"Can you manage this by yourself after I am through?" I asked.

"Yes," Ru'andarko said. "It is easier to drop down than lift up."

"Then this will be goodbye," I said. "Take care of D'Quilla and yourself."

"I will." Another blast in the city behind us briefly lit the undersides of the clouds and the falling water.

With that, I was through the gate, skimming over the muddy path that ran along the side of the cliff. I was barely aware of the gate closing behind me.

CHAPTER FORTY-ONE

IN THE DARK AND THE RAIN, IT WAS A MIRACLE I COULD SEE THE TRAIL ONCE I WAS away from the gate. Finding it was one thing; staying on it and not going down the steep slope was another. At one time this route had been paved, which was some help. Fortunately, the floater Ru'andarko had given me had a headlight in the stanchion where the steering was mounted. It wasn't much, and the beam was lost in the downpour a scant few feet in front of the floater, but as long as I kept my pace to a crawl, it let me pick out the path. I decided not to worry about the light giving me away. The likelihood of anyone being out to see it in this weather was less than of me plunging down the cliff in the dark.

Eventually, the rain began to slacken, then it dwindled to a light drizzle. By that time, an early morning glow was peeking over the ridge behind me. The underside of the cloudbank ended in a sharp line, even with the ridge above me. Clear sky beyond the ridge lit up the trail and allowed me to make better time.

The floater I rode was an interesting device. I couldn't see any of the machinery in it. The entire structure was sealed and smooth. I had no idea what kept it up, or propelled it forward, or even enabled it to turn in response to my twists on the steering handle. Magic? I didn't laugh. I remembered someone writing that if you were confronted with technology advanced enough beyond what you knew, it might as well be magic to you.

How advanced had the Jandi technology been? Well beyond ours on Earth, that was obvious. Yet that hadn't stopped them from destroying themselves—multiple times, apparently. Their current-day tech seemed mostly at the level of nineteenth- or twentieth- century Earth, but they still made use of parts of their old technology.

I wondered if the biggest difference between them and us was that our computer networks were so fragile, and we had been so dependent on them, that a cyberwar nearly wiped us out, while the Jandi had lasted long enough to be reduced to killing themselves with explosives and poison. If we could ever decipher what Ru'andarko had given me, we might learn. Assuming, of course, that by the time we returned to the solar system, humanity wasn't as extinct as the Jandi would be.

The trail I was following merged with the main route I had taken down from the pass and was upslope from the twin blocks I had seen before I was stunned. I stopped the floater there and examined the intersection. It wasn't really hidden, yet I had no memory of having seen it on my way down. That was probably a good indicator of my mental state at that time. I went back up the old, cracked road with my eyes fixed on the ridgeline above.

By the time I reached the pass, the clouds had receded back over the ocean, and the suns were bright in the sky. The ground was the same crumbly brown dirt. It did not appear to have rained in or beyond the pass.

The gray walls of the Octagon loomed ahead of me, also unchanged. I wondered if the bodies I had left inside would be intact. I was far from happy to enter the Octagon to find out, but I had a duty to perform and I was going to do it.

All three of them were where I had left them. They had not been disturbed. That did not mean they were unaltered. It doesn't take long after death for decomposition to begin. Tissue breaks down. Bacteria, especially from the gut, generate gas. Bodies bloat and change. I was no stranger to death and I had seen battlefields where it had been days before we could recover the dead. Even so, I couldn't think of my dead young friends as soldiers killed in battle. I had to summon up all my callousness to deal with looking at them. Well, there was no help for it.

I picked a spot past the back entry to the Octagon and away from the road. The earth was soft there. I took the shovel and dug. I excavated a good-sized pit, deep enough that I believed they could stay undisturbed. Then, one by one, I carried them out and put them in the grave. There was only one of me, so I could fire only a single shot instead of a volley, but I did fire three times. Then I saluted at the grave, as I had done in the Octagon before. In my mind, I saluted other graves as well: my mates on Mindanao; lonely graves on High Noon; too many in too many places. Yong could not have a grave, but my salute was also for her.

The suns were lowering in the west by the time I had filled in the grave and finished with my service. I had nothing to use for a marker. I don't think I would have put one up even if I could. While I was certain the nu'Jandi would not pass the Octagon to reach the grave, I couldn't be so sure no one would come up from below. I wanted Sho, Caleb, and No Nonsense to rest. It wouldn't be on Earth, but they could rest.

I leaned on the shovel and looked out over the ocean. Deep blue water out to the horizon and blue sky above. It could have been Earth. I shook my head, tossed the shovel into the floater, and maneuvered the floater through the entry to the Octagon.

I was struck by how empty it was. With the floater hovering over the surface, there was no sound except my own breathing. No echoes bounced off its stark and sterile gray walls. If I hadn't known about the circuitry, machinery, and weapons hidden in those walls, I would never have suspected they were there. The Jandi were very skilled at the technology of war and destruction. Or they had been.

I stopped at the end of the passage out on the other side and gazed downslope to the ruins beyond. Nothing left there except the nu'Jandi, who lurked underground, living off each other and whatever support the slowly failing old technology would provide. Yes, the Jandi had been very skilled at destruction, even more so than we had been. It was finally catching up to them.

Stop being morose, I told myself. I still had a mission: saving my own life and fulfilling my promise to Ru'andarko about saving the history of the Jandi. I had no time to mope about self-destructive behavior.

The twin suns were now almost down to the horizon. I had spent most of the day being a gravedigger and burying my team. The floater could make, perhaps, thirty miles an hour. That was faster than the rover, but I wouldn't clear the remains of the lower city with what daylight was left. After I was out of the lower city, I would need more than a single day to return to the LZ, no matter how I planned the trip. What advantage would this Warrior download of Ru'andarko's give me in a real fight? It had to be significant, based on the importance Ru'andarko had attached to it and the little I had seen of old Jandi capabilities, but I doubted invulnerability was part of the package. I would spend this night in the Octagon, where I didn't need to worry about a nu'Jandi attack. It would cost me an extra day's worth of food, but I could afford that. It was worth the delay to have been able to give my threesome their burial.

·   ·   ·

I WAS UP WITH THE SUNS AS THEY ROSE OVER THE EASTERN HORIZON THE NEXT morning. The sky was mostly clear, burning orange-red at the horizon with patches of grayish cloud turning white as the light strengthened. Except for the double sun, it could again have been a scene on Earth. *Stop thinking like this.* I started the floater.

I slid down the slope on a cushion of air, the passage of the floater marked only by tiny crumbs of dirt that rolled away from the breeze it caused. If the only way the nu'Jandi underground learned of something on the surface was with sensors that picked up vibration through the earth, maybe the floater would go undetected. I wasn't going to bet on that, however. Ru'andarko would have passed along that intelligence.

From the images I had downloaded, I knew the eastern end of the ruined lower city would front open desert. I planned to skirt the ruins until I came to that point. Then I would turn northwest, effectively a sharp left. With the slope on my right up to the higher ground where the upper city sat, it would be a straight shot to where the monument stood. That would be easy to spot across the flat and open desert valley. This route would add still more time to the journey overall, but it would minimize the time I had to spend among the ruins. That should improve my chances. As long as the floater's power stayed on.

Unfortunately, whatever the genius technology was that let the floater float, it didn't include traction. If I tried to traverse any slope, the floater slid down to the side. The exploratory rovers we had were stable on a slope as steep as 40 percent. The floater would slide down grades of only a few percent. It cheered me to think that machinery from Earth was superior in this respect, even as I was forced closer to the old walls than I wanted to be.

Those ruins had a depressing sameness. They stretched out for mile after mile of low ridges that varied from a few inches above the ground to waist high. All were covered with the same layer of granular beige dirt. Some of the grains glinted under the suns and threw off sparkles, but the only difference from one section to another was the amount of sparkle. Randomly spaced openings in the ridge nearest me were, I assumed, the remains of roads that led into the heart of the old Jandi city. A smooth layer of dirt covered those. The only movement was grains here and there dislodged by a gust of wind.

It was that very monotony that gave away the fact I was being watched. It was a flash of black in one place, a low curve of black in another that moved in the wind. The nu'Jandi were there. What were they waiting for?

Ru'andarko had told me they weren't very bright. I knew their grasp of small unit tactics was poor. Did they expect that I would, at some point, turn into the ruins? Were they waiting for more numbers? I didn't think that was reasonable. After all, I was alone. How many would they need? Was it nothing more than they were waiting for me to reach an area where they had outlets from their tunnels? I strained my eyes at the ground ahead, trying to discern a break in the surface ahead of me that might indicate one of their damn holes was about to open.

Driving along, expecting to be attacked—knowing I was going to be attacked—was nerve racking. For hours, nothing happened, just the occasional glimpse of black that told me one of them was there. The afternoon shadows began to lengthen. Were they waiting for dark? Again, I did not understand their thinking. Was the memory of their losses when they came out of the ruins to attack us in front of the Octagon inhibiting them now?

Ahead of me, a low mound rose out of the sand and was distinct from the upslope to my right. Rock stuck up through the sand. This was not part of the ruins. The presence of rock meant, I hoped, that a tunnel was not likely to come up in the middle of it. It wasn't a great defensive position, but it was better than open, flat ground.

I angled the floater away from the ruins toward the mound. There was movement by one of the ridges and a flash of blue. A dark char appeared in the sand in front of the floater. Steam rose from that char. To my left, more figures in black appeared above the low ridge walls. The nu'Jandi were coming for me.

The Warrior *emerged*.

This was the rush of adrenaline, the sense of being fully alive that I'd had in combat before, but it was multiplied a thousandfold, a millionfold. I was high on violence; I was drunk on combat. Every sense was sharpened. I *knew* from the slightest glimpse, the most muffled scrape, exactly where each enemy was. I *was* the Warrior. I fired the M8c without thinking. Every shot was true. I stopped the floater and leaped over the side to use it for cover, grabbing the shovel as I did. I didn't know why; I only knew it was right.

A hole began to open ahead of where the floater hung motionless above the sand. I fired before either of the two figures rising had more than the top of their heads above the surface. Two nu'Jandi. Two shots. Two kills. Then I was off on a dash for the rockpile. I had never burst into a sprint so fast. I had never made such crazy and random zigzags as I did on the dash to that little rise. Even in the midst of that run, when I saw a target, I fired without slowing down, and whatever I fired at, I hit.

The cover the rocks afforded was minimal. Projectiles hit rocks, and splinters of rock shot through the air. Blue flashes were followed by puffs of steam from dirt and rock. I was in continuous motion, but always glued to the ground as I shifted from one bit of scant cover to another. As I went, any target I spotted, I killed. I was Death wielding a firearm.

A group of them circled behind me to take me from the rear. I knew they were there by sounds; knew how far they were and how fast they were closing. I spun, saw four with long knives out. The nearest one leaped at me. My hand was on the shovel. I thrust it with so much force I split the center of their head. A second one was right behind the first. While I impaled one on the shovel blade, I fired the M8c one-handed and killed the next one. In an instant, I had their knives in my hands. The remaining two were only a step behind, knives out, looking to carve my flesh from my bones. My wrists moved of their own volition. I parried both attacks. I counterattacked; they both died. I had the M8c back in my hands. I turned and fired; knew I'd hit yet another. And then it was silent. Nothing moved.

I trembled. I wanted more. I reveled in the bloodlust. I wanted to lick their blood from the knives. I wanted to drink the blood from their veins. I wanted to butcher their bodies and bathe in the blood of my enemies. I wanted—

"Stupid Soldier Boy."

Yong's words penetrated the insane berserker rage that gripped me. She was seated on an upthrust rock in front of me, smiling. That saved me. My controls returned. I forced the Warrior instincts away. It was like putting the genie back in the bottle or the toothpaste back in the tube. I had to fight to put the Warrior away. Yong disappeared as I engaged in the struggle.

I don't know how long it took. Over an hour, I'm sure. From the outside I was motionless, although sweat stood out on my forehead and soaked my clothes. The turmoil was all in my mind. At last, though, it was done. My emotions, my thinking, my controls, were all back to normal, back to Leif Grettison.

Except that wasn't quite true. The Warrior wasn't some foreign entity that had been implanted in me. The Warrior was *me*. It was, as Ru'andarko had told me, a type of machine learning. The Warrior was what my mind could do with my body. Nobody else inhabited my head except me. I was awed by what my body had done as a fighting machine. And I was sickened in equal measure by the thirst for blood that had accompanied it. Did the emotions that came with the Warrior say something about the Jandi who'd created this learning technique, about what a Jandi Warrior was, or did they speak to what was already inside me? I wasn't sure I wanted to know the answer. Perhaps Ru'andarko had understood me a little better than I'd wanted him to. I knew I would need to keep tight control of myself. I only wished I could be sure of how to do that.

What I was certain of was that I was mortally tired. My adrenals had been pressed and dried to raisins. Every muscle and every joint ached. Where I had scooted around my position while hugging the ground, I had torn holes in my clothes and ripped the skin underneath. I had paid no attention to any of that during the fight. One of those blue flashes had caught me across the back of my left calf. The pant leg was burned and there was a blackened groove through skin and muscle. I hadn't noticed that either, when it happened, but I sure noticed it now. Chicken satay on a grill probably felt the way my lower leg did. When I flexed my foot, the blackened tissue in that burn cracked and leaked blood. My pack in the floater had some gauze I could wrap around it, but that was extent of what I could do for first aid.

Time is a funny thing when you're fighting for your life. It's a little like relativity, I suppose. The time of the fight seems to expand to forever. In fact, very little time had passed. I still had at least a couple of hours before the light would fail.

I did not want to spend the night at the rockpile. Whatever its dubious merits as a defensive position, the bodies of the nu'Jandi I had killed were going to attract other nu'Jandi in search of dinner. I did not want to be nearby. The floater had a couple of holes in its sidewalls, but whatever it used for an engine still worked. I slung the M8c and tossed the shovel into the floater and resumed my travel.

By the time the suns were down, I was into the open desert past the eastern tip of the ruined lower city. I didn't want to go to sleep, because there was no one else to take watch, but I didn't have a choice. I was exhausted. I think as the Warrior I would have been able to keep going, to ignore the need for sleep, rest, or food, but I wasn't sure if in that mode I would keep going until I dropped dead without realizing I was reaching that point. In the end, it didn't matter. I couldn't summon the Warrior as though it were some other being. As best I could tell from that one experience, the Warrior was simply an aspect of me that came forward in response to a threat. Absent a threat, I couldn't make it happen.

This wasn't quite the way Ru'andarko had explained it—not in the way I remembered the explanation—but they had said they were guessing how the imprint would affect an alien. I did believe that anyone trying to sneak up on me in the dark probably would bring out the Warrior response. Even if that was wishful thinking, it allowed me to curl up in the bottom of the floater with my head on my pack. I was asleep immediately.

CHAPTER FORTY-TWO

I AWOKE TO FIND THE DOUBLE SUN IN MY EYES. THE SKY WAS DEEP BLUE AWAY FROM the blazing yellow balls, truly more a lozenge than discrete circles, because one was starting to eclipse the other. The wind was picking up.

I let out a groan as I pulled myself to a seated position. The desert was empty around me. That was a good start. Checking myself over, the rest was not so good. All my muscles that had been sore were now stiff. The cuts and scrapes had begun to dry up. The bandage I had put on over the burn on my leg was bloody. I didn't take the dressing down. I knew it was going to hurt when I stood up, but there wasn't anything I could do about it.

I pulled some food out of my pack and chewed mechanically. Once I'd swallowed all of it, I pushed myself upright. Yes, the leg hurt every bit as much as I expected. I ignored that and started the floater moving. I could see in the distance a rise in the land that had to mark the location of that monument and the ruined upper city beyond it. It was hard to be certain, because even with one sun blocked behind the other, it was like trying to make out details across a snowscape reflecting sunlight into the eye.

While I floated across the desert, waiting for that rise to clarify, I thought back to the day before. More specifically, I thought about what the old Jandi tech had done to me. We had never had AI on Earth with the capability of doing something like that. How advanced had the Jandi been? The computer capability that remained in Ru'andarko's office told me they had been very advanced. Had their egocentric philosophy that assured them they were the sole intelligent species in the universe been the only thing keeping them from reaching out across the stars, the way we had? If they had been curious—if a Jandi ship at the height of their powers had shown up in the solar system— would that have been a first contact of nightmare proportions? Had we been lucky? The answer was probably yes to both.

As I thought about what a Jandi visit might have been like, my mind went to the contents of the leather case Ru'andarko had given me. They had said it was a history of the Jandi, so that the memory of their people would not die out. Did that fit what I knew of the Jandi? Could it be more than that? For obvious reasons, this was not like a printed book we could look at and puzzle out the meaning. It would need to interface with a computer system in order to be read. The AI in Ru'andarko's system had been able to use my chip to make me learn their language and give me a Warrior imprint. It did this despite operating across an alien interface and on an alien brain. What was the real capability of the machinery in the pouch Ru'andarko had given me? What would happen if it interfaced with humanity's computers? Somehow, I doubted it would be a passive transfer of information.

It was a delicious irony that humanity no longer had any computers. That was the one part of the equation Ru'andarko did not know and would not have believed. After all, how could a species fly starships if they didn't have computers? But that didn't mean we would never have computer systems again, sometime in the future. Possibly by the time we returned to Earth. What could happen? Could this re-create the Jandi? Was this a way to transfer the Jandi to our planet? If so, would this bring their eternal warfare to Earth and turn it into a second Hell? The fact that I couldn't conceive of how that would be possible didn't mean it couldn't be done. It might be magic to me, but basic technology to old-time Jandi.

I felt an odd tingle. My skin crawled. Suddenly, I wasn't alone. Petey, Luke, and Jamaal from my old squad were walking alongside the floater. They were in full combat gear, rifles at the ready, scanning side to side. Somehow they were walking as fast as the floater was going. Well, Ru'andarko had told me I would see ghosts. I guess ghosts can walk as fast as they need to.

Petey dropped back to be even with me. He had a stalk of some plant in his mouth and was working it between his teeth. He turned to face me and spat out the stalk, which vanished immediately.

"Hey, Sarge," Petey said, "you know this mission's been a fubar from the start. Right?"

"Yeah," I said. "I think I've got that figured out."

"You think we're gonna make it back?"

"I don't know, Petey. Honest to God, this time I don't know."

I guess I wasn't only going to see ghosts, I was going to have conversations with them. My squad was with me, "bloody but unbowed" as the poet wrote, trying to make it back despite the wasteland in front of us.

That was when I noticed someone was up ahead, walking point. When I looked at them, they stopped and turned around. It was Yong. She wore the garb of an attack plane pilot, but her visor was up on her helmet, and her oxygen mask hung loose so I could see her face.

"Soldier Boy," she said, "do you remember I said I would fly any mission?"

Yes, I did remember her saying it when we had less than forty-eight hours to keep a crazy man from blowing up the only plant that could make the antimatter fuel for the starshots. I told her that.

"I would fly any mission," she said, "and I did. But the missions I flew were our missions, not anyone else's."

With that, the ghosts were gone. I was left with the empty desert and my thoughts. Whose mission was I carrying out right now? I knew that Ru'andarko's mission had been to save the Jandi. Their mission was not about saving my sorry ass. That realization brought a few others. In a city under attack, in a society where war was second nature, how absurdly convenient that the gate I needed to use had been unguarded and the path beyond it clear. How generous of Ru'andarko to hand me this floater, a piece of working old Jandi tech that was highly prized.

Then there was the Warrior learning itself. Ru'andarko had said the technique had been lost to the Jandi, that only his system retained the capability. Had Ru'andarko ever gone to their leadership? Did they need to? Was that why I was making this trip with only my Warrior self for company? They had hustled me out of the city as fast as they could and without letting anyone but D'Quilla meet me. Who planned the mission I was now on, and what was its real purpose?

The Society of Watchers had been built on a pipe dream: send an appeal out to the stars and a truly advanced species would show up and save them from themselves. The Jandi had given up on that fairy tale until we appeared on the *Ranger*. Except … Ru'andarko had realized quickly that we could not save them. Had they used those days when I hadn't seen them to come up with a plan B? Was I carrying the plan B?

I thought I knew the answer to that.

All of which brought me back to the question of what was in the pouch Ru'andarko had given me. I knew the answer to that one also. I wasn't angry at Ru'andarko. They were in an impossible situation, and they had grasped the slender reed of a chance they saw. They owed nothing to me or to humanity. To think otherwise was nothing more than me being narcissistic. The problem was that none of that told me what to do. Should Pandora open the box?

I took the pouch out of my pocket and looked at it. Inside it was a smooth black block, a square maybe three inches on a side and half an inch high. If I stared into the block, I could see a shifting, squirming green light inside. The edges were all smooth. I saw no obvious means of connection to anything. I knew that didn't matter. Ru'andarko's computer had connected to my chip.

I laughed, if only to myself, as I remembered worrying when I came back to Earth and boarded that transport that the old Hollywood vid staple of hacking someone's chip and taking them over had become reality. Ru'andarko had done it. Well, sort of. I didn't understand how, and that didn't matter. Call it magic. It still worked. That block would connect, and I was certain, absolutely certain, that it was designed to do far more than passively transmit a history. I stared at the swirling green light in its innards. What was I going to do?

A decision that could determine the future of not only one but two intelligent species had been put in the hands of Leif Grettison. I lacked—totally—any qualification to make a decision of this magnitude. Too bad. It didn't matter. Whatever I did, that would be the decision. I couldn't avoid it, and there was no one else to make it.

You do the best you can with the situation you have.

I stopped the floater and jumped out onto the sand. With the shovel, I dug through the granular sand until I struck hard-packed dirt below. I kept digging until I had excavated a hole a good six feet deep in the dark brown earth. It was as deep as the grave I dug for Sho, Caleb, and No Nonsense. At the bottom of that hole, I buried the legacy of the Jandi.

CHAPTER FORTY-THREE

I STEERED TOWARD THE RISE IN THE GROUND. THE DESERT BETWEEN THE TWO SETS OF ruins was so devoid of any feature that there was nothing else to go by and no way to get lost. Ru'andarko had commented that this area had once been a lush and fertile plain. What had the Jandi done? Had they changed the weather as well? How many years and how many wars had it taken to produce a desert, sterile but for the subterranean remnants of genetically engineered murderers and their dwindling support?

The cliff was there, rising out of the desert, with only more ruins and desert beyond it. The statue was there, just as we had left it. Conqueror or liberator? Tyrant or revolutionary? Ru'andarko had never said. It didn't matter, in the grand scheme of the universe. Whatever triumph it commemorated had been ephemeral.

What did matter was that our rover tracks around the statue from the journey out were as evident as if we had been there the day before. Even our footprints were still there. Time and wind would eventually fill them in or scour them away, but that would take much longer than the time I had spent in the city. I could even tell where Sho had been because her prints were clearly smaller.

The tracks had a much greater significance than a reminder of the dead. They offered me an easy path through the ruins, maybe even through the desert beyond.

I followed the path of the rover away from the statue to the slope we had descended. That drop was a problem for the floater. It wanted to slide down. However, when I aimed it perpendicular to the slope and gave it a running start to reach its maximum velocity before it hit the steep part of the slope, it reached the crest with the same lack of elegance as an old self-driven car on an icefield. It was a good thing too. I don't think I could have pushed the floater up the hill.

At the top, I could see the rover's tracks leading back into the ruins. The dirt there was looser, more granular than at the base of the cliff. The sides of the tracks were beginning to slide down to fill in at the bottom. But with nothing else to mar the surface, the path was still plain.

I was uneasy going through the ruins, but I didn't see any reasonable choice. We hadn't sighted any nu'Jandi before we were past the upper city. Possibly they haunted only the lower city. I pushed the floater as fast as it would go, with my rifle propped on top of the steering stanchion, and followed our trail back to the open desert.

The easy way forward came to an end where the ruins did. Beyond those low walls, no barrier existed to the swirling winds. The loose sand grains of the dead land shifted easily under the force of even gentle breezes. Even the deep tracks the rover cut when we'd come through vanished into the sands no more than twenty yards past the last of the walls.

That meant back to basics for me, back to a basic skill. I knew where we had entered the ruins, and because I could follow our tracks through the walls, that was where I came out. I had that location on the images I'd downloaded from the *Ranger*. Those same images gave me the location of the hab we had set up at the LZ. My chip had a compass app. The desert held no obstacles. All I had to do was set a straight-line course to the hab. Except I wasn't on Earth.

The axis of the magnetic pole pointed to the south on this planet. The direction of Earth's magnetic axis would shift back and forth, north to south, over geological time periods. The same mechanics, presumably, worked here. The app had been built based on a magnetic needle pointing north. Here such a needle would point south. When I realized this, my first reaction was *Who cares?* I'd just pretend north was south and set my course that way. All would be fine.

Not quite. The app used a built-in magnetometer and accelerometers to create the compass that displayed on my projection field. My army chip, all the way back in 2055, had done the same. However, since the magnetic axis pointed the opposite way here compared with Earth, when the app tried to combine the data from the magnetometer with those from the accelerometers, I got error messages.

Alone in a bleak land was not the time for error messages.

With some effort, I was able to get into the app's settings. A toggle switch that allowed me to switch the polarity would have been a thoughtful option, but why would anyone have thought of it? By going to the "custom" menu, I was at least able to turn off the accelerometers. That cleared all the error messages but earned me a warning message that the compass heading would not be accurate and I should consider it approximate. When you are trying to find a tiny hab in a vast, unforgiving desert, *approximate* is not what you want. Well, I didn't have a choice. The next aggravation from the stupid app was that in order to use the custom menu, I had to enable notifications. Intermittently, it cluttered my field with ads telling me which store pages to check for my Christmas shopping. Even if Christmas was coming on Earth, those stores were long out of business and a couple of hundred light-years away. I suppose it was funny, but I failed to appreciate the humor at the time.

This would have been so much simpler with a handheld magnetic needle. I hate technology.

Then the floater died. It happened suddenly and without warning. One minute I was cruising along fine, the next the floater dropped to the sand and lurched to a stop. I slammed against the steering stanchion, rebounded, and fell across the pack and shovel. The thing did not have seat belts.

My first thought was that I was under attack, but when there were no shots, neither blue flashes nor projectiles, and no movement anywhere in sight, I knew that wasn't the case. As if to confirm that impression, I didn't sense any stirring of the Warrior side of me. I picked myself up and checked for damage. My sternum was bruised from hitting the stanchion. The side of my head hurt, and when I probed it, my hand came away with a smear of blood. I had fallen against the blade of the shovel. It could have been worse.

What was wrong with the floater? All I could tell was that it had no power. I could not make it lift off the sand; the steering controls were frozen. Since I didn't know how it worked in the first place, I couldn't tell if it had malfunctioned or simply exhausted its power source, which was also a mystery to me. Ru'andarko had not been certain how long the floater's power would last. One of the problems with advanced technology as magic is that when it fails, you can't fix it. It's not a matter of finding the right-size Allen wrench. By my estimate, the floater had brought me fairly close. That would have to be good enough.

I pulled my pack onto my back, hung my water bottle from the pack, slung my rifle, and hopped out onto the sand. My boots sank into the surface. This was going to be more of a slog than if I had a hard surface to walk on, but I told myself it could be worse. It could have been mud. I wiggled my shoulders to settle the pack and marched forward. The leg where I had been seared by the blue flash burned with pain every time the muscle flexed. I was on foot, wounded, alone, in a hostile desert, and on an approximate course. Wonderful. How much better could it get?

Once the wreck of the floater was out of sight to my rear, the weight of my solitude pressed down on me. I have always thought of myself as a tough nut, and I was. I'd found my way in the wild before. I'd survived combat, including times when I didn't understand how I could have lived through it. However, I don't care how tough someone is. At times like these, especially when there is time to think, a frisson of fear will seep in. Anyone who denies that isn't being honest.

I discovered that this fear brought out the Warrior. Apparently, I shifted into that mode when I was in danger or under attack or when I felt fear.

It had some advantages. As Ru'andarko had said, the Warrior would ignore fatigue, not feel the pain of the burned leg, devote every scrap of energy to its purpose, and make the body push on when there was nothing but will to keep it moving. However, rest breaks, food, and water were also important to maintaining a human body, and the Warrior ignored all the body's cues.

It was more useful for an immediate crisis than a long haul. I also hated the bloodthirsty state of mind that came with it. I did find that the more I had to work with the Warrior, the easier it was for me to force it down and put it away. The Warrior was another side of me, the way I could sometimes be tender or compassionate. I could not make it appear voluntarily, but I could shut it off. It was like playing with my own settings panel, and it gave me something to do as I trudged along.

As time went on, I had to wonder if approximate wasn't good enough, if I was going to end as a pile of bones in this desert. One patch of sand looked like any other. It was only the movement of the suns in the sky that provided some change in my surroundings.

Then suddenly, with only one additional step forward, a notification flashed on my field: NETWORK AVAILABLE. Yes! That was the system in the hab. Approximate had been good enough, because all I had to do was come within range of the system. Once I chipped in to it, I had the exact direction and distance. It was still several miles away, but knowing the destination was there for sure quickened my step. That sorry little hab was a sight for sore eyes.

·   ·   ·

THE FORLORN HAB DIDN'T HAVE MUCH IN IT, BUT THAT DIDN'T MATTER TO ME. IT MIGHT have been the most basic, spartan ISC-standard piece of construction in the universe, without a picture on a wall or a coffeepot on a desk, but in its banality it was familiar. Stepping through the door into familiar human architecture was a relief in itself. It spoke of home. I enjoyed that emotion.

We had stored a few days' worth of food and water in the hab. A quick glance showed that both were untouched. I didn't bother with either at the moment; I wanted confirmation that there had been no intruder. I turned my attention to the transmitter.

The power was on—not just the local network at the hab but also the transmitter that could reach the ship. "*Ranger*, this is Grettison," I said into the pilot's comm channel. "I have reached the hab and need to be extracted. Come in, *Ranger*."

When I didn't hear a voice immediately on the comm channel, I sent a notification to everyone in the crew who had a chip. Had I somehow arrived during ship's night? I didn't think so. I switched to the general comm channel for the ship and sent again, both on the comm and on the speakers.

"Leif." That was Shane at last. "It's good to hear your voice. What's your situation?"

In my opinion, his voice could have sounded more enthusiastic. "We've had casualties," I said. "I'm the only one left. You need to get me out of here."

"There was more fighting after you left the rover?" I could hear the uncertainty in his voice. "You're sure about the other three?" I wondered if he realized we were on the general channel.

"Damn it! I buried them!" I was angry and it showed. I didn't expect to be questioned about anything like this. "I'll make a full report when you pick me up. When can I expect the spaceplane?" I made certain I was back to an unruffled tone.

"Are you saying the locals are hostile to us?"

"There's a remnant of a population that lives in, I guess, caverns under the lower city area where we were attacked. They're what's left of a gene-engineered army, and, yeah, they're hostile to anybody. Otherwise, the fighting here is among political groups I don't really understand, but I don't think they care about us unless we can give one of them a military advantage."

"But these modified soldiers you talked about—are you sure the landing area is secure?" His voice quavered, and I was certain it was not the connection that made it sound that way.

"What do you mean? The LZ is in the middle of a completely empty and lifeless desert. We didn't even have trouble in the upper city. It was only in the lower area, by the Octagon."

"But what if they have surface-to-air?"

"Christ, Shane, we've been over that before." I thought I heard an intake of breath that came from someone else. "We had no trouble when we came down before, and from what I learned from them in the city, air travel is almost nonexistent. They don't have any such capability." It would have been a bad idea to say that the little remaining capacity was reserved for military use.

"But you can't be sure. And you can't be sure none of those fighters tracked you, and you said that they came up from underground, and we don't know, we can't know, how far their underground network might go. We just can't know." Shane's voice rose an octave within the space of those last four words.

"What are you getting at, Shane?" My voice was becoming louder and sharper.

"It's everything I pointed out that were risks before, but now, with what you've said, they're even greater. We can't take a chance with the spaceplane, Leif. And I'm the only pilot for it. Magda can't fly; she can't manage the controls or handle the accelerations. But even if we're not talking about me, we need the spaceplane when we return to Earth."

"Shane, I'm down here on the surface. You need to come get me."

"Leif, you shouldn't have insisted on this expedition to the surface. Not when we saw how things were on this planet. This is really on you. We can't risk the spaceplane." He sounded like he was losing control.

Talk him down, I thought. Calm him down. "Shane, I understand your concern about the spaceplane. But the hibs are just as important for getting us back. You need me on the ship for that."

"Pilots have training in putting people into hib, and Hannah's learned enough to help. I won't deny there's some risk, but I don't see it at the same level as risking the spaceplane. You have to understand."

"Shane, we don't leave people behind." My voice was ice cold.

"I'm sorry, Leif, so sorry. I really am. I need to put the ship and the crew first."

"Shane, you can't mean to leave him there." That was Kwame.

"This is on the general channel, Shane, and the speakers." Hope's voice. "We've all heard it."

"I have to do what's right," Shane said. With that, his voice was finally even.

"Shane, you can't—" I stopped when I realized he'd closed the channel.

He was going to maroon me on a dying alien world.

CHAPTER FORTY-FOUR

WAS IN SUCH A STATE OF DISBELIEF THAT I DIDN'T SPOT RIGHT AWAY THE BLINKING notification on my field. It was marked Private and encrypted. From Magda.

I looked at it and it opened to show I'LL BE ON THE BRIDGE WITH HIM. GIVE US A FEW MINUTES displayed on my field. It had gone to the entire crew other than Shane.

I could certainly give her a few minutes. It was not as though I was going anywhere. We didn't leave people behind. We just didn't. At least, not voluntarily. That was a tenet of faith in our mates and our command, the bedrock that supported so many missions in so many dicey situations. The concept that you could be in a bad place and someone could say, "Nah, it's too risky to come for you," was anathema. Except it had happened.

Did Magda think she was going to talk Shane into changing his mind? I doubted that would work. Not after everyone else on ship had heard that conversation and he still ended it the way he did. I did wonder what had happened to Shane. Cowards don't become space pilots; it's not a profession that attracts people repelled by risk. Something had happened with the wreck upon landing at Earthbase, and that had become entrenched in his mind in the long years he had to ruminate on it. Oh, his outward bravado had been intact, but the signs of his real feelings had been there all along. I saw them in retrospect, in his words and actions, starting from his hesitation when we were fired on while leaving Earthbase. I had no time for recriminations over missed signals or what I should have done then. I had no time to worry about Shane's psyche. I had to work out whether there was anything I could do.

My eyes fell on the M8c. No. Once the *Ranger* left orbit, I would have no choice, because I couldn't survive on the world its own inhabitants called Hell. But I wasn't there yet. Not yet. The transmitter still worked. The *Ranger* network was still available, and I was still chipped in. Perhaps I could buy Magda and the others more than a few minutes to change the situation up on the ship.

What if the hibs were shut down? If a starship had enough food for its crew, and if the air and water systems would support it, there was no absolute reason a crew had to go into hib. They could sit in the caf and play cards and age the SFOR years it took a ship to make the journey. In the case of the *Ranger* and this crew, it could be done because the *Ranger* had originally been stocked to support colonization. The supplies to support the planned two hundred for their awake time on the ship would cover our tiny remaining crew for five years. Arithmetic would show that. However, the starships weren't designed for the crew to be awake the whole time. It would be like spending five years in an underground prison with only five other people, and it would take five years off their bio lives. They were already old, bio-wise.

I had access to all the hib screens. I opened the settings panel. Then I sent a notification to all crew that the hibs were inoperable and sat down on the floor of the hab to wait.

It didn't take too long. A notification popped on my field, saying the spaceplane bay was depressurizing. That was followed in short order by one that said the spaceplane was separating. When I saw that, I let out a whoop and danced a little jig around the hab.

I went outside to watch for the spaceplane. The sky was deep blue, unbroken by any clouds. The twin suns gleamed overhead. The planet had a cruel beauty to it. Was the cruelty fundamental to this place and had it seeped into the Jandi over time, or had the Jandi made it that way? That was a question we would never answer.

At first, it was a black dot against the blue canopy above. To me, the big, ungainly spaceplane could have been an angel descending from heaven as it grew larger against the sky. I ran back into the hab and grabbed the M8c. I'm not sure I had a clear reason; it was just my state of mind.

The last set of parachutes burst from the rear of the spaceplane as I came outside again, a flamboyant orange against the off-white and sere plain around us. Then the skids hit and sent up sprays of sand and gravel, as though this were a water landing on a lake. I was running for where the ramp would come down even before the spaceplane came to a halt.

The comm channel was silent as I walked into the spaceplane and the ramp began to retract. I figured Shane didn't have a lot to say, and I didn't care. I was going to have a lot to say, but that would come later.

However, when the hatch closed behind me, I heard, "Leif, why don't you come up to the cockpit?" It was Magda's voice.

Yes, it was Magda in the pilot-in-command seat, her left arm in a sling, and she was the only one on the spaceplane. "Why don't you take the copilot seat? You won't be needing that." She looked at the M8c.

"Probably not much, where we're going." I found a strap next to the seat to secure the rifle and belted myself in. "I thought you weren't cleared to fly."

"Given my physical condition, I wouldn't be if there were anybody other than me who had to clear me." She favored me with a thin-lipped smile. A wince replaced the smile and she rubbed at her left shoulder. "Hannah said this would hurt. I like a doctor to be right, but not all the time."

I tried to read her face for the meaning behind what she'd said, and couldn't. "You don't sound as though Shane changed his mind, either from when you spoke to him or from the notice about the hibs."

"Correct." She stopped there and looked at the desert through the windshield. "Bleak place. You can, I hope, fix whatever you did to the hib systems?"

"I actually didn't do anything," I said. "A hib unit isn't like turning a light on or off. I was able to make control screens flash red alerts without doing anything fundamental, and I sent everybody a notification that I had screwed them up. I didn't think anyone would know differently, except maybe Hannah, and I thought she would play along."

"Hah!" This smile was a real one. "You're certainly right about Hannah."

"You said it wasn't the notifications, though. What did happen?"

"We'll tell you when we're back on the *Ranger*. We do need you for some decisions." Magda tried to adjust her position in the seat, but nothing she did seemed to make her more comfortable. "I can't talk now. Until we're back to zero gee, I can't use my left arm very much, and my hands don't work the way they used to. I probably shouldn't be flying."

I decided my curiosity could wait.

.   .   .

Magda was more comfortable once we were in zero gee; however, she was still having difficulty with physical manipulations. A control that might need only a finger tap still called for concentration when the fingers did not flex or move easily. Her jaws were clenched and her lips pressed bloodless through the process of docking the spaceplane in the bay.

"We need to go to the bridge," she said as soon as the bay repressurized.

Hannah was there to greet us, along with Kwame, Hope, and Ian. I was not prepared for them to clap when I walked through the bridge doors, but that is what they did. Then they looked at me as though it was my turn to speak.

"I want to thank all of you for bailing my ass out of that place. The locals actually call it Hell, or they use a word that translates to that, and that's where this place is going. Very soon." I looked at who was there and thought about who was not there. "I assume there is a reason Shane is *not* here," I said.

"That's because he's tied up at the moment." Magda laughed when she said that.

"Doing what?" I asked.

"No." It was Hannah's turn to laugh. "He's tied up. Literally. Because that's how I left him."

They were laughing, but I wasn't quite sure if it was a joke. "Are you trying to tell me that we've had the interstellar version of mutiny on the Bounty?"

"It's not really funny," Magda said. "You know we all heard that last conversation of his with you. I suppose he's never been quite right since the Earthbase landing all those years ago. We all know what he wanted most out of this starshot was to return to a different Earth. We're all guilty of that except Hannah.

"But once the return was there for the taking, he couldn't think about anything else, couldn't consider any risks. You know, with what has happened, I think if Shane thought he could have gotten away with it, he would have just made a huge loop through interstellar space at near cee, really made this a time machine."

"That never occurred to me until you said it," Kwame said. "If we did that, though, and then came back to a revived civilization on Earth, we might not have been received very well for having used the starship that way."

"I said as much, I think, before you went down to the planet," Hannah said.

Faces darkened and silence gathered for a moment as Hannah's words brought up the memory of Sho, Caleb, and No Nonsense.

"You're right," Magda said, and broke that spell. "I'm sure Shane realized that much about not even going at all. I should have seen that there was something wrong with him. I should have done something, said something, starting with the way he acted in getting to the

Ranger, but I've been so incapacitated, I feel like cargo. I'll stop there with anything that sounds like I'm avoiding my responsibility in this.

"Anyway, the message I sent about going to talk to Shane by myself was stupid. I should have had all of us go, but I wasn't thinking of a fight. I was thinking to find some way for him to get you and keep some dignity. Stupid. He hit me, told me to belt myself into a seat and stay there or he would tape me into the seat.

"He was in command, and we were the only two pilots. He was going to order Hope and Ian to bring the antimatter rockets online and have us leave orbit. By mission rules, his orders would have been valid. But, of course, Hannah never saw the message to let me talk to Shane by myself."

"No chip!" Hannah burst out. "I've got a practical mind. I went to the Med Unit and made up a syringe of one of the sleeper drugs you had reviewed with me. Then I went to the bridge. His back was to the entrance when I came in. I saw him hit Magda. So I stuck him."

"You put him out?" I asked.

"No. I think I got the dose wrong." She had to work to get the words out around her laughter. "He turned around. After all, I'd stabbed him from behind. I grabbed him by the balls and squeezed. Hard. I grew up using farming tools."

Low tech beats high tech every time.

Hannah had lightened the mood again, and everyone on the bridge was laughing. I wanted to thank each one of them a thousand times.

"Kwame brought some cable and I tied him up," Hannah continued. "I'm very good with knots."

"I've got him locked in his room. The door is set not to open for him," Magda said. "Then I went down for you."

It has occurred to me that I have had few friends over the course of my life, but I have been very fortunate in the ones I have had.

"Very nice work," I said. "But you said you needed me to help with a decision, Magda. If it's about heading back to Earth, the answer is 'Yes, we should.' We've answered all the questions we came here to answer. This place and the beings here—the Jandi—are dying; they have been destroying themselves for centuries—millennia, actually—and it's close to the end. There's nothing we can do about it." What I had buried was going to stay buried. I saw no need to mention it.

"The issue isn't about the planet. The question is what should we do about him?" Magda said.

"You're pilot-in-command now," I said to Magda.

"Technically, you could say what we did was mutiny," Magda said. Scattered laughs now were nervous ones. "We're also a long way from anywhere and I'm still angry. It would be easy to do something we will all regret later."

"You're not the only one who's still angry," I said. Then I took a deep breath and slowed my racing thoughts. I had been in a similar situation before, and if it hadn't been for Yong, I would have made a grievous decision. "I could make a case for pusillanimous conduct in the face of the enemy," I said. "Especially in circumstances that result in death of another service member, that can carry the death penalty under the military justice code. However," and I slowed the word down even more, "there's a lengthy and very strict process under the code to pass a sentence like that.

"Now, this isn't a military expedition; the US Army and its code have long vanished into history, and the pilot-in-command of a starflight has virtually absolute authority. Still, those codes have value, and we set the precedent on the first starshot not to make life-and-death decisions in an arbitrary way. If we dump Shane out of the air lock, it won't be justice. It'll be revenge. I'm a soldier, not an executioner."

I think they looked relieved.

"What do you want to do?" Magda asked.

"He goes into hib," I said. "Right now. And he stays there until we make Earth orbit. I don't know what we'll find at Earth, if there will be any authorities to do anything with him, but at the very least he will have to live with everyone knowing him for exactly what he is. Is that satisfactory?"

It was.

CODA

"Dies irae," 13th century

CHAPTER FORTY-FIVE

A MONTH LATER, I WAS SITTING ON THE BRIDGE WITH MAGDA AND HANNAH. The twin suns of Hell were now only a single bright point on the screen marked AFT. The FORE screen showed an undistinguished starfield, points of white against the black. We had reached 6 percent cee, fast enough to ignite the fusion ramjet but still nowhere near the velocity needed to see relativistic condensation of the starfield. The hum of the antimatter rockets still permeated the ship.

We three were the last ones awake on the *Ranger*. Once the ramjet was lit, Hannah and I would put Magda into hib. Then Hannah would go in. I would be last.

"So, what do you think, Leif?" Hannah asked. "You're the only human who has met the Jandi face-to-face. Are they smarter than us? Are we really like them?"

I had asked myself those questions in the privacy of my mind, but they were not the kind of questions I had ever been trained to answer. I took it slowly. "I don't know how to grade different levels of smart, so I can't answer that one. At one point, they had more advanced technology than we do, more advanced than we ever had. Much more advanced. I don't know if that means we can't reach the same level someday."

I sighed. "As for the other, we are more alike than I want to think, given what they've done to themselves and their world. But I saw differences. They had no interest in exploring space because in their reasoning system, there could be nothing of interest. They did not search for other intelligent species, because they had concluded that two suns were required for intelligence and therefore the possibility of other intelligent species was vanishingly small.

"I won't say we've never been that dogmatic, but not when we had technology. The idea that we would explore another star system out of curiosity shocked them. Okay, I'm aware we had cynical reasons for our starshot programs, but we relied on an underlying curiosity. Maybe there are enough differences that we won't end up the same way."

"I hope you're right, Leif," Magda said. "I guess we'll have an idea when we return." She shifted back and forth in her seat. "What happens if I come out of hib with even less mobility than I have now? I don't want Shane awake and making decisions."

"We'll get you moving, Magda," Hannah said. "It may hurt, but we'll mobilize you."

"I have no intention of turning to Shane," I said.

"Maybe I should just stay awake," Magda said. "The ship has plenty of food. One person won't stress the systems. I mean, it's five years, not forever, and honestly, with how I am and the way Earth was, I don't mind losing five years." Her voice was soft but firm.

"No," I said. "Never mind the psychology of five years in what would be absolute solitary confinement. You're in your sixties, biologically. You have medical conditions already, and we don't have drugs to treat you properly. The risk to having you alive and functional after five years is greater if you stay awake than if you go into hib."

Magda smiled. "You do have such a cut-and-dried way of putting things, Leif, but I'm sure you're right. It's just a good thing that what we needed was a solution to a problem, not empathy."

"I've been told empathy isn't my strong suit."

"I've seen you have your moments." Hannah grinned. "Don't let that ruin a good persona, though. Now, how many years till we return?"

"Another 236," Magda said. "I wonder if anyone will even remember we went."

"Or if there will be anyone left to remember, or any civilization worth coming back to. Is intelligence a ticket to extinction? I can't get this place out of my mind," I said. That was literally true when it came to the Warrior, but that was not a topic I wanted to discuss with anyone else. "Well, there's only one way to find out what Earth will be like, and it's time we do it."

.　　　.　　　.

WE LIT THE FIRE. THE RANGER WAS COMING HOME.

DRAMATIS PERSONAE

STARFOLK AND THEIR SHIPS

MAX BERRINGER—Senior Ship Physician, *Invincible*

HOPE BLANCO—Senior Nuclear Systems Engineer, *Invincible* and *Ranger*

SHANE CRYSTAL—Pilot-in-command, *Invincible* and *Ranger*

MAGDALENA CRUZ—Copilot, *Invincible* and *Ranger*

LEIF GRETTISON—Exoplanetary Scout, *No Name*, *Dauntless*, and *Ranger*

IAN GROSS—Junior Nuclear Systems Engineer, *Invincible* and *Ranger*

RUTH JONES—Junior Ship Systems Engineer, *Indomitable*

MIKHAIL SITNIKOV—Senior Ship Systems Engineer, *Invincible*

KWAME STEVENSON—Junior Ship Systems Engineer, *Invincible* and *Ranger*

EARTHBASE

MARIO ABBRUZZESE—Blue Director and Senior Scout Administrator

ALEXANDER BARTTLEBY—Green Director

PAULA BISCHOFF—Red Director

AURORA CHISOLM—Cadet, Blue

BERT COLANGELO—a Red

HANNAH JIN—Physician

CHRISTIAN LANDRIEU—Chief Administrator

CALEB PETERSON—Certified Senior Scout, Blue

SHOSHANNA (SHO) PETERSON—Junior Scout, Blue

ROSANN SITNIKOV—Mikhail's wife, a Red

RAMÓN UGARTE—Base Security, a Green
SYDNEY YAEGER—Green Director and Senior Base Security Administrator

FROM THE EAST

BARE BONES MCCLINTOCK—Wagon train leader
JUSTICE SERVED MCCLINTOCK—Bare Bones's wife
NO NONSENSE JOHNSON—Leif's friend and Charity's eldest son
PRAISE WORTHY JEFFERSON—Manager, Settlement Association at Gateway Arch

THE JANDI

D'QUILLA—Ru'andarko's child
RU'ANDARKO—The last Watcher, Society of Watchers

ABOUT THE AUTHOR

COLIN ALEXANDER IS A WRITER OF SCIENCE FICTION AND FANTASY. HE HAS HAD A career as a physician, biochemist, and medical researcher. He now lives in Maine with his wife, where he also studies and teaches taekwondo.

A Planet of Wrath and Tears is the fourth adventure of Leif the Lucky and follows directly on the events in *The Lucky Starman*. If you have enjoyed Leif's adventures, trials, and tribulations, stay with him and see what happens on his return home in the next book.

Find Colin Alexander on the web at:
www.afictionado.com
www.facebook.com/ColinAlexanderAuthor
www.goodreads.com/colinalexander

www.ingramcontent.com/pod-product-compliance
Lightning Source LLC
Chambersburg PA
CBHW051315190726
48290CB00001B/160